Wrapped in the Stars

by

Elena Mikalsen

Wrapped in the Stars

Cover Art by *Diana Carlile*

The Wild Rose Press, Inc.
PO Box 708
Adams Basin, NY 14410-0708
Visit us at www.thewildrosepress.com

Publishing History
First Vintage Rose Edition, 2018
Print ISBN 978-1-5092-1860-8
Digital ISBN 978-1-5092-1861-5

Published in the United States of America

Dedication

To my husband—we were always meant to be.

~

To my grandparents—you will never be forgotten.

~

To the amazing writers
of the Women's Fiction Writers Association—
thank you for inspiring me and supporting me
through every step of becoming an author.

Acknowledgements

I am very humbled by writing this list as I realize how many people have been generous throughout my journey as a debut author. Huge thank you to my publisher, The Wild Rose Press, whose team has been incredibly supportive at every step. My editor, Nan Swanson, has been kind and generous with her time, wisdom, and words. My fantastic colleagues in writing, the Women's Fiction Writers Association, have held my hand through this entire process of struggling through learning the craft of writing and putting all my ideas together into a novel.

I am forever indebted to my cheerleaders at the Outlander Nook who never once questioned my ability to write a book and answered random questions at all times of day. Thanks to Lori Christian Renfro for the hours she spent making suggestions on how to make the novel better. My wonderful helper from Scotland, Irene Paulton, was kind enough to assist with the dialect. Thank you, Ginger Wiseman, for checking on the German grammar. Thank you, Carroll Chapman for looking up historical facts. Big thanks to New Yorkers, Sandra Petrucco Sena and Wendy Gold Rossi, for finding some perfect New York locations for the novel. Gayla Cole Feachen—thank you for the research on family photos. Thanks to E.V. Svetova and Lori McConnell for their invaluable feedback that made this novel shine. Rachel Lipetz MacAulay, I am forever grateful for your careful edits.

Thank you to my family, for allowing me to write for hours at a time and never making me feel guilty.

And, finally, thank you to all the readers who buy this novel. This story is for you!

I would like to say that I noticed the ring in the display right away, but I know now that it had recognized me first. After all, the ring's features were not displayed in any special way that would catch the attention of shoppers. In fact, it was turned slightly around, as if somewhat shy. An old yellowed price tag half-covered it, suggesting it had been ignored by all but the rare Scottish sunlight for years. But I was unable to take my eyes away, somehow held by its power.

The wooden door of the Royal Mile Antique Collection creaked as I opened it, my arms straining with effort. The shop smelled of the familiar aroma of most places in Edinburgh—mold and whisky. The dark interior revealed several open-shelved cabinets displaying mismatched teacups, whisky glasses, and various jewelry items. A small ray of light from the door in the back was making dust dance over the displays, and I moved toward it with hope.

Praise for Elena Mikalsen's Fiction

WRAPPED IN THE STARS made the shortlist
for the 2017 Del Sol Press First Novel Prize.

"Written with passion and expertise, Elena Mikalsen's *WRAPPED IN THE STARS* is an intelligent and beautifully crafted story that proves the power of love while illuminating the historical struggles of women in medicine. I love books that teach me something while also being thoroughly entertaining."

~Kelli Estes, author of
The Girl Who Wrote in Silk

"Loved this story. Read it straight through in one sitting. Such a unique and charming work. Endearing characters and the plot is bewitching."

~Fleeta Cunningham, author of the Santa Rita series
available from The Wild Rose Press, Inc.

"Mikalsen effortlessly weaves past and present in this engaging tale…. A delightful debut!"

~Jessica Topper, author of Louder Than Love

"*A* gripping tale…. The author's mastery at story telling and the beauty in her words kept me reading!"

~Negeen Papehn, author of Forbidden by Faith

"An intriguing twist on the idea of a found object that connects the past and present. Smartly drawing from Carl Jung and quantum physics, Mikalsen evokes shared memories…a love story that lasts a century."

~Jennifer Klepper, author of Unbroken Threads

"I am very impressed with the scope and depth… viable, alive characters, …a well-paced and lively story. The author made me care…an incredible amount of serious research…."

~E. V. Svetova, author of Print in the Snow

Prologue

In Quantum Physics, our bodies are described as walking energy fields. Our souls are imagined as systems of spinning particles, negative potential energy electrons with memory. Physicists say that, when we touch an object or a person, we exchange our energy fields. Some of our soul's energy goes into the object or another person, and we gain some of theirs. Every touch changes us, as we are all connected through our minds and physical selves.

What if you wished to share more of your soul?

What if you wished for your memories to live forever?

What if great love couldn't die and its energy remained in the universe?

"I seem to have loved you in numberless forms,
    numberless times...
In life after life, in age after age, forever."

~*Rabindranath Tagore*

Chapter 1

Edinburgh, August, Thursday—Present Time

I was lost. In my life in general, but also in the dark narrow alley of Edinburgh's Old Town.

This sudden realization nearly knocked me down, and I stopped short. I choked on thick fog, and my throat sealed shut. I shouldn't have taken the shortcut. I shouldn't have run away to Scotland.

I've obviously made a mistake. Typical.

I hated not knowing where I was going. I hated walking in the dark alone. I hated being alone. Years of getting home in the middle of the night, as a medical student in New York City's hospitals, still didn't take away my fear of danger lurking in dark alleys. I scanned my surroundings, fear pounding in my chest, making my rib cage ache. Was the street below a safer choice?

I stood on the uneven, well-worn steps of a narrow walkway. Gray buildings towered over me on both sides. The stone beneath my feet was wet and slippery from the moisture dripping off the walls. There were a few small windows above me and an old streetlight up ahead, making the alleyway a little less dungeon-like. I willed my mind to focus on these small sources of light. My lungs unlocked, and I inhaled the cold wet air.

The smell of mold immediately overwhelmed me. I

hurried up the steep slippery steps toward the light. But no matter how fast I climbed, it seemed to get farther and farther away, and my stomach twisted tighter with each step.

Moments later, I felt the world suddenly fall away beneath me as I landed on my right hip, hitting the sharp edge of a stone. I cursed, the words echoing off the moldy walls. Shifting a bit on the icy wet ground, I palpated my aching parts, making sure that my pelvis, femur, and acetabulum were only bruised and not fractured.

Sitting still, I listened to the slow "drip, drip, drip" of water from the buildings and felt sorry for myself. I was in Edinburgh to have a break, after all; this was not fair! It was when I tried to get up that I heard the chirping. This tomb-like passageway surely couldn't be the home of a bird? But there it was—on a bright green branch, growing over the wall of one of the buildings, sat a puffy little bird.

Another old streetlight next to me suddenly turned on, filling the alley with a soft yellow light. I got back up on my feet slowly after some awkward maneuvering and tested my ability to walk. The bird chirped again, startling me so that I jumped, rather painfully for my bruised leg. Then the slight creature moved to the step directly above me.

"You scared the shit out of me!" I yelled at it, holding on to the wall with one hand and rubbing my leg with the other.

I leaned my back against a building. The bird turned its head and looked directly at me, chirping again. I sighed and squinted my eyes to see it better. It had a round white belly and a bright orange chest. I hadn't seen a regular city bird in a long time. For the last seven months there had been only tropical ones around me. My breath stabilized, and my heart and stomach settled.

"Listen," I said to it. "You're cute, but I need to get back to my hotel, okay?"

The bird turned its head toward me, sang another verse of its song, and gently flew into the passageway in front of me, as if showing me the way.

"Do I follow you or something?"

I did. I followed it out to the street above, with no further trouble. To be honest, I was glad for its temporary friendship. Being lost had unsettled me thoroughly. Finally out of the alley, I found myself in the middle of the main street of the Old Town, Royal Mile, with crowds gathering for the Military Tattoo's marching band performances. The lights were lit on Edinburgh Castle, and its flags waved to me in greeting.

"All right, so where do I go next?" I asked. But the bird had disappeared.

With my mind depleted of all rational thought and my feet begging for some relief, I looked around for a place to sit and realized I was standing in front of the dusty display window of a small antique shop.

I would like to say that I noticed the ring in the display right away, but I know now that it had recognized me first. After all, the ring's features were not displayed in any special way that would catch the attention of shoppers. In fact, it was turned slightly around, as if somewhat shy. An old yellowed price tag half-covered it, suggesting it had been ignored by all but the rare Scottish sunlight for years. But I was unable to take my eyes away, somehow held by its power.

The wooden door of the Royal Mile Antique Collection creaked as I opened it, my arms straining with effort. The shop smelled of the familiar aroma of most places in Edinburgh—mold and whisky. The dark interior revealed several open-shelved cabinets displaying mismatched teacups, whisky glasses, and various jewelry items. A small ray of light from the door in the back was making dust dance over the displays, and I moved toward it with hope.

"Hello?" I called out.

A gawky teenager emerged from the door. "Um, were you needing somethin'? We're getting ready to close."

"Can I please see that ring over there in the window?" I pointed.

The teen fumbled with the display case and sighed. "It's locked, miss. I don't know if we've even got the key. Those items are just a decoration for the shop."

"I'd really appreciate it if you'd look," I said and attempted a smile, my patience wearing thin.

He shrugged his shoulders and disappeared back behind the small door, leaving it creaking and groaning as it closed slowly behind him.

I paced in irritation, rubbing my injured hip and wondering whether this store didn't get many customers or just didn't care whether they made any sales at all. Lousy customer service, for sure. I walked to the display containing the ring, examining it closely. My reflection stared back at me—a tired and flushed face with a now-fading tan, frizzy brown curls escaping a loose ponytail, and a brand-new tartan lamb's wool scarf befitting a tourist.

The door opened, but, instead of the teen's face, a head full of silver hair appeared, leaning low to avoid the doorframe. The head belonged to a handsome and ridiculously tall man. He resembled a college professor, with his pleated brown wool pants and the collar of his white shirt folded neatly over the neck of his sweater. Large glasses and a well-groomed cropped silver beard completed his rather academic appearance.

"Good day. My grandson is telling me ye're interested in one of my rings?" He gave me an appraising look and offered his hand. "Name's Ian Fergusson. Which one is it, then?"

"It's the silver one with the white stone in the middle," I said.

"Why does this one catch your eye, may I ask?" He raised his brows, but his eyes were kind.

"I'm not sure, actually. It's just—calling to me."

He nodded his head a few times. "Aye, that's the best way to find your pieces. Let them speak to you and tell their story. This ring must've found the right owner, then."

My heart beat faster as he opened the display, carefully removed the ring, and handed it to me.

"What kind of stone is it?" I gently touched the glowing gemstone in the center.

"A moonstone. It's said to bring protection during travel. There's another meaning to it also," he continued. "Lovers exchange moonstones in the hope of eternal love. But you choose what meaning suits you best."

I laughed. "Who wouldn't wish for eternal love? But I'd settle for travel protection."

"Been traveling, then?"

"A while, yes."

"Are you staying in Scotland for a bit?"

"I think I have to get home soon." *Eventually.*

"Your accent is difficult to place. A bit of the American and a bit of the…French?"

"I live in New York," I said. "But I was born in Ukraine. What are these?" I pointed at the sparkling rows of stones around the moonstone. I was anxious to switch the conversation back to the ring.

"Marcasite. Made of pyrite, a type of iron. Used commonly in the last century. See how carefully it's mounted in its place? Very delicate work. Gives the stone some extra sparkle."

"How old is it?"

"Given the marcasite and the moonstone, I'd venture a guess it's likely an Art Nouveau ring. Made somewhere between 1912 and 1920."

I turned the ring to look for an inscribed date and squinted to see something etched on the inside. "There are words here!"

"Well, that's unusual. Can I take a look?"

I waited impatiently as he examined it with a magnifying glass.

"German, certainly. I can sort out *Ich,* but the rest of the words are too faded and in need of cleaning. Very tricky to clean it properly though—may lose some of its tarnish. Do you want me to try to clean it a bit for you? Do you speak German?"

"No, I don't. Only Russian and Spanish. But that's all right, you don't need to clean it." I stopped him from taking it again. "I'm not really shopping; I just wanted to look at it. I don't buy very much jewelry." I hesitated. "Do you know where this ring came from? If it has German writing in it, I wonder what it's doing here, in Scotland."

He looked at me for a moment, head cocked to the side. "I have a few minutes. I can look in my records."

"I'm sorry I'm asking so many questions."

"It's nay bother. My supper will keep." He winked and walked behind the counter to a black desktop.

"You have computer records for your inventory?"

"This is modern times, you know. We've had a database for over ten years. If we bought the ring in that time, I can tell you a bit about where it came from." He checked the faded tag, and I heard him typing numbers on the keyboard after he placed the ring back on the counter.

I picked up the ring and held it up to the flower-shaped wall sconce to see the inscription. It caught the light and sparkled, blinding me for a second. As my vision cleared, my eyes were greeted by a tiny rainbow reflected onto the window of the shop. My heart skipped a beat, then another, then started again, making me shudder.

My twin sister Ella had loved rainbows. She'd drawn them on every scrap of paper she found.

The rainbow blinked and disappeared, its power captured back within.

"There it is." Ian handed me a page from the printer.

"Paris!" I nearly jumped. "The ring came from Paris?"

"Indeed. It was part of a purchase from a store we often work with, Les Trésors Enchantés. We bought jewelry and a few furniture pieces from the same estate at the time."

"Do you have anything else from that estate?" *I wonder…*

"Unfortunately not; everything's been sold. I can give Paris a call, if ye'd like, and find out if they have any information about the seller or any more objects from that estate?"

I motioned for him to stop. "I'll buy it!" The words burst out of my mouth.

I walked out of the shop a few minutes later with the ring and the receipt from its purchase from Paris in my backpack. My earlier fears of the evening had been forgotten, as I now felt a strange sense of satisfaction. The streets had filled with more people. Normally, I would've walked over to hear some of the music and watch the spectacular fireworks, but tonight I rushed through the crowds. I could still see the blue lights of Edinburgh Castle on top of the hill, but I was quite done exploring. I gave the ring, now safe on my finger, a quick touch. It was my only companion at the moment, and I couldn't afford to lose it.

The truth was, I had been pounding my feet on the cobblestone streets of Edinburgh for days, but despite the bloody blisters on my feet, I was no closer to finding a solution. A solution to my current issue of having no good return plan after running away to Guatemala and then to Scotland from my pediatric residency in New York.

But now, at least, I knew what I was doing tonight. Tonight, I was going to clean the ring and read that inscription. And find out why I had felt so compelled to buy it.

Chapter 2

Edinburgh, August, Thursday—Present Time

My body jerked awake violently, and I stared unseeing into the darkness. Icy shivers pulsed through my spine. I grabbed my blanket from the floor and wrapped it tightly around me, but the shivers continued.

What day was it? Thursday? Yes, definitely Thursday. Edinburgh.

My body was back in my hotel room, but I still smelled the nauseating scent of wisteria blooming wildly in the garden I was just in. I still heard the crunch of the gravel under the wheels of my bicycle.

I hadn't touched a bike since I was eleven. Since the day I insisted that my twin sister race bikes to the beach with me on a sweltering summer day. The day I watched Ella collapse, gasping for breath, on the path covered in gravel and sand, with wisterias dropping their purple blooms on her white face.

Hypertrophic cardiomyopathy was the first condition I learned about when I got to medical school. Ella's heart muscle grew abnormally thick and her heart couldn't pump well. Patients with this condition were supposed to avoid bursts of physical activity, especially in extreme temperatures. I hadn't thought of Ella in a long time. Too long. I guess that was the idea. Go to medical school, become a doctor, save lives. Earn my right to be alive when she was dead. I wiped the tears rolling down my cheeks.

The dream. I needed to think. I'd had strange dreams before, but not this vivid.

The garden I just rode through in my dream looked similar to the gardens we liked to ride through as children. *But...not quite the same.* I rode my bike through a large entrance with an arch, then past well-manicured bushes bearing different kinds of flowers. Then I went through a black iron gate and onto a gravel path, past the fountain and toward the wisteria trees, where I knew someone waited.

A woman stood by the bench, leaning on her bicycle, while several birds played at her feet. Her gray flared skirt cascaded gently over her laced-up boots, and her jacket was almost the same color as the wisteria. The woman slowly lifted her head, allowing me to see her face, slightly shaded by a hat. She was strikingly beautiful, with skin that seemed to glow in the light of the morning sun. Her large, dark, brown eyes were framed by long lashes. And full of tears.

She said something in a language I didn't understand, then got on her bicycle, and we rode on together. I tried to keep up with her because I knew she needed my help. I also sensed I had hurt her feelings, and I felt desperately sorry. As I finally reached her on my bike, I noticed her hands on the handlebars. On the long outstretched fingers of her right hand she wore a ring—the same one I had bought earlier today. I pointed at it, speechless, and that's when I woke up.

I didn't know this woman. I didn't know why I may have hurt her. Was this related to Ella? I hadn't had any nightmares about my sister in a long while, but maybe it was time they returned. But, no, this didn't feel at all like a nightmare. This felt very real. *Too real.* I stopped shivering, but I still couldn't think clearly. I tried to remember what the woman said. I was fairly sure it sounded German. She didn't look at all like my sister. And she wore my ring.

I got out of bed and turned on the lights and the TV. Despite the constant noise of the Edinburgh festival, my room's silence was unsettling. It wasn't even midnight yet. I had fallen asleep from fatigue, still wearing my street clothes. I changed into a clean shirt and a pair of yoga pants and made a cup of tea, as sleep seemed an impossible idea at this point. I sat on the chair by the window, looking at the darkness of the street below.

Maybe I've spent too much time in Scotland.
Maybe this dream was telling me to go home.

Of course, I was in Scotland because I couldn't go home to New York. *Not yet.*

I walked to the bathroom to clean the ring and try to read the inscription. Maybe there was a clue. Not that I felt superstitious, but I was glad to get it off my finger. Some scrubbing with my baking soda toothpaste, and the letters began to shine beautifully, even in the dim bathroom lights. I took the ring into the bedroom and held it under the bedside lamp.

I turned on my laptop and carefully typed into the search engine while squinting to read the tiny letters. "*Du Bist Mein, Ich Bin Dein.*" Several pages popped up, each one telling me that these words were from a medieval German love poem found in the Tegernsee monastery and written by an unknown author. I couldn't understand the poem in German, but the

13

English translation read:

"You are mine, I am yours,
Thereof you may be certain.
You're locked away
Within my heart.
Lost is the key,
And you must ever be therein."

So I was right about the woman speaking German. I searched for "meaning of moonstone." Apparently, the moonstone was a symbol of protection "on land and sea" and could guarantee eternal love or help lovers after a quarrel. It could improve intuition and bring good luck. It worked differently depending on the type of person who used it, but its power was greatest when used by a woman. The ring lay peacefully in my hand, the moonstone shining silvery-white and then suddenly more opalescent. Its calmness slowly transferred to me, and my body relaxed.

I was coming to the realization that the dream had nothing to do with my sister. The wisteria and the bikes were just a coincidence. Was it possible the woman in my dream was a real person? She must've received this ring from someone who loved her. But why did she show up in my dream? Was it possible for me to dream about this woman and her life because I owned her ring now?

Was it possible for objects to store their owner's experiences?

I touched the ring carefully, then slowly put it back on my finger. I wondered why the woman had sold the ring. Surely, if it brought good fortune, it wouldn't end up in an antique shop, being sold for a mere thirty pounds? The shopowner had said it was made sometime between 1912 and 1920, so I must have dreamt of someone from a long time ago. Why was she sad in my dream?

The cell phone vibrated loudly, its buzzing echoing through the room, startling me.

"Hello?"

"Hello. Dr. Radelis?"

I jumped up, my heart thumping in my chest. Not a single person had called me "Dr. Radelis" since I left New York. I'd been Maya, simply Maya, for the past seven months.

"Yes," I said quietly and closed my eyes, leaning against the window frame.

"Well, it's been very challenging to find you, Dr. Radelis." The woman's voice was familiar, but I couldn't quite place her. "I've been trying to track you down for over a month. You haven't been answering your phone."

"I'm sorry. Who's this?" I asked.

"This is Madeleine. I'm the administrative assistant to Dr. Haber, the Dean of Graduate Medical Education. Please hold for Dr. Haber." The phone went silent.

"Wait, wait…" Still silent.

Shit… Shit. Shit!

I paced, the ring forgotten, wondering if I had the guts to end the call. What time was it in New York, anyway?

"Dr. Radelis? This is Dr. Haber," a forceful voice announced in my ear.

"Yes, Dr. Haber. This is Maya Radelis," I said, nearly dropping the phone.

"I normally hold these meetings in person, but Madeleine informed me you were out of the country.

So, unfortunately, it had to be a phone meeting. Is this an acceptable time for you?"

I had a feeling I wasn't really being given a choice. "Yes, this is fine." I sat back down on the bed. Dread grew in my stomach like a monster, beginning to devour my insides.

"This won't take long. I'm calling to inform you that you've exhausted your six-month leave of absence and your forty-four-day vacation allowance. You're now in violation of the ACGME Leave Policy. We have no choice but to place you on probation at this point, with a required completion of the remediation plan. The GME Academic Committee met a few weeks ago and prepared your remediation plan, but we haven't been able to reach you to discuss it. I need you to come in to sign it if you agree. Then, of course, you'll need to complete all the points on it if you wish to resume your residency with us. I'm afraid this meeting is required to be held in person. Any questions?"

Probation. Did he actually say probation? Remediation? Was I being kicked out? Was this the end?

Why was I not saying anything to fight back?

"I understand, Dr. Haber," I heard myself say. "I'll be there and... I'll see what I can do to fix this."

"Very good. I'm going to transfer you back to Madeleine, so she can schedule this. And... Dr. Radelis?"

"Yes," I whispered.

"The committee did discuss that your ability to complete a remediation plan is questionable, given your previous record. I'm referring to your actual performance during your residency. You did have an investigation recorded in your file, if you remember?"

"Yes, I remember." I swallowed hard. The monster had reached my throat now and was sealing it shut.

"And you never took your USMLE examination as expected in your first year of residency."

"Yes, I'm sorry, I…" I choked on my words.

"I hope you know we do try to help all our residents be successful in their medical careers and we wish you all the best as well, but you've really struggled since you've been with us. It may be prudent to examine whether you truly wish to continue on the path of becoming a physician, especially a pediatrician. I'm switching you back to Madeleine."

Click. Silence. The end.

A few minutes later, it was over. I heard only a few of the words Madeleine told me. I was to show up at Dr. Haber's office at noon Friday. Or else.

Lunchtime. He expected it to be a quick meeting.

I lay on the bed, face down, suffocating. I had a week. A week before my medical career was in the toilet. I would no longer be Dr. Radelis—I would be just Maya, for good. I had made yet another mistake. I should've returned to my residency when the Family Health Volunteers Mission in Guatemala ran out of money. Instead, I had stayed as long as possible, trying to delay my return. I ran away to Guatemala in the first place because I thought it would be enough time to cope with my residency failure, but it wasn't. As I waited for my connection to New York a week ago, I still couldn't imagine going back to the hospital. When I saw an Edinburgh flight posted on another gate, it seemed like the perfect chance to postpone facing Dr. Haber, fellow residents, and Dr. Ryan Asher, who was my Attending when I killed my patient.

The monster had reached my brain and began spinning my thoughts. My body felt violently ill, with my stomach battered by sharp pains, my lungs struggling to breathe, my heart beating rapidly in panic, and my head spinning out of control until the fear finally expelled itself in a series of loud sobs against my pillow. I climbed under the blankets, curled myself into a ball, and fell asleep as the only escape I could think of.

I woke when daylight filled my room. The pain was still there, settled permanently in my heart. So now I had to be back in a week to face it all.

I had never escaped.

And my life would be over in a week.

Then I remembered. The ring. The dream. I did have a week before my life would be over.

I had until Friday before I had to return; seven days before I had to get on a flight to New York. Just enough time to try to figure out the ring's mystery. After all, I had nothing else left to lose. I searched my backpack for the receipt Ian Fergusson had given me, the one from the store that sold him the ring.

Paris. The ring was from Paris. Was that a sign? Ella and I spent all our childhood reading books about Paris and dreaming about the things we would see there together. There hadn't been a day in my life when I didn't wish to go to Paris. Paris was also where my best friend, Pauline, lived.

After a shower, I put on the last clean outfit I owned and called my grandmother, Zoya, in New York. I held the phone a few inches away from my ear. It had been twenty years since we arrived in New York as refugees from Ukraine, but she still couldn't get used to the excellent phone connection in the U.S.

"Allo? Allo?"

"Baba, it's Maya."

"Maya, child. Are you all right? Where are you?"

I interrupted the string of questions about to follow. "I'm fine, Babushka. I still didn't catch any malaria. I'm in Scotland now, in Edinburgh. I'm doing just fine. Don't worry."

"Scotland? Edinburgh? You said you were going home a week ago. What are you doing there? It's the other end of the world!"

"I'm taking a little work trip," I lied. Again. I'd never explained why I left in the first place. No need to worry her.

"A work trip? Why would it be in Scotland? I don't understand… You're an American doctor. Why do they send you to Guatemala and now to Scotland? How long before you come home?"

"Next week. I need to do some things here, and then I'll be back next Friday. I promise this time." I tightened my jaw, sure of what she'd say next.

"If only your mother was alive, you wouldn't be running all over the world."

Many things would've been different if my mother were still alive. But my mother died giving birth to Ella and me twenty-nine years ago. She wasn't there to stop me from taking Ella on the bike ride that killed her.

"Please come back home for sure this time. It's not good for us to never see each other." My grandmother sniffed, and I imagined her wiping away tears with one of her embroidered handkerchiefs.

"I will. I'm trying, I promise." I struggled to think

of what else to say.

"You're just like my father. He could never be in one place. Always wanting to travel around and never happy to be home. And he was a good doctor, too. You'd think being a doctor would keep you busy enough," Babushka said.

"I'm sorry, Baba." I did miss my grandmother terribly. I almost felt the warmth of her hug right then and imagined I caught the scent of her hair. Suddenly, I felt so lonely I could hardly stand it.

"Be safe, and please call me more often." Another sigh, but she always forgave me, even when I didn't forgive myself.

"I love you, Baba," I said, but she had already hung up.

The noises outside my room signaled the beginning of a busy tourist day in Edinburgh. I texted Pauline to let her know I was coming. Dozens of emojis popped back up on the screen, her favorite way of communicating these days.

Paris. I was going to Paris. Until I had no choice but to face the worst.

Chapter 3

Bern, September 1911

The sun was starting to set, so Rebecca hurried to finish her hair. A flower would make it look better, the way she wore it in the summer, but today was Rosh Hashanah, the first of the High Holy Days, and Mother would not approve of her vanity. Not that Mother ever approved of the way she looked. Well, at least her clothes were clean today, and she did manage to get a bow into her unruly curls. It was unseasonably warm, and Rebecca was quite glad she wore a cotton blouse and a loose skirt instead of a velvet gown like the one in which her mother was surely suffocating.

Rebecca's dress for the synagogue tomorrow was laid out on the lounge chair. It was expensive, made of white lace, and ordered from some famous dressmaker in Vienna. She had protested the dress when it was first made, thinking of lace and ribbon wasted on what Mother always called her "rather plain figure." It would've hung much better on her sister Hannah's curvier shape. But Father simply waved his hand when she pleaded with him. He knew better than to argue with Mother.

She turned at the sound of heels. Hannah ran into the room, holding her chest.

"Your corset's too tight," Rebecca said, watching

Hannah collapse into a chair next to her.

"You…have…to…come."

"I'll be down shortly. I have to find my new shoes or Mother will be angry with me for the rest of the evening."

"No." Hannah stopped, gasping, and pointed to the window. "Now. There's a man outside. He's going to take our photograph." She examined her hair in Rebecca's trifold mirror. "My hat. Please help me pin it. It's too heavy for me to manage."

Rebecca picked up the hat and stood behind Hannah's chair. The hat was piled high with velvet pleats and flowers. She wasn't quite sure whether she could secure it on top of Hannah's elaborate hairstyle. But it wasn't Hannah's shiny hair she thought of as she began to work with the hat. Her mind filled with dread at the thought of taking the first photograph without their brother. Her fingers shook.

"Ouch!" Hannah's face contorted in pain.

"I'm sorry. I'm distracted by my thoughts."

"Well, don't be. We have to hurry or Mother will be angry."

"I'm just so surprised that she's going through all the trouble this holiday. First the dresses, then the dinner, and now the photograph." She paused, a pin in her hand. "Do you think she's finally decided to stop mourning Karl?"

"It's been five years. How long can she be so melancholy?" Hannah asked.

"Sometimes I think it's because she loved him the most."

"Of course she did. Father preferred him, too. To both of us." Hannah twirled a stray strand of hair.

"It's only because Karl wanted to study medicine, like *Papi.*" She touched Hannah's shoulder.

"Is that why you always study so much? Because you want *Papi* to like you more?" Hannah's eyes narrowed. "It's never going to work. *Mami* will never let you go to the university."

Rebecca bit her lip to stop herself from saying something she'd regret later. Hannah was only sixteen, after all, and it wasn't her fault that their parents had neglected her since Karl died.

"Everyone's talking about us, I'm sure. How will we ever find good marriages if we're not allowed to hold dinners or wear pretty dresses? Look at your friend Sarah—she's eighteen like you, but already engaged." Hannah was back to looking at her reflection.

"You know I have no plans for marriage. Let's hope it's just the end of Mother's melancholy."

Rebecca looked around for a suitable hat for herself but found only her enormous straw hat. She wondered for a moment if her mother would approve, but then heard voices increasing in volume downstairs.

Hannah took her hand, saying, "I love you, you know I do, but please don't spoil the holiday by talking all night about your examinations and how you never plan to marry. It gets Mother in such a vile mood. Let's say a quick prayer for a happy evening."

Rebecca was too distracted for prayers. Karl's death from influenza had held her family in gloom for many years. This was the first time Mother was even willing to have a proper Rosh Hashanah dinner. Was it indeed possible that Mother was feeling better now? Would she finally notice that Rebecca had stopped attending social events? Would she also notice that her oldest daughter had been spending all her days studying for the Matura examinations so she could be accepted to the University of Bern?

"Hurry!" Hannah was already on the stairs.

In the hallway, Mother gave Rebecca a quick look of disapproval—she was used to it, really—then pushed her out the door and into the small garden. Per Mother's instruction, Rebecca, Hannah, their parents, and their grandmother were seated in various poses on chairs and benches, and even on the yellowing September grass. Rebecca's right shoulder ached, reminding her that Karl used to sit at her right in family pictures. No one else seemed to notice that he was gone.

When she entered the parlor later, waiting for the cook to announce that supper was ready, she sat next to her father, who was resting on the sofa with a peaceful look on his face. The family wasn't very religious, but they did observe Rosh Hashanah and Yom Kippur, and Father had stayed home from his medical practice today. Rebecca put her arms around him.

"Shana Tovah, my dear," he said, his arms around her.

"Shana Tovah, *Papi*. Are you looking forward to the feast?"

"Oh, yes. The cook's been working all day." He patted his stomach in anticipation. He had worn his best suit for the pictures, and the button of his jacket was open now, revealing a crisp shirt and silk vest.

The house was filled with the smells of freshly baked challah and other delicacies. Rebecca loved their weekly challah, but there was something very special about the sharing of the sweet bread on Rosh Hashanah, especially with all the honey dripping from it. She licked her lips.

"How did you persuade Mother to hold a real holiday dinner?"

"It was her doing; I didn't have to persuade her at all. She might be finally ready to celebrate holidays again. What do you think?"

"I'd like that very much. I've missed the holidays. But, I also miss him being here with us," she said.

"Karl is part of our family always. Just because we hold a holiday dinner it doesn't mean we've forgotten him, my dear child."

Father brushed off a tear from his cheek, and she gave him a tighter hug. "Do you think when I go to the university next year, I'll still have time to celebrate with you?" she asked, listening to the sounds from the dining room.

"Well, of course you'll be very busy. But you'll also be in charge of organizing your studies, so you'll find time for your family. How are you coming along? Will you be ready for the Matura next week? Is your Latin getting better?"

"I am doing very well in Latin. Herr Rothstein says my Greek is now excellent, too. And I've been doing algebra every day for two hours. My examinations are on Thursday. I will be ready."

"You have indeed been working very hard." He patted her hand.

"Not as hard as you work every day, *Papi*." She snuggled closer to him to inhale the familiar carbolic and camphor that seemed to have soaked into his skin permanently, no matter how much Mother demanded that he wash with her scented soaps.

"Do you really think they'll accept me at the

25

Faculty of Medicine, *Papi*?"

"Of course! You're as smart as any medical student we have. I'll be so proud to know my daughter will become a doctor."

Their conversation was interrupted by loud voices outside the parlor. Mother entered, followed by a richly dressed couple Rebecca had never met before. Her father got up quickly for introductions, and she stood near him, puzzled. Mother had changed for dinner, again something new—a blue beaded gown Rebecca had never seen before.

"My dears, these are Herr and Frau Goldstein. Herr Goldstein is my father's new business partner, from Vienna, visiting Bern this week. I'd like for him to feel welcome in our home for the holiday. And this is their son, Peter."

Rebecca rubbed her forehead. This was a very unusual occurrence, even for their progressive family, to invite guests for a Holy Day. Especially since they hadn't had a big dinner for Rosh Hashanah in years. It was always a family meal on the eve of the holiday, and they only ever had their grandmother or aunts to visit. It was actually quite unusual for them to invite guests for any meal at all.

Mother's intentions became obvious after the introductions were over and they proceeded to the dining area. Rebecca found herself seated next to Peter. She'd discovered a long time ago that she was not good at social conversation and, since men didn't seem interested in her looks, she generally stayed away from their company. No one ever noticed, and it suited her just fine. Perhaps her corset was too tight after all, she wondered, as she suddenly struggled to catch her breath. Her stomach flipped uncontrollably. She wished she hadn't skipped tea and cake earlier when she hid in her room to study. And now she couldn't think of anything better to do than go through algebraic calculations in her mind until the candles were lit.

With the dinner prayers finally finished, Rebecca placed the first slice of the honeyed apple into her mouth, chewing hurriedly and saying her own prayers for the dinner to be over as quickly as possible. She noticed, out of the corner of her eye, that Peter was watching her, and the momentary pause caused the honey to drip down her chin. Her cheeks heated, and she hastily wiped her chin with a napkin.

Peter leaned closer, his breath burning her ear. "I wish I was the sweet apple touching your lips."

Rebecca froze, her cheeks quickly losing their warmth. She looked down at her fidgeting hands. "I beg your pardon?" she whispered.

"You're very beautiful," he continued, smiling slyly.

She was mortified. The smell of his sweat suddenly reached her nostrils, and she just knew she would vomit.

She stared at Mother, who was engaged in laughing at something Peter's mother was saying. Were they aware of this inappropriate conversation? Did Mother know this would happen? She picked up her glass of wine and quickly drank most of its contents. She was unaccustomed to wine, and it burned her throat, but she momentarily felt her stomach and legs relax, and the sensations gave her something else to think about than Peter.

She leaned closer to Hannah, sitting on her other

side.

"Watch out! You're going to spill your wine on me!" Hannah hissed.

Rebecca's discomfort increased with every piece of challah her father ceremoniously sliced. She took her slice and began to break off pieces in a hurry, placing them in her mouth two at a time.

"I love a girl with a good appetite," Peter said. "It means we'll have good dinners when we're married." He raised his wineglass to toast her.

She choked on the bread, the taste no longer sweet on her tongue. As he leaned closer to her again, she swiped at his wineglass in desperation. The full glass upturned, spilling the rich, ruby-colored liquid all over the embroidered white tablecloth and Peter's gray trousers. Little rivers ran down onto the dining room rug. Hannah gasped. Mother rose from her chair with hands covering her mouth, and Father issued orders to the cook about how to clean up the mess. Rebecca flew out of the dining room. She took the stairs two steps at a time, tripping on her skirt, and slammed the door when she finally got to her room.

She lay on her bed without bothering to turn on her kerosene lamp, listening to the laughter and conversation in the dining room. She couldn't believe the guests did not leave and, instead, continued with their dinner. Grief and anger filled her heart until she could hardly stand it, and she hit her pillow with her fists, then mouthed some very bad words, in Latin, that she had learned from Karl before he passed away.

If Karl were alive, this ugly boy would never dare insult me like this at dinner!

When she heard the guests finally leave several

hours later, she waited for her parents to come and punish her, but no one came. She was so very hungry. She quietly opened her door and snuck back downstairs to the kitchen. She slowed her steps as she heard her parents' voices in the living area.

"Joseph, you must stop this nonsense. She's learned enough schoolwork. She must learn the skills of a proper Jewish wife and mother. After today, I wonder if it's too late."

"My dear, the girl has no interest in clothes and dinner parties and other frilly things, like Hannah does. But she has the gift for healing."

"You used to say Karl had the gift."

"I may have been wrong. Or maybe it's possible for two people in a generation to have it. I don't know how it works. But I know she has it. I can feel it. And you can't deny the girl is intelligent," Father pleaded.

"I can't deny that. But the life of a doctor… She will regret not having a family, I'm sure of it."

"You can see she has no skill with men. How will you get her to take an interest in marriage?"

"She is stubborn, but she knows her manners and can make a good hostess."

"It's a waste of her mind and her gift if you lock her into a marriage! Look at her friend Sarah. She's only eighteen and already engaged, barely out of Gymnasium." Father's heavy steps meant he was pacing the room now.

"Well, the Badens know it's a waste of money to pay for a daughter's university education. She'll most likely meet a nice boy, marry, and abandon her education. Or what if she becomes an *emanzipiertes Frauenzimmer* and never marries or has children?"

Mother's voice was sharp in Rebecca's ears.

"She'll not become a bluestocking! She'll make an educated and popular wife. And she will help so many people."

"What good is a wife who can discuss mathematics?" Mother's voice got louder now.

Rebecca pushed her back into the wall, horrified. What if Mother won this argument, just like she won any other argument with Father? What if Mother wouldn't allow her to take the examinations next week? What if she were forced to marry that horrible boy?

"Well, she'll go to the university because she's hardly going to impress any decent family we know with her manners. You might as well allow her to do what she excels at," Rebecca heard her father say, followed by her mother's muffled cries.

It is true, Rebecca thought, walking slowly back to her room and forgetting to get food from the kitchen. She was not very good at anything but learning. No man would ever accept her as a pretty woman or a good dancer. She stood by her window, watching the wind swing the branches of the oak tree. She had no choice but to take her exams next week. She'd have to apologize to Mother and obtain her approval. There was no other road open to her.

And what was this gift that her father spoke of?

Chapter 4

Bern, September 1911

"I really hope I faint and Mother sends me home to bed," Rebecca whispered to her best friend, Sarah.

"I hope my mother is right about my weak constitution," Sarah said, fanning herself with her hands vigorously. Her red hair, arranged beautifully in a chignon earlier in the morning, was now hanging in loose strands.

Their mothers sat only a few rows away, forcing the girls to whisper or risk a reprimand. Sarah was engaged to be married and, therefore, was observed for proper behavior at all times. It was sweltering in the women's gallery of the synagogue, yet they'd been forced to sit at the Rosh Hashanah service for most of the day. The service was held on the ground floor, which was reserved for men, and Rebecca could see her father's head, clad in his silk yarmulke, on one of the benches close to the rabbi.

Rebecca tried to distract herself by counting panes of stained glass on the other side of the synagogue, behind several rows of other women banished just like her, far from the sight of the men, the rabbi, and the cantor. Her new lace dress itched fiercely, and the collar suffocated her. Sweat dripped slowly down her sides. At least she had refused to wear the corset today.

Hopefully, Mother would continue not to notice.

She checked on Hannah. Of course, her sister was pretending to listen to the readings. Anything to look proper. None of them could understand a word. Why wouldn't Rabbi Hirsch allow the teaching of Hebrew to women? If rabbis finally accepted that women were smart enough to connect with God, then the women might stop looking at the Holy Days as just a social occasion. When Rebecca was accepted to the university, she knew she'd never again set foot in the synagogue until women were treated as equal to men.

"Look down over there." Sarah pointed discreetly with her chin.

Rebecca followed and saw a group of young men sitting in the back corner downstairs. They were dressed noticeably poorer and were making some noises, attracting attention and hushes from the elders.

"Who are they?" she asked.

"Russian university students," Sarah whispered. "Mother says they're trouble. The university trustees are letting them study here."

"They don't look so dangerous."

"Oh, they are. They march through the streets and sing late at night. They live right in the center of the city in boardinghouses, but some houses are starting to refuse them now."

"But do they study too?"

"Perhaps, although Mother says they pretend to study, and that they're really all revolutionaries. The governor tried to ban them from the city a while ago, but the university refused, and now more of them are coming. They don't have to take the Matura to enroll, just show that they received some sort of education wherever they came from."

"They seem to be having fun." Rebecca observed in envy as the young men bumped each other's shoulders, laughing and obviously ignoring the hushes. She could hardly stop herself from laughing while watching. One of them seemed oblivious to the fun, leaning with his elbows on his knees, his eyes covered in small, round glasses, intent on listening to Rabbi Hirsch. Someone patted him on the shoulder, and he turned, brushing his light brown hair off his forehead. The man who disturbed his concentration then pointed straight toward the gallery.

"Is he pointing at us?" Sarah asked.

"Why would he be pointing at us?"

Rebecca watched, eyes wide, as the man with the glasses rose a little from his bench, bowed, and blew a kiss straight to her. She sank into her seat, mortified, and prayed harder than she'd ever prayed that she was mistaken and the kiss was meant for someone else. She prayed even harder that her mother hadn't noticed. The kiss surely wasn't meant for her! It must've been for Sarah; no man had ever noticed her before.

The loud sustained blast of the shofar, the ceremonial ram's horn, saved her. Now they'd walk to the creek and she could speak to Grandmother about yesterday. Mother had hardly said a word to her this morning. It was understandable, of course. Rebecca felt incredibly guilty for her behavior. It wasn't proper, even if it was an accident. And even if it *was* Mother's fault for inviting that despicable boy to dinner without warning. But she needed Mother to forgive her. And allow her to take her examinations on Thursday.

She spent the rest of the time in synagogue

alternating between anger, guilt, and self-pity. As she left the synagogue, holding hands with Sarah, she couldn't help it—she looked back to see if the Russian men were still there. The benches were empty now. Her friend was forced to walk home with her fiancé's family. Rebecca gave her a hurried kiss, sad as always to see her taken away by Friedrick, a man she considered Sarah's inferior, overall.

To her dismay, on the way back Mother continued to ignore her. Father and Hannah were in the best of spirits, and Rebecca felt some relief as they threw their bread crumbs into the creek and she imagined her guilt floating away with the crumbs. After all, according to tradition, her sins were gone and Mother had to forgive her now.

She walked home slowly, strolling down Kapellenstrasse with her grandmother, Rahel, who leaned on her arm. She was quiet for a few minutes, thinking of how best to approach the topic of last night's dinner. She was pleased to spend some time with Grandmother. She lived only a few minutes away by carriage, but Rebecca had been so busy lately, studying for her exams, that she had hardly spent more than a few minutes with her.

She felt a pat on her arm. "We all make mistakes when we're young, dear. Just try a little harder to please your mother."

"You've heard, of course." Rebecca sighed.

"You didn't think something like this would escape my ears?"

"No, of course not."

"It's nothing to be embarrassed about, dear."

"Hannah behaves so much better in company

because she really wants to be married, and I don't."

"Hannah is a different person. I have no desire to see an intelligent girl like you get married. Education is what's important in these modern times and not marriage. Look what education has done for your father. Your mother would do well remembering that."

"But I don't know how to please her and Father at the same time. I seem to always disappoint someone, mostly Mother," Rebecca said.

"You won't go wrong with showing proper manners and pleasing your mother. Behaving rudely in front of company is not acceptable in any home." Grandmother's tone was firm.

"*Grossmami*, I'll never have great manners as you do, and I will never be as beautiful as Mother or Hannah. *Papi* says if I go to the university, I can make sure to have a job and money all on my own and at least then I can be worth something."

Grandmother stopped and turned Rebecca to face her. "You *are* already worth *everything* to me, my dear. Don't ever think you are worth less than someone else. And you have a gift passed on to you from your father. It's been in our family for a long time."

A few minutes later they arrived at home. Rebecca felt a kiss on her cheek and was grateful. "Maybe this is a good opportunity to check on your mother." Grandmother pointed in the direction of the parlor. "I'll sit with Hannah and your father in the garden."

Rebecca nodded but paused in the hallway. What was she going to say? How to apologize when you hate doing so? She looked at her face in the hallway mirror and whispered silently to her reflection. *Rebecca, if you can't face your mother and speak for your choices now, how can you do it when you're learning medicine among men?*

She watched her cheeks turn pink, her eyes narrow, and her chin turn up. She had to get Mother's permission for Thursday's Matura, or what else was she going to do with her life?

She walked quickly to the reading parlor. Mother was having tea and rubbing her temples in exhaustion. Rebecca sat next to her on the sofa. In the end, it wasn't so difficult to find the words.

"Mother, my behavior was improper last night. I don't know what came over me. I'm very sorry."

Mother's eyes were icy. "We had a well-respected family to dinner last night, and you greatly disappointed your father and me. Your prospects for getting married are not very good, and you'll need to remember your manners and your family's honor when you're introduced to eligible young men from good families." Her words cut sharply through the air.

"Mother, you know that I have no wish to be married!" Rebecca bit her lip. She needed to control her temper and endure this quietly.

"And what is wrong with being married, I'd like to know? You'll have a family and a home to care for. And a respectable place in a community. What is it that we didn't provide you with in this home?" Mother's lips were pursed.

"But Mother, I'm not interested in being a wife. I see what marriage is like. Father is ten years older than you. You don't care for his work, and he doesn't appreciate your love of art and music."

"Oh, you silly child," Mother said. "It's true we have different interests and he's older, but it doesn't mean our marriage is deficient. We might not understand each other all the time, but we respect and care for each other. In truth, I can't imagine life without Joseph."

"You respect and care for him, but you don't love him."

"Pfft." Mother waved her hand in dismissal. "What do you know about love? Love does not buy you a nice home and a good place in society. Love brings you trouble and heartbreak. And it doesn't last long, either."

"It's not that I want to avoid marriage." Rebecca tried to find the right words. "It's just that I want to learn about the world and become my own person. Before I get married."

Tears grew in Mother's eyes and began to roll gently down her tired face. "If your brother didn't pass away, your father would've never filled your head with this university nonsense. You don't have to take your brother's place."

"Oh *Mami,* it's not because of my brother. Do you not remember? Karl and I were always studying together. I've always been this way."

Rebecca wiped her own tears, kneeled by Mother, and took her hand, truly hoping for forgiveness now, and not just for the permission to take the Matura. It had been a long time since they had gotten along, and she really missed her mother and the way things used to be between them.

"I feared this would happen one day. When I married your father, I knew his family had this curse," Mother said.

"What curse? What are you talking about?"

"In every generation in his family, there's always

someone who carries a gift for healing. It's a calling they are born with, and it's what they must do. We were sure it was Karl, but it appears we were wrong…"

"I don't think I have any special gifts. I just want to know things. Did you ever want to learn, like me, *Mami*? You always say such smart things. I just know you must've wanted to learn more."

"Oh, I did. My mother allowed me to finish the Gymnasium, so that I would play piano and speak French and know how to write and read well. When I was your age, women in Vienna couldn't go to the university. I always wanted to get married. I liked the idea of a quiet life, of being the mistress of my home."

"I don't think I'm very much like you, *Mami*. I don't want a quiet life," Rebecca said.

"I know, child. You're just like your father."

"It's just that I really need to understand life, and the science of how humans work, and how I can make things better for them. I think I could make you, and *Papi*, and our family proud. Maybe I could even help fulfill God's purpose for me," Rebecca suggested.

"You'd be very lucky if you heard the universe tell you what your purpose is," Father said as he walked into the room.

"My voice will not be heard, I see. You've decided against me, and you're sending her to the university." Mother rubbed her temples in agitation.

"My dear, your voice is very much heard. But we need to hear Rebecca's voice as well, and she has spoken on the matter clearly many times."

He walked to his favorite chair and sat down, stretching his legs. "It is 1911, and we have several hundred women at the university. Doing very well, I might add. Many have successfully defended their dissertations now."

"These are not Swiss women studying at the university—it's those Russian revolutionaries the Faculty of Medicine is allowing in. What if your daughter forms friendships with those political refugees and spends all her time at their meetings instead of the science lectures?"

Father shook his head and looked at Rebecca. Winning an argument with Mother was never easy.

"Dear *Mami*, I wish I could make things easier for myself and for you and for our family. But I can't. I can't have an ordinary life. I'm scared that this is not the right path for me, but I'm also scared not to follow it. I have to do this. Please allow it." Rebecca tried again.

She felt her mother's soft embrace. She knew she was forgiven but likely not understood.

"I don't understand," Mother confirmed. "I might never understand how a beautiful, gifted woman would choose to waste her life in a schoolroom. But if you must do this…"

This was the first time Mother had ever called her beautiful, Rebecca thought with sadness. She felt she was pleasing one of her parents but betraying the other, and there was no easy way for her heart to reconcile this. She gave Mother a kiss and asked to step out before dinner to compose herself.

In her room, Rebecca sat by the window and cried her heart out with guilt about hurting Mother's feelings, fear over what the future held for her, and relief at knowing she was on her way to accomplishing what she wanted more than anything in the world. When she was done crying, she wiped her eyes on the bottom of her new dress, watching the wet smudges of tears ruin the delicate lace.

Chapter 5

Paris, August, Friday—Present Time

The grumpy taxi driver I hired at the airport smoked as he zigzagged his tiny Peugeot in and out of traffic circles with a clear death wish. Finally, the taxi pulled up to a street corner and jerked to a stop. I paid without asking for change and stumbled out of the car, looking for a nearby bench as my motion sickness rose to a concerning level. With my head between my knees, I observed that the cobblestones of Paris were much dirtier than the cobblestones of Edinburgh.

I had met Pauline Girard in Guatemala in the Family Mission's cafeteria. It was a humid, sticky kind of day, but she was painstakingly painting her nails while waving away flies. I had plopped down on the seat next to her and stared.

"Do you want to borrow some?" She pointed to three other bottles of nail polish in bright colors.

"Are you serious?" I asked, showing her my fingernails, which were black with several layers of grime underneath.

"But of course! I have enough." She wrinkled her nose, likely from my smell. "Do you need some different color? Or soap?"

I had been determined to keep to myself since I left New York, and I was never much for making friends in the first place. But, somehow, she managed to make me depend on her for company within days. Unfortunately, Pauline was with the Mission barely long enough to fix everyone's nails. She was there for the simple reason of worrying her parents, and apparently that didn't take more than a few months.

Pauline's family owned a luxury hotel in Provence, with a private beach on the Gulf of Saint-Tropez. During some sort of spoiled-rich-girl rebellious episode, she took off to Guatemala, following a crush on an American backpacker heading there. She was smart enough to dump him as soon as the airplane landed in Guatemala City and smart enough to negotiate the terms of her return with her overprotective family. She got a temporary job at the Mission designing malaria education pamphlets, and it took her parents several months, an apartment in Paris, and a promise that she could pursue her artistic interests before she agreed to quit.

As spoiled as she was, she was kind and fun-loving, and tended to gather the most intelligent and creative people around her. I had missed her greatly since she left for Paris, carefully wiping her tears to prevent mascara from smudging. We spoke at least once a week, and she wasn't surprised in the least when I told her I was dropping by. Because nothing ever surprised Pauline.

As the nausea subsided, I got up from the bench and looked around. Pauline lived in a very charming square in the Marais, well hidden by several tall eighteenth-century buildings. A bistro was well-placed in the middle, filling the area with the smells of cheese, wine, and fresh bread. Her building was a smaller one, tucked into a corner in the back. A kitten sat by the painted front door to the building, looking at me between licks at its paws. Ella would've loved seeing this.

I walked through the door and up the stairs and was nearly knocked down by vigorous hugs and kisses from Pauline. She looked as beautiful as ever in a perfect bob and what was likely a designer dress, jewel blue and showing off every one of her curves.

"Pauline, this is gorgeous! You're absolutely sparkling!"

"You're in France now. You can start looking pretty!" She smiled and pointed at my oversized khakis. "But I cannot see your legs! We must go shop soon." Then she gave me a concerned look. "Have you got a bite to eat? Scotland is not a good place for food. Let's drop your things in my flat, and then we shall feast!"

An hour later, I stretched my legs lazily under a small café table, smiling at the curly-haired dog underneath the table next to us. The wicker chair was surprisingly comfortable and the wine cool and relaxing.

"Okay. Now tell me all about your ring." Pauline took my hand and examined the ring, turning my finger slightly and letting the marcasite shine.

"Well…" I took a sip of wine. "It seems to have a story to go with it."

"Like a mystery story, with someone dying or stealing it?"

"No, not quite that dramatic, but who knows? All I can say is that I bought it because I felt this strong need to have it. I felt as if it belonged to me."

"Belonged to you? As in past-life-belonged-to-you?"

"No, it wanted to belong to me *now*." I hesitated. "After I bought the ring, I had this dream. Except it felt very real—as if I were right there. Have you ever experienced dreams like that?"

"Yes, of course."

"In my dream, I walked through a garden and saw a woman who said some words in what I think was German. Then we got on bikes and rode somewhere. I could see she was sad and needed my help. I also felt very guilty for some reason, as if I had hurt her in some way."

"So, who were you in the dream?"

"No idea. I think I may have been someone she loved, since this ring has an inscription from a love poem, and I felt love toward her."

"Wait, but you said you also hurt her?" Pauline gulped her Bordeaux.

"I'm not sure. I felt all these conflicting feelings. But I really couldn't tell. I woke up all confused."

"What did she look like? Ghostly?"

"Not at all! So beautiful! Her skin glowed, and her eyes were big and pretty. She had this very old-fashioned outfit on: a long skirt and light purple blouse and a hat. But I saw some brown curls of her hair underneath the hat."

"So you think the ring has a memory of her lover?" Pauline asked.

"Well, the ring was on her finger. So it must be her memory. But maybe my brain got confused somehow and I'm seeing something that happened, but from a different point of view?"

"And what are you trying to find out here in

Paris?"

"The ring was sold from a store in Paris, so I figured I'd come here and go to the store to check what other items they may be selling from this woman. Maybe I can find out more about her? I'm only curious, that's all."

"If the ring came from Paris, are you sure she wasn't speaking French?" Pauline asked.

"No, not sure, but the ring has a German inscription, and it didn't sound French at all."

"So you came here not to only see your best friend, no?" She pouted.

"Oh, come on. You know I was planning to come see you soon anyway. What's new with your gallery plans?"

"It is going very well. Almost finished the ceiling now. We must open for the fall. I think I might go to Madrid and New York soon to buy some new photography. I want our first show to be photography."

"Oh, I love photography. Great idea!"

"Can I ask a question of you, though, my friend? Why are you here?" Pauline asked.

"What do you mean? I just told you. I have to find out about the ring."

"We're friends, right? You were supposed to go back to being a doctor a month ago. Am I wrong? What's going on? Why were you in Scotland?" She leaned closer, eyes searching.

I hesitated a moment. She knew I had taken a break from the residency, but not why. "I was on my way back a week ago... I made it as far as the airport in Houston. But then I couldn't bring myself to go back..." My eyes itched, and I wiped them quickly. I didn't like to show anyone my feelings, not even Pauline.

"I know you never talk about it, but I can see you want to cry every time I ask about New York. What happened? Did you have a bad boyfriend? Is it your family? Why do you need to run away?"

"I'm not running away!"

"Sure you're not! When was the last time you went home?"

"I'm going back in a week. Don't worry."

Our dinner plates arrived, and I ate with joy, soothing my hurt. The duck was delicious, and the steamy crusty bread was perfect for dipping in the sauce.

Pauline persisted. "So. You're here for a week. Is this only an extra break? Sounds as if you needed to gather strength or courage."

"I have to have a meeting with the dean on Friday. He is placing me on probation," I mumbled.

"Oh, I am right." She raised her brows and whistled. "I love when I'm right! What's happened?"

I leaned back and rubbed my temples. Might as well tell her; she'd never give up asking. "I killed a patient."

Pauline spit out her wine. "You did *what*?"

"Last January."

"What do you mean you *killed* a patient?" she whispered, wiping the red wine stains off the table vigorously.

"Well, not with-my-hands killed her." I paused. "She killed herself, technically. But it was because of something I said…or did…"

"Now you have to tell me the whole story. You say

nonsense!"

"Fine. I was learning pulmonology, since you learn all different specialties as a pediatrician. Hailey was a sweet, frail, fifteen-year-old. She had cystic fibrosis, and her parents were going through an ugly divorce. She wouldn't talk to a therapist, but somehow she opened up to me." She reminded me of my sister, but Pauline didn't know about my sister.

"What is this 'cystic fibrosis'?"

"A genetic disease you're born with. Your lungs are drowning in mucus all the time and your stomach can't digest food normally. You have to take enzymes when you eat, and breathing treatments, and wear a vest that shakes your lungs and makes them expel the mucus. And still you get violently ill with deadly bacteria all the time, and your life expectancy is barely into your twenties. Unless you manage to get a lung transplant, but that only prolongs your life temporarily."

"I can see why you'd wish to end your life. How did she do it?"

"She went home, walked into her closet, wrapped a belt around her neck, and hanged herself." I emptied my glass of wine.

Pauline was pale as she asked, "And you think it's because of something you said? Sounds as if her life was awful!"

"The parents filed a complaint. They thought I told her she was dying and it made her feel desperate. Which I didn't! They thought this because her disease was very advanced. And she hadn't been taking her medications, so her lungs were failing."

"What *did* you tell her?"

"I've been going through what I said to her, every

single day since it happened. Every single fucking day. I can't figure it out. We talked about a boy she had a crush on. She wanted to go to the school dance with him, but she was worried her palms would sweat too much. Because kids with CF have a problem with sweaty palms. And I gave her advice about getting around that issue. And then we discussed changing some meds around so she'd be more motivated to take them and would be strong enough to go to a dance."

"You describe someone happy."

"Yes, but that's what I remember. What if I forgot something I said that really affected her? Teens think differently."

"Maybe she killed herself because her parents were getting divorced? They were happy to have you as someone to blame!"

"You think I was a scapegoat? Doubt it. They loved her."

"People do evil things." She sighed. "Well, you really tried to get her better, and you were only a resident."

"There's no excuse. I had a patient and I took on a responsibility. I should've sent her to get help. I should've realized that day how depressed she was. That's what a physician does."

"So, did the hospital blame you?"

"Not really. There was an investigation. Her parents couldn't possibly prove that this was the hospital's fault, so they couldn't bring a case against anyone." I stifled a sob. "I had to give a statement to the Education Committee and the Peer Review Committee. And they wrote in my file that I had 'questionable clinical judgment.' Because I did. I shouldn't have missed this."

Pauline covered her face with her hands. "Oh, Maya, this is horrible. Is this why you went to Guatemala?"

"Yes, I found a leaflet in a pub in the East Village for the Mission. I told my Residency Director I wanted to do a Global Health track for six months and he'd better let me go. I think he was happy to send me away. He never even verified that the Mission was a real place of work."

"And are you ready to go back? What does this probation mean?"

I swallowed my pride. "I don't know what it means. I was supposed to be back a month ago. That's why they're placing me on probation. I'll have to do all this extra work, I guess. I really don't know if I want to. There seems to be no point."

"So you left and never wished for going back? Poor Maya." She stroked my hand. "But this wasn't your fault, right?"

"Yes, it was. It's always my fault."

"What do you mean 'always'? Was this not the first time?"

"No," I said. I wasn't about to tell her about Ella. No one could ever know about Ella. It was my burden and mine alone. "I just mean that the residents always get blamed. And you understand? I really couldn't go back to the hospital, facing the other residents and my supervisors, day after day, knowing that I let that girl die."

"But you didn't! This was just a mistake. Look, I don't know what it is to be a doctor, but don't they prepare you for this at medical school? You must learn that some of your patients will die, no? And this was not because you gave her wrong medicine. She was simply sick in her head; she was too sad!"

"Pauline, they teach you how to handle it if you make a medical mistake, but not this kind of mistake. I never learned what to do if it was my fault that my patient died and she wasn't sick enough to die."

"You're talking to a queen of making mistakes, Maya. You deal with your mistakes by learning from them and trying to do better next time, that's all."

"My lessons were not good from this." I looked away.

"Well, one day I think you will feel different about this."

"I hope so."

Back at my friend's apartment later that evening, I fell asleep as soon as my head touched the soft pillow, soothed by the sounds coming from the TV. When I woke up a few hours later, it was dark and quiet except for the sound of my sobbing. I was covered in sweat. Hot tears were streaming down my face, burning my skin, and I felt enormous grief squeezing my chest. But it wasn't for Hailey Reed, my patient with CF, or for Ella. I was crying for someone named Sarah. Thoughts were racing in my head about her being abused by her husband. The pain for Sarah was sharp and real. I remembered seeing her in an old-fashioned hospital room, bruised and depressed, telling me a story about her husband beating her. I wanted to protect her, but I couldn't think of a way to do it.

I've never met anyone named Sarah.

What was happening to me?

Chapter 6

Paris, August, Saturday—Present Time

Pauline poured me a cup of coffee. "Do you feel as bad as you look?"

"Worse," I moaned and sat next to her, sipping the lifesaving liquid.

Pauline's two-bedroom apartment on Place du Marche Sainte Catherine must have been at least two hundred years old. Her decorating style gravitated to modern, but she had left the Art Deco chandelier in the living room, and the old mantelpiece held a few carefully arranged antiques. Utensils and kitchen ingredients in matching jars neatly lined the counters. Herbs in small pots were planted outside her kitchen window. Everything from the stainless-steel countertops to the antique range hood looked picture-perfect.

I envied Pauline. I've never had a sense of home as an adult. Dorms, shared apartments, and resident on-call rooms at the hospital were my life. It would be nice to have a home one day, where I could feel at peace. Would it ever be possible?

"I never saw you look so bad. What's the matter?" Pauline asked.

I took another sip of coffee. "The ring gave me another dream. Except that I'm not exactly sure it was a dream. It felt more like a memory flashback, to be honest."

"Oooh." She poured another cup of coffee for herself and sat down next to me.

I continued. "This time, I was just sad, and I couldn't stop crying. I kept thinking…and the thoughts…they weren't mine. They belonged to someone else. I was crying about a friend. Her name was Sarah. I've never had a friend named Sarah…"

"Are you sure? It's a frequent name."

"I'm sure. Never heard of any Sarah."

"A child you maybe saw as a doctor?"

"Nope. It wasn't a patient. It was a friend. I was sad her husband was hitting her."

"*Mon Dieu!*"

"And here is the thing that's the most confusing. When I was dreaming last night about this Sarah, I believe I was the woman who owned the ring. But, last time, I think I was dreaming as the man who loved her. How does this make any sense?"

"So you're dreaming as two different people?" Pauline asked, eyes wide.

"Yes, I'm having flashbacks to two different people's lives." My hands shook, and I set down the coffee cup.

"*C'est merveilleuse!*" She clapped her hands.

"Not very *merveilleuse* when you get no sleep and you get frightened by crying and seeing things at night, and you are already a person who gets nervous at night," I grumbled.

"No, listen," she said, turning her laptop toward me. "I searched today for why this could happen. Look what I found. There's this science of parapsychology, and people that study it say that objects and people—

they have, like, this energy around them. When we meet people or touch objects, we can take or give some of this energy. So when you buy something that belonged to a person a long time ago, possibly it has some of her energy, and now you feel it. You understand?"

I rubbed my forehead. "So this ring could be like a memory stick? It kept this woman's experiences and feelings in it, and somehow I'm accessing that? But who is this other person?"

"Maybe their memories are linked together."

"Because they were a couple?"

"Right. But it could be what the woman remembers, also."

"Possible. I wonder if anyone can touch it and then access it? Here, you try it." I twisted the ring off and handed it to her.

"Oh, no. Thank you. I have many of my own feelings and dreams to experience. You can keep it." Pauline backed away.

"So if I get rid of this ring, I'm going to stop having these dreams, right?"

"The question is—do you want to?"

"I don't know. What if her life is terribly sad? So far everything I've dreamt has been so sad, and I ended up sobbing last night. I'm not strong enough emotionally to take on someone's heartbreak. Maybe that's why her memories are trapped in there?"

"Because she had heartbreak? Possibly. But it could be also her memories were saved because her life was very happy. I'd think for someone's energy to transfer to an object, they have to be a person with strong happy feelings," Pauline said.

"I'll just keep it on for a few days and then sell it at home if it still gives me dreams that keep me up at night crying. For now, I desperately want to find that shop where the ring originally came from."

"All right. I'll help you." Pauline got up and gave me a quick hug. "But first you must borrow some clothes, *chérie*. You're out of the jungle and this is Paris. And…" She touched my curls with some distress. "When was last time you styled your hair?"

"Styled my hair?"

"Never mind." Pauline sighed.

She, herself, of course looked radiant, in full makeup despite the early morning, hair beautifully styled, skinny jeans, and a flowing blouse. Even dressed casually, she looked better than I could ever hope to look.

To my surprise, two hours later, I was looking in the mirror at a complete stranger. Pauline had managed to wrangle my hair into shiny cascading waves, and I looked rather fashionable in one of her dresses. She was pleased, and I had to say that wearing something clean was a welcome change. The rest of my clothes were in the process of being freshly laundered in Pauline's washer and dryer to remove the smell of Guatemala, where I had last washed them in a public washbasin by hand with goo that was supposed to pass for soap.

"I promise we can go shopping for clothes later, but can we please go to the antique store now? I've been waiting all morning," I pleaded. "I only have five days before I have to leave!"

"Yes, fine," Pauline finally agreed, silencing her cell phone.

"You've been texting all morning. Boyfriend?" I

teased.

She winked. "Maybe."

"I was right? Tell me, or I'm not wearing the dress!"

She laughed. "Well, I have been having some nice evenings with someone. And maybe even nights."

"Oh, this is such great news! I'm so happy for you!"

"He is a movie producer, so he travels. Not such an easy man to see. His family has a vineyard in Provence. We met when we were children, and then we met each other at a party here, in Paris, almost a month ago."

"So you've liked him your whole life?"

"No, not at all. I hated him when I met him. He put a frog in my dollhouse!" She pretended to pout, but her lips were smiling.

"Well, he's not going to do that now. Or at least we can hope he won't." I raised my brows. "Is he handsome?"

"Gorgeous."

"Kind? Funny?"

"All those things. Fantastic lover. His name is Nicolas, by the way." She grabbed her purse, and we left the apartment.

"Score, then. I'm so happy for you." I gave her a quick peck on the cheek. "Are you falling in love with him?"

Pauline giggled.

"You are, aren't you!"

"Nicolas wants to meet us later. He is in Paris now. Would you like to meet him?"

"Of course I want to meet him! *After* we go to the antique store."

I rushed my friend through the square to get a taxi. Then I paused. A little bird with an orange chest and a white belly sat on one of the benches, looking at me. It sang as we approached.

"I know this bird."

"What?"

"See that bird with the orange chest? I know this bird," I said with certainty.

"*Le rouge-gorge?* You know the robin? It's a bird. They are everywhere, especially in Paris."

"Oh, that's what it is? A robin? I got lost in Edinburgh a few days ago, and this bird helped me find my way. It was the day I bought the ring." I walked slowly toward the bird. It continued to sit and look at me, with no fear.

"Come on, leave the bird alone." Pauline shook her head. "I think you need some rest, *chérie*, but seeing *le rouge-gorge* is a good sign. It means you'll have a new start, maybe a new chance."

My imagination ran wild with all the information we were likely to find out about my ring. I felt a pang of sadness as the taxi drove past Notre Dame. Ella and I had drawn so many pictures of Notre Dame. It was going to be our first stop in Paris. And now I was off on some selfish quest. Before my career and my life were over. In six days.

Chapter 7

Paris, August, Saturday—Present Time

We made our way down Rue St. Honoré to the antique shop. Les Trésors Enchantés was a treasure trove of Edwardian powder boxes, tiny perfume vials, and china. Beautiful glass-covered tables displayed Art Deco and Art Nouveau jewelry in the center of the store, making me hold onto Pauline in excitement. A few small paintings immediately distracted my friend.

"Look at this—so beautiful!" I picked up a gold pocket watch with a cover depicting two fairies collecting tiny strawberries into baskets.

"You have a good eye." An impeccably dressed woman came by with a tray holding a few more Art Nouveau pieces. "American?" she asked.

Pauline answered in a string of French that made no sense to me, so I continued to look around. I wasn't sure what exactly I was looking for. I hoped that, if there was anything in the shop that belonged to the ring's owner, I'd feel it somehow. I walked slowly from table to table and touched various items but nothing seemed right.

"This is Colette." Pauline motioned for me to return. "Her family has owned this store since the '30s. She wants to look at your ring."

"Let me see," Colette said. She took the ring

behind the counter, where we watched her examine the stone through a magnifying glass. "Hmm, yes. It is Art Nouveau period. Made in Germany. Did you notice the inscription?"

"Yes, it's a love poem," I said. "An old German love song."

"This kind of ring would likely be given for love. Moonstone was believed to be a sort of special symbol then, to—how do you say it—give you forever love?"

"Yes, we think this ring has a love story with it. But do you have any other things that belonged to the woman who owned this?" Pauline asked.

Colette returned the ring, and I handed her the receipt from Edinburgh. "All right," she said. "It will take me some time to look through my records. Do you want to come back in a few hours perhaps?"

"This is impossible." Pauline sighed as we left the store. "We would do better looking for your girl's belongings at the Saint Ouen flea market. Well, now we have time to be Paris tourists. Where would you prefer to go: Le Louvre, Musée D'Orsay, La Tour Eiffel?"

"Notre Dame," I said quietly.

Nicolas joined us ten minutes later, walking over from a bookstore he owned in the Left Bank. I learned he owned several of them as a hobby. It was immediately obvious why Pauline adored him. He was knowledgeable and witty, not to mention terribly handsome.

"We can walk through Pont de L'Archeveche," he suggested.

"Oh, yes! You can see the famous love locks." Pauline smiled.

We walked slowly, enjoying the Paris sunshine,

sneaking into the narrow streets of the Latin Quarter. Nicolas and Pauline pointed out famous buildings to me and gave me a brief history of the city. When we finally came to the bridge, I recognized the view. The Point de L'Archeveche was one of those Parisian bridges you always saw on postcards, with Notre Dame in the background. But the metal mesh sides of the bridge were covered in thousands of locks, hanging on top of each other in a tangled mess. I looked closely. Each lock had names written on it. Some had hearts etched or drawn on them or the word "love." Dates from the past several years were underneath the names.

"I heard these locks had been taken down," I said.

"The city has tried to take them down several times. I'm afraid it's doing some damage to the bridges. Too heavy for the delicate ironwork. But people return with more," Nicolas said.

"I think it's rather romantic. See how it says, *You're my forever.*" Pauline pointed to one.

"So people who are in love come here, put on a lock, write down their names, and then throw away the key into the Seine?" I asked. "Do they hope their love will last if they clip a lock on here?"

"*Exactement.* I always wonder what they do when *l'amour* is over," Pauline remarked. "Jump in the Seine and get the key?"

"I hope not," I said. "I love it. Did this tradition start in Paris?"

"It did. Right on this bridge. We are the City of Love, after all," Nicolas replied. "But it's happening all over Europe now."

Pauline looked at a few of the inscriptions. "Maybe you can feel the memories from these as well? I would think there are strong energy and emotions attached to them."

I ran my hand along the locks, some shiny, some rusted now, some with ribbons or hearts attached to them. "Nope, nothing. It doesn't work like that with the ring, either. It's only when I go to sleep."

"Maybe you can only do it with this ring and not with any other object?"

"Oh, yes, the magical ring," said Nicolas.

"Ugh. You told him." I glared at my friend.

"She told me because I happen to love unexplained phenomena," Nicolas explained.

"So does it mean you can help me understand this?" I asked.

"No, not necessarily. But perhaps reason through it. Pauline said you're experiencing memories of the previous owner of your ring, is that correct?"

"Yes. And sometimes I'm her and other times I'm watching her. Well, I've only had two dreams, so I don't know what will happen next."

"And you have no idea who this person is? No sense of what the connection is between you and her?"

"None at all. I walked into a random antique shop in Edinburgh and bought a random piece of jewelry." I gripped the railing. "Wait a minute. It wasn't quite so random, now that I think about it. It was late evening, and I was trying to get back to my hotel, but then I got totally lost and this little bird, the robin, showed me the way out and then disappeared right in front of an antique shop. Then I looked at the display and this ring…I just knew I had to have it."

"Told you this was a great story!" Pauline said to Nicolas.

"This sounds like the beginning of a great script," Nicolas said. "I can see the trailer in my mind. Wait. So, you just had this feeling that you had to buy the ring? Have you ever heard of synchronicity?"

"Synchronicity? You mean as in Fate? Things happening because Fate wants you to realize something?" I asked with curiosity.

"Synchronicity means meaningful coincidences. It was a term discussed at great length by Carl Jung, a psychologist. It's like when you miss your friend because you lost their phone number, and then suddenly your friend calls you because they've been looking for you for a long time."

"Or when you bump into a guy in a bookstore and later find out you grew up together?" Pauline gave him a quick kiss on the lips.

He pulled her closer to him. "Well, Jung and some of his followers think we should pay attention to this phenomenon, because maybe we're all connected in some way, through some layers of consciousness. And all coincidences have a purpose, very likely."

"If we're all connected, wouldn't life get terribly confusing as we're constantly bombarded by synchronicities and trying to make sense of them?" I rubbed my forehead.

"True, but not all of them would have a meaningful impact on your life. The point is," he continued, "there may be a reason we're connected and why these coincidences happen. People who take time to notice synchronicity may find some interesting meaning to their lives."

"How does this help me with my problem?"

"Maybe there's a reason you decided to go to

Scotland and then you found this ring?" Pauline chimed in.

"So you're saying that it wasn't just chance that I bought the ring. I was meant to find it?"

"It could even be that all the events in Edinburgh were connected and not random. You got lost so that you would see the robin, so that he would lead you to the shop, so that you would find the ring," Nicolas said.

"And the ring needed the right person to read its memories. *Voilà*!" Pauline added.

"I suggest you pay some attention to other coincidences from now on and see if more things will start having meaning. The universe might lead you to an explanation as to what kind of connection there is between you and this mysterious woman." Nicolas gave Pauline a kiss. "I'm afraid I have to get back to my work now, *mon amour*. Too many phone calls to return. See you later tonight?"

"We might have plans."

"She'll see you tonight," I interrupted. "We won't have plans."

"It was great to meet you, Maya. Enjoy your trip to Paris."

"He is fantastic," I said to Pauline as we continued our walk toward Notre Dame.

"I think I might love him," she admitted.

"Does he love you?"

"He told me he did."

"Have you told him you loved him?"

"I will. Tonight. If that's okay that I see him tonight? Can he come over after you and I are done with dinner?"

"Of course, silly!" I hugged her. "I'm so happy for

you. Tell your man you love him."

"What if I'm making a mistake? How long do you wait before you tell?"

"I don't know. I've never been in love. You're very lucky," I said with a sigh.

"One day it will happen, you know it will. Well, here it is."

I stood in front of Notre Dame Cathedral, with its two towers as majestic as Ella and I had ever imagined, and with three grand sets of doors open and inviting. This was all wrong. I shouldn't be here with Pauline. I was supposed to be here with Ella. I'd been here with Ella a thousand times, in my mind. It felt wrong. Every single moment of this felt wrong.

There was a gentle touch on my shoulder. "Come, I want to show you something."

Pauline led me inside, which was dark and musty, with sunlight streaking through the red-and-blue stained-glass windows. I inhaled the smell of incense and burning candles and touched the urn of holy water as we passed it.

"Here." Pauline handed me a candle. "Anyone can light a candle in Notre Dame. Think of the patient you're grieving. You do this in her memory."

I watched her light a candle and firmly place it in its stand. I followed her with my candle, but it wasn't for Hailey. It was for Ella, who would never get to see Paris.

Later, at the antique shop, Colette met us with a look of regret. "I am so sorry, but I have no news. I found no other jewelry or other pieces that came in at the same time. I simply have no record of anything else from that estate."

My heart fell. "Do you have a record of the name of the person who brought you the ring? I don't know if that's something you can tell me or not…"

"Well, that's the problem. We don't have the name of the owner of the ring. All we have are the initials 'C.T.' We don't know if it was a woman, a man, the real owner of the ring, or a servant of the owner. We have no way of finding out."

"The initials 'C.T.'! Well, that is some news." Pauline was excited.

" 'C.T.' I suppose that's something. Are there any other shops I could go to for information?" I asked.

"Oh, dear. There are hundreds of antique shops in Paris. You could be looking for years. I could only wish you *bon chance* in your search."

"Thank you," I whispered, near tears. I walked out of the shop heartbroken. I turned to my friend. "There goes Nicolas' idea about coincidences and meanings. There are no more threads to follow. What am I going to do now?"

"You'll spend some time seeing Paris with me, and then you go home Friday, right? You have to go be a doctor again. You're a very good doctor." Pauline's hand on mine was very gentle. "Children need you. Families need you. You can't be running away from Fate."

"Pauline, I'm on probation with my residency. They are going to kick me out. I'll never be a doctor."

"Those are stupid words. You will fix it when you get back home. You will do what needs to be done. I put my life together and so can you."

"I'm not as strong as you."

"You are stronger than me. I've seen you be

stronger. You're just sad right now. I know what could cheer you up! I remember how much you love your books. I'll take you to one of Nicolas' bookstores—they have great old books, many in English. You're going to love it!"

Shopping for books sounded just as good as anything else at this point, so I let Pauline push me into a taxi.

Chapter 8

Paris, August, Saturday—Present Time

The taxi dropped us off in front of Le Coin du Livre. The bright blue door was an entrance to a labyrinth of brick and wood beams and books of all sizes, piled up in every possible square inch of the space. People filled the multitude of spaces with chatter, laughter, and poetry readings. Chandeliers of different colors and styles hung from the ceiling, and drawings decorated the walls. Worn plush chairs stood next to the disorganized shelves, encouraging readers to get lost within pages of a book.

Pauline, having been here previously, was unfazed by the chaotic magnificence and quickly moved through the rooms. She led me to a small area toward the back and pointed at a shelf filled with antique medical books.

"I think you'll be happy looking around here, no?"

I didn't wish to disappoint her, but the medical section was the last place I wanted to be in right now. "Yes, I'll be fine. Go shop," was all I said.

"I leave you here for a while, okay? I need to look for a good design book. I'll come back soon?"

She was gone before I could respond.

In truth, I was glad to have a moment to myself. I should've been thrilled about being in this strange but wonderful store, but I sat down on a tiny stool propped in the corner, hid my face in my hands, and gave in to panic. The ring chase had led to nothing, and I now had no further excuse to stay in Europe. I had to go back and face what had happened in New York.

They had told me that I wasn't directly to blame for Hailey's death. The other residents said I was "lucky" that I wasn't asked to leave right away. But no one blamed me for my sister's death, either. My grandparents said Ella had had a condition since birth and it was going to end her life at some point. But why wasn't I born with the same heart condition? We were twins, identical in every way. We should've died together, as we had spent every minute of every day together. They said I was "lucky" that my heart was perfect. I guess it was difficult to feel grateful for my "luck" sometimes.

I heard voices and lifted my head to see a young couple entering the room. I was about to get up and pretend to search for a book, when a very dusty brown leather volume caught my eye. I cleaned the dust off with my fingers, revealing the title, *Text-Book of Operative Surgery by Dr. Kocher, 1907*. Next to the volume was the same textbook, but in German, *Chirurgische Operationslehre von Dr. Th. Kocher, 1907*. I could just hear the voice of a third-year surgical resident demonstrating the use of the Kocher clamp, used to grab slippery tissue. Kocher was a surgery pioneer in Switzerland.

What else was he famous for? I took out the German volume and searched through the illustrations in the book. Oh, yes, the thyroidectomy! Kocher was the first to perform the full removal of the thyroid without killing the patient. The German copy was also covered in beautiful dark leather, but the cover was fragile and faded at the seam. The pages were yellow and stained, but the text was still bold and black. One of the pages had a black-and-white photograph of a surgery in progress. I didn't know even one word of German, but my mind did not need translation. I let my fingertips trace the arteries and tendons, quietly whispering the Latin names my brain had memorized so long ago. Flipping through the pages gently, I noticed a handwritten paragraph at the bottom of a page.

"Maya, you find something?" Pauline's voice from the next room startled me away from the book momentarily.

"I'm here, Pauline. I'm trying to figure out something written in German in this really great old—" I didn't finish. The words were stuck in my throat. In tiny and very neat letters, it was written in German:

"Du bist mein, ich bin dein,
dessen sollst du gewiss sein.
Du bist verschlossen in meinem Herzen.
Verloren ist das Schlüsselein:
du musst immer darin sein!"

I knew the first line of this poem very well. The faded signature underneath the writing said in cursive, "*Mark, Bern, 1913.*"

"Find something good?" Pauline was behind me, with her head on my shoulder.

"Look at this!" I said. "There's a poem written in this textbook and the first line matches the inscription on the ring!"

"*C'est merveilleuse!* Wait, it says Mark and Bern! Switzerland! So now you have initials 'C.T.' and name

'Mark'. Well, with some luck, you can find your girl, right?"

My heart thumped in my chest. "What if it has nothing to do with the ring?"

"How could it not? Have you ever heard of this poem before? Now you see it two times? That is a lovely coincidence. Or 'synchronicity,' as Nicolas would say, right?"

The same thoughts flew fast through my mind. I searched frantically for more writing or any signs of its previous owner. There was nothing else, but I didn't tell Pauline, that, as I was looking at the pages, I saw myself not in the bookstore but in a large, dimly lit library, sitting at a table, studying this book with much less faded pages and feeling my heart skip with joy when I found the hidden poem. So the ring owner was a medical student. Did she even survive her medical training? Or did she fail? Fail like I did…

"You look pale." Pauline sounded worried. "We need to get air. So dusty in here. Then we can look through more of this book and see more clues, right?"

I stared at the book for a few seconds, then replied. "Yes, you're right. I feel strange. Can you wait for me by the register? I just need to get one more book really quick."

"Don't be long. I'll go get us some postcards."

Bern, Switzerland, was my next destination, then. I searched for travel guides in a rather messy section of the store. Maps, antique books, and newer travel guides were everywhere, shoved haphazardly into the cubbies that passed for shelves. The books on Switzerland were piled on top of the shelves, almost near the ceiling. Cursing my shortness, I climbed the small ladder propped up near a small dusty window, but they were still out of my reach. I stretched my arm and the ladder swayed.

"Darn it!" I burst out.

"Can I help you get that? Before you kill yourself on that rickety thing?"

The male voice startled me, pushing my heart into my throat. My foot slipped on the ladder, and I practically fell on top of the man behind me. A tall, warm, strong man. Laughing at me.

I scrambled to stand up straight. "I was just trying to get a travel book up there. I need one for Switzerland. I couldn't reach."

He held my elbows until I was steady. Warmth spread from his touch throughout my body, and I felt my cheeks burning.

"Hold on. I'll get a good one for you." He let go of my elbows and reached up.

He had no trouble getting to the top cubbies. I fanned my face. Honestly, how much more could I embarrass myself?

"This is a good one." He handed me a small volume. "I've used it before. Tells you how to find places off the beaten path." He looked down at me, eyes examining.

"And what makes you think I'm looking for places off the beaten path?" I said.

"This bookstore isn't exactly on any tourist map." His eyes were smiling.

"All right, I'll take it." I needed to get away from him. He was unnerving me. I turned and started walking.

"If you have time for a drink, I'll give you some

tips about Switzerland. Been there many times," he called after me.

"No, thanks," I replied quickly, then decided to be more polite. He did help me after all. "I'm here with a friend. She's waiting."

Pauline arrived on cue. "Oh, there you are." She eyed the man, then gave a knowing smile.

"Hi, I'm David." He waved.

"Pauline Girard. Her friend."

She pushed me back, and I nearly bumped into him again.

"David Fischer," he offered his hand to me.

"Maya," I returned the handshake and held my breath. The shock travelled up my arm, through my shoulder, and to my chest. It wasn't painful, more like electricity, pulsing through my blood and muscles, making it hard to breathe.

David looked at me with narrowed eyes. Had he noticed?

"Wait a minute." I looked at the travel book in my hand and back to him, raising my brows. "Is this your...?"

"Yeah," he said, eyes laughing. "My brother."

The photograph on the back of the book depicted a man who was a younger version of David, in hiking gear and on a hillside. "I can't believe you gave me your brother's book!" I wanted to feel anger, but for some reason a laugh burst out of my mouth.

"Nate is really a very good writer. You'll love the book. I wasn't conning you." He laughed too.

"Fine, I'll buy your brother's book. But he better not put me to sleep!" I said.

He turned to Pauline. "I was just asking Maya if

she'd like a drink. I offered to give her some tips on travel to Switzerland. Obviously, the invitation extends to you, as well."

I mouthed *No* to Pauline, but she ignored me. "But of course! That would be lovely. I've been breathing too much dust in this bookstore. I must tell the owner to do something about it." She winked at me.

I blew more dust from a nearby shelf into Pauline's face and whispered, "I can't believe you did this!" as we walked to the register.

"He is so handsome! You can't pass this opportunity," she whispered back.

We walked to a nearby café with small tables under blue umbrellas. I gulped my Bordeaux, trying to distract myself from watching David's lean body stretched comfortably in a tiny chair. I was still rattled by the electricity of our earlier contact.

"Maya, David asked you a question." Pauline touched my shoulder.

"Oh!" I sat up, dazed. "I'm sorry, the wine went straight up to my head."

He laughed. "Nothing like a strong Bordeaux. I was asking about your ring." He pointed at my fingers, wrapped around the wineglass.

"Oh, I bought it in Edinburgh."

"An antique? My mother has moonstone earrings just like this, I think maybe with the same silver-and-marcasite design," he said.

"What a coincidence!" Pauline smiled.

I touched my ring protectively and motioned to the waitress for more wine.

"Why Switzerland?" David asked.

"I heard it was a beautiful country," I answered.

"It sure is. Which cities are you visiting?" David asked.

"She'll start with Bern. Easy connection from here," Pauline answered.

He took a sip of his wine. "It is. It's a pity few people visit. It's a beautiful medieval city, and the Aare River cools it off nicely in August. Are you going together?"

"No, she's going alone. I have work to do in Paris," Pauline said. "Maybe you keep her company?"

"And why are you in Paris, David?" I asked. Time to switch the topic.

"I'm here for work."

"What kind of work?" Pauline pushed.

"I'm an attorney in New York, but I came here to work on contracts for a US company with offices in Paris."

I took in his relaxed pose, faded jeans, clearly fit upper body covered by a light blue T-shirt, chestnut hair, and large brown eyes covered by brown-rimmed glasses. "You don't look like a lawyer," I observed.

He laughed. "What do you think lawyers look like?"

"Well, gray pinstriped suit, gold glasses, black polished shoes, leather briefcase, that sort of thing."

He shook his head. "It's Saturday. I'm allowed to wear casual on the weekends."

I motioned the waiter for more alcohol and wiggled in my chair. The sweat trickled down my back. When the wine arrived, I finished it in a few sips and sat back in my chair, legs feeling fuzzy now.

"So, what brought you to Paris, Maya?" David asked, while gesturing for another round of wine.

"Oh…I'm just here visiting her." I pointed at Pauline. "We've been friends since we worked together in Guatemala."

"It wasn't work. It was terrible suffering, let me tell you. I don't know how we survived there. I couldn't wait to leave. Now, Maya, of course, couldn't do enough for the children. She is a doctor. Also from New York," Pauline chimed in.

"Oh really? What kind of a doctor are you?" David asked.

"No kind. I haven't finished my residency." I gave Pauline a stern look. *Why can't she ever keep her mouth shut?*

"She is a pediatrician." She winked at me.

"I've only done a year of pediatric residency at Kips Bay Hospital," I said.

"So they let you go to Guatemala as a resident? That's awesome. When will you be back in New York?"

"Soon." My skin felt cold suddenly. "Next week." I stood up. "Well, I think I'm done with the heat and the wine for the day. Very nice to meet you, David. Good luck with your contracts."

"Great to meet you both. Maybe we'll run into each other again one day?" He stood up.

"I doubt it." I shrugged my shoulders. *I hope we will* was what I wanted to say but wouldn't admit it to myself.

Pauline leaned over to kiss him on both cheeks, in French fashion, then stepped aside. I held back, shy and weary, memories of the recent strong physical reaction still there. He nodded, eyes demonstrating understanding, and touched my shoulder lightly with his fingers, saying goodbye. The contact, however brief, sent another electrical wave of warmth through my body. This time, I knew he felt it too. His head went up suddenly, eyes examining mine for a reaction. I pulled away, grabbed Pauline's arm, and waved at him. It was time to leave. I couldn't afford this distraction.

"Did you see how he looked at you? Like he knew you already? Like you had an instant connection?" Pauline asked.

"He also handed me his brother's book. I can't stand lawyers."

"What's wrong with lawyers?"

"They care about no one but themselves. They'll break your heart and destroy your soul before you realize you're even in trouble."

Pauline laughed. "Fine, you don't have to date him. You can leave him in Paris for some lucky French girl. Let's talk about you going to Switzerland."

"Do you think I should go?"

"*Absoluement!* Nicolas said you must pay attention to coincidences and see what happens and—*voila*—you found the book with the writing. You must find out more!"

"I guess it was a sign," I agreed. "I was so ready to give up and go home, and then—there it was!"

"I wish you'd stay with me longer." She sighed.

"Me too, but I only have six days until I have to go back. And I have to figure this out. Can you come with me? It's the weekend."

"I can't go with you, I'm sorry. I'm in the middle of all this construction. And I have an art auction to go to in two days." Pauline hugged me close. "But remember you can't keep running. You'll have to go back to New York at some time."

"I know." I sighed. "I have to be back by Thursday. I'll probably be back before then. So you and I can catch up some more. This shouldn't take long."

We finished our walk to her apartment. I took a quick look to see if the robin was in the square, but it wasn't, and I went peacefully to sleep that night, with no more dreams.

Chapter 9

Bern, December 1912

The icy winter wind propelled Rebecca down the street and bit her cheeks. She had studied late with her new friend, Lara, who had come to Bern from the city of Odessa, in Ukraine, and lived in a boardinghouse with poor lighting. Lara preferred to study at the library, with its excellent electricity, which suited Rebecca fine, as she could never concentrate at home with Hannah's constant chatter about her outings to the theater or the symphony. Mother was busy searching for a proper match for Hannah, and it occupied them both well enough to leave Rebecca alone to spend as much time at the university as she needed.

This was from early morning until late night these days. She was taking Anatomy, Physiology, Pathology, and Chemistry. She wished she had time for X-Ray Interpretation, but it just wasn't possible in her first semester of studies. It was not that her classes were particularly challenging. It was only that she found it difficult to accept that some of the professors seemed to ignore her presence and her questions but answered the male students often enough. Professor Beitke was especially gruff in his attitude toward women, although she was doing well enough in his Pathology class.

She slowed and sniffed the air around her—

Snow!—and her excited glance went to the blue and silver clouds. Minutes later, large snowflakes began to drift from the sky, only just touching the orange roofs of the houses. Nothing could cheer her up more than a fresh snowfall! She had always drawn power from nature, but these days she needed it more than ever. Her body was often depleted by the stress of learning, and she had to find new ways to connect with natural elements and release the pressure building inside her.

Rebecca waited until the snowflakes fell gently on her face, like soft kisses.

More and more came now, and the whole world seemed to be turning silver and white. Her heart filled with joy, and she opened her arms and spun slowly, completely oblivious to the passersby on the busy street around her. There were a few moments of bliss, until she felt a rough shove, lost her balance, and found herself on her knees on the filthy pavement, with her books sliding out of sight.

There was no time to feel embarrassed—she cried out as a sharp pain shot through her left ankle. Rebecca bit her lip and tried to get up, her hands slipping in the cover of fresh snow. She fought back tears of frustration and pain but then felt herself lifted by a pair of strong arms and supported enough to be able to balance on her uninjured foot. She looked in gratitude for her savior and saw a handsome young man's face with brown eyes and small, round glasses speckled with snow. He looked foreign but also kind. And then she remembered the man. He was the one who had blown a kiss to her that day in the synagogue a year ago! She would have blushed, if not for the pain and the cold.

"I lean you over?" the man asked, suddenly letting

go. She almost lost her balance until she leaned back on the building near her. He rushed to pick up her books, which were lying in the muddy slush, in danger of being stepped on and ruined.

The sight of the books made her feel even more sorry for herself. Rebecca was nearly sitting back down on the ground, struggling to hold her balance. She shook some of the mud and wet snow off her coat. At least she hadn't worn one of her best coats today. This black one could be easily cleaned once it dried. She took off her hat, as the pins were off anyway. She felt like a child who needed to be scolded. What was she doing spinning around in the snow in the middle of the street, and now sitting in wet slush, covered in dirt, and talking to a stranger? What would her mother say about this behavior?

The man picked up her books, took a handkerchief out of the pocket of a shabby-looking coat, and cleaned them up carefully. As he handed them back to her, he examined her intently and she wondered if it was from pity or kindness.

"My name is Mark Minchin," he said. "I am also medicine student." He opened his coat and showed her a textbook safely tucked in there.

"Rebecca Miller," she whispered. She accepted his hand to allow him to pull her up. As she stood, a piercing pain shot through her ankle again, and she whimpered, struggling to hold back tears.

"Can I check your ankle?" Mark asked with concern in his voice.

"I've never seen you in my classes," Rebecca said.

"I see you." He smiled. "You sit in the front in Physiology. You stay late always, and you make pretty pictures in your notebook." Mark looked up. "It's getting to be more snow. Can I look at your ankle, please?" He bent down before she had a chance to protest, causing her cheeks to flush as he appeared to poke underneath her skirt. "It does not seem broken, but I see swelling. You can walk, yes?"

"It hurts too much to put pressure on it," she admitted.

Did he not remember her at all from that day in the synagogue? Well, she would have to forget about solving that problem just now. She needed to figure out how to get home.

"Can I help you go home? Are you far from your home? Do you need me to get a carriage?"

There were no carriages or cars in sight; not on a windy, snowy night like this. Rebecca realized she had no choice but to accept Mark's help.

"I live only a few minutes' walk from here. Can I maybe lean on you while we walk?" Rebecca prayed silently that her mother did not look out the parlor window tonight.

"Of course. Here." He offered his arm.

She tried to be comfortable without leaning too much on him, but it wasn't possible. She had to tightly hold onto his arm or the pain was unbearable. She took a careful step and Mark gently followed, supporting her elbow. She stopped crying and concentrated on walking. The streets were dark now, and having this man so close was somehow very comforting on this cold, wet, and now very miserable night. He was strong and steady under her arm. His warmth radiated through his thin coat and seemed to float straight to her heart, making it beat much faster than normal.

"You're very kind," she said.

"I am used to helping my sisters."

She thought she caught a note of sadness in his voice. "Where does your family live?" she asked gently.

"They are far away, in a country called Ukraine. Maybe you heard about it?" He supported her as she pointed to a street crossing.

"Yes, I have. I have a friend from Odessa. We study together. Maybe you know her? Her name is Lara Silber."

"Of course. Lara and her fiancé, Vlad, are my close friends."

"Oh. I suppose that makes sense. Lara said you're all part of a small student community. Are you here because of Tsar Nicholas and the politics, like Lara?"

He appeared uncomfortable for a moment. "No, I am not political. I am here only to go to university. Tsar Nicholas made law that only seven percent of Jews can go to universities at home, and there was no more space for Jews like me. You don't have such law in Switzerland. Anybody can come study here."

"It's a terrible law. Lara told me. But of course she is here because the Tsar won't allow women to study at universities in your country at all."

"It is how things are when you have the Tsar. He makes law and everybody follow the law. So I come and study here. People are kind here. It is easy here. There's so much freedom."

They reached Rebecca's house in Monbijou, and she looked nervously for any sign of her parents' activity inside.

What should she do to avoid her mother? Her father's office!

It was next door to the house, and she knew just where Father kept the spare key. The windows looked dark—he was surely home for supper now. She'd be able to give Mark a hot drink and wrap a compress around her ankle before going home and causing her mother a headache.

"This way. Can you help me up a few steps, right to this door?" She pointed and limped to the door with Mark's help. She searched around the door knocker and found a little slot that contained a key.

They walked in clumsily, with Rebecca struggling to get past the door frame. She was relieved that the hallway was indeed dark. There was sure to be a scolding about being late to supper, but that would not be as bad as the scolding for arriving with a poor Ukrainian student holding her up.

"I think I can get what I need to tend to my ankle in this room to the right," she said, starting toward the main surgery office. "Come, let's not take too long. I can't tarry."

But Mark was not moving. His body seemed frozen, so she looked in the same direction as he was and found her father standing at the end of the hallway by the open door of his private study. She froze as well.

"And what do we have here?" Father asked calmly, approaching them while wiping his glasses.

"She fell with the snow, and her ankle twisted." Mark found his words after first making a polite bow to Father. "I check on it, and it is not broken. I am medical student at the university."

"Of course you are," Father remarked calmly, while taking Rebecca's arm, putting it around his own shoulders, and leading her to the surgery. He propped her somewhat less gently than she wished on the examining table, then took off her boot and examined the ankle.

Rebecca stared at him, defiant, expecting a lecture. The ankle hurt terribly from the examination, and she bit on her lip a little to keep from crying out. Mark moved toward her slightly as she winced, but she shook her head, willing him to stay put.

"You are correct. It is not broken," Father pronounced, with a glance at Mark. Then to Rebecca he said, "But you'll need to keep off it for a few days, my dear," giving her an examining look as if wondering if she'd be able to stay out of trouble for that long. "This seems to be the season for young ladies to injure their bones. Your friend Sarah was just here, with a fracture to her wrist."

"What happened to Sarah?"

"She told me she had fallen on the ice by her front steps."

"But we haven't had any ice. Until tonight, I mean."

"That's what I said to her." He cleared his throat. "So do you think you can be careful with your ankle for a few days?"

"Yes, *Papi*. I can study at home," she said, looking down.

"I will go then." Mark nodded and turned to leave.

"No, young man. Wait!" Father surprised them both by waving Mark back in. "Why don't you have a seat, and I'll get you a hot drink. You look half frozen."

"Thank you. It's much appreciated."

Rebecca pointed at a chair near her, but Father quickly pointed at another, much farther away, in an adjoining room. He gave her a stern look, then walked out.

"I'm sorry," she whispered to Mark. "It's just that he's my father, and he's being protective, you understand? I'm not really supposed to be walking around alone at night and then showing up at home with a strange man."

Father came back with a steaming cup of tea and handed it to Mark. Mark took a careful sip and closed his eyes in delight.

"I put a small amount of brandy in there to warm you through. Do you have any clothing warmer than this thin jacket?"

"Oh, this is very warm clothes," Mark assured.

"It's certainly not going to keep you warm through the winters here. Rebecca, we should really talk to your mother and her ladies about organizing a coat donation event for these students from Russia. You are from Russia, right?"

"I am from Ukraine."

"Ukraine. Either way—I can't allow you to leave on such an evening without a warm coat." He walked away, then returned with a thick jacket. "This is my orderly's spare jacket. It's old and worn, but much warmer than what you have on."

"You are very kind, but there's no need," Mark protested.

"Please take it, I—that is—we don't want you to freeze while you're here. Especially if you want to become a doctor."

Rebecca smiled her best smile at him, hoping to convince him of her father's best intentions. She felt genuine affection for him, and she desperately didn't want him to go out in the cold without the jacket. Mark met her eyes. She blushed and looked down at her ankle, still throbbing but much less now.

"Thank you," he said.

"I see you have Professor Kocher's book on surgery," Father remarked, while putting a compress on her ankle.

"Are you studying surgical techniques then?" Rebecca stretched her neck and saw a large text with the title, *Chirurgische Operationslehre,* lying on a chair next to Mark.

"Yes, he was kind enough to allow me to take his course this autumn. I hope to continue my studies in surgery. I like it very much!" The young man bubbled with excitement.

"Theodor and I are old friends. He is a demanding teacher, but he will make you a great surgeon, mark my words. You must work hard to advance in his courses."

"I will, Doctor. I will always work hard. I have no other choice. I can't go home until I'm a doctor."

Father finished with her ankle, and the two men chatted about the state of politics in Ukraine and the Tsar's Russia. Rebecca couldn't hear over the sound of her heartbeat. She hoped his tea wouldn't last too long and he would go soon. And then she also hoped his tea would last forever. But soon it was done. Mark got up and bowed his goodbye, and her entire being ached to see him go. She wasn't sure, but she thought she felt him looking at her from the edge of the doorstep as he was leaving.

Father walked her home a few minutes later, supporting her on his arm. He hesitated on the steps. "Perhaps it would be best not to mention this to your mother."

"Yes, *Papi*. Thank you." She bent her head. She knew Mother wouldn't approve of her bringing a Ukrainian student home. She had heard many hushed conversations between her mother's society friends, discussing the *Russenproblem* of so many Jewish students coming to study at the University of Bern. She was grateful that Father would keep this secret for her.

Later that night, she stared at her window until the late hours, but it wasn't from the discomfort of her ankle. She thought of Mark walking in the snow and feeling cold, and she hoped he would make it safely to wherever he was going.

Chapter 10

TGV Lyria, *August, Sunday—Present Time*

In the early afternoon, we took the Yellow Line Metro No. 1 from Saint Paul to Gare de Lyon train station. The early twentieth-century building with its large clock tower was a busy travel hub on a Sunday. I thought it rather resembled a tropical beach inside, with the sunlight pouring in through the domed ceiling and settling on the tall palm trees arranged all throughout the platforms. Silver trains zoomed quietly in and out like large dolphins, and school groups, families, and business travelers floated in as ocean waves.

We picked up my cheap *Loisir* fare for the high-speed TGV *Lyria* at the sales kiosk. The adrenaline pulsed through me as I anticipated arriving in Bern in just under five hours. I needed the fast train. I only had five days left to figure out the ring's mystery. As my train pulled into the station, Pauline and I exchanged quick kisses and, with a pang of regret for not spending more time with my friend, I said goodbye to Paris.

I found my seat with no difficulty. I still had only a small carryon and a backpack, which now held the Kocher book wrapped carefully in tissue paper. The train took off slowly from the station and glided through the suburbs of Paris, revealing a graffiti-covered, tenement-like side of the city, with laundry hanging on ropes between the buildings. It wasn't unlike the apartment building complexes in Odessa, where Ella and I grew up in Ukraine.

Thoughts swirled in my head. What exactly was I going to do when I got to Bern? David's face jumped into my memory. I took out his brother's travel book and decided to look up the universities in Bern. My girl was a medical student—I was certain of that, at least. I found the right pages and began to read carefully.

Ouch! My head had hit the window with a bang. I always did tend to fall asleep on trains. I sat up, heat rising up my neck and spreading to my cheeks. I peeked with embarrassment at the seats across from me. Someone slept across both seats, his head covered with a suede jacket. I stretched my neck, which was stiff from falling asleep in an uncomfortable position. The travel book, still open to the University of Bern page, lay on the table, pages lifting up and down with each puff of the air conditioner's fan above my head.

I checked my phone. I had been asleep for about two hours. The window scenery still showed only trees flying past at dizzying speed. At some point, the train would slow down to go through the Alps, and there would be a lovely view, but, clearly, we were not there yet. A couple passed near my seat with snacks and sodas, and my stomach rumbled. I slowly walked to the restaurant car, enjoying the feel of the slight rocking of the floor beneath me. The restaurant held a few tables but was mainly a bar selling alcohol, sodas, and snacks. I bought a cheap muffin with the change I had in my pocket, gave a quick glance to the tables occupied with happy couples and families, and decided to eat back at my seat.

As I started walking back, the train suddenly jerked, and I tripped very neatly on someone's foot, landing sideways on the table.

"Darn," I muttered, picking up my muffin from the floor while rubbing my injured side. Stumbling through a hasty apology in a mix of English and broken French, I looked into the passenger's face and took a step back.

"Are you stalking me?" I hissed.

"What?"

He was smirking. David Fischer was definitely smirking!

"You knew I was going to Switzerland!" I said, the pain in my side forgotten. "Did Pauline tell you which train I was on?"

"No, she didn't tell me. I've had the ticket for two weeks."

"Sure you did! Are you laughing at me?" I couldn't believe it! He was laughing now!

"I'm laughing because you keep falling on me, yet you're standing there with your hands at your hips, all indignant, accusing me of stalking *you*!"

I put my arms in my pockets. I *was* beginning to feel slightly ridiculous standing in the middle of the dining car, causing a scene. People had been staring, for lack of anything better to do, but looked bored now as it seemed like our fight was not going to pick up in intensity.

"Look," David said calmly, "I'm going to a family reunion. Why don't you sit down?" he offered.

I tried to think of a way to walk away gracefully but felt at a loss for words. I sat down on the edge of the seat across from him. My blood was still boiling.

"How do you have family in Switzerland? Didn't

you say you were from New York?"

"My family came to America from Bern about a century ago, and they like to get together with their Bernese relatives every few years," he explained calmly.

"Well, you still don't look like a lawyer," I said.

"It's Sunday?" he said, raising his brows.

"Well, most lawyers I've met looked conservative even on Sundays. You've got this whole jeans and T-shirt look that doesn't work for a lawyer."

"What do you have against lawyers, anyway? You get this disgusted look on your face when you say the word. Have you lost your inheritance due to an attorney or something?"

"Do I look like someone who'd have an inheritance?"

"No, not really. But that's why I thought maybe an attorney was involved." He winked at me.

I actually laughed at that. "Nope. Never rich enough to hire an attorney. I've just dated enough lawyers to realize I don't match very well."

"Oh, I get it. We—lawyers—are conservative, precise, by the book. You consider yourself a free-spirit, liberal, and all that," he said.

"You know," I said, getting up, ready to walk away, "I really don't think this was a good idea. I'm going back to my car. And you'd probably love to go back to your first-class seat."

"Wait. I'm sorry. I really am." He touched my arm lightly with his hand. "Can we start over? I'm really not such bad company, I swear. Stay for a drink at least. I'd like someone to talk to. This train ride is really boring."

I ignored the jolt my body seemed to feel whenever

he touched me. I hesitated, then sat down. "Fine. So tell me, what kind of lawyer are you?"

"I'm an environmental attorney. I was in Paris working on some contracts for a company that wants to make sure it's not contributing to climate change."

"Environmental? I had no idea there were environmental lawyers. How exactly is this company trying to avoid impacting the climate?"

"Well, many companies are trying to go green now. The CEO of this one, ALB Industries, wants to make sure they use renewable energy and give off lower emissions."

"And how are they going to do that?"

"What I am mainly assisting them with is drafting contracts to ensure that the land near the company doesn't get damaged. There are some wetlands and forests that could be affected, and the company wanted some say in how this will be handled by the French side of the business."

"So—how did it go? Did the French cooperate?" I asked.

"They sure did. They are helpful when it comes to working on environmental issues. It went faster than I expected, actually. That's why I'm able to make it to Bern to see the family."

"Sounds interesting. I had no idea lawyers could have an impact on the environment. And you get to travel too," I said.

"Thanks," David said, smiling. "I hope you despise lawyers a little less now."

He leaned back in his seat, his arms behind his head, stretching while looking out the window. I struggled to take my eyes off his face, so handsome and so strangely familiar to me. He looked back, catching my eyes, examining my face now. I began to fidget and busied my hands with unwrapping my pathetic-looking muffin.

"Are you going to eat that? It looks disgusting," David said.

I sighed. "No. I think I can wait until Bern. Hopefully, food is better there."

"You're welcome to share my dinner." He pointed to his paper bag, from which he proceeded to remove a small baguette, a round box of Camembert, and a bottle of Bordeaux.

"Do you always travel like this?" I asked, watching him expertly slice the baguette and the cheese with a pocketknife.

He grabbed a few glasses from the bar and poured the fragrant wine. After a few slices of fresh bread with cheese and a glass of wine, I suddenly felt much more relaxed. David pointed to the window, where the scenery began to change as the train finally slowed down through the Alps. We stared at the bright greenery on the mountains quietly for a long time and sipped the wine, until he startled me with a question.

"So, why Bern?"

"I told you, I heard it was pretty," I said, avoiding his eyes.

"If you wanted to see Switzerland, you'd be going to Geneva. Bern is too small a city to attract visitors. No one goes to Bern as a first stop unless they have a pretty good reason." His eyes searched mine. "Don't trust me enough to tell me, huh?"

"I just met you yesterday. And it's quite likely you are a stalker," I retorted.

"Hey, you are the one who keeps falling on me! Strange coincidence!" He raised his wineglass to me.

Meaningful coincidences, Nicolas had said. That's what synchronicity was. *Like meeting someone in Paris and then seeing that person again on a train to Bern. But what would be the meaning of this coincidence? I don't like or need this guy, except maybe for some more of his wine and snacks.*

"How long will you stay in Bern?" David asked.

"Two, three days."

"And where are you off to next?"

"Back to Paris and then home."

"Back to your residency? Didn't you say you were doing pediatrics?"

"I was. I am." I struggled to swallow my sip of wine.

"Bern is great. You'll like it. The Old City has a bit of a magical quality to it. Did you look over my brother's book? It has some fantastic pictures of the city center."

"I actually did. I saw the clock." I didn't tell him I had only read a few pages.

"Where are you staying?"

"I think that's none of your business, is it?" I raised my brows.

"I just want to make sure you're staying in a safe place. August crowds can get a bit crazy, and some hotels are not appropriate for a beautiful single woman."

"I don't need a chaperone, thanks."

He leaned over the table, his face was close to mine. Very close. His hand, holding the wineglass, was next to mine. Was he flirting with me? Did he just call me beautiful?

He swirled the wine, then leaned even closer, his eyes mere inches away. "I have a dinner planned with my relatives tomorrow night, but I'm free otherwise until Friday. Would you like me to show you around? I think it'd be fun for two New Yorkers to hang out."

I hesitated. The thought of walking around an old town in the company of this man who stirred so many feelings in me was both appealing and incredibly frightening. I wanted to, badly, but knew I couldn't possibly allow it. My life was just too complicated at the moment.

And then—he would definitely ask more questions that I didn't wish to keep answering.

"I like to travel on my own. I'm sorry." I got up before the flirting got to the point where I couldn't resist him. "I better get going. Thanks for the food and the wine."

"Wait! Here." He took out a pen from his shirt pocket and a small notebook and wrote down numbers. "This is my cell. Call me if you change your mind. I mean it."

I thanked him and walked away in relief. I desperately needed to get to the bathroom and wash my face with cold water. And then convince myself to throw away the phone number.

In the end, though, I didn't do either. I went back to my seat and stared out the window, going through all the logical reasons in my mind for why I should never talk to him again.

I'd had enough failures lately; there was no reason to risk my heart. This man really seemed like a great candidate for breaking it. I was on a mission after all. I had only a few days to solve a puzzle and I needed to focus.

But then I felt his phone number, tucked safely into my pocket.

Elena Mikalsen

Chapter 11

Bern, April 1913

Rebecca inhaled the fresh air deeply as she walked into the Falkenplatz, which was alive with spring greenery. The early morning wind had the tree branches in the small park waving their leaves at her in greeting. She always made a stop by her favorite linden tree in the morning to touch its smooth trunk and gain some power from its height and stillness. She was taking Anatomy, Physics, Biology, and X-Ray Interpretation this semester. Some days, the studying gave her terrible headaches, until she sat in the garden or walked by the river. There were times she worried that all the years of hard work and studying had been for nothing. Maybe she should've listened to her mother and sister and concerned herself more with hats and dresses.

She sat down on a small wooden bench and inhaled the fresh smell of nearby evergreens to clear her lungs. There it was—her body filled with strength and her mind with clarity. She watched birds dancing happily around a nearby puddle left from yesterday's rain. One of them, a robin with a bright orange chest, hopped close to Rebecca and looked at her with some curiosity and without any fear. She listened to the songs of the birds and watched them splashing, and could almost imagine herself being just as carefree and happy. If only she could turn into one of these lovely birds and play in the garden happily! Maybe a robin! She could easily see herself as a robin, not a very flashy bird at all, with just a splash of orange. It was a kind and smart bird, she could tell. And a bird that wasn't afraid.

She heard footsteps approaching and tried to hide behind her hat, pulling it down to cover her face slightly. She was glad for the size of it, which was just enough to shade her eyes. Curiosity won over, and she peeked at the approaching figure of a handsome young man in a brown suit several sizes too large, wearing shoes that were clearly worn out.

Mark! She had tried to speak to him ever since that day last winter when he'd saved her by walking her home when she injured her ankle, but she couldn't find a way. She noticed him often, talking to his friends after classes or walking to the university. But he never seemed to notice her.

He came close to the puddle, kneeled down with his hand on the ground, and began making chirping sounds. Seconds later, one of the birds hopped near his hand and pecked at it. Rebecca laughed.

"I love robins," he said. "They mean new happy things are coming."

"They seem to like you, as well," she observed.

"Do you remember me, Rebecca? We met before?" He smiled.

She nodded her head and looked down. Did he not notice her all this time at classes? "It was you who helped me when I fell last winter. I've been wanting to thank you, Mark."

"Well, that is no problem. You're very busy, of course. I never expected to hear from you. And it is you and your father, the kind doctor, I need to thank. I still have the coat he gave me. I expect your ankle is all well now?" He bent down and touched her ankle with his fingers gently, making her skin tickle in pleasure from this unexpected, but strangely welcome, contact.

"Oh, yes, it's all better," Rebecca said, then wished it were still hurting, so he would be forced to examine it some more.

"I am glad to hear it. I've thought of you since then," Mark admitted. "I see you are taking Professor Kolle's Anatomy." Mark whistled and pointed at the textbook next to her on the bench. "I hope you are well prepared."

"I am indeed well prepared," she said defiantly. "As you can see, I'm studying this morning. Just because I'm a woman doesn't mean I wouldn't prepare." Her voice shook a little, and she coughed to cover it.

"I didn't mean to imply that you being a female made you study less. I have many women friends. They study harder than I ever will. Kolle just demands a particular level of effort." Mark sat down next to her on the bench. "He also does tend to communicate better with male students. It may be the case that he worries that a female will outsmart him."

Rebecca smiled, appreciating his effort at trying to make her feel better. "I do believe that some of your female 'comrades' can outsmart any of the professors at the school. I've never met any women so intelligent and passionate. I can't believe how far they have had to travel to study because they've been denied their right to education in Russia."

"Well, you would do the same if you were in their

position, right?"

"I'm not sure that I'd have the courage to leave my family or that I would be clever enough to study in a language not my own," Rebecca admitted.

Mark shook his head. "I think women have an easier time recognizing accomplishments of others and give little credit to their own. I see my sisters and my friends here do this all the time."

"You have many sisters?" She knew he had plenty of female friends. He was very handsome, if clearly poor.

"I have eight sisters. Also four brothers," Mark replied.

"There are thirteen of you all together? But how do your parents have enough money for you all to come here?"

"Not all," Mark said, looking down. "The family could only afford to send one. My parents had to choose which one of us would go. I was lucky they chose me, but any one of us was smart enough to come. My brothers and sisters worked for two years to save enough money for me to go. I am trying hard to make them proud."

"Why you?" Rebecca couldn't help asking.

"They knew I would be the one who would manage being away from the family so long. My sisters wouldn't leave my parents or my grandparents. My brothers help with the family's business, and the girls have been promised in marriage. I had no such commitments. I was lucky." Mark looked down at his hands, which were folded on his knees.

"And not so lucky. Because you had to leave your family," Rebecca added.

"Yes, I miss them very much. But I have a new family here, in the student colony."

"What's it like? It must be wonderfully exciting to live with all your friends."

He laughed. "It is exciting, true. I share a room with Vlad, Lara's fiancé. You know Lara, right? We live in the boardinghouse, in Mattenhof. There are many of us there—we are like sardines. Everyone helps each other. There is food to share, clothes, books. We have tea in the evening, and discussion."

"How do you earn the money to pay for the boardinghouse? Do you teach music like Lara?"

"I give lessons in Latin and Greek. But next year, I hope to work in the hospital."

"Does giving lessons pay well?"

"Well enough to buy tea. And pay for my room."

No wonder he looks so thin, she thought. "I don't know if I could live on my own. On the other hand, I really would like it if my parents didn't tell me what to do all the time. It must be so freeing to make your own decisions."

"I have been making my own decisions a long time. It's easier for a man. My sisters were given away to their husbands before they were old enough to have braids. Women have more difficult lives. That's why so many come here to study. To be independent," Mark said.

"Yes, that's what I hope for as well. If I can be my own person, with my own way of making money, I wouldn't have to be given away to a husband who orders me around."

"I don't see how anyone can order you around." He laughed.

She blushed. "Thank you. You are kind." She noticed the textbook under his arm. "Are you still interested in surgery, then?" It was easier to discuss academics.

"You remembered? Yes, I'm now a surgery student with Professor Kocher. It is a great honor to me. I hope to one day become a resident with him, if I earn his approval. I passed my preliminary medical examinations already."

"He is very difficult to please, and you must be very gifted if he selected you to be his student," Rebecca said. Indeed, Professor Kocher often dined at their house. He and Father argued into the late hours about the necessity of surgical procedures for various ailments and ways to ensure proper postoperative recovery. She was slightly terrified of him, since he was always gruff and stern, although less so after a few brandies and cigars late in the evening.

"Will you study surgery, do you think?" Mark asked.

"I'm not sure. I'm just studying for my exams right now. I worry about dissections. I find anatomy to be so dull, overall. And the idea of surgery really turns my stomach."

"I understand. I hear Lara say that to me also."

"I'm relieved you are not offended."

"There's nothing you can do to offend me." He looked at her with understanding, and she found that she couldn't look away.

"It was good to see you again, Mark. But I must get to my lecture now," Rebecca said.

"You are trying to run away." His eyes danced with laughter. "But you must answer if we are to be friends."

"Yes, of course we can be friends. We're all students here together, aren't we? I'd better get to my lecture now." She picked up her books and brushed a few stray leaves off her jacket.

"I walk with you. I need to get to surgery."

They started walking down Länggassstrasse. His presence nearby rattled her and she found it difficult to think. Thankfully, the walk was short. As they made a left on Bühlstrasse, they approached the doors to the Anatomy building, where other students were rushing in.

"May I have permission to meet you later after your classes?" Mark asked.

"You may," escaped her lips before she had a chance to think it through.

Mark took her fingers between his two hands and held them delicately, not letting go when she thought the proper amount of time had gone by. Rebecca's heart beat rapidly from the sensation of the warmth of his skin. She looked around, but no one seemed to be paying attention to them. Anatomy was about to start, after all.

"You have beautiful fingers," Mark said.

She pulled her hand away, her heart jumping in her chest. "You shouldn't say things like that."

"Why not? Is it not proper in Switzerland to give compliment about hands?"

"It's not proper to compliment a woman who is a stranger to you."

"But we are no longer strangers." He smiled.

His smile was definitely charming and she struggled to turn away. His brown eyes seemed to read all her feelings at once. Something in her kept stirring, over and over. He planted a small kiss on her hand, nodded to her, and walked away.

"Goodbye!" Rebecca called after him, not sure of what else to say. She touched the spot on her hand that held his kiss. Why did he stir such feelings in her? How could she possibly concentrate on taking notes on the dissection of the heart now? She sighed and rushed into class, hoping she wouldn't be scolded.

At dinner that evening, Rebecca still couldn't stop thinking of Mark. She'd managed to avoid him after classes were done for the day, as she wasn't sure how to react to his affection just yet. She hoped to phone Sarah and speak to her about this. She needed to ask whether it was appropriate for Mark to hold her hands and ask to meet her without her parents' permission. Sarah was married now, but they still talked and had tea every once in a while, although less and less now that she was so busy at the university.

"Before you go," Father stopped her. "There's someone you need to visit next door. Sarah, she is still your friend, is that correct?"

Rebecca sat back down. "Of course she is. She's married now, but we still talk sometimes. Why is Sarah in the hospital, Papa?"

"She appears to have fallen down the stairs yesterday morning. Two of her ribs are fractured and there's some bruising on her right side that concerns me for internal bleeding to the spleen."

"Why didn't you tell me earlier, *Papi?* I would've gone to her straight away when I came home."

"There was no need to hurry. I'm keeping her for observation overnight and will release her back to her husband tomorrow if she fares well. She had some trouble breathing earlier today."

"Is she all alone?"

"Her family were visiting, but it wasn't good for her to have too much company, so I sent them away. Her spirits are low…" He paused. "I think a visit from you may cheer her."

"Of course. May I go, Mother?" She didn't wait for permission.

Sarah lay stretched out flat on her bed with her ribs wrapped in white bandages. Her eyes stared straight at the ceiling, open and unmoving. Rebecca was sure her heart stopped, as her friend appeared dead to her for a moment, as pale and still as she was. The nurse stepped toward Sarah with a glass of water, and she stirred.

"I'm so sorry I didn't come to see you earlier," Rebecca said, bending over and touching her hand gently.

"Rebecca." Her friend smiled, but then winced in pain from the effort.

Rebecca shuddered at seeing Sarah's beautiful face with a large blue bruise on the right side of her chin spreading to the cheekbone. The nurse brought over a fresh compress for the bruise and held it in place carefully.

Rebecca sat down on a chair by the bed and stroked her friend's hand. "*Papi* told me you fractured your ribs, but he didn't tell me you have injured your face as well."

"Dr. Miller has been very kind to me, but I can't stay here. I must go home. Our chauffeur is coming to pick me up. My mother can do the nursing perfectly. My husband is very angry that I'm not present at dinner tonight." Sarah looked away.

"How could your husband be so selfish? You're lying here bruised and in pain. Your ribs are broken, and I'm sure you can hardly breathe. Any husband would be heartbroken! Oh…"

Rebecca stopped, suddenly aware of tears streaming down Sarah's cheeks and puddling on the clean white pillowcase. Her blood ran cold. Anger and then rage surged through her.

"Sarah, please tell me Friedrick is not hurting you. Oh, no! Please tell me that's not true. Because if it is, I'm going to kill him!" She got up in fury, the blood pulsing through her veins.

"Please stop, Rebecca. Stop yelling. It hurts my head. What are you going to do, you silly girl? You don't know what marriage is like."

"I know it's not supposed to be like this! You need to get free of him!"

"No, you're free to do what you want, but I'm not. I'm tied to this man forever. I'm Frau Grossman. I have no rights. I have no property of my own." Sarah's tears poured down in a steady stream now.

"You can divorce him!"

"And then what? I have no skills, no education, no way to earn my money. I'm not smart like you. I made my choice and I just have to make sure he's never angry with me again."

"You're young. I'm getting my education, and so can you! We're barely twenty—we have our whole lives ahead!"

"But I never studied as much as you. I can't learn science. I'm not as strong as you or as gifted," Sarah pleaded, wincing in pain as she tried to shift her position in the bed.

"You did better than I in Gymnasium! You can't let Friedrick ruin your life. You are so much better than he is!"

"He says I'm not even smart enough to be his wife," Sarah said quietly.

"He's not even smart enough to hold onto you! Wait, did this happen before? My father told me a while ago that you came with a fractured wrist."

Sarah turned away. "I think I've been making him more and more angry every week we're married. Nothing I do seems to please him. I just hope that once I have a baby he'll stop. Surely he won't hit me if I'm with child."

"How could you be sure that he won't? What happened today?"

"I told him I wasn't pregnant. Again. And he pushed me down the stairs. And then…" Sarah's voice got quieter. "He kicked me, over and over. I fainted. When I came to, I threw up and then walked here. I was afraid he'd kill me. But then he came here, and he was so sorry. He said his temper got the best of him and he'd never hurt me again. I have to give him a chance."

Rebecca kneeled by the side of the bed and hugged her friend's shoulders gently. "You are safe here. We can keep you safe. I can ask Father to convince your husband to leave you with us, while we all try to help you figure out what to do. *Papi* will tell him that the recovery needs to be long because you have internal bleeding. It will all be worked out, don't worry!"

"Dear friend, I can't let your family get involved with this. I must go. I can't anger him any more. It's my duty to try to fix this." Sarah cried into Rebecca's shoulder.

"All right. But I'll try to fix your face first. And you must promise to call me if he lays even a finger on you ever again!"

"I promise."

Rebecca washed her hands and bent over Sarah's face. She wasn't sure if it would work, but in the past she had been able to make her own bruises lighten and heal faster.

"Hold still, Sarah," she ordered. "I'm going to use a technique to draw the blood away from your face."

She placed the fingertips of her right hand on the ugly bruise and closed her eyes. She concentrated very hard on imagining the capillaries drawing the blood back into Sarah's body under the warmth and energy of her fingers. She felt the surge of electricity from her fingers, the pull of it, the tingling.

Stronger! Faster! Keep going! she commanded.

When her fingers were nearly finished pulsing, she withdrew her hand and shook the rest of the feeling off. She looked at her friend. The bruise was light yellow now and much smaller. She could see the bones of Sarah's beautiful face much more pronounced now. But Rebecca could do nothing to heal the pain in her friend's heart, and it broke her own.

"Thank you." Sarah kissed her fingers and slowly got up from the bed, wincing in pain, waving to the nurse for help.

Rebecca closed the door to the room and went home, allowing Sarah to get dressed and wait for her husband. She knew she must talk to Father about getting her poor friend out of this horrid marriage. She hadn't the slightest idea of how she could possibly explain this to him, but she knew she had to. Who else was going to help Sarah? She was terribly grateful that she had never married, and horrified at the injustice of it all.

Chapter 12

Bern, August, Sunday—Present Time

Bern was cleverly designed with covered, arched passageways for walking and window shopping. Red-and-white streetcars glided quietly on rails in the middle of the street, and trolleybuses followed. I enjoyed the walk to my hotel, only a few blocks from the train station. It had the same gray stone facade decorated with colorful flags as many other buildings along my way. The reception area was efficient, with the computer kiosks checking travelers in and out with the push of a few buttons and a clerk only supervising the process and handing out the room keys.

"You'll need your credit card and passport, please," the clerk instructed me.

"Oh, sure."

The passport was quickly in my hand, but my wallet wasn't in its usual spot. I kept searching, wishing I hadn't overstuffed the backpack.

My wallet had to be here, didn't it? When was the last time I used it?

I'd bought a muffin on the train, I remembered. Right before I ran into David. A sudden chill went through me and gripped my throat. I didn't use the wallet when I bought the muffin; I used those small euro coins in my pocket. I sat down on a chair nearby, spilling the contents of my backpack onto the floor, to the obvious displeasure of the clerk. I searched furiously.

It wasn't there.

Makeup—check. Phone charger—check. Kocher book—check. Good luck charm—check. Everything else seemed to be in its place.

I clapped my hand to my mouth, a scream ready to escape.

Something *else* was missing. Something I never bothered to check if it was there anymore, because it was *always* there in the backpack or any purse I carried. A tiny photograph of Ella and me standing in front of a cherry tree, our hands and faces stained with cherry juice, wearing matching peony-print sundresses. It was always zipped safely into the same pocket as the wallet, safe from rain and from accidentally falling out.

I tried to breathe, panic rising, dizziness settling in my head like a thick fog. I put my head between my shaking knees. I refused to believe this was happening. I'd had the picture since I was a little girl. I had carried it in my backpack throughout high school, brought it to the U.S. as a refugee, and taken it to college and then to medical school every day. It had survived travel through the cities and villages of Guatemala.

I searched my mind frantically for how this could've happened. I shopped at the bookstore yesterday, and then we went to have drinks. Today, I bought the ticket at the Gare de Lyon. Then I remembered: That person who was sleeping across the seat from me on the train, when I woke up from my nap! Whoever that was likely stole my wallet and the picture, and then pretended to be asleep!

I hit myself on the forehead. What an idiot! How could I have fallen asleep? I was always so careful. I knew to watch over my stuff. I knew to watch out for pickpockets. I've never had anything stolen in any cities or in South America. I must've let my guard down now that I was in Europe. *How could I have let this happen?*

"Hey, you okay?" Two dusty hiking boots appeared in front of me.

I looked up, forcing myself to take in enough air to answer. A young woman in a beanie, with earbuds in her ears and a piercing in her lip, was looking at me kindly.

I shook my head to clear the fog. "My wallet was stolen on the train on the way here." Tears came, but I didn't care.

"You got any other money?" she asked. Her eyes appeared sympathetic.

"What for?" I wiped the tears on my sleeve.

"You need a room here, don't you?"

It hadn't even occurred to me that I had no way to pay for a room now. It was evening and I had no place to sleep. I stood up and kicked the couch I was sitting on, desperation giving way to anger.

She took out her earbuds and handed me her cell. "Better call someone to bail you out."

"No. Thanks. I still have my phone."

She shrugged her shoulders and left.

Shit. Shit. Shit!

I bit my lip and called Pauline. She paid for my room and breakfast, after giving me a quick lecture on watching out for pickpockets. I didn't tell her about the picture. She never knew I had it.

I dragged my suitcase and backpack into the elevator, down the hallway, and into my room. At least I had eaten on the train, as I had no way to pay for any food tonight. A few phone calls and identity checks later and my new credit and debit cards were on their way to the hotel. The thief had only purchased a few items so far. I should've felt relief, but I felt awful. An aching in my chest kept reminding me of my sister's picture, gone forever because of my utter stupidity.

I allowed myself to wallow for another few minutes, then washed the tears off my face, brushed my hair into a ponytail, and bravely went out to the tourist information center. The streets were lively in the warm summer evening, with people enjoying the weather and dining out at small tables filled with fragrant food, wine, and beer. My stomach growled as I passed by a chocolate store and spotted perfect round truffles of all colors. I inhaled the sweet aroma and thought of killing the thief if I ever got my hands on him. I really wasn't very hungry at all, I kept telling myself. It was the thought of not having money to buy food that was so distressing. Especially when I was alone in a strange city where everyone was out and eating. Somehow being alone no longer felt like an adventure. A fleeting thought to call David occurred to me, but I had had enough embarrassment for one day.

It happened when I left the tourist information center at the Bahnhofplatz. My mind ordered me to turn and look at a grand building across the street, with a wide green lawn in front. I knew exactly what the structure was in my heart, but my rational mind searched for confirmation. I ran back inside and jumped in front of a man restocking street maps.

"What is that building across the way?" My heart was beating rapidly.

"That's the University of Bern. The main entrance. Would you like a map of the campus?"

"No need, thanks." I was already off.

A week ago, I would've been frightened. But today I stroked my ring gently, then found myself walking down Länggassstrasse, making a left on Bühlstrasse, and standing in front of another university building. I knew the archives would be closed this late at night, but I was desperate to see something—anything. With my multiple layers of grief about so many things, I had completely forgotten why I was even here. I didn't need a map, as I had a perfect memory of the campus in my mind, although a thought did occur to me that perhaps things might have changed since the beginning of the last century.

Now what? I asked no one in particular, then saw the plaque on the building: "Institute of Anatomy, Bühlstrasse 26." It didn't take long for the memories to come. The images came almost like a slideshow, except at the speed of a hundred slides at a time. Wooden seats in a small lecture hall, full of men in suits and women in long-sleeved lace blouses and their hair in chignons, all listening intently. A man at the center of a lecture hall, in a white apron, holding a human heart and talking. Women's faces as they ran up the steps of the auditorium while picking up their long skirts. And a young man with small round glasses and love in his eyes.

I stood still, letting this play in my mind. Was this young man Mark? Suddenly, as quickly as this slideshow began, it was over. I tried the handle on the door. Open! I looked around for any security, but there was none. I walked in cautiously, nervous about being caught. The place was deserted, but lights were on in a large corridor with a ficus tree and a bust on a white pedestal.

My nervous heartbeat echoed my footsteps on the stone floor as I approached a door next to the bust. Emil Theodor Kocher. I carefully opened the door next to the bust, and it revealed a large room finished with woodwork and paintings, set up as a theater. An anatomy lecture theater! I walked in, all fear of discovery forgotten, and sat down in one of the seats in the middle row, listening to the ticking of the wall clock and looking at the skeleton in the corner. I didn't have to wait long to see the image of a professor, in a long white coat over an old-fashioned suit, lecturing at the center. My fingers ached suddenly, as if I had been taking notes for a long time. The professor looked sternly in my direction and my heart sank, with a sudden desperate desire to run. But I knew the woman whose memories I had inherited never ran away. I felt her resolve and pride and determination.

I walked out a few minutes later, all fears gone. It felt good to be her. She was strong. She was loved. She was not afraid. And she was definitely not alone.

Chapter 13

Bern, September 1913

Rebecca pressed the handkerchief to her face and breathed slowly through her mouth. Very slowly. She was grateful the large corridor outside the dissection hall was nearly empty now and few students would notice her weakness.

"I don't know how I'll ever get through this," Lara said, leaning against the wall next to Rebecca. "My cadaver's eyes stared at me the entire time!" She touched Rebecca's shoulder. "Are you quite all right? Do you need to vomit again?"

"I think I do, yes." Rebecca ran, nearly tripping on the skirt tangled between her legs.

Thankfully, the lavatory was nearby. Her stomach heaved, expelling its contents violently. Afterward, she collapsed on the cold tile floor in exhaustion. She felt slightly better, although she was sure the stench of the bodies would never leave her nostrils. She got up, legs trembling, and managed to get herself to the sink, where she splashed cold water on her face.

Better. She was much better now.

Mark and Vlad were waiting alongside Lara in the hallway when she returned. She didn't want Mark to see her like this!

He held her shoulders and examined her face. "Do

you need to sit down for a while?"

She shook his hands off. "I'm all right now. I can bear it. There's no need to fuss."

"It's disgusting," Lara said to Vlad. "I think the horror of that room will stay with me always."

"Are you sure you don't wish to sit down for a while?" Vlad asked Lara, brushing her blonde hair off her face gently.

"We have to get used to this," Rebecca said. "It's just that…they all had eyes—looking at us. As if they were still alive. And the entire time I was dissecting, I imagined my man's life. I saw him getting dressed, going to work, smoking a cigarette." She looked around to ensure no one else was listening.

Lara laughed. "Did you think you murdered yours, then?"

"Yes! I felt like I was cutting into his live arm. I thought any moment he would start screaming. I think that arm will haunt me for ages. And that smell…" Rebecca said in a horrified whisper.

"I'll make some scented handkerchiefs for us to wear over our faces. I heard this helps."

"Good solution," Vlad said, rolling his eyes. "You'll have your faces covered so you can't see anything. How will you learn?"

"What do you know? You have no understanding of what it's like to be there. You sit with your books, then argue back and forth about law all day. Pointless. Pfft," Lara said.

Vlad's eyes blazed, and he straightened up, standing up to Lara. "You need to learn to show some respect. My wife will not disrespect me."

"I'm not your wife yet. And I will disrespect you

all I want or all you deserve. So you better not deserve." She gave him a kiss in reconciliation. "I know, I know. You study law to become a politician. Arguing and giving speeches is not easy, either."

"Stop being small children," Mark chided them, smiling.

"Remember, Rebecca. We can't let Professor or the men know that we are disturbed by the cadavers. They'll laugh at us and think we're weak females. We must show them we can survive this dissection room."

"Maybe next time it'll be easier," Rebecca said. "Do you ever stop thinking of who those people were when they were still alive?" she asked Mark.

"I don't think of them alive," said Mark. "You have to think of how you will save some person's life one day because of what you do here."

"Well, I just hope all of this learning leads to something good. Every day that I'm in Anatomy I feel as if I'm an embarrassment to my father. Professor Kolle almost growls at me when I attempt to answer his questions."

"Just do the best to please yourself." Mark hugged her.

As the group approached the exit, the front door opened and Professor Kocher walked in. Mark bowed his head and greeted him. Rebecca was about to greet him, as well, when he started talking in his quiet but stern voice.

"Mark, I'll be performing a complete thyroidectomy tomorrow morning on a forty-four-year-old female who's been suffering from a goiter. She's been experiencing heart palpitations, weakness, and general debility. This would be an excellent case for you to observe."

Mark nodded. "Of course, Professor. Thank you for the opportunity."

Kocher dismissed Mark's politeness with a wave of the hand. "She and her husband are exiled Russian politicals, in hiding from the Tsar. I suppose this may be of interest to some of you? They reside in Poland, but I expect they'll need to remain here for three to four weeks after the operation."

Lara and Vlad looked at each other in excitement, then asked in unison, "What's the patient's name?"

"You'll find out if you show up to observe the surgery, Fräulein Silber. You're welcome as well." Kocher turned to Rebecca. "Fräulein Miller, are you interested in observing this operation also? I believe your father told me you expressed some desire to offer physician services to female patients. In that case, surgical cases of goiter may be of interest to you?"

Rebecca really had no interest in surgery, especially not after today, but an invitation from Kocher was an honor not to refuse. "Of course, Doctor."

With a small nod of his head, the professor was on his way, and the students proceeded outside. Lara grabbed Rebecca's arms and spun her around so swiftly she nearly dropped her books.

"Stop, silly! You'll find anything fun, won't you?"

"A secret person from Russia? Watching Kocher remove a thyroid? What could be better?" Lara said. "Do you know a patient never dies in his care? He is an absolute magician at surgery. Very tedious to watch— students have been known to fall asleep. But remarkable if you can stay awake!"

"You've seen him operate, haven't you?" Rebecca

asked Mark.

"I have. Many times."

"What was it like?"

"He makes everyone wash hands for long time and even scrub nails. Then he wears special gloves that have been cleaned to prevent bacterial infection. He believes very much in cleanliness to prevent infection."

"But that must take so much time!"

"It does, but his patients stay alive after the operation. He works slow and explains every step to the students. He has special clamps to close the arteries and prevent bleeding."

"I would really like to watch him," Lara said in awe.

"Well, you will. Tomorrow, at eight sharp, in the surgical theater. He doesn't allow latecomers," Mark said.

"I'll be there." Lara said.

"Goodbye." Rebecca hung around for a moment, wondering, hoping.

"Can I have permission to walk you home?" Mark asked.

She nodded to Mark, her heart dancing with joy. Mark had been walking her home more and more over the last few weeks. It was a long walk, past the main university buildings and then along four streets to Rebecca's home. She had learned to walk slowly, stretching the time they had together. Sometimes they stopped at a park across the street, where the linden and oak trees gave them cover. She wasn't sure if she could tell her parents about him walking her home yet. *Papi* had made it quite clear never to tell Mother about Mark helping her that day last winter. Rebecca wasn't even sure that Mark's attention to her was much more than friendship. She figured she had enough time to find out before telling anyone but Sarah.

"What will you do after you become a surgeon?" Rebecca asked as they crossed a narrow street.

"I will get a license from the Tsar to open a practice in a big city, and then my family can come and live with me," Mark said.

"So you will leave Switzerland?" A pang of sadness made itself known.

"I will have to go take care of my family. They have sacrificed a great deal to help me learn medicine. I can't abandon them." He squeezed her hand.

"I understand. If you don't take care of them, they won't be able to leave the Pale of Settlement you've talked about. What's it like there?" She asked.

"There is great poverty for the Jews. They are kept to the poor area of each village and not allowed to get land, to do trade outside, or to get help from authorities. If everyone gets ill, gentiles receive medicine but Jews are left to die. Police tell Ukrainians to attack the Jews every so often, to make sure they remember they are not welcome there. I think Ukrainians wish the Jews would die or leave. And sometimes there are 'pogroms.' Villagers come and break our things, set fire to the grain, and steal the horses and chickens."

"But that's absolutely unacceptable! How can people do such things to other human beings?"

"It's amazing of what evil people are capable. Especially if paid well with vodka by the police and promised money. But we put out fires, buy more horses and chickens, grow more grain, and clean up our things for the Shabbat. We must endure and go on."

"I don't see how you can endure this quietly."

"That's why I'm here. I know I can give my family a better life."

"It must be a very great burden to have to take care of so many relatives," Rebecca said sadly.

"Thank you for listening," he said, taking her hands.

She squeezed his hands gently. He was beginning to mean a great deal to her, more than she should allow him to. Suddenly inspired, she stopped, pulled up on her tiptoes, and kissed him on the cheek. Come to think of it, she really liked the idea of keeping Mark a secret from her parents for now. Especially when he held her hands and kissed them gently, like he was doing right now. And what was the point in telling anyone about him if he planned to return home anyway? But how would she ever cope with him going away?

Chapter 14

Bern, August, Monday—Present Time

As I walked through the main entrance of the University of Bern, my mind raced through someone else's memories of rushing up and down the stairs off the main hallway. My plan was to go straight to the archives that morning to search for possible names matching what I had to work with: "Mark" and "C.T." The woman at the information desk directed me next door, to Hochschulstrasse 6. After a short walk, I was quickly settled at a computer and was given instructions on how to search records by first or last name and years of attendance. My explanation of working on a dissertation about the medical students of Professor Kocher was enough to satisfy the assistant.

I twisted the ring on my finger as I waited for the search engine to produce results. Twenty Marks popped up on my screen. Most names sounded Jewish, a few German. I was further able to click on each Mark's name and verify which program they were enrolled in and when. I knew Kocher wrote the book in 1907 and died before 1917, so that narrowed things a bit. Only eleven were enrolled as medical students at that time. I did a quick search for history on Kocher as well, to check on any possible class list under his name.

However, I wasn't sure what to do next. I had no

phone numbers, no addresses, nothing to go on except for the fact that they all went to the medical school. I did have one more piece of information for each of the Marks. The archives registered the names of the town and country each student came from. I needed to clear my head, so I left the building, walked along the sunny street, and planned how to proceed next. I stopped and looked at my piece of paper. Eleven towns; it looked like some Ukrainian, some German, and some Russian. Two of the Marks came from Odessa, where I was from.

Meaningful coincidences… Was I meant to find this Mark? Was he from Odessa? Should I only look at Marks from Odessa? If he came from Ukraine, why did he write a poem for the woman in German? I didn't remember from Odessa's history anyone ever wanting to learn German. The city was built by the French and preferred to affiliate with the French. The woman in my dream also spoke German. Maybe I shouldn't look for a coincidence in this case. I walked back to the hotel, hungry, hot, and puzzled. I decided to try some computer searches for the rest of the day. I was sure something helpful would turn up.

The clerk stopped me. "You have a message here. You're Maya Radelis, Room 204, right?" She handed me a small folded note.

"That's strange. I wasn't expecting messages. Thanks," I said. I opened the note. It was from Pauline.

Maya, call me. Trying to reach you all last night. Pauline.

"Will you be checking out today?" the receptionist asked.

It occurred to me then that I had no way to pay for

the room after today. "Did any mail come for me?"

After looking through a stack on the reception desk, she shook her head.

"Give me a moment, all right?" I walked away and called my friend. I'd have to beg for more money, just for tonight. I could only prolong my stay for so long. I was due back to Paris for my flight to New York by Thursday.

"Finally, you call me? Where were you? You lost your phone?" Pauline sounded less than pleased.

"I'm so sorry. I was at the University of Bern archives and turned my phone off. It was super quiet in there. I didn't mean to blow you off."

"Not a problem. I just was worried about you. Do you have money yet?"

"No, not yet." I sighed.

"This is ridiculous! Do you have a pen? I'm going to call a good friend of mine. She has a hotel in an old castle about two hours away from Bern. She will send her driver to pick you up. You'll like her, she's very nice. Has a handsome brother, too."

"Wait, slow down. I can't leave Bern, and I don't want to go to a castle." I hesitated. I hated begging. "Can you please loan me some more money? For another night in a hotel here in Bern? I'll pay you back when I get back to Paris."

"Sure. That's no problem. So does it mean you are finding something about your woman? 'C.T.'?"

"Not much. But I feel her here almost everywhere I go. And I got some names from the archives at the university that I can follow up on. I just want to stay another day. I'm sure I'm close."

"Fine, but you are not staying at that cheap hotel. I

know this really old place, you'll like it. It has very good food. I stayed there once. I'll text you the address."

My new hotel was a three-story brick house tucked away on a quiet street near a park full of linden and oak trees. A small wooden sign that said "Wildflower" and a door knocker decorated its front door. Two large window boxes full of red geraniums sat on each of the windowsills. Two robins landed on the flower boxes as I was getting ready to knock. One was awfully familiar.

"Made it all the way from Paris, did you?" I asked, setting my suitcase down.

The robin chirped.

"If we're going to be friends," I said, "I should probably give you a name. Are you a boy or a girl?"

The robin turned its head and chirped.

"That doesn't help me. How about…"

I didn't get a chance to announce the bird's name, as I heard footsteps on the other side of the door, and the robin and its friend flew away. The sound of several locks slowly clicking was followed by some generous tugging of the heavy door, and then it finally opened to reveal a short and bony older man with a set of large keys in his hands.

"Well, come on in." He ushered me and stepped aside without offering to help with my luggage.

I hesitantly walked into the small hallway. "Hello. My name is Maya Radelis. I have a room reserved for two nights?"

"Yes, yes. Sign here." He closed the door and pointed to a large register book on a narrow hallway table. A fountain pen sat in a stand next to the book.

I set my suitcase down and sighed, looking around

for other guests. The house clearly had many guest rooms, as it looked large on the outside, but the hallway we stood in was dark and quiet at the moment.

"Leave your things. I will give you a tour." He spoke very good English, but his German accent was quite obvious in the way his "r's" were just off-putting enough to my ears. The man moved quickly, and I ran behind him, our footsteps echoing in the empty rooms.

"My name is Radner, Franz Radner. Dining room, sitting room, the study." He opened a creaky door into a small study. "Don't touch anything in here; these are all antiques." He gave me a sharp look.

I shook my head and tried to remain patient as we walked down a narrow hallway with an uneven floor. He continued the tour. "The bar—you can come here later to have a drink. Dinner is served at half past seven, breakfast is at half past eight. Your room is Number 5, up the stairs—here is your key." He handed me a large metal key. "You must lock your door. Any questions?"

My mind went blank, staring at the ancient key as I tried to think of questions. "No, thank you," I said, thinking it was best to go check on the state of my room.

He offered no help with my suitcase. I dragged it up the stairs, the wheels bumping against the wooden steps. The landing upstairs was slanted, and I nearly tripped on the two small steps someone thought to place by the entrance to the hallway. The ceiling lowered toward the end, and I almost had to bend my head not to hit it. Why exactly did Pauline like it here? What was this place in the past, anyway?

The door to my room was cracked slightly open. It was surprisingly lovely, with white lace curtains on the window and a large window seat that held a tray with books and an electric kettle with a teacup and cookies next to it. A large bed with a flower-patterned duvet stood in the middle with a glass-covered nightstand next to it. A newly remodeled bathroom with luxury toiletries was attached to the room. I shivered, wondering if I could possibly convince my strange host to turn the heat on. I looked at my watch: It was only six o'clock. Too early for me to go out, with no money whatsoever.

I was about to go speak to Franz about the heat when I noticed a bit of the old wallpaper in the corner of the window frame. I sat on the windowsill and leaned in for a closer look when my world shifted. The tray with the books and the tea kettle was gone. So was the large bed with the flower duvet, replaced by a narrow bed with a thin white blanket and a small white nightstand. A man sat at the desk, writing. The man looked remarkably like...

Lenin? The head of the Russian Revolution?

I bolted out of the room. A loud moan followed me out of the hallway, making the hair on my arms stand up. I ran to the landing, tripping on the uneven floor, and then even quicker downstairs. I found the narrow hallway behind the stairs Franz had showed me earlier and rushed to the bar, where a light was beaming through.

The bar was full of cigar smoke, making it difficult to see two men sitting there in large armchairs. It was Franz and a drinking partner, a tall middle-aged man with a face that would have been handsome except for a very large bold head, reminding me rather of a pumpkin. The pumpkin nodded to me, as if he was not surprised to see me at all.

"It… was… cold… in my room," I said, trying to stop my chattering teeth.

"Ah, the heater never works right in those rooms upstairs, does it, Franz?" The man got up and went behind the bar area. "It's been known to spook people up there, as well, when it gets cold," he mentioned casually. "A drink for you, maybe?"

"A whisky," I said. "What do you mean 'spook people'?"

"A real whisky drinker, look at that!" He brought me a glass of amber liquid and shook my hand. "I'm Jacob. My house is next door."

"Don't listen to his ghost stories. He doesn't know what he's saying," Franz said.

"Thank you so much." I took a large gulp, my hand still shaking.

"Fine, no ghost stories, but you should make it warmer upstairs for your guest," Jacob said.

"It will go out again as soon as I fix it. I'll get you an extra set of blankets after supper, how is that?"

"How old is this house?" I asked. The alcohol was doing its job to calm me, but my mind was furiously trying to figure out the paranormal upstairs.

"Oh, it's well over a hundred years old. I only bought it ten years ago and have been trying to fix the damn place ever since," Franz said gruffly.

"Don't mind him," said Jacob. "He doesn't appreciate old houses; don't know why he bought this one to begin with. It used to belong to my family, and we never had a problem with it until he got his hands on it. I don't think the house likes him."

"Nonsense!" Franz puffed angrily on his cigar.

"Oh, I don't think so. I never had trouble heating the rooms upstairs." Joseph bent closer to me. "You know, this used to be a doctor's practice a century ago."

I set my glass of whisky on my lap. "What kind of doctor was it?"

"Hmm... I believe he was a general type of doctor, for any kind of illness. What do you call that in America?"

"A general practitioner?"

"Yes, that's it. Broken bones, babies, gout, bad heart, that sort of thing. We inherited the house from my wife's family. The doctor was her great-uncle. Here, have some more. You look like you could use it," Joseph said.

"It's been a difficult day." I took another large sip of my drink. "Did this doctor ever have patients stay here, as in a hospital?"

"He did, actually," Joseph said. "Some wealthier patients who didn't wish to be taken to the large university hospital and preferred private care."

"Did anyone..." I paused. "Did anyone famous ever stay here?" My heart thumped.

"Well, the rumor is"—Joseph took a sip of his drink—"that one time the wife of Lenin stayed here for a week. You know who Lenin is? The man who was in charge of the Russian Revolution?"

"Of course," I said, gripping my chair arms.

"So what is it making your day bad? A young boy? Money trouble? Work?" Franz asked.

"Franz, don't pry. Young girls like their secrets." Jacob wagged a finger at him.

"No, it's quite all right." I was in control of my body again. "It's been many things, really: men, work, money, all of it. Just all got to me today. Did anyone ever die in this house?"

"I'm sure many people did. The doctor began his practice during the influenza epidemic. And then there was tuberculosis and cholera and a host of other things they couldn't make right back then."

I shivered, thinking of the moan I'd heard upstairs.

"But don't worry. No matter what he tells you, the house is not haunted," Franz said. "We have yet to see any ghosts. He only sees them when he's been into his drink."

Jacob laughed. "That's true. The spirits do show up more around the holidays. But no worries, girl. You're safe here. You'll sleep soundly. Everyone does. Especially after you've had some of his roasted lamb and potatoes for supper. Nothing like a full belly to get you to sleep well."

I rather doubted I'd sleep at all after what I had seen and heard upstairs. But the drink was helping, and my body was relaxing well.

"Well, let's have a toast to you having some luck tomorrow." Jacob raised his glass.

"Yes, I could use some luck, for sure." I smiled and took another sip.

After dinner, I had no choice but to go back upstairs. I walked up slowly, the flashlight on my phone turned on, listening for any noises. But it was quiet now. And my room was much warmer. Joseph was right; after I burrowed myself in the blankets, I slept great. Maybe it was the drinks or maybe it was the best lamb dinner I'd ever had. Or maybe it was because I knew David's phone number was still tucked into the pocket of my jeans.

Chapter 15

Bern, September 1913

Rebecca walked into the operating theater with great curiosity. It smelled strongly of having been freshly disinfected with mercuric chloride. There were several tables with basins full of steel instruments, sponges, and gauze around the empty center of the room. Sterilizers were set up off to the side, and another table held cauterizers, suction pumps, and unfamiliar surgical machines. Everything gleamed white, and she wondered how surgeons' eyes could stand the brightness.

Rebecca searched for a good place to stand. There were four tiered observation rows around the center, but only a few students present so far. She looked toward the door, hopeful that Mark would come in soon. She didn't have to wait long. He walked in with his confident stride, and she waved to him. She watched his face light up when he saw her, and then he slipped into the stand, touching her fingers lightly.

"You came!"

"Why wouldn't I?" she asked.

"I thought maybe you weren't ready to see a surgical procedure yet. Even dissections make you ill."

"I wouldn't miss it for the world," she said defiantly.

"You are brave to stand in the front."

"I want to be able to observe better."

"He asks questions of people who stand in the front."

She paled, but wouldn't admit her fear. "If you can answer questions, so can I. I studied his textbook on operative techniques. See?" She showed him her brand-new copy of *Chirurgische Operationslehre*, and he nodded in approval.

Someone tapped her on the shoulder, and she turned to the other side. It was Lara, handing her a handkerchief scented with rose water. "Oh, no need. I think I can handle the smell just fine. Yesterday was a weakness that I shall never repeat. And I've smelled ether before."

"It's not the ether smell you're going to be troubled with. You'll be grateful for this later," Lara said.

"Why are there so few students observing?" she asked Mark.

"This operation wasn't announced to all the students. Professor prefers to keep it quiet. It's the wife of a famous socialist from Russia. They're exiled."

Suddenly, the room hushed. She looked toward the door and watched a woman being wheeled in by two nurses in starched aprons. The woman's body was draped with white sheets, but her face and neck were visible. Rebecca couldn't help but check for any sign of fear. It wasn't fear, but rather resignation and fatigue that she observed. She wondered if the woman's suffering from her goiter was great.

The team of four surgeons and two more nurses walked in minutes later, and Rebecca held her breath as her heart beat faster. She tried to pay attention to everything, from the way Professor Kocher held his hands up for the surgical gloves to the way the anesthetist positioned the ether mask over the patient's face. She watched the nurses prepare the instruments and clean the woman's neck.

"Your patient, Dr. Kocher," the anesthetist announced.

Professor Kocher picked up a surgical knife from a nurse, turned to the students, and spoke. "Does anyone know what is the great advantage of ether over chloroform in general anesthesia?"

Mark answered, "A larger quantity of ether can be administered safely to a patient, Professor."

"Entirely correct. While both substances can be poisonous to a patient, the toxic dose of ether is much larger than that of chloroform. Therefore, we can use ether more safely for longer surgeries. Now, what would be the contraindications to using ether?"

"It irritates the respiratory tract," Rebecca heard herself respond.

"It does indeed. Your father is very familiar with this." Dr. Kocher nodded in approval. "Prolonged uses may cause bronchitis, and you would not wish to use ether with patients who show signs of catarrh." He continued, "When making an incision, we must avoid unnecessary injury to the adjacent structures. In this case, we'll make a long transverse incision."

Mark's eyes focused on the operation intently. He seemed to be holding his breath.

Rebecca turned to Lara. "What's the name of this woman? And who is she married to?"

"Her husband is Vladimir Ilyich Lenin, and her name is Nadezhda Krupskaya. He's the head of the

Russian Socialist Party," Lara whispered.

"Why were they exiled?"

"Anti-Tsar activities. They're in charge of many protests against the Tsar. They've been living abroad to escape being arrested and sent to prison."

The surgeon continued, "As we'll be resecting the goiter, ligature of the main vessels above and below on the left side and above on the right side will be necessary."

Things were moving fast, and a cautery iron was called for to stop the bleeding. Rebecca suddenly felt faint from the smell of burning flesh and was grateful for Lara's handkerchief. She heard the calls for suction, clamps, and sponges through a haze. Mark's warm hand covered hers, stroking in small circles, bringing circulation back. The room came back into focus, and she made sure to breathe through her nose.

Kocher's voice slowly became clearer in her ears. "As you can see, we're doing a partial removal on both sides to prevent hemorrhage. We must leave a small piece of thyroid tissue intact or the patient will suffer severe physical and mental deterioration—what we term *cachexia strumiprivia*."

"Do you and Vlad have to hide from the Tsar as well?" she whispered to Lara.

"Not I, but this is why Vlad came here," Lara said. "There were police watching him for holding meetings to discuss a newspaper that posted articles about people starving while the Tsar prospered. He knew he was going to be sent to Siberia any day. So he hopped on the train and came here."

"He doesn't wish to study law?" Rebecca asked.

"Think of it. What good is Swiss law to him in

Ukraine? He's a journalist. He studies and waits for his chance to return," Lara said. "If you tell anyone about this, we'll be in big trouble."

"You're wrong about me if you think I'm the kind of person to tell your secrets to anyone," Rebecca said.

"It's just that…we have so much at stake." Lara squeezed her hand. "Please forgive me. I just don't want to lose him. I love him, you see. If there's no more threat from the Tsar, maybe one day we can get married."

"I'm not a child who runs to her parents to tell what she heard all day. You can trust me."

Kocher worked slowly and meticulously. Rebecca's legs were tired from standing, but she endured. Mark was called on to answer more than a dozen questions, all correctly. She was as proud of him as if she were the one providing the correct answers.

"And now we must bring the divided tissues into apposition again by means of sutures," Kocher finally pronounced much later. "Good nursing care will now ensure that our patient will have sufficient recovery. Antiseptic wound treatment is essential for surgical success." He wiped his forehead and threw the last instrument into the blood-filled basin. The observers stood up and clapped. The nurses wheeled the woman out.

They walked out of the operating theater, careful not to step in the puddles of blood. Rebecca was surprised that the smells no longer bothered her, and her only thoughts were focused on Mark and his friends and the threats they faced in their country. She knew now that the rumors had been correct and these students had been involved in political activities. But was Mark?

He sure seemed interested only in medicine. Was he in danger, like Vlad? Should she worry about her heart being given to someone who was in danger from the Tsar's secret police?

****

"I have the most unusual patient arriving tomorrow morning in my recovery room," Father announced at supper two weeks later.

"Who is it, dear?" Mother asked, placing her soup spoon down and waving to the cook for the main course.

"Well, my dear. You know that I seldom accept patients for rehabilitation any more, but I find it difficult to reject Theodor. He is most persistent. Not to mention—I do wish for him to teach our Rebecca."

"Who is it, *Papi*?" Rebecca interrupted.

"She is the wife of a political refugee from Russia, would you believe it? Her name I really can't pronounce. But her husband is someone quite known to the socialists here." Father sliced the beef, and the cook began to serve the steaming slices that smelled of fresh garlic and herbs.

"Professor Kocher allowed me to observe her surgery a few weeks ago." Rebecca clapped her hands. "I would so much love to help care for her and observe her recovery. May I, please?"

"This is precisely why I have to continue granting him favors. He'll watch over your education for me." Father sighed.

Mother sighed as well. "You know, I'm starting to wonder if some of our medical faculty might be socialists themselves, with all the support they're giving to the Russian political students."

"I think you may be correct, my dear, but hardly anything like that matters, as long as they give Rebecca good preparation for her medical boards."

"I just don't know how you can stand watching them cut into a live person. The blood alone would make me faint on the spot," Hannah said, wrinkling her nose.

"Don't worry yourself about it, sister. No one is asking you to observe surgery. You can keep yourself to fashions." Rebecca rolled her eyes at Hannah. "So can I help you, *Papi?*"

"Yes, of course. But I do believe one of his surgical students will be coming, as well. And she'll have my nurse. So I'm not sure how much help will be required."

"Sounds as if our Rebecca would be rather a nuisance, then," Hannah said, popping a piece of a fresh roll into her mouth and smirking.

Rebecca ignored her. "Thank you, *Papi.* May I be excused from dinner? I have some studying to do."

"Why don't you finish your meal first? You're thinner every time I look at you," Mother pleaded.

"She's fine. Doctors always eat on the run. You must remember what it was like when I was young, my dear?"

"I do, but she's a woman, and she'll ruin her health forever. She'll catch an illness and it will put an end to her education and to any hope I ever had of having grandchildren."

"But what about me, Mother?" Hannah's cheeks puffed in anger.

"Of course, darling. I didn't mean to forget about you. Speaking of which, I've heard of some balls being planned for this winter. We will need to decide which ones you will attend."

Mother and Hannah bent their heads together and proceeded to discuss winter entertainment as Rebecca gave her father a kiss and went upstairs. She had a great deal to think about. But first, she needed to call and check on Sarah. She hadn't heard from her in a few weeks, and Father hadn't made any great progress in speaking with Friedrick about being kinder to Sarah. Her friend continued to look worn, thin, and ghostly pale. Although there hadn't been any new bruises or broken bones since that awful night, still Rebecca believed that Sarah's situation was quite desperate. There had to be something she could do to help her. They simply had to meet alone and come up with some solutions. Maybe she could talk to Mark and Lara about this.

Thinking of Mark, tomorrow she'd meet Lenin's wife and try to find out more about all this socialist talk and how much exactly Mark was involved with the revolutionaries. Mainly, she needed to estimate how much danger he was in. From what she has heard from Lara, she was not entirely optimistic. This woman being in her father's care was just the perfect opportunity for Rebecca to obtain information.

Chapter 16

Bern, October 1913

Rebecca closed the door to the dining room, effectively tuning out Mother and Hannah discussing upcoming winter balls, and ran to Father's medical practice. She hurried straight upstairs to the recovery rooms, skipping steps as much as her long skirt allowed. At the landing, she stopped to catch her breath and adjust the stray hairs coming out of her tight chignon. Damn this long hair! She should have cut it short, as some modern women were doing.

"Is someone chasing you, dear Rebecca?" Mark stood at the bottom of the stairs, waving at her. Joy filled her chest immediately. As it rose to her lips, she couldn't help smiling.

"I'm here to help my father today. Were you sent with Dr. Kocher's patient?" she asked.

"Yes. I am to watch over her today. It was the woman you observed having surgery, Nadezhda Krupskaya."

How foreign that name sounded! "Yes, I remember well. That's why I'm here too."

Mark was up the stairs and next to her now. His hand on the banister moved nearly on top of hers, his face barely inches away. Rebecca felt somewhat faint, whether from the lack of breakfast, from running

139

upstairs, or from Mark's face so close to hers—she wasn't quite sure. His other hand briefly touched her cheek, and she closed her eyes in pleasure. Could he tell what effect he had on her? Did she want him to know? Was he planning to kiss her? Would she allow it?

"I'm so glad you'll be here today," he said and walked away, leaving her breathless. *Why didn't he kiss me?*

Rebecca composed herself and followed him. In the largest recovery room, Father was bent over the same woman she'd observed in surgery only recently. A man sat in a chair by her bed. His face appeared concerned, but then he laughed at her father's joke. Mark was talking to a nurse in a starched white apron and hat. The room had been freshly cleaned, the smell of disinfectant still strong.

Papi looked back, hearing her at the door. "Oh, Rebecca! Come in, come in. I will introduce you to Herr Lenin and his wife, Fräulein Krupskaya, who will be in our charge for the next week."

"Nadya, please." A hoarse voice spoke from the bed, and the nurse hurried with a glass of water.

Herr Lenin stood up and bowed to Rebecca, greeting her with a warm smile. So this was the Socialist her friends told her about. He was rather short and unimposing; just a bit shorter than she was, actually. His bald head and a rather large mustache didn't disguise the fact that he was still young.

Throughout the day, Rebecca realized that, other than bringing Nadya meals and tucking in her blankets a few times, there was hardly any other way she could be helpful. The nurse took care of bathroom needs, bathing, and stretches to ensure Nadya was recovering muscle function. Mark changed the dressing, examined the drains, irrigated the sutures, and applied ointment to speed up the healing. Mark also mixed a special tonic and administered it to the patient at certain times. Rebecca moped around the hallways, waiting for instructions and getting none. She hated that she hadn't had any time alone with Nadya or her husband to ask them questions about her friends' involvement with revolutionary activities. Mainly, she did not like feeling useless.

She did enjoy watching Mark, though, so sure in his procedures, his long fingers doing exact actions in confidence. They exchanged many glances and slight touches of hands throughout the day, but she worried someone would notice and tried to keep her distance. It was the right course, she decided, until she was certain how she felt about this progress in their affections. In the early afternoon, in exasperation, she sought solitude in one of the empty recovery rooms upstairs, planning to write a note to Sarah, telling her she hoped to visit with her as soon as it was possible.

"Oh, I'm terribly sorry," Rebecca said, when she realized the room's chair and desk were already occupied by Herr Lenin. He'd clearly had the same idea about writing.

"I should apologize as well. This is your father's hospital, and I intrude with my letters." Lenin spoke hurriedly, standing up and bowing to her again.

"You're welcome everywhere, no apology needed. I was simply looking for some space to write a note, but I can go elsewhere."

"I am almost finished. I'm happy to give up the desk to you for your writing." Herr Lenin began to pack up his papers and inkwell.

"Oh, no need to pack up. My note is not as important as your work," she protested.

"You're familiar with my work?" He sat back in the chair and looked up with interest.

"Mark—Doctor Minchin—told me you're exiled by the Tsar because you've been protesting his laws."

"That is indeed correct. However, it's much more than the Tsar that we're trying to fight. The Russian Social Democratic Labor Party attempts to liberate the working class from the oppression of the Tsar and bourgeoisie. The other leaders of the party and I are leading the exploited workers of Russia into the revolution that will overthrow the bourgeoisie rule and establish Communism in our country and then throughout the world."

"Vladimir Ilyich, do you believe that's possible? That your party can start a revolution against the Tsar?" Mark spoke behind Rebecca.

"It's not just possible, but it's already happening, my dear doctor. Just this year, we had May Day strikes in Saint Petersburg that showed the world that the industrial proletariat is following its revolutionary course. We're very close, Doctor Minchin, very close."

"How can you lead an uprising in such a large country? What will you do to spread the word?" Rebecca asked.

"There are many members of our party here in Bern, Geneva, and Zurich, planning and organizing, at the moment. We have underground networks and newspapers. Here is an issue of *Iskra* for you to read." Lenin took out a fragile set of papers and handed them to Mark.

"Thank you. I'll read them carefully."

"There are meetings in the student colony here in Bern at least twice a week to discuss Bolshevik plans. You need to participate. The Revolution is coming." He gathered the rest of his papers, closed his inkwell, bowed again, and walked back to his wife's room.

Rebecca looked at Mark, who was busy scanning the papers. She was truly concerned now. Lenin sounded so certain that this revolution was going to succeed. Was it possible? Or was he a lunatic, leading people to prison and ruin? How much danger was Mark actually in?

"What do these papers say?" She looked over Mark's shoulder, worry spreading through her chest and stomach.

"It talks about the poor starving in Russia, Ukraine, and Belarus, while the rich are buying new houses and vacationing in Europe at the seaside. It says there are enough people willing to rise up against the rich to make the working class the rulers instead." Mark's voice was grave.

"Is this true? Is the paper just trying to maybe rile people up to serve the political party?"

"It is true, and it breaks my heart to be away from home at a time like this. I need to start going to these political meetings. I feel so separated from my community sometimes, always at my classes, always at the hospital, and never contributing to my country." Mark paced across the room and looked out the window, setting the copy of *Iskra* down on the now-empty desk.

"But you *are* contributing! They will need surgeons in your country, even if they do succeed with this revolution. Surely you must realize doctors are always needed everywhere. Look what's happening now. If Dr. Kocher hadn't performed the operation on Nadya, she wouldn't be able to do her political work."

"If the uprising is to happen, they'll need every man and every woman to fight. Don't you understand?"

"I do. Yet nothing is happening right now." She came close and put her hands on his chest. "All you see is a newspaper telling stories and people giving speeches. Finish your education, so you can be useful to this Bolshevik Party when they finally do need you. If you go to prison, you'll be no help to them, ever." *And you'll be lost to me,* she wanted to add but didn't.

"You are correct, of course. I am grateful, as always, for your wisdom." Mark held her face gently.

His eyes were teary. Then they changed, the deep brown turning as black as the winter night sky. She searched them, hopeful and fearful at the same time. His lips reached hers, and the warmth traveled all the way down to the pit of her stomach and then to her legs. She wrapped her arms around his neck and inhaled the surgical scent of him, so familiar. She gasped as his lips withdrew, then touched her fingertips to her lips.

"You don't need to worry about me thinking of politics. All I ever think about is you. I try so hard to do my work at the hospital, but you fill my thoughts. I think, 'Where is she? What's she doing? Who's she talking to? Is she happy?' I cannot sleep sometimes." Heat pulsed through his skin and radiated into the space between the two of them.

"I don't know if you should say all these things." She tried to move away, but was held by the power of his eyes. Of his love.

"I love you. How can I not say it?" He kissed her again.

She couldn't think at all. The world around them melted and fell away. All she knew were his hands on her back, shoulders, neck, head. *Please don't ever stop,* she prayed silently and almost cried when she felt him move away. Although her body still burned and shook, she wasn't sure this was not all her imagination.

He held her face gently. "I'm sorry I kissed you without permission."

"No, please, don't be sorry." She turned away for a moment, willing her body to settle down. There. Better. "I love you too," she whispered, burying her face into his chest and inhaling the smell of his clean white shirt.

He picked her up and spun her around the room, making her squeal. "You've made me so happy."

"Put me down!" She pounded on his chest in pretend protest.

Mark collapsed on the empty bed and put her on his lap. He hugged her close and kissed her in earnest. She ran her fingers through his hair. She'd never imagined love could feel like this, where you no longer wanted to be your own person but wished to fully belong to someone else. She wanted Mark to possess her body, and it wasn't frightening at all.

"Rebecca! What do you think you're doing?" Father's voice boomed from the doorway and exploded in her ears.

She jumped up from Mark's lap, cheeks blazing. "Father, I'm so sorry…"

"Dr. Miller, my apologies," Mark said. "I have good respect for your daughter."

"You will not speak. You will leave immediately.

How dare you behave in such a way? I trusted you to care for my patients!"

"But Father, we love each other!"

"You will go straight home, Rebecca."

Mark was on his way out of the room, but he tried again. "Dr. Miller, I did not mean disrespect."

"Must you be so cruel?" Rebecca yelled out. "It was only a kiss. What do you think you saw?"

"You don't have the right to disagree with me, at the moment. I'm afraid your mother's fears came true, and she'll be furious tonight. Go home. Now. We will discuss this later." Father walked out, knocking a chair into the wall on his way out with a loud crash.

Rebecca walked home as slowly as she could. Mark disappeared through the back door. She was hurt that he didn't attempt to speak to her father to defend himself. Or to her, for that matter. She sniffled. It wasn't fair she had to face her family all alone, while he ran home to the safety of his friends. She stood in front of her home, wondering whether to enter or to run away. And where would she run? Sarah had enough troubles without her. And besides—she'd never been a coward. She opened the door and marched in. Thankfully the hallway was quiet, the housekeeper and cook nowhere to be seen.

She snuck upstairs, to avoid being noticed by Hannah, and closed her door quietly. There was really no point in changing her clothes prior to the scolding she was expecting at dinner, but there was also no point in coming to dinner quickly. So she brushed her hair and arranged it with combs and put on a clean dress and shoes. It certainly didn't hurt to feel clean when one was being yelled at, she decided before heading to the dining room, her back held straight in defiance.

The family went silent as she walked into the dining room.

They had heard, then.

She sat down in her chair, placed the napkin in her lap, and faced the enemy.

"Have you had an offer of marriage from that man?" Mother began.

"I have not."

"Do you expect one?"

Rebecca hadn't thought of marrying Mark. She loved him, but why did everything in Mother's mind have to turn into marriage? Why couldn't they just enjoy being in love?

"I don't know, Mother. We only had just one kiss," she protested feebly.

Father coughed at her mention of the kiss, and Hannah giggled. Mother turned a bright color. Rebecca looked down, then looked up at everyone again. She had nothing to be ashamed off. It was only a kiss! Well…several, but still.

"Your father found you engaged in improper behavior with a man who has not made you an offer of marriage. And while you were expected to perform duties for your father. Responsibilities you begged for over and over, as you claim you wish to become a doctor."

Mother always knew ways to make her feel guilty.

"I'm so sorry, Father."

"Rebecca," Father said, "I do believe that it may be time for us to look for a husband for you. You are twenty now, and I can see that your mother's been right. Education is not everything; you may desire to be married as well."

"Of course I'm right," Mother huffed. "And if we don't find her a husband, she'll continue looking for improper behavior herself."

"So can we go to more balls, then? How about the one at the new Hotel Bellevue Palace? Everyone is going to be there! Please?" Hannah interjected.

"Am I to be auctioned off at the ball? Have you lost your mind?" Rebecca thought she might explode in anger at Hannah. "And Mother, I have no plans to be married, at the moment. I'm not ready to marry anyone. *Papi*, you know how hard my studies are. I don't have time to care for a husband."

"And yet you have time to kiss strange boys?" Mother raised her voice.

Her head was beginning to throb rather painfully. "Mark Minchin is almost finished with his studies, and he is a student of Professor Kocher. He's going to become a surgeon, a respectable profession. A kiss from him surely couldn't be too improper."

"He's not asked for our permission to marry you. And he'll not receive it either," Mother said.

"I remember now." Father's voice boomed with anger. "You brought him here when your ankle was hurt. You said he was a student from Ukraine. Do you understand you'd have no future with him? He has to return home; he can't stay here. His future belongs elsewhere. And you'll not be welcome in his country. Jews are hated and killed in Ukraine."

"But why can't he stay here, *Papi*? We can keep Mark safe here in Switzerland. You are right, he can't go back home. It is not safe." Rebecca felt her eyes fill with tears. "If he and I married, he could stay here, and then he could bring his family here and none of them would ever be in danger again."

"You can see it's gone too far. We must put a stop to this immediately," Mother said to Father.

"A ball is a great idea," Hannah said again, shoving a piece of chicken into her mouth.

"Stop with your stupid ball!" Rebecca shouted.

"You'll watch your manners," Mother said. "You will be going to balls with your sister. You'll also be supervised more closely in all your activities now. And you may not see this man anymore."

"You can't do that, Mother! You can't prohibit me from seeing someone. I'm an adult now!"

"I can do as I wish until you are a married woman," Mother said dryly. "So it's in your best interest to marry quickly and run your own household. Then you may do as you please."

Rebecca was desperate to win the argument and defy her parents. They were wrong, plain wrong about Mark. Her anger burned a hole inside her. However, if she argued and fought more, she'd likely get more restrictions and wouldn't be able to see Mark at all. Rebecca bit her lip. Hard. She knew her eyes were blazing.

"Fine! I'll go to the balls. But I'm not getting married until I find someone I really like—love, preferably."

"No one is forcing you to marry a person you detest, my dear. By all means, choose well," Father said. "Let us finish our dinner in peace now."

Chapter 17

Bern, August, Tuesday—Present Time

Sunlight streamed through the windows. I lay on the cool white sheets, trying to remember the last time I'd slept in this late. I had dreamt of David last night. It was a delicious dream, the kind that filled my stomach with warmth and put a big smile on my face. Finally, my own dream and not someone else's. I stretched luxuriously, allowing myself time to get up slowly and not rush.

Then a nagging sadness filled my chest and my enjoyment of the morning was over.

My sister's picture. My money. Probation.

My medical school career was as good as over. I had no idea what that remediation plan was going to list for me to do, but I was pretty sure I wasn't going to like doing it. I also had a nagging suspicion that I wasn't going to *want* to do it. A small part of me was beginning to consider the possibility of not returning to the residency. *Ever.*

The phone buzzed. I looked at the caller ID. Grandma. Ugh, she always knew when I was feeling vulnerable.

"Baba, I've been meaning to call you. I'm sorry, it's just that the time difference is very confusing," I said.

"Always excuses for your Babushka."

"I'm sorry. Is everything okay?"

"Are you healthy?" she asked.

"I'm in perfect health. I'm fine."

"Where are you?"

I hesitated. Safer to tell her I was still in Scotland. Less questions, for sure. On the other hand, more lies.

"I took a little trip to Switzerland, just for two days. But I'm flying back to New York on Thursday night, so I'll be back home on Friday. I'll see you Friday," I emphasized.

"Switzerland? What are you doing in Switzerland?"

She wasn't fooled, damn it. "I heard it was pretty here, and a friend of mine suggested I see it. I'm in Bern. It's an old and pretty town."

"Wait a minute. I've heard of Bern. I think my father, your great-grandfather, once lived there. He always said he had many good memories of the city."

"Really? That's interesting. When did he live here?" I asked. Coincidences seemed to follow me everywhere these days. Maybe this was what happened when you began to pay attention to them.

"I think as a young boy. I'll look for his journal. He left it for me when he died. I've never read it, as his writing is very difficult to read. Maybe when you come back we can read it together?"

"Sure, that'd be great. Especially now that I've seen the city. Oh, since you're looking through things, Baba…" I paused. "I lost the one photograph I had of Ella and me. Can you please find another one for me to keep?"

"Of course." She sighed. "You know I have many.

You might wish to have a picture of your mother, as well. I'll look through my albums this afternoon."

"Thank you," I said, relieved. "I love you and miss you. See you in a few days."

"Call me when you're at the airport. And call me if your airplane is delayed," she instructed.

When I went down to the dining room, Franz was busy yelling at the housekeeping staff. I quickly ate a cheese pastry resembling a Danish and drank a delicious black coffee. I still had no money, so I wrapped two pieces of toast in a napkin and placed them in my backpack for later. I hoped that at least one of my credit cards would arrive today, and I would be able to buy food and pay for my own room again.

Feeling the sunshine as I opened the door and smelling the fresh flowers outside gave me some renewed energy. My web searches this morning for Mark, the medical student of Theodor Kocher, turned up nothing. I had no particular plan for where to go, but I decided to let Fate and my ring guide me. I followed the crowds to the open-air markets of the Old Town, enjoying the sights and smells of the fresh flowers and fruit, and wishing I had some money to browse through the colorful accessories for sale.

Some time later, I turned to the main street, Kramgasse, which displayed the medieval town clock on top of a large tower. I arrived at the clock just as a large crowd gathered to watch the figurines in the clock move as it struck the hour. A balloon seller attracted my attention, and I had a sudden desire to buy one of the brightly colored globes with long strings. It was such a childish wish that I actually giggled quietly to myself before spending the last of my coins on a smooth pink balloon. I was inhaling the smell of the latex with pleasure when a familiar voice sounded from behind me.

"A balloon?"

"Haven't you ever bought a balloon?" I spun around.

David was here! My heart danced with joy; every cell of my body lit up in excitement at his being near me.

"Oh, tons of times."

"Sure you have!"

"You make a lot of assumptions, but you don't know anything about me." His mouth curved in a half-smile. "So why do you happen to be everywhere I go?" he asked, sitting down next to me on the empty bench spot.

"I believe you are the one stalking me, let me remind you." I laughed. "What are you doing walking around the tourist areas, anyway? Don't you have a family thing? Are they sick of you already?"

"Yeah, they kicked me out. Told me to go find a tourist to bother. You got any other plans besides buying balloons?"

He wants to spend time with me, my heart sang. I ordered myself to calm down and be rational. David could, of course, be useful in this town. He did seem to know his whereabouts. "Do you know Bern well? Can you show me around?"

"It's a small city. I should be able to give you a bit of a tour. I have a few free hours. Where do you wanna go?"

"What do you recommend?" The truth was—I was willing to go anywhere with David. The warmth radiating from him made it difficult to think. I just wanted to get moving.

"Still haven't looked at that travel book, have you? It's all right, I'm not offended." He touched his right hand to his heart in a mock gesture. "Well, it's a nice sunny day. How about we start with a walk through the Old Town right here, then to the University Botanical Garden, and then grab a bite to eat? If we're still talking to each other after all that, maybe we'll walk somewhere else."

He took off his sunglasses and leaned closer to me while talking, so that I could hear him over the hum of the crowd. I smelled the light scent of shampoo, coffee, and laundry soap on his T-shirt. I struggled not to inhale too deeply.

"Sounds great." I moved back, overwhelmed by how strongly I reacted to him.

"All right." He stood up and pointed at my balloon. "Let it go and make a wish."

I let go of the balloon. David was already moving out of the square, and I gladly followed, trying to keep up with his fast pace. Why was I so drawn to him? He stretched his arm back, and his hand found mine and gently clasped it. The touch sent waves of heat through my arm and into my stomach. I fought the sudden sense of déjà vu and focused my attention on the sights.

"You know, all the buildings look similar to me," I observed. "All the gray stone and the covered sidewalks."

David was oblivious to my turmoil, or maybe he was just pretending not to notice. "They *are* all the same in style. They had a great fire here in medieval times, in 1405, I believe. The entire city burned down.

It was rebuilt entirely out of stone, so that it would survive in case of another fire."

"Very practical."

"Yes, focus on survival, not beauty. But the city has its charm, too. Let me show you this great view of the old bridge. We just need to walk a few blocks over this way, to the Aare River."

A few minutes later, we took in a breathtaking view of a calm emerald river with an old stone bridge separating two sides of the city: the old and the new. The old city's houses lined the riverbank tightly, their orange rooftops resembling hats, their roof windows looking at the houses on the other side, watching over their inhabitants.

"I love the colors here," I said, inhaling the fresh air brought by the wind from the river.

"This bridge we are standing on is called Nydeggbrücke, and the one we are looking at is Untertorbrücke. Untertorbrücke is the oldest bridge in Bern. It was built in the 1400s."

"What does Un-ter-tor-brücke mean?"

"Lower bridge."

"Practical again."

"Should we get going to the Botanical Garden?" David asked.

"Sure."

"The Garden is part of the University of Bern. We'll walk back through the Old Town and then down by the river."

We arrived at the Botanical Garden as the afternoon clouds rolled in across the sky. David confidently led me through. "My mother always says it's her favorite place in the city."

"Where is your mother, by the way? How come she is skipping the family reunion?"

"She had a knee replacement and thought it would be best if she rested a while instead of running around on cobblestones here."

We were approaching a small archway at the end of the Japanese garden when I smelled a familiar scent. I looked more closely at the lush purple blooms on the archway.

Wisteria.

I swayed. The smell filled my nostrils and became intoxicating. I pinched my nose.

"You don't like the smell of wisteria?" David asked. "I love it. It reminds me of sour candy. My mouth is watering for some right now." He touched the blooms over our heads, making a few brightly colored petals fall gently on his hair.

"Candy?" I blew air in strangled breaths. The horrid blooms smelled like the sweat and tears and dirt that were on my sister's face when she lay dying and I hugged her small body to me, begging her to stop pretending.

And then, as David touched another bloom, unaware of the impact the scent was having on me, the view of wisteria shifted, and I was no longer in the same garden. But I wasn't in the garden with my sister either. I was back in the garden from the dream I had in Edinburgh. My mind traced the path to the right of the wisteria archway, and I knew it led past the bushes and the oak tree, around the fountain, and to the bench surrounded by more wisteria and rose bushes. I knew that path like the back of my hand. I knew I was waiting for someone with some urgency.

My head was spinning and I felt disoriented, unsure of my surroundings, as if I had just walked off a fast-spinning ride. I grabbed onto David's arm to steady me.

"I've been here before. I can see this garden, but not from right now. I smell flowers that are not even here." I felt tears on my cheeks. "I know I'm not making any sense, and please don't think I'm insane. I'll explain in a minute... I need...a minute."

I sat down on a chair nearby, put my head in my hands, closed my eyes, and allowed the memories to wash over me. The smell of wisteria was replaced with fresh rain, and then I smelled something else. Perfume—a very gentle scent of roses. I found myself oddly calm, despite the experience. My heart beat steadily, and my senses were sharp. I expected to feel cold, as in the presence of a ghost, but I continued to feel the warm sunshine.

Images flashed through my mind, too fast to understand, swirling. Then sounds: birds, a man's voice, children's voices, crying, a woman's voice. I took a few deep breaths and willed my mind to still the images. I watched a man, with little round glasses, riding his bike on the path toward me. I knew I was happy to see him. My mind told me I loved him, and I wanted to tell him something very important. I knew it was something very urgent, because my face was wet with tears and my chest was hurting in grief. I was sad, desperately sad, but relieved to see him, because I was sure he was there to help me.

And then the images broke and I was back with David. I lifted my head and noticed we were sitting at a small café. I could still smell the wisteria and the roses, but the power of the memory began to fade. The nausea and dizziness were also gone.

David was stretched out in the chair across the table from me, a coffee cup in his hand. When did he get coffee? He didn't look concerned or frightened, but he wasn't looking at me either. I knew I'd have to tell him, but how?

"I'm okay now. Thanks for sticking around," I said slowly.

"No problem! I'm enjoying my coffee." He turned his coffee cup in his hand and gave me a sideways look. "You wanna tell me what this is all about?"

"I just need a minute."

"Sure." He pushed a cup of coffee toward me. "I added cream and sugar."

I took a sip and gave him a grateful look. "Thanks. David, it's not an easy thing to explain."

"I figured as much."

"This is gonna sound really crazy."

"I can do crazy."

I laughed nervously. "Just give me a minute to explain! Okay. So, I found this antique ring in Edinburgh." I pointed to my ring and continued, "And ever since then, I keep having dreams or, like, memories of a woman who…I believe, owned this ring."

David nodded and set his coffee cup down on the table. "How do you know this woman owned the ring?"

"How do I know the woman…? Is that the only question you have about this?"

"Well, that's a reasonable question, isn't it?"

"You don't want to know if I'm making this up?" I raised my brows.

"Well, I just watched you turn pale, as if you'd seen a ghost, and act as if you'd lost your wits." He waved a hand at me. "No, I didn't mean as if you had actually lost your wits—it was more like you were in shock. Or more like if you weren't even here."

"I wasn't. That's the whole point. I wasn't really here. Or at least not here with you."

"I know." He looked at me curiously. "The question is, will you tell me now what's going on? Or am I not trustworthy enough?"

"Well..." I was stumped at how to explain exactly what was happening to me, without sounding even crazier. "I wasn't exactly... It just seemed like... Oh, hell! I know this looks bad. But I swear, I'm not psychotic!"

"Look, is there any possible chance that you may be taking something? Like just a little bit of something for stress?"

"Are you asking if I'm doing drugs? Oh, great! I must look even more out of control than I thought." I stood up and paced in frustration.

"Hey! Hey!" He lifted out of his seat and touched my arm lightly. "It's all right. I don't think you're crazy. I do believe you."

"Fine. I'll be better in a second, and then I can explain more," I said, sitting back down and wiping away my tears with the napkin he handed me.

"How about we get out of here?" He looked at the children running between the tables. "I know a nice quiet place where we can talk."

He didn't wait for my answer, but got up and gently took hold of my arm, pulling me to come along. It felt very comforting to lean on him, even though I didn't need it. I could walk just fine, but I didn't want him to know. I let him lead me gently down the path and away from the wisteria and the garden, as the power of the memories faded fully away.

Chapter 18

Bern, August, Tuesday—Present Time

I was glad David insisted on a taxi, as my legs kept buckling despite my best efforts to pull myself together. The ride was quick, but I soon wished it was longer. As the car bounced on the cobblestone streets, David wrapped his arm around me, stroking my shoulder with his fingertips. I could've used a few more minutes of this prior to having a serious discussion or, as I worried, having another round of questions regarding my sanity.

As he helped me out of the taxi, I gasped at the sight of the six-story neoclassical building rising in front of me.

"This is Bellevue Palace," David said, noticing my look.

"Wait, why are we here? I was hoping we'd go to a small place—somewhere quiet. This looks like a fancy hotel."

"They have a very quiet bar. They serve politicians, so they understand how to keep secrets. I thought this place would be good. Trust me, you'll approve of it."

"But I'm not dressed for a hotel like this," I protested, pointing at my casual summer dress. "This isn't cocktail attire."

"You're fine. It's lunch hour, not cocktails. And you look beautiful." He grabbed me firmly by my elbow and led me to the massive doors. "People who stay here don't dress in fancy gowns. I'm telling you, it's all politicians and people who do business with the government. Let's go have that drink."

I pulled my elbow back. "I'll have a drink with you, but… Listen, I… This is really awkward. Remember how we were on the train together? I fell asleep when I was sitting in my seat. When I got off the train, my wallet was missing."

"What? Someone stole your wallet?" He stepped back, shaking his head.

"I know, I know. I was really stupid to fall asleep. I've ordered replacement cards. But I don't have any cash right now. So do you mind paying for my drink?"

David's mouth hung open for a second. Then he spoke, much louder than before. "You've been hanging out with me this whole time, and you've been in Bern for two days, and you didn't say anything to me?" He ran a hand through his hair. "What the hell, Maya? Why wouldn't you say something? I gave you my cell!"

"Look, I've been taking care of myself since before I ever met you."

"But what have you been doing to get by? Where are you even staying?" He began to pace on the steps.

"I called Pauline. My friend in Paris, remember? And she paid for my hotel and food. She actually made me move to a hotel where they had better food." I sighed. "So I guess I haven't been taking care of myself. Pauline has."

"Well, I'm glad you've had someone helping you out. It's okay to ask for help, you know, when your wallet gets stolen. It can happen to anyone—it's nothing to feel embarrassed about." He stopped pacing and touched my shoulder.

"I'm not embarrassed. Are you going to buy me that drink now?" I was anxious to finally get off the front steps of the hotel.

David shook his head again. "Sure, let's go in."

We walked into a lobby with marble floors reflecting the light of a crystal chandelier hanging from the stained-glass ceiling. Perhaps David was right and this was a good, quiet place to talk. There were several people in the lobby, but you could hardly see them or hear their voices, let alone know their conversations.

"Follow me. The bar is through this door," David said.

I wanted to follow him, but my feet refused, suddenly glued to the floor in front of the large open doors to an empty ballroom. But it wasn't empty in my mind.

"Does it make you feel like dancing?" David's voice said quietly in my left ear. "They used to have many balls in this room. Now mainly just large meetings. Not much society in Switzerland, so hotel ballrooms don't get used for weddings as they do in New York."

I turned away, trying to break the spell. I didn't wish to appear as if I had lost my mind again. At least not until I explained to him what had been happening. But the face of a man I'd danced with in this ballroom was very clear to me. Was this Mark?

"They have really good champagne and gin. What do you like to drink?" David asked, pointing to the bottles as we walked into the small, dark bar.

"Whisky." I looked around for a seat.

"Come over here. This table is the best."

"This is perfect. You were right," I said to him, slipping into a seat by the wall and stretching my legs comfortably.

Our table was in a dark corner, away from the window. The bar held only a few round tables, surrounded by upholstered chairs. There were tall leather bar stools and mirrored walls with small windows, candles, and what appeared to be an excellent collection of Scotch, gin, and other spirits. A large golden sculpture of some winged angel-like creature stood on the side of the bar. David was right; the space was quiet, with only two casually dressed men at the bar, whispering. Our drinks arrived quickly, and I took a larger-than-necessary gulp of my whisky.

"Why are you even here with me, David?" I started, attempting to postpone the conversation about the ring. "Aren't you supposed to be with your family for all your 'family reunion activities,' whatever they are?"

"The reunion is not until this weekend, and it's not here in town. It's at a lake nearby, at my uncle's lake house. We're going Friday."

"What are you gonna do until Friday?" I was relieved he said he had to leave Friday. It would make it easier for me to return to Paris.

"Walk around, sit in coffee shops, drink wine, and rescue you from trouble, pickpockets, and visions, apparently."

"I hope you have better things to do."

"Not really." He leaned closer.

"I really do appreciate you showing me around and putting up with my strange story."

"I like spending time with you. It's not a chore."

He looked straight at me, reading my response, and for a moment I struggled to breathe.

I tried to control my face, but it wasn't possible. I liked him, and I probably radiated my thoughts.

"How many times has this happened to you? With this ring?" he asked.

"Only a few." I hesitated. "It's gotten worse since I came to Bern."

"All right." He tapped his fingers on the table. "So it started happening when you found this ring, you said? In Edinburgh?"

I told him the whole story then. He kept a blank but serious expression on his face. I was sure that as a lawyer he was used to hearing all kinds of stories. "So what did the woman say when you—I guess—*saw* her in the garden today?"

"She didn't say anything. I felt as if I *was* her. I just knew I felt sad, and also that I was in love. As her I was in love, not me." I felt the redness spreading through my cheeks. "Why is this happening to me?" I shook my head. "Why am I the one having these experiences? I'm a scientist, for God's sake. I don't believe in this magical nonsense!"

"Are you sure you don't believe in this? Because I'm having trouble pretending I didn't see you, earlier." He seemed to half-smile with his eyes. "What a strange experience that must be. Do you know who she is in love with?"

"Yes. She is in love with a man whose name is Mark. He gave her this ring and wrote the inscription. I saw his face this morning. It was sort of fuzzy—just a round face with glasses."

"All right, let me think it through. I need to be

logical about this. So you have a ring that belonged to a woman, and it has an inscription on it. And you have a medical textbook from 1907 that possibly belonged to this man, Mark, who possibly lived here in Bern. And the book and the ring both have the same words in them. Right?"

"Right. And Mark was in love with this woman. He must've been the one who gave her the ring."

"As an engagement ring?"

"Very likely."

"Incredible. Really," David said quietly. "Did you look into the possibility he was a medical student at the university here?"

"Yes, I went to the University of Bern's archives yesterday, and got the names of all the 'Marks' who attended during the right years. There are eleven. I did a search for Marks who were students of Kocher, because that's who wrote the textbook, but I found nothing."

"So here's a question. Why do you want to look into this? Do you want to keep seeing these dreams and memories?"

"I feel like there is a reason I needed to buy this ring. And there's a reason these memories are coming to me. This ring was at that shop for many years and no one bought it. What if it waited for me, and it's showing things to *me*? If I stop paying attention, what if some important story doesn't get told?"

"What if you learn that something terrible happened to these people?" David leaned closer and whispered, "What if Mark murders her in that garden? What are you going to do with that information? You don't even know who she is."

"Well, that's why I came here, right? I followed the

clues the ring gave me, and then I found the book in Paris, and now I'm here."

"But you have no money, no clear plan, and little to go on but these experiences. I just don't get it." He sighed.

"I don't expect anyone would," I said.

"I'm sorry, but you have to be a little practical, at least. How long will you spend here? Don't you have to get back to your residency?"

"I do," I said. "I'm leaving tomorrow." I thought for a moment. Why *was* I leaving tomorrow? If my cards arrived today or tomorrow, there was no reason I had to leave so soon. And now I wasn't alone. "Or maybe the day after."

"All right, so you only have two days? You do realize that's a ridiculously short amount of time to find any evidence?"

"Spoken like a true lawyer." I dismissed him with a wave of my hand.

"Spoken like a practical person, which you should be more of—as a scientist. Fine. Will you take off the ring after?" he asked.

"Probably. Depends on what I find out," I said, my chin raised in defiance.

"Look," he began, "don't think that I don't believe you. I just don't meet many people who'd hang around an old town, hoping to trace a hundred-year-old story based on an antique ring and an inscription in a book. But maybe you're right and there's a reason why this happened to you."

"Well, thank you for giving me the benefit of the doubt." I looked at him carefully to check whether he really believed me or was just trying to make sure I

167

didn't get angry and cause a scene.

He leaned back in his chair, forehead wrinkled in thought. I had a sudden deep desire to sit next to him and rub his forehead until it relaxed. The desire was so strong, I had to hold onto my chair. The truth was, I suddenly felt that I had done this same motion many times before, with David, and that he loved it. I excused myself to the restroom, and he pointed the way, with a gesture that also felt so familiar that I nearly stumbled trying to get out of the chair in a hurry. It took me a few minutes to regain my composure in the bathroom.

When I was on my way back, I stood, stunned, at the entrance to the bar. My seat was occupied by a tall, gorgeous redhead in a suit and heels, sharing a drink with David and bending her head very close to his, whispering. *A girlfriend*—a voice whispered in my ear. Worry traveled to my stomach, twisting into painful coils. I wasn't sure whether to run or march in there indignantly and sit next to them, demanding my rightful place in the conversation. Finally, I marched to the table, dragged a chair from the next table over, and sat between them.

David put a hand gently on my shoulder. "Maya, this is Emelie, my cousin. She works as a manager here at the hotel. I wanted you two to meet."

"Your cousin?" I mumbled, feeling foolish. The coils within my stomach slowly unwound, but my pulse still raced. "Why do you want me to meet your cousin?"

"She's lived here all her life and may be helpful to you in some way. Like, in finding out more about your Mark." He winked at me.

"Oh." I felt my face getting warm, and I looked

down, hoping neither of them would notice me blushing. "Okay, thanks. It's a real pleasure to meet you, Emelie."

She looked at me with a kind smile, clearly reading my thoughts. "Don't feel bad. David loves to surprise people, and not always in a nice way. But we love him."

"It might take me some time to get used to him," I said.

"So David tells me you're trying to find a couple here, from a long time ago. They were in love, is that right?"

"Yes, but all I have is a ring that belonged to the woman. And her initials, 'C.T.' And I have the man's name, Mark, and some possible surnames and towns of origin from the registrations at the University of Bern."

"I have access to some databases on my computer. Can Maya maybe come for dinner tonight, David, and then we can all look?"

"Oh, I couldn't impose like that! You have a family gathering. Maybe at your office?"

"Not at all. You're not imposing." David dismissed me with a wave. "Emelie and Ruth, her mother, cook entirely too much for dinner anyway. They'd love to have a guest. You can entertain them with your lost ring and love story."

"Well, that's settled then. I apologize, but I have a meeting to get to." Emelie walked to the bar and returned quickly, handing me a folded piece of paper. "This is our address. Just give it to the taxi driver. Wait, I have another thought. If your woman was a medical student, you should stop by the Inselspital; that's the hospital connected with the University of Bern. It's been in the same location since the 1800s. I think they destroyed most of the original buildings to make it modern, but maybe there are still some historic aspects left."

"Thank you." I tucked the address into my pocket. "Really, thank you both so much. I feel terrible for imposing, but I'm so grateful for your help." I stood up. "I'd better go and see if my credit cards have arrived. They were stolen a few days ago," I explained to Emelie.

"Wait!" David got up. "I need to get you a taxi. You don't have any money, do you?"

"Oh, no, you don't need to. It's a really beautiful day, and I'd love to walk."

He bent his head low, whispering. "I'm worried you may still be a bit unsteady. I'd like to go with you, to make sure you get to your hotel okay."

I did want him to walk with me, his hand holding mine again, that electrical feeling traveling up my arm one more time. But I needed some time to myself, to think about what had happened, and to calm down. With significant mental effort, I refused him.

"I'm fine. I'll see you later at dinner."

"Which hotel are you staying at? In case you don't show up."

"I'll show up. I need your cousin's help, remember?"

Overbearing ass, I muttered to myself as I started to walk to my hotel. I needed time to chastise myself for feeling jealous earlier. What rights did I have to David? There was absolutely no relationship between us. He was helping me out because he was clearly bored in this small old town, waiting for all his relatives to gather. One New Yorker helping another. Why did I even assume she was his girlfriend? Then I stopped still because I realized I'd never asked if he actually had a girlfriend.

Chapter 19

Bern, March 1914

The ballroom of the Bellevue Palace was bathed in blinding bright light from the crystal chandeliers. The space immediately overwhelmed Rebecca with its noise, body heat, and the obvious anxiety of the young women, standing near their mothers and waiting to be noticed. Curse Mother! She scanned the room for a place to hide.

"How magnificent!" Hannah exclaimed, tugging at Rebecca's arm.

"I feel as if I'm going to go blind. All this electrification!" Grandmother covered her eyes with a fan.

"Our pupils can adapt to the brightest light, *Grossmami*," Rebecca said, frantically searching for Sarah, who was supposed to attend with her younger sister. She needed to tell her that Father had promised to speak to a friend of his, a lawyer, about the possibility of divorce for Sarah. Sarah's own father refused to hear anything about the matter.

"You'll stay with your family tonight," Mother demanded, noticing Rebecca's searching.

"Mother, you can't possibly expect me not to greet my friends," she said.

"I can expect you to behave as your parents wish."

Father wasn't even there yet. He was still finishing up with patients and would join them later. He resented these social events. And so did she!

"There had better be wine or champagne," Rebecca whispered to Hannah.

Walking on the slippery, polished floor, she cursed the hideous pale-green dress she had been forced to wear. The color wasn't the worst of it—the heavy brocade was draped all around her, making it impossible for her to sit down. The dress's heavily beaded bottom tangled constantly around her ankles, forcing her to walk in tiny, measured steps. Hannah suffered a similar fate, but her gown at least had a lovely cream color that highlighted her skin tone.

Rebecca found refuge by a window, leaning awkwardly against it and hiding behind a curtain. Spring snow was falling gently outside, and she watched the floppy snowflakes landing on the bushes. The heat in the ballroom was intolerable, and she imagined the snowflakes landing on her flaming face instead. She wondered how long it would take for her mother to notice if she took off her itchy long gloves.

"I hate these things, don't you?" A male voice with an American accent pulled her away from the window.

"More than anything in the world," Rebecca said, then quickly covered her mouth.

He laughed. "You shouldn't feel embarrassed. I wasn't trying to catch you. I truly meant it. I resent this type of social event."

Rebecca recovered and examined the stranger with interest. He was impeccably dressed, dark-haired and handsome. Clearly, an eligible bachelor.

"Then why are you here?" she asked.

"I have a mother and a sister who live for entertainment. My sister's been ill, and we brought her to Switzerland for treatment. We should've gone home, but the doctors insist that a few months in the mountain air will do her good."

"There are worse places to be than Switzerland."

"Certainly. But I have work to do, you see, at home. My apologies. I neglected to introduce myself. Edward Fischer, of New York."

Rebecca stretched her hand to meet his. "Rebecca Miller, of Bern."

"And are you here with your family?"

"Yes, all of them." She sighed.

"And why are you hiding?"

"I have no wish to be married." She clapped her hand to her mouth again. "I apologize. I don't mean to be rude. But I do tend to speak my mind."

Edward laughed and sat down on the windowsill near her. "It's quite all right. I have no wish to marry either. You see, I wish to choose my own wife and not have someone forced on me at a ball. But what about you? Why don't you wish to be married?"

"I'm studying to be a doctor. I have no time for marriage and children right now. I have patients to care for, and I'm preparing for my clinical exams."

He whistled. "Admirable. We don't have too many female doctors in America. At least, I've never met any. I'm guessing your family's not in agreement with that, though, given that you're here, at this matchmaking event?"

He was intelligent, she had to give him that. "No. My mother's trying to marry me off, so that I'll give up being a doctor and just become a wife and a mother."

"Mothers don't always know what's best for their daughters. My sister is very smart—probably much smarter than I am—but our mother won't allow her to study at a university. She wants her to marry and bear children, and that's it. We argue about this all the time."

"Thank you. And I'm sad that your sister can't be educated."

"Yes, things are different in America." The music changed, and Edward offered his hand to her. "Would you mind? Just one dance? Waltz is the only one I know."

"I'm a terrible dancer." Rebecca shook her head.

"So am I, but we can both fake it. You can step on my feet all you like. I won't complain."

He took her hand gently and led her away from the window and onto the crowded ballroom floor. Her heart was beating wildly. It had been years since she attempted to dance at a ball. She had always been terrible at dancing and swore she'd never do it again. She hadn't had to, either, since going to the university. Why did she agree to dance now? What was she thinking?

The music started. She felt his hand slide gently around her waist. Suddenly, she was flying on the dance floor, despite her clumsy feet and her terrible, heavy dress.

"You deceived me. You're a great dancer," Edward whispered in her ear, his mustache tickling her and his breath warming her neck.

"I did no such thing." She smiled.

"Maybe you've never had a good dance partner."

She looked at him and felt herself blushing, noticing the open admiration in his eyes. No one except for Mark had ever looked at her this way. But Mark loved her mind, her fortitude in medical studies, her courage, and her knowledge. This man didn't know her at all! But he really was very handsome, with his dark eyes sparkling at her and a smile that seemed to know just what she was thinking.

"Do you find it difficult to live in Switzerland? Is it much different from America?" she asked.

"Not very. The bank I work for has offices here in Bern, and I'm able to continue working as always."

"You are a banker?"

"I'm a bank broker, for J.P. Morgan."

"Sounds like a fascinating job."

"Not as fascinating as being a physician, I'm afraid." He turned her with ease, and she noticed some jealous stares from the other young women.

"I think any honest job is admirable and fascinating," she replied.

He laughed. "That's very true."

The music ended, and Rebecca found she regretted it as he led her back to her spot by the window.

"It was a pleasure to meet you and dance with you." Edward bowed and kissed her hand, holding it gently.

"Yes, it was a pleasure for me as well," she said.

"Perhaps we may meet at another time and you'll allow me another dance, or just the pleasure of your company."

"Yes," she said. "If we meet at another time."

She watched him walk away and wondered if she'd ever see him again. She was imagining the feel of his warm breath on her neck when Sarah came up behind her and hugged her.

"I didn't know you still remembered how to dance," Sarah teased.

"I didn't."

"Must've been your handsome prince then."

"Not a prince—an American banker. I only danced with him so that Mother would know I'm making an effort and leave me in peace for a few weeks," Rebecca explained. "The truth is, it's been quite awful at home. They send a car to pick me up after the lectures, and they don't allow me to go anywhere. Maybe if I dance with a few of these men, I'll have some peace."

"How are you surviving with not being able to see Mark, then?" Sarah asked.

"I haven't seen him in months." Rebecca wiped at the tear rolling down her cheek.

"Is he that afraid of your father?"

"He's been gone. Lara said he received a letter that his mother's been ill and left right afterward. But there's been no word on when he's coming back. If ever." She hid farther behind the curtain, tears pouring freely now. "I feel him. All the time. Like a thin thread is connecting us. I wish it would break, and I could forget all about him."

Sarah sat next to her on the windowsill. "He never said goodbye?"

"He wrote a poem in one of my textbooks," Rebecca said. "I found it the other day, when I was studying. It said,

You are mine, I am yours,
Thereof you may be certain.
You're locked away
Within my heart.
Lost is the key

And you must ever be therein.

Sarah hugged her. "I haven't been a good friend to you. I should visit you more often."

"You've been a great friend. You've had your own problems to contend with," Rebecca said. "I need to tell you something. I finally spoke to Father about your situation."

"You did what? How could you?"

"No, don't worry. He understands and is very sympathetic. You've known him since you were a little girl. Why do you think he wouldn't help you?"

"Because all men want the same thing of women—to trap them into marriage and childbearing," Sarah said, sighing.

"Shhh. You know my father's not like that. He sent me to medical school, not to get married."

"And what are you doing here, then?"

"It's all my mother. She's the one poisoning his mind. And I'm still allowed to go to my lectures. Listen to me for a second. Father said there was someone he could consult regarding the possibility of divorce for you."

Sarah grabbed Rebecca's hands and squeezed them. "Do you really think this might be possible? That I'll be free of Friedrick? That I can start my own life?"

"I don't know. But I have to hope. For you."

"Then I'll allow myself to hope as well. Let's walk to have a drink and pretend to be merry. We can't keep hiding here all night. Our mothers will notice."

Sarah pulled Rebecca away from the safety of the window alcove and to the crowd of people talking, dancing, and matchmaking. Rebecca stretched her neck to look for Edward but couldn't see him. She spent the rest of the evening with Sarah, hiding from Mother and trying not to think of how much she missed Mark. Tomorrow, she resolved, she'd sneak out from one of her lectures, go to the student colony, and find out if anyone had heard from Mark. He couldn't have just disappeared. Someone was not telling her the truth.

She'd get to the bottom of it.

Chapter 20

Bern, March 1914

Rebecca walked confidently into the women's ward. She hoped today would be quite ordinary, and she would be able to slip away in the afternoon to talk to Lara and then visit the student colony to ask questions about Mark's whereabouts. She was certain that the string she had felt connecting them all this time had become shorter today. She felt him closer, thinking of her. She had to find out if he was returning soon.

Rebecca had been training at the hospital for the last three months in preparation for the qualifying exams and was now familiar with the routine of the wards. She was well-prepared for the daily rounds and comfortable working with the nurses. She had been allowed to review the charts, make notes, and recommend patient care. She had expected to be drawn to the children's ward, but discovered that she most enjoyed caring for the women.

She only wished something could be done about the routine of requesting the husbands to make all the medical decisions for their wives. And then there was the matter of how male doctors treated female patients; with brief examinations, disregard for their feelings, and a preference of asking the husbands all the questions. The worst of the physicians was Dr. Lohrer.

Rebecca absolutely hated the days that she was assigned to follow him. He ordered women to strip their clothes and lie still and quiet on the examining table. He ignored any complaints of delay in recovery, calling them "hysteria" and prescribed increased housework as treatment.

Today's rounds were no different. "Do you think he only sees Fräu Mühler as a body harboring disease?" Rebecca whispered to Lara.

"I think he may truly believe that women only exist to harbor disease," Lara whispered back.

"Dr. Lohrer, may I ask Fräu Mühler a question about her condition?" Rebecca stopped the doctor as he was about to move on to the next patient.

"This woman is dying; there's no need for further questions. There's nothing that can be done here. We have three more to see."

Rebecca glanced at Fräu Mühler, a frail woman in her late forties who, sadly, was in the last stages of tuberculosis. Dr. Lohrer was likely right—there was little medicine could do for her now. But Rebecca wouldn't accept that nothing could be done to ease the suffering of the patient and her daughter, who was sitting by her bedside and crying quietly into a handkerchief.

She kneeled by the patient's bedside and spoke quickly. "I do believe the doctor is correct and your illness is very serious. I don't think this hospital can help you very much at this time. But I want to advise you that resting in the mountains, in your own home, may ease your breathing. You can also try a hydrotherapy clinic. Our nurse can tell you more about it. It will allow you extra time with your family."

She turned around to see if any of the doctors or interns were watching, then quickly placed the palm of her hand on Frau Mühler's back and concentrated. She counted to fifteen, imagining the healing energy traveling to the suffering woman's lungs, correcting the wheezing. As the woman's breathing gradually eased, she pulled away her hand, got up, and joined the rest of the students, hoping no one had noticed.

Her group finished the rounds and then settled to observe a procedure on another patient. This unfortunate woman was stripped naked and straddling a chair, her breasts uncovered and her back turned to the residents and doctors. She shook as she struggled to hold onto the back of the chair, appearing to be losing her balance. Her face was pale and covered in sweat, whether from embarrassment or fever was not known, but Rebecca guessed both.

"You're observing a pulmonotomy—a simple drainage of the lung cavity of an abscess due to pneumonia," Lohrer announced. "It's possible to make an incision in the abscess area and drain it without causing pneumothorax. The treatment destroys the bacteria, speeds healing, and allows us to introduce antiseptic solution."

A long needle was inserted into an incision in the woman's back, and Lohrer began to suction the pus from the incision. The woman moaned, her eyes shut tightly, and Lara held Rebecca's hand.

"Is there no medication that could be given for her discomfort?" Lara asked.

"Medication would impair the drainage and healing of the abscess. Besides, women don't feel pain at the same level as men, especially after their nervous system has been damaged by birthing," he replied, giving her a stern look.

Rebecca barely made it through the rest of the rounds, listening to more of the same nonsense coming from Lohrer and watching more suffering from his patients. One could only be thankful that he wasn't in charge of the children's ward.

"I need to ask you about Mark," Rebecca whispered to Lara, making notes in a patient's chart.

"I heard a rumor he'll be back any day now," Lara whispered back.

"I knew it!"

"Rabbi said he's had a letter from the rabbi in Mark's village. Mark's mother has recovered and sent him back. He's on his way."

"I felt him today, as if he is close." Rebecca washed her hands and pulled Lara into a small hallway. "I know it sounds strange, but sometimes it seems as if we're connected in some way."

"Not strange at all. It's like that for me and Vlad also. If he's not here, I'm only half a person, with half of my soul missing."

"Exactly. I never knew it would feel like that. I sometimes can hardly take a breath without thinking of him."

"He'll be here soon. Any day. Maybe even today." Lara kissed her forehead. "I have to go assist a laboring woman. With any luck, Lohrer will be having his meal and not interfere. Don't worry so much. Mark is safe."

Rebecca went through the day half-dazed, worried, and excited about seeing Mark soon. But how soon? By the early afternoon, the feeling that Mark was near became stronger. She felt the warmth of him in the very pit of her stomach, smelled his hair, heard his words in her ear. She turned around a few times, looking for him, but to no avail. He wasn't in the hospital. Lara was nowhere to be found either.

Finally, she could stand it no longer and left the hospital. The student colony was not too far; she could walk there easily. But would she be welcome? The relationship between the students in the colony and the Swiss wasn't exactly the best at the moment. There were rumors that the university had been urged to stop admitting foreigners unless they passed more rigorous examinations. She was dismayed at Mother's ridiculous worry about the dilution in the quality of the instruction. The students she knew worked exceptionally hard to learn, and in a language that wasn't their own.

But there was other talk as well. The Bernese were increasingly worried about the students' revolutionary activities. Lara and Vlad have mentioned that the colony was becoming a place where politics were debated more frequently in gatherings in pubs and private houses. Father had said recently that he'd heard the Bolshevik Party was doing recruitment of the politically interested students. Rebecca refused to believe it. She knew most students were not in Bern for revolutionary activities. They simply had no other place to go to receive an education.

The walk through the muddy streets was harder than she imagined, and she was half-frozen by the time she made it to Mattenhof, where rows of dimly-lit boardinghouses stood. Rebecca knew Mark shared rooms with Vlad and wasn't expecting to find any decent lodgings, but she was still surprised at the general poverty of it all. The neighborhood was run down and filthy, and the smell of smoke hung thick in the air. Several rats scuttled below the steps of one house. Some of the houses had signs of "No Slavs" or "No Russians" on them.

She stood, observing, regretting her impulsive decision to search for him, wishing she had waited to follow Lara home. Why did she think he was back? Why did he have to be gone and put her in this situation? A soft touch on her shoulder made her jump, but she knew it was him even before she heard the voice she loved so much.

"Rebecca!"

There was just enough time to say, "I love you!" before his lips closed in on her own. There it was! The warmth of him, the smell of him, the joy of him being near her.

"I'm so sorry," he said. "I was gone for so long. My mother—"

"Yes, Lara told me. Your mother was ill. Is she all right?"

"Yes, Mother's recovered. There was a cholera epidemic, and I brought her medicine. She can't get medicine in her village; there is no money and no help in the Pale."

"I'm so sorry." Rebecca stroked his face.

He pulled her upstairs, into a tiny room with two narrow beds and small tables. He sat her on his lap, not letting go.

"How could you leave me without saying goodbye?" she asked. "My heart nearly broke."

"Did you not see my poem? In your surgical textbook?" he asked, face concerned.

"I did. Of course I did. You know I study that book every day. It was a lovely poem."

"I've missed you so much," Mark said. "I couldn't say goodbye, as there was not time enough. I had a letter from my family, and your father was so angry with me. I thought I should just quietly go and come back soon."

"You didn't worry I'd forget you?"

"I felt you right here." Mark pointed to his chest.

"I love you," she said, her eyes wet.

"But your hands are frozen, my love. Let me make you some tea." He busied himself with preparations. "I have no food, but I think we can find some cake somewhere."

She suddenly noticed how thin he was. "You haven't been eating well!"

Rebecca looked around and saw nothing but bare surroundings. Grief and guilt squeezed her heart. She's been feasting with her family and going to balls, while the man she loved had been traveling to Ukraine to care for his sick mother, starving, and living in poverty. She accepted tea from him in a small glass and enjoyed the warmth spreading through her cold fingers. He sat next to her, smiling so brightly that it warmed her more than the hot water.

"I'm sorry to fault you for not saying goodbye," Rebecca said. "I understand you had to travel to care for your family."

"I'll never leave again like that. It broke my heart too," he said, touching her hand to his lips. "Can you stay a while?"

"Just for a little while. I have to be back at the hospital. Father will pick me up before supper."

"There is a music concert this afternoon—a very good violinist. Maybe you'd like to listen? Then I'll walk you to the hospital."

"A violin concert? Here?"

"We are poor, but we have culture," he said proudly.

She finished her tea and was about to ask him about his family when a blond-haired boy poked his head in the room, asked something in Yiddish, and then apologized when he saw her.

"Lenin is giving a speech in a house next door." Mark took her tea glass and pulled her up on her feet.

"Lenin, the socialist?" she asked. "He's still here?"

"He comes to speak to the colony all the time, as the head of the Bolshevik Party. The Bolsheviks have to hide at the colony; it's not safe for them anywhere else because of the Tsar's secret police. Come; you have to see him speak. His speeches are very powerful."

"I was afraid of that," Rebecca muttered to herself.

They walked to the next boardinghouse and entered a small room packed with people, young and old, sitting, standing, smoking, and laughing. Lenin was in the corner, on some sort of pedestal. She recognized him right away; he looked the same, if perhaps more tired. Rebecca searched for Nadya but couldn't find her in the crowd. When Lenin began to speak, she was moved by the power and conviction in his quiet but strong voice, even though she didn't understand a single word. She looked over at Mark's face, which was full of excitement and hope.

Later, Mark walked her back to the hospital, their faces covered tightly with scarves against the icy wind.

"I'm assisting Dr. Kocher in the gynecological

surgery tomorrow," Rebecca said.

"But that's very good news. I'm very proud of you," Mark said. "I'll find you at the hospital after."

"What was Lenin talking about?"

"He was talking about the Bolshevik Party's latest action. They've just adopted a resolution calling for the liberation of all people oppressed by the Tsar, and for the confiscation of the wealthy landowners' estates. They want to change things for the working class—to establish better working conditions and an eight-hour working day."

"Do you think all this is really possible in your country?"

"Lenin says it is."

They approached the hospital, and she looked for her father's car nervously. "We'd better say goodbye here."

"Your family can't accept me." He looked at her with eyes filled with sadness.

"It doesn't matter," she said. "It'll never matter what they think. I love you."

"I respect Dr. Miller. It does matter to me what he thinks. I hope I can win his approval. I try hard at the hospital." He bent down and kissed her lips, melting them with his heat.

As she walked to the large doors of the building, Rebecca was full of thoughts and feelings; they swirled in her mind like vines. The rumors she'd heard—her fears had been correct then. The Bolshevik Party was indeed trying to recruit the students in the colony, and they clearly had Mark's ear. How long did she have before Mark wished to join them and decided to return home for good?

Chapter 21

Bern. August, Tuesday—Present Time

I stopped at the Inselspital, following Emelie's suggestion, but the modern set of hospital buildings affiliated with the University of Bern triggered no memories of the past. A polite woman at the information desk informed me that the old buildings had been demolished in order to upgrade the hospital. Another dead end.

There was a long white envelope tucked underneath my room door when I finally arrived at the Wildflower. A quick squeeze of the envelope confirmed a plastic card inside. Finally, things were turning around for me! A few minutes later, I ran downstairs to the bar with my newly activated credit card.

"Oh, here you are, Maya," Jacob, the neighbor, greeted me. "Did you have a good day exploring?"

"I did. I sure did." I plopped happily into one of the chairs next to him and stretched my tired legs.

"And what can I get you?" Franz appeared from a small area behind the bar, startling me.

"A soda, please. And if you have some cheese or any other snack, I'd appreciate that as well. Really hungry."

Franz gave me a curious look, but a few minutes later, a plate of sliced bread, butter, cheese, and olives appeared.

"If you are this hungry," said Jacob, "you should come for dinner. My wife makes a much better schnitzel than Franz's cook. We have a grandnephew visiting from New York, so she'll probably make her best recipe tonight."

My mouth watered at the thought of schnitzel, and I swallowed. I thought of my grandmother's schnitzel and felt a tug at my heart. It was too late to call her tonight, though.

"I'm sorry, but I already have plans for tonight. Thank you."

"Another day maybe," Jacob said, taking a slice of cheese from my platter.

I pushed the platter closer to him. I thought of David then and how I'd handle sitting next to him at dinner and spending an entire evening with him. What did he really think of me? And why did I feel such a strong need to be with him?

I distracted myself by getting up and walking around the small bar area. I felt strangely comfortable in this room, just as I felt uneasy in the rest of the house. What was it about the room? I touched the dark paneling and the old shelves holding glasses, my fingers gently gliding on the worn wood.

There it was—that slipping-from-reality feeling I was beginning to get used to…

"You like what I've done here?" Franz's voice brought me back to the present world.

I shook the feeling off. "I love this room. I feel…at home in it, somehow."

He looked pleased. "The bar was my special project. Most of the rest of the home was remodeled.

Everything is new and rooms have even been added on the side and on the top floor. But for this room, I saved the old wood from the furniture I found in the doctor's office. I made the shelves here myself, and I paneled the walls." He touched the paneling gently. "I even saved the old doctor's desk. Come see here." He waved insistently. "I modified the desk to make it taller, so that it could be used as a bar now. But I did save one feature. It had a—"

"Hidden drawer!" I exclaimed and covered my mouth in surprise.

"It sure did." Franz placed his hand underneath the bar.

Click. I didn't need to see, because I knew exactly how the secret hinge worked. I could tell him all the things that I'd seen hidden in that drawer, as well, over the years that I'd been in this house. When it was still a doctor's office. When I was someone else.

"And here is what I found in the drawer when I finally managed to open it," Franz's voice broke through my thoughts. He held out to me an old photograph of a family in beginning-of-the-century clothing. My pulse speeded up and tears welled up in my eyes. I grabbed the edge of the bar and tried to hold still.

"And this is how we became friends," Jacob chimed in. "He came to me asking if I wanted the picture or if it was all right for him to keep it. I told him this was indeed my wife's family, but we had many pictures of them, and he can keep it for his hotel and bar. It was nice of him to ask, though."

"So I keep it here, to tell stories. Isn't it a great picture? Look how happy they all look! Maybe just not this one girl." He pointed.

I took the picture, hoping my fingers wouldn't shake. "What are their names? Do you know?" I managed to ask in a cracked voice. They didn't seem to notice.

Jacob looked over my shoulder. "The family's name was Miller. This girl here, the one who is not smiling much in the straw hat, is Rebecca. She was the older daughter. We don't have too many pictures of her. The youngest daughter, next to her, is Hannah. Then, here are their mother and father; their names were Helene and Joseph. Joseph was the doctor, so this was his office we are in right now. Then this is the grandmother, and I don't know her name. You'd have to ask my wife. She likes to be the keeper of the family history."

I studied the photo, every detail of it. *There she was. Rebecca. The ring's owner. The woman who's been sharing her life with me. But she's only a girl in this photograph.*

In the photograph, Rebecca sat on the grass, next to her sister. There was a remarkable difference between the two girls. While Hannah reclined in a relaxed pose, smiling and comfortable in her fine clothes, Rebecca sat awkwardly, looking down at her folded hands, large hat lopsided on her hair, legs folded underneath her. Their mother sat rigidly behind them, frowning, tense.

"I wonder why Rebecca doesn't look so happy," I said, studying her face.

What was it that made you so sad, Rebecca Miller?

"I think they were happy enough," Jacob said. "Well off, and the girls made good marriages. There was a son, too, but he died from some illness."

"Is your wife related to Rebecca or Hannah?" I asked.

"To Hannah. Rebecca moved to America sometime after the Great War. That's how we have a relative coming to visit us from New York. That's where she lived."

"Wow, she left her family behind," I whispered. I knew how Rebecca must have felt. An immigrant. Alone. I knew why I'd had to leave my country. I wondered why she had to.

"Jacob," I said, thinking carefully of how to phrase my words, "I love history and especially old photographs and family stories. Is there any chance your wife would be willing to meet with me for a bit tomorrow? To tell me more?"

"Oh, she would love nothing more. We're busy with family this weekend, but tomorrow should be no problem. Maybe you'll take me up on my dinner offer then?"

"Thank you so much!" I could hardly contain myself from going over and hugging him tightly.

"Well, it's settled, then! You can help with the cooking and hear the stories. My daughter can tell you whatever my wife forgot."

I rushed upstairs, planning to return to the bar early in the morning before Franz got in. I wanted to discover if I could bring up some of Rebecca's memories from her father's office. Rebecca! I knew the name now! *Rebecca Miller.* I skipped all the way to my room. Everything was falling into place. I had to tell Pauline! And I couldn't wait to tell David.

Newly armed with my shiny bank card, I walked out to the market I'd noticed a few blocks away and bought a box of sweets and a bunch of flowers to bring to dinner. Then I pulled out the folded piece of paper that Emelie had given me with her address. And nearly dropped it.

I looked at it twice, turning the paper around in disbelief. I walked quickly back to my hotel to check that my eyes weren't deceiving me. I was staring at two nearly identical houses sharing a wall: one with a blue front door and one with a red. My hotel had the blue door. The address on my folded piece of paper identified the one with a red door. I dropped my purchases on the ground, torn between the desperate desire to run away and the desperate need to find out whether I really *was* looking at the house where Rebecca, the woman whose life I'd been remembering, used to live.

Jacob's face and words suddenly flashed into my mind.

My house is next door…This house used to belong to my family too…Rebecca moved to America sometime after the Great War…We have a great nephew visiting from New York…

Not possible…but then…was it?

Meaningful coincidences. So David was Rebecca's great-grandson. David, who made me lose my mind every time he touched me. David, who I was pretty sure I should be staying away from, was currently waiting for me.

"So are you planning on coming in?" David popped out from the bright red door, and he waved at me.

I picked up the bag and bravely walked toward him. My mind was racing. Should I tell him? Did I really have a choice? Jacob surely would be there to tell him. I felt cornered. The entire story was about to be revealed to a large group of people. What would they think of their strange dinner guest? On the other hand, what did I have to lose?

Breathe.

"I need to tell you something," I said as I approached.

He turned around, eyes curious.

"I swear I'm not making this up," I began.

He listened quietly, as he always did, then whistled and ran a hand through his hair. "Do fantastic things always happen to you?"

"No, my life is normally really shitty and ordinary."

"It's hard to believe." He rolled his eyes. "So you have my great-grandmother's ring? Let me see it again." He carefully examined my outstretched hand. "I knew the design reminded me of the earrings my mother had. Great-Grandma must have gotten the earrings to match the ring. I'd like to know how the ring ended up lost from the family in the first place."

"You're going to have to ask your mother. If Rebecca went to America after she got the ring, how did it end up in Paris?"

"I haven't the slightest idea. Wait! You said the man you were searching for was Mark. My great-grandfather's name wasn't Mark. It was Edward. Rebecca's husband was Edward Fischer."

"Edward Fischer? No, it has to be Mark. And there's still the mystery of 'C.T.' who sold the ring."

"Are you sure you're searching for Mark? And not Edward? Or maybe it's not even the right Rebecca?"

"No, of course I'm not sure, but I *think* that's who I'm looking for. It's the poem. It matches the inscription on the ring." I was worried, however. "Should I keep looking, or do you want me to stop? Now that it's your family. I know it's her. I'm sure. When I was at the house next door, I knew exactly where that secret drawer was. I remembered clearly."

"You don't have to stop. I'm somewhat worried about what you'll find out, though. Maybe you shouldn't tell all the details to Ruth, Emelie's mother."

"Sure. Thank you."

"For what?"

"For taking it so well. I keep throwing all kinds of crazy-sounding information at you. And you just listen…and help."

"You mean, someone else would be reacting with some negativity?" He smirked.

"I mean, someone else would've run away. Very far away by now."

"Maybe you're introducing some level of fun into my trip that I wasn't expecting." David looked straight into my eyes, and I struggled to breathe.

"I'm glad I'm making your life more interesting," I said slowly.

"You are." He moved closer to me and bent his head.

"Here you are!" Emelie's bright voice emerged from behind the door. "Oh, am I interrupting something?"

"I was just inviting Maya in." David stepped aside and motioned me in.

As I walked past him, squeezing through the narrow doorway, I stopped, just for a moment, and peeked at David. He winked. As Emelie was now back inside, I stood up on my tiptoes and gave him a quick kiss on the cheek. He smelled heavenly. It had been a long time since I had kissed a man.

I rushed inside. "Come on, you need to show me around," I called back to David, still standing at the doorstep.

Chapter 22

Bern, November 1914

Rebecca ran out of the hospital and sat on the icy window ledge by the ambulance garage. She needed fresh air, even if it was freezing outside. It was one of those dreary fall days when the clouds were an ominous gray color and not a romantic silver one that people talked about in wonder. The sun had gone missing for at least a week. The relentless icy rain had covered the city in puddles, and the hospital was full of patients suffering from catarrh and pneumonia.

Rebecca closed her eyes and tried to calm herself down. She couldn't go back until she got hold of her feelings. She must restrain herself or she wouldn't be helpful to her patients. Suddenly, she felt someone's hands on her shoulders and heard a familiar voice.

"I think you could use this." Mark's face materialized through the stinging icy wind. He wrapped a thick gray scarf around her shoulders and neck and sat down next to her.

"Thank you," she said. "Where did you get this?"

"My mother sent it. These wool scarves are the way we keep warm when the winters get harsh at home."

"I can't take it. This was meant for you." She pulled it off.

"I'm never cold. But I know you suffer from the cold, and I don't like to see you suffer," he said, kissing her frozen nose. Then he wrapped her back in the scarf, holding her tightly in his warm arms.

"What is wrong? You look so pale. Are you feeling ill?" Mark grabbed her wrist to check her pulse, but she shook his fingers off.

"No, not ill, only in a temper. I can't stand it! I'm afraid it's very difficult to control myself at times."

"What happened? Why do you need to control your temper?"

"It's Lohrer, he is…despicable! He treats his female patients like—I don't know—like objects for him to practice on. He doesn't see them as human beings at all! He talks about them as if they don't even exist outside of their disease. He doesn't care about their suffering!"

Mark sat down next to her. "I'm afraid many academics like him don't care much about patients. They only wish to study the disease and observe what it does."

"They don't actually wish for the patient to be free of disease?"

"They do, but not in the way you think. They want a mechanical or medicinal cure only. You want more of a—what's the correct word?"

"Healing," Rebecca helped. "I want them to be healed. Emotionally, as well as medically. I wish for them to feel happy to come to us for help and medical care. I want them to have hope and know we'll take care of them."

"Correct. Dr. Lohrer likes to tell truth. You will live and you will die. He doesn't worry about tears. He does know about their disease, and he gives good diagnoses and medicine. He's not a healer, though."

"I don't think his patients want or like his truth." Rebecca sighed.

"You can do better, for certain."

"It's just that working with real people is so different from simply looking at the pictures in textbooks for all these years as a medical student. You understand?"

"Of course I do. It is a shock to see real disease, not just read descriptions of it. You feel helpless often. That's why I prefer surgery. I feel I can practice medicine that way better somehow."

"Do you truly believe I can do better?"

"I know you do. These hands have the gift of healing." Mark picked up her hands and kissed them. "I've seen you touch patients and relieve their suffering."

"You've seen me?" She was mortified. She thought she had kept it hidden. Even from him.

"Of course I have. I love watching you heal, *liebe*."

"I'm so embarrassed." She covered her face with her hands.

"Why? I grew up with a healer in the village. We weren't allowed to have a doctor. But healing is a great tradition in our culture, and I understand what it's like. You have to use any gift you have. Surgery and medicine will only help so much." He pulled her hands away from her face. "If you can relieve a patient's suffering in other ways, you must do it."

"You always do know how to help me feel better." She got up. "I'd better go back."

"Can I walk you home today?" Mark got up as

well.

"Not tonight. I promised Sarah to meet her after her law classes. I haven't talked to her in a while."

"Is she really planning to become a lawyer?"

"She is. I'm so proud of her! It's not easy for women to find employment as lawyers, but she'll persist, I believe."

"Is her divorce all done?"

"It's not. At least her family was willing to take her back and protect her from that brute of a husband," Rebecca said, opening the heavy door.

"I can walk both of you home?"

"We enjoy a chance at our own private female conversation sometimes. So, no, not tonight, my darling."

"I miss you," Mark looked around, then planted a quick kiss on her lips. "However, I do have something else to do tonight. More students are arriving from Berlin," he whispered.

"More? Didn't almost fifty arrive last week? Why are so many coming suddenly?"

"All German universities have a *numerus clausus* now, just like Ukraine and Russia. They can only admit so many foreign students. All foreigners must go to Swiss universities or go home. But if they go home, they'll become soldiers."

"So the German universities are discriminating against the Jewish students now as well?"

"They are. Just the same. Well, not the German Jews, though. I hope the Swiss universities let us stay, or we'll have no place to go. Vlad heard a rumor that Zurich is going to allow only sixty foreigners a year. That's why so many from Germany are coming here and not going to Zurich."

"I have to speak to my father and see if he's heard anything." Rebecca felt so worried she hardly remembered her anger at Dr. Lohrer now. Was it possible for Mark to be sent away?

"Vlad, and I have to hurry and obtain *Aufenthalters* for these newcomers. That's a temporary residence permit."

"I'll send you a note after I talk to Father."

"When can we see each other longer?" He held onto her arm, not letting her go.

"My family will be going to a wedding in Vienna next week. I can stay at home. I'll say I have hospital responsibilities."

"I can hardly wait until next week then. No need to worry, I won't be going away any time soon." He gave her another quick kiss and rushed away.

"I love you!" she called after him.

That evening, she told Sarah about the German universities sending foreigners away.

Sarah asked, as they walked home slowly, "Do you truly think the university will send all these students home?"

"I won't believe it; I simply won't. We have at least five hundred here. And now even more are coming," Rebecca said. "Lara did tell me that some of the women were thinking of leaving on their own, since schools in Russia now allow them to study. I'm sure many of them are homesick."

"I hate that the other universities would do this," Sarah said. "You know, I heard that there used to be protests here too, in the 1890s, against Russian students. The community didn't want them to take spaces at the university that should be available to the Bernese."

"That's nonsense!" Rebecca protested. "It's because the faculty allowed these Russian women to come and study here that they realized the women of Switzerland were intelligent and strong enough to study at the universities."

"I think you're right. If it weren't for them, I'd never have been able to leave my husband and study law. At least the Russian colony respects women, not like the Jewish community of Bern."

"Yes! The *Gemeinde* believes all we're good for is volunteering for charity or heading women's organizations. That may be good enough for Hannah, but certainly not for me. I wish to do grand things. I thought simply being a doctor would be enough for me. But I see the disrespect male doctors give to female doctors and patients, and I desperately want to show them that women deserve much better treatment. By all males—not only by the doctors."

"So do I, of course. That's why I wish to become a lawyer."

They entered the small park near their homes and sat on the bench by the trees, inhaling the crisp fresh air. It was much warmer than earlier that morning, with no more icy rain. The mist still hung around the branches and the carpet of yellow, red, and orange leaves was soft and soggy under their boots.

"Are you enjoying your studies?" Rebecca asked, wrapping Mark's scarf tighter around her neck.

"I love it. I really do. And I'm starting to volunteer at a legal aid clinic for women. Wives similar to me, who get hurt by their husbands and want to leave them, yet don't know how to accomplish it."

"Oh, Sarah, how wonderful! I'm so proud of you!" Rebecca gave her friend a warm hug.

"I can't stand it that our marriage laws lead to such inequality between husbands and wives. Women are doomed to live in oppression, without a right to vote, sold into marriage by their fathers, then controlled by their husbands. If you hadn't convinced me I had a choice to leave Friedrick and get an education, I don't know what would've happened to me!"

"Well, I hope you'll teach them to get an education as well. I think that's the answer for the Swiss women in modern times. It's the only way we can stop being men's property."

"Yes, we must advocate for new role models for Jewish women. Maybe, one day, I can even help fight for our right to vote. If we were not so dependent on our husbands and fathers for the taxes they pay for us to belong to communities, and if we could place our own votes, we'd have greater freedom to speak our opinions," Sarah said.

"That we have so many educated women but still don't have the right to vote is so out of step with our times. What good is education if you can't change the injustice you observe?" Rebecca hit the bench angrily with her fist.

"The war will change everything all over Europe. It may be the right time for us to ask for more rights for women."

"Do you really think the war can change things?"

"Of course! With so many men gone, there are less of them to stop women from doing what they want. Many will die, and women will take their place—in all kinds of work, even in government. Not in Switzerland, of course, but in other countries at least," Sarah said.

"I never thought of the war as being positive in some way. I just worry whether Mark will have to go back to Ukraine."

"I'd think he is safer staying here. Vlad, Lara's fiancé, is in one of my classes. He says revolutionaries are against the war and they're all staying here to plan protests."

"This would be wonderful, if it is true. If Mark and his friends go home, the Tsar will force them to join the army and fight. He'll never be able to finish his education," Rebecca said.

"Vlad said that he'd never return while the war is going on. He plans to go to Italy if he has to leave Bern. I wonder if he'll convince Lara to go with him."

"She'd follow him to the moon if he went. I have to talk to *Papi* to find out what the university is doing." Rebecca sighed.

"Do you think your parents will ever accept that you and Mark are in love?"

"I don't know." Rebecca got up and adjusted her hat. "You're right. The war will change things. For now, I go wherever Mother orders me to. I pretend, I dance, I talk with other men. I just tell her the men don't like me. It's easy to be disliked."

"Is it just his poverty your parents object to?"

"No, it's also the fact that they believe all the foreign students are revolutionaries."

"They are probably right, you know."

"To some degree. But Mark is also an excellent doctor. So is Lara."

"Vlad is also very smart. I don't think he actually

studies, however. He seems to do more arguing than studying during lectures."

"He has no use for the Swiss law. He just enjoys going to lectures in between his political activities. And Lara makes him go." Rebecca laughed.

"Well, I don't appreciate him interfering when I'm actually trying to learn," Sarah grumbled, getting up as they began to walk toward their homes, the rain picking up again. "Professor Reichesberg, one of our law professors, is a big supporter of the foreign students and allows them to pretend to study at the university while doing their political activities. I only hope they don't stand in the way of my becoming a lawyer. I actually plan to do something useful with my education."

Rebecca stopped, a thought occurring to her suddenly. She rubbed her forehead with her gloved hand, concentrating on explaining her thoughts to Sarah. "Do you think that, maybe, we can think of opening a place for women where they can come to receive health education from me and legal education from you? Women who can't afford to go to the doctor or who don't wish to go to see male doctors who berate them and treat them as less than human? Women who can't afford to pay a lawyer?"

"Women who are being mistreated by their husbands?" Sarah finished. "You really think we could do something like this?"

"Yes, why ever not? I could teach classes on preventing pregnancies and diseases, and on hygiene in the home. You could educate them on their legal rights. Maybe *Papi* will allow me to borrow his clinic for one evening a month so we can do this."

"He'll never allow it. His patients would be

outraged."

"He has a very kind heart. But if he doesn't allow it, I can rent a set of rooms somewhere. We could start with just a few hours a month and then do it more often as the need arises and we have interested patients. What do you say?" Rebecca's heart was beating wildly. She couldn't believe she hadn't thought of doing this before.

Sarah smiled. "How could I say no to such an enthusiastic offer? And what else do I have to do in my free time? Embroider?"

Rebecca hugged her best friend. "I'm going to run and ask *Papi*. Will you make it home safely from here?"

"Of course. It's only a block away." Sarah kissed her and left.

Rebecca picked up her skirt and ran home, oblivious to the muddy puddles on the way. Worries about Mark forgotten, she now knew how to apply her efforts and healing abilities to something useful. For the first time since entering the university, she was aware of a sense of real purpose.

Chapter 23

Bern, August, Tuesday—Present Time

Jacob's wife, Ruth, seemed unfazed by my disjointed explanations of the coincidences of me finding a ring belonging to her relative. Emelie clapped her hands, but chose not to discuss the entire story right away with her mother, and I followed her lead. Jacob shook my hands and winked, while Ruth led me to the kitchen and gave me the job of chopping apples, next to Emelie who was peeling potatoes. David was sent to help Jacob set the table in the family's small dining room.

A few minutes later, I looked through a small pass-through window and found David on the floor of the living room, with the family's dog, a small spaniel. The dog was presently on top of David's chest, licking his face vigorously, as David wiggled and laughed.

"David, Ula hasn't been eating very well lately and seems to refuse most foods we give her. Can you check on her?" Ruth called out to him.

I looked at her in surprise.

"He loves animals," Emelie explained.

"I can see that." I giggled as David and Ula seemed to be playing tackle now.

"He also has this gift for knowing just what's wrong with them. They trust him. Did he tell you he wished to become a veterinary doctor?" Emelie asked.

"A vet? I only know he's an environmental lawyer."

"He was accepted at a veterinary school, but it was far away from home. He didn't want to leave his mother after his father had a stroke and died. He thought he should stay close and help her. Nathaniel was still quite young, so David chose to study law close to home," Ruth explained.

"Who is Nathaniel?" I asked. "Oh." I remembered. "His brother! The writer." I realized I hadn't asked David much about his life. I only bothered him with mine.

"Yes, his younger brother," Emelie said, passing me a large bowl for the apples. "They're nine years apart. David feels very much like a father to him. I think he's done a nice job with him, too. Nate just finished college and has already written a travel book."

"David and I only just met a few days ago. I don't know much about him," I said quietly.

"You will. He doesn't hold secrets. He's a good man. Kind, loving, and smart. You can't do better than our David." Ruth gave me a questioning look.

"We're not really dating, you see," I said. "We met by accident, and he's just been kindly helping me. My life is a bit uncertain, at the moment."

"You do realize he's falling in love with you?" Emelie asked.

My fingers shook so hard I dropped the knife I was chopping apples with. What did she mean he was falling in love with me? How did she know? Is that what I'd been feeling? I picked up the knife and rinsed it in cold water, letting the coolness spread through my body, calming me. I looked back at Emelie, quietly arranging potatoes in a pot, pretending she hadn't noticed my discomfort.

"I don't know what to do about that yet," I finally said. I didn't. I really didn't.

"It's all right. You'll figure it out. Life always finds a way to let us know." Ruth smiled encouragingly.

"Ruth, the dog needs more protein and less fillers in her diet. More walking wouldn't hurt, either," David called out.

So he'd wanted to be a veterinarian. Not a lawyer. Sacrificed for his family. Who knew?

"Are you almost done with those apples?" Ruth asked. "We need to start layering them into the dough if we are to have the strudel for dessert tonight."

I gasped as I saw how she had laid out large sheets of thin dough on the kitchen table and was brushing them with melted butter.

Apple strudel! That's what I am making.

"Are you all right? Did you cut your finger?" Emelie asked, wiping her hands with a towel.

"I haven't had apple strudel in a long time. I used to bake it with my grandmother. And my twin sister. But not since...my sister passed away." I looked down.

"Oh, you poor dear." Ruth gave me a hug. I struggled not to shrug away from the unexpected comfort. "David, why didn't you tell me Maya didn't want to have the strudel?"

"What are you talking about?" David materialized by the kitchen entrance.

"It's nothing, don't worry about it," I said, stretching my lips into a smile.

Ruth pointed at me. "Maya doesn't like to have

strudel. It reminds her of her sister."

"What sister?"

"He doesn't know, *Mami*. They've only just met. Go back to playing with the dog, David. Dinner is almost done."

"You both should've let me know what Maya likes to have for dinner." Ruth shook her head. "Now look how sad she looks!"

I protested. "I'm fine. Really, I am."

Ruth gave me an appraising look. "If your grandmother made the strudel, that means you are a Jew."

"Yes, my grandmother was a Jew. I don't really think of myself as a Jew. I wasn't raised Jewish."

"If your grandmother was, then your mother was— and that makes you a Jew." Ruth stated definitively.

"Being a Jew comes from the mother," Emelie explained.

"I probably should've known that," I said.

"How did your sister die?" she asked.

I swallowed the lump in my throat. "Ella had a heart condition. Her heart muscle was too large. Her heart stopped when she rode her bike for too long in the heat."

"How terrible… She was little then?"

"She was eleven."

"Well, if you haven't had the strudel since you were eleven, it's time you had some. We can remember your sister today when we eat it," Ruth said brightly.

"No, Mother, please. Let's not do that," Emilie begged, likely noticing my horrified look. "Maya, I don't think we need any more help. How about I show you to *Mami*'s office? There are some old photo albums of the family there. Maybe you can find some pictures of David's great-grandmother."

"You have her pictures? I thought she moved to America."

"We should have some from when she was a child, at least." Emelie led me to a small room set up as the office and pointed to a bookshelf full of worn leather albums. "You'll find plenty of pictures here. After dinner, Mother can tell you what she knows about Rebecca. While you look, I'll go tell *Mami* the whole story about the ring."

I chose an album from the shelf and was looking around for a good place to sit down when the feeling grabbed me. I touched the wall by the window in a gesture that seemed so familiar to me that my arm shook suddenly. I sat down on one of the armchairs and looked toward the chair opposite. I knew I'd sat in this exact spot before. My hand stretched toward a small table in front of me, and then I tasted tea in my mouth and challah bread. I swallowed and licked my lips. It had been years since I'd tasted challah. But this room wasn't an office in the past. I closed my eyes and saw a women's parlor with sofas and armchairs and small tables with teacups on them.

Who did you drink tea here with, Rebecca? Your sister? Mother? Grandmother?

"Did you find the photo albums?" David interrupted Rebecca's memories.

"Yes, I did. Your cousin is very kind," I said, back in the present.

"She's the best. She's telling Aunt right now about how you can…imagine things when you are in places Rebecca has been." He sat down on the arm of my armchair. "So, any pictures of my great-grandmother in there?"

"Imagine" was one way of describing my odd sensations, I supposed. I looked through the album, finding no pictures of Rebecca. David pulled out more albums but still found none, although there were many pictures titled "Hannah Miller" but none of her sister.

"Hmmm," I said. "No photographs of her besides the one in the other house. You probably have most of them in your home in New York."

"Maybe the family here in Bern didn't like her much?" David proposed.

"Maybe she didn't like being photographed," I said.

"Why don't we have dinner first and then ask Ruth?"

I was actually starving. After a very satisfying dinner, which also involved David sneaking food to the dog, despite repeated reprimands, David, Ruth, and I returned to the office again.

"This is mainly my reading room," Ruth explained. "But I was told it was a women's parlor in the past. I feel a calming presence in here sometimes." She crouched by the bookshelf and began to search through it. "I wonder why you couldn't find the pictures. They should be here."

A few minutes later, she turned, frustrated. "The album should be right here. I don't understand. Emelie!"

"What is it, *Mami*?" Emelie came in, wiping her hands on a towel.

"I don't see it—the album with a silver frame in the middle with that picture you always liked to look at?

You remember, with the wedding?"

"Oh, that one. But *Mami*, there are so many albums in there now, how are we ever going to find anything?"

"Oh, no!" Ruth exclaimed. "You just reminded me that the last time we tried to find pictures of your aunt and uncle you said the same thing. That there were too many albums on the shelves. So I moved some of them to the lake house."

"Oh, no!" Emelie looked at me. "I'm really so sorry. But maybe *Mami* can tell you about Rebecca."

"Yes, I can tell you anything you want to learn about any of our family." Ruth sat down in a chair next to me. "Rebecca is a little more difficult. She married Edward Fischer in 1918 and they moved to New York in 1919. But I do wish I could show you the pictures. I had a beautiful one of her wedding."

"Why did she marry an American?" Emelie asked.

"She didn't get married until she was older. It was probably difficult for her to marry. She was one of the first women in Switzerland to become a doctor. The Jewish community would've frowned on a woman working. I have pictures of her in front of a free women's clinic she ran with a friend."

"She continued to work as a gynecologist in New York: one of the first women physicians in New York City. She ran a free clinic there, too," David added.

"Sounds like she was quite a pioneer for women in medicine," I said.

"David, why don't we invite Maya to Spiez with us for the weekend? That way she can see the pictures and learn more about our Rebecca." Ruth asked.

"Oh, that would be lovely! Everyone could meet you, and Lake Thun is so beautiful at this time of year.

It will be a great addition to your trip," Emelie said.

"Thank you, but I'm afraid I must leave on Thursday. I have to return to Paris and catch a flight to New York. I need to...be back at my job on Friday morning," I said, looking away. The truth was I didn't feel I deserved to learn any more about Rebecca. She was strong and brave. She was a physician during a war and ran a free clinic for women and children. I couldn't even finish my residency.

"Well, the lake house is in Spiez. It's about an hour away. We could be there and back by tomorrow evening," David said.

"Don't worry about it. I'm sure you have other things to do. All I wanted was to find out who the owner of the ring was, and now I know." I took off the ring. "Here, you should have it." I handed the ring to David. "Give it to your mother." My eyes felt watery.

"You're not going to take it, are you?" Emelie raised her brows.

"Of course not." David narrowed his eyes at me, examining my face. "I have nothing to do tomorrow. Completely free to take a ride to the lake. And I know my mother would love for you to have the ring—it was clearly meant for you."

I wasn't sure how to resist him. "Are you sure you have nothing else to do tomorrow?"

"You're saving me from complete boredom."

"You're all being very kind to a total stranger."

"Nonsense," Ruth said. "You're not a stranger. You're David's friend, so you're part of the family. And you want to learn more about our Rebecca's story. That's an honor to us." She walked back to the living room. Discussion over. Emelie followed.

"David," I said, as something occurred to me, "if your great-grandmother married your great-grandfather Edward and moved to the States in 1919, we still don't know who was this Mark she was in love with, here in Bern."

"See? You have to come and look at those pictures in Spiez. I remember what Edward looked like, of course. I've seen many pictures of my great-grandparents back at home. I'll for sure recognize a photograph of Rebecca with a strange man. That's how we might find Mark."

I laughed. "I already said 'yes.' I'd better go pack. Let me say goodnight to everyone."

After he walked me to the front door a few minutes later, he held me by my shoulders. I lifted up on my tiptoes a bit, bringing my face closer to his. He looked gently at me and tucked a stray curl of hair behind my ear, then gave me a friendly hug, leaving me with a lingering sense of disappointment. I felt his body moving farther away as he opened the front door, and I missed the sensation of him being close and the warmth of his hand on mine from earlier that day.

Later that night, I paced around my room, twisting the ring on my finger, torn in thought and indecision. My scientific mind fought with my emotions. The opportunity was here now. But what was the point of all this, and what if I were to discover something really upsetting about Rebecca and Mark that I'd have to tell Ruth and everyone else? After all, Ruth thought Rebecca married Edward, but I knew she loved someone else.

Wouldn't it be safer to just take the ring off, leave it for David, and return home? I could be on the first train to Paris tomorrow morning and would have some time to spend with Pauline, forgetting all that had happened here. Running away always seemed like such an easy option. I'd done it before, many times. My life had become so complicated already. What if more were at stake than my impulsive mind realized? And yet I wanted to learn Rebecca's story more than anything in the world. A nagging, aching feeling in my chest reminded me of another reason I was clinging to someone else's story right now.

Goddamn residency.

And then, of course, I couldn't stop thinking of David. Memories of our near kisses and his touches on my body found their way firmly into my thoughts and made my blood heat. Was Emelie right? Was he really falling in love with me? Was it possible for someone to fall in love with me? Even after all the mistakes I'd made… I went to the bathroom and splashed water on my face.

I simply had no choice but to keep the ring on my finger for at least one more day, and go visit the lake house in Spiez with David.

Well, how much more complicated could my life possibly get?

Chapter 24

Bern, February 1915

The winter cold seemed to have settled into Rebecca's very soul, making her shiver constantly and have a dreary, grouchy disposition. She was afraid to cry for fear her tears would freeze, and she pushed herself to walk toward the hospital. There was never enough warm clothing to shield from the snow and frozen wind on the way to the hospital, no matter how hard she tried. She would never dare complain to Hannah or Mother about her misery, though. It wouldn't do to allow Mother to gloat about how going to the university was dangerous to her health. She simply had to survive this part of her training, no matter what!

Lara was waiting for her by the stairs as she entered the hospital. "The women's ward. Hurry!"

"Yes, Dr. Silber," she said, already running down the hallway behind Lara.

"How many times did I tell you not to call me Dr. Silber!" Lara yelled back.

Rebecca smiled as they both arrived at the ward. Lara had finished her training and was now a full-time resident. She had earned her title.

Rebecca pulled her coat, scarf, and hat off and threw them on a chair as she entered the large room.

The ward wasn't usually full; few women had time to be ill and away from their families. It was the same today, with only a few beds occupied, their inhabitants trying to rise and observe the excitement in one of the beds by the far wall. Several nurses and students were gathered there, where a labor was clearly taking place, given a woman's anxious cries and moans.

Rebecca hurried, following Lara past the crowd. She pushed a medical student out of the way and found herself by the bedside of a large and rather disheveled woman who appeared entirely too old to be giving birth. The woman was held by her arms by two orderlies as she frantically struggled to get up off the bed, while several nurses attempted to talk her into staying put.

"Help me get up! My dance card is full, can't you see? Ahhhh!" The woman screamed and strained her back as her stomach contracted, her uterus working to expel the baby.

"How long has she been in delirium?" Lara asked one of the nurses.

"For the last hour, Dr. Silber. She's been asking to go dancing. Before that, it was swimming in the Aare."

"Toxemic?" Rebecca asked.

"I think so. Frau Kuntz was here a year ago and had toxemia then." Lara was busy checking the woman's cervix for dilation, as she continued to scream and strain against the orderlies.

"How many children has she had?"

"Eight she gave birth to, but only three alive," one of the nurses said. "Dysentery took the last boy."

"I told her last year she could die if she had any more children," Lara said, crossing her arms.

"It's not her choice, it's her husband's. You know how it is," another nurse said.

"Oh, I do. I very much do. And now she's going to die because of him."

"Is there really nothing we can do?" Rebecca asked, watching the woman tearfully. The woman's whole body seemed to be spasming in agony.

"Did you test her urine?" Lara asked the nurses.

"We haven't had the time yet. But she has the fever."

"Well, there's really no time now. You see the edema on her, Rebecca? That and the delirium are definite signs of toxemia. The child is not ready to be born but it has to be delivered or the mother will die. She may still die, but we can at least try. Take the patient into surgery," she ordered the staff. "Rebecca, will you tell Mark we are coming?"

"Of course."

"And you can observe if you'd like."

A rough hand grabbed Rebecca's arm as she ran out of the women's ward.

"You are going to fix my wife, right? I don't have time for this."

"I'm sorry, Herr Kuntz. Your wife requires an operation. The pregnancy is making her ill. Your child has to be born surgically," Rebecca said, narrowing her eyes, trying not to judge a man who was about to lose his wife.

"Surgically? What does that mean?"

"Your wife is sick. She can't continue carrying your child safely." Rebecca tapped her foot in agitation. There was no time to waste.

"I won't agree to it!"

"Then your wife and child will both die," Lara's voice struck from behind them.

"God will protect my son and damn my wife for not doing her duty!" The man hit the wall with his fist. Rebecca had a strong feeling that he really wished to pound either her or Lara.

"You have lost five children already. Do you wish to lose another?" she pleaded with him.

"You're women. You don't understand what a man has to do for his wife and children. Are you going to be the ones doctoring my wife? Is that why Anna is having trouble?"

"Yes, I'm your wife's physician. My name is Dr. Silber. I'm the doctor for all the deliveries here today."

"I want a man doctor or I'm not paying for any of this!"

Rebecca touched Lara's arm and whispered, "We have to rush to surgery, ignore him. Just obtain his permission."

Lara squeezed Rebecca's fingers tightly. "I understand your feelings. Do you wish for your child to be born with our assistance or do you wish to take her elsewhere? I need the decision now." She opened the door to the women's ward, and Frau Kuntz's screams poured into the hallway immediately.

The man paled and sat down on a bench. "Take her. I want my son saved."

Lara nodded, and the women ran to surgery. An hour later, Rebecca sat in the washroom with her hands in the sink, watching the bloody soap rivers slowly run into the drain. Mark and Lara were still working on the child, trying to revive it, but she knew it was hopeless. The mother had died midway through the operation.

The baby was pulled from her uterus unable to take its first breath, too weak and too small to live.

She finished washing her hands and walked out into the hallway, where she leaned against the wall, exhausted.

"What's wrong? Where is my son? Is he all right?" She heard the man's voice.

"Do you not even care to ask about your wife?" she said, eyes watering.

"Did you save my son or not?"

"Your *daughter* was born too small and not breathing. The doctors are trying still…"

"Another daughter? I don't need another girl!" The man pounded the wall again.

Lara came out of the washroom and narrowed her eyes at the man. "Your daughter and wife are both dead. How could you allow her to become pregnant again? You knew how ill she was the last time! Haven't you gotten her pregnant enough times already? She was too old to do this again. I told you this last year!"

"How dare you speak to me like this? My wife is none of your business. You need to go home to your husband or your father and learn respect!"

"No, *you* need to learn respect for women. You'll need a new wife to take care of the living children, and you won't easily find another one to do your bidding. You need to take care of your women and not kill them!" Rebecca raised her voice.

"You insolent little bitch! I'll show you what respect means!"

"I suggest you rethink your words." Mark stepped in front of the man quickly, causing him to waver and nearly fall backwards.

"What's this?" Dr. Lohrer approached the group, smiling from ear to ear.

"These stupid women have killed my wife and child and dare to be terribly rude to me. This one is defending them!"

"I'm terribly sorry for the unacceptable behavior by my junior doctors. You're grieving and you don't deserve such disrespect. Why don't you step into my office, and we'll have a drink and talk things over?"

"Finally, a real man to talk to." The man gave an angry look to Mark and stumbled off with Lohrer.

Mark was still breathing hard. Rebecca touched his shoulder. "It's over. Nothing else we can do."

"Why did you put yourself in front of this gorilla?"

"I was furious, and still am. It's his fault that his wife and baby are dead," Rebecca said.

Lara interjected. "It's not his fault any more than any other man's fault in this town. He only did what he believed was right—get his seed into her so she could make him sons. They don't know any better."

"Then we have to teach these women to think of their health."

"How are you going to teach them? Their husbands won't allow them, and the physicians won't allow *us*."

"Sarah and I have been talking about opening a clinic for the prevention and education of women. Now I think we will finally be pushed to do it. As quickly as possible," Rebecca said firmly.

"*Liebe*, when will you find time, with all your responsibilities at the hospital?" Mark asked. "I have to get back to surgery." He touched her shoulder. "I'll walk you home later?"

"Yes." Rebecca kissed his lips and watched him

run off as usual.

"He loves you," Lara said.

"I love him too," Rebecca replied.

"You should let him marry you. That's all he wants, you know. That's why he is still in Bern, away from his family and his village."

"You're still here too," Rebecca said, her heart beating wildly at the thought of marriage to Mark.

"I'm here because of Vlad. We do anything for people we love. Do you want to marry him?"

"I do, desperately. I just haven't figured out how to convince my family yet."

"Well, you'd better figure it out, or he will give up hope. A man needs encouragement."

"Do you ever worry about Vlad being in danger because of his work for the Revolution?"

"All the time," Lara said. "He's being watched by the secret police now. I can't sleep at night sometimes, I'm so frightened."

Rebecca hugged her friend. "I'm so sorry. Please let me know how I can help. I love you both so much."

"Thank you, my dear friend." Lara hugged her back.

"You should help me in my clinic. It will distract you from your worries. I hope it will distract me."

"What if I put you in danger by bringing the Tsar's police to your door? They might be following me, too."

"I'm Swiss. I'm not worried about any secret police!" Rebecca laughed. "You must help me. I can't possibly manage without you."

"I do want to help you. I have to do something about these senseless deaths we have in the hospital. There has to be a way to prevent these women from becoming pregnant if they're too ill or too old."

"There is. Sarah and I have been talking for a while about it. We found some cheap rooms we can rent nearby. Come have some tea with me, and I'll tell you everything." Rebecca wrapped her arm around her friend and pulled her along to the dining lounge.

She didn't see Mark until it was time to walk home. The night air was biting with frost. She was almost sorry her father had finally stopped picking her up from the hospital in his car. He no longer worried about her inappropriate behavior, as she had made a considerable effort to listen to Mother and attend as many social events as possible. She was working up the courage to tell them she was dating Mark. She hadn't been able to come up with any way to actually phrase this to them. *Mother, Father, I hope you have changed your opinion of the man you forbade me to date. I'm in love with him and wish to marry him.* Yes, that would go over very well indeed.

"You're really thinking of opening a clinic?" Mark asked, interrupting her thoughts.

"Yes, absolutely! Sarah, Lara, and I will do it together. We're very excited."

"I admire you for wanting to help, but how can you possibly do this? You're so busy as it is."

"I'll have to think through my schedule, of course. I can see patients at my clinic early before my hospital rounds, or in the evening, after my work is done."

"I'll walk you there and back home. It's not safe for women at night in the city," Mark said, taking her hand.

"There are three of us; we can take a car. We'll be fine. I just hope that we can do something to prevent unnecessary deaths from Lohrer's maltreatment."

"You have to learn how to handle these deaths, Rebecca. Many women die here, many children, many men. It's not your job to save people. You can only diagnose and alleviate their suffering," Mark said.

"But maybe we can do something to prevent the disease. Lara and I do know how. We have many ideas."

"That's not a physician's responsibility. We diagnose and heal what we can. We hope for future cures. Prevention is not possible."

"I don't know." Rebecca rubbed her temples. "I disagree. I believe prevention is absolutely possible. I can't keep coming to the hospital every day and watch awful things happen. I heard Lohrer say the other day, when we asked about contraception, that it was the woman's destiny to have children and we all must get to it to make more soldiers for the war."

"He is an imbecile. That doesn't mean you must be a hero and sacrifice yourself."

"But isn't that what you do? When you help in your colony, or when you went home to care for your mother?"

"That's different." Mark looked down.

"I see no difference at all. We all do what we can to fight injustice, to make things better for other people." She stopped and took his shoulders to turn him around. "Look, let's talk about something else. I know you've been doing more political activities. Lara told me."

"I've only been helping a bit. I didn't tell you because I know how you worry," he said.

"What exactly are you doing? Is Vlad getting you into the revolution he is planning?" Rebecca brushed the snow off her face.

"It's not Vlad I am assisting. I'm working with Lenin." He looked down, snowflakes settling on his eyelashes.

"Lenin? He is still here? I thought he left a year ago. How often are you talking to Lenin?" She couldn't believe her ears.

"We've been having more gatherings at the colony. Lenin is reorganizing the Bolshevik Party. They're not getting along with the German Socialist Party. He's asked for my help."

"Mark, you're getting distracted from your work as a surgeon. And you'll be in danger."

"I'm not in any trouble at all. They just asked me to be involved a little, that's all. There is going to be a conference to discuss the war and its effect on democracy, and I've been asked to assist with organizing. It's nothing, really."

"Can you promise me that you'll be safe?"

"Of course. I promise. I'm not seen anywhere with Lenin or the other prominent party leaders. I'm just an unimportant helper. I don't do speeches or recruitment. I'll be fine." Mark bent to kiss her, his lips warm, reassuring, distracting.

"I have to go now. You remember your promise?" she asked.

She watched him walk away, a large lump of fear in her throat. What was in Mark's mind? And could she persuade him to change his mind and focus on medicine? Did she have a right to insist on him doing anything if she didn't even possess the courage to tell her parents about their relationship?

Chapter 25

Bern, April 1915

Rebecca wiped perspiration and dirt off her forehead. It had been a long winter and a wet spring. She wasn't scheduled to be at the hospital today, so she had been making home visits to her clinic patients since before dawn. To filthy houses with very ill children and mothers, many of them dying.

She held the babies as long as possible, concentrating her energy and wrapping it around their fragile bodies. But her power wasn't enough to save them. Not when their mothers didn't have enough milk and they were exposed to so much disease. She had long forgotten about her earlier hunger, but her aching feet did occasionally make themselves known.

She and Lara had rented two rooms for their free clinic, open to any woman or child in need of medical services but not wishing to seek them at the hospital. They found out quickly that few families could visit the clinic because they were often too ill to travel there, especially when it snowed or the temperature fell. By the time the mother arrived, either she or the child was more often in need of a coroner. Still, some women came, hiding their faces, not wanting anyone to know, asking for a pessary to prevent pregnancy or asking what could be done if a husband drank or hurt the child.

Sarah provided legal aid, and Lara kept the clinic going. Rebecca had discovered that the best use of her skills was to go to the women's homes. Once she entered the squalid neighborhoods, the word spread, and women came to wherever she was, alone or with their children. And they brought friends. Sometimes her skills and the medicine she brought made a difference. And so she went. Day after day.

"Rebecca, did you read about the silk intrauterine device they are selling in Germany? It's more effective for pregnancy prevention than a pessary. Do you think we can get our hands on a few?" Lara asked, coming in from an examining room.

"I did, but it's expensive." Rebecca sighed. "I don't know where we'd get the money for it. My father gave me enough for rent, but he said he doesn't want to know anything about what we're doing here. We are on our own."

"I'm afraid my salary at the hospital will not be enough to support the clinic," Lara said. "Maybe we can ask the other residents and physicians to donate money."

Rebecca washed her hands with carbolic. "Most of our fellow doctors are ignorant of social issues and don't support our efforts."

"Well, there is the Zimmerwald conference in September. What if we ask the Socialists to donate funds? Or write to the Association of Socialist Physicians?"

"Yes. Mark mentioned a conference he was helping to organize. What kind of conference is it?"

"It's an international gathering of Socialist parties, to unite in their protest of the war. They are going to make an official stand against it, together. I hear Trotsky is coming. Vlad worships him and desperately wishes to hear him speak."

"How much is Mark involved in all this? He told me he was only helping in a minor way." Rebecca sat down and leaned against the wall.

Lara looked away. "The rumor is Mark is working very closely with Lenin on a resolution that will be presented at the conference."

Rebecca felt the tears welling up. "Mark is a surgeon. Why would a Socialist leader need his help in writing speeches? This doesn't make any sense. This revolution of yours is going to take him away from me."

"Mark is a gifted writer, and I think he likes receiving attention from Lenin. You should be very proud of him." Lara stroked her head. "We all are. He is being honored by this."

"I love him and I need him. I can't lose him."

"You won't lose him. He and Vlad and the others just want to make the world better for everyone. If the revolution succeeds, there'll be no more divide between the rich and the poor. Everyone will prosper. And you'll be the wife of a hero."

"But he is a hero to me already," Rebecca whispered to herself.

"Oh, there he is now," Lara announced with a smile as Mark walked in.

Rebecca threw herself at him, nearly knocking him down. She felt she was already losing him.

"I missed you too," Mark said, giving her a kiss.

"I missed you more!" She wiped a tear escaping down her cheek.

"What's the matter?" He lifted her chin and forced her to look at him.

"Lara was telling me how much you are working with Lenin. You haven't told me. I'm worried. What if the university sends you away if they find out about your political activities? Or what if Lenin needs you to go to Russia with him?"

"I have no plans on leaving Bern or you, *liebe*. The Bolsheviks are here for a while. Nothing but talking is happening with the Revolution right now. I will tell you anything you wish to know. I have no secrets. Only please don't cry." He sat down next to her and held her close.

"What is Lenin like?"

"Lenin is very kind to me. He treats me like family. He lives in Distelweg, by the woods, where he invites me to take a walk with him and his wife and some other Bolsheviks sometimes. He knows all the plants in the woods and points them out. Their friend, Inessa Armand, comes with us frequently. We discuss plans for articles and speeches on the Revolution."

"What is it exactly that you are working with him on? You are a surgeon, not a politician. Why can't he ask Vlad?"

"Vlad is helping too. Many people are. I am only helping Lenin write, yet it's very exciting what we're writing."

"What is it?"

"I'll show you one of the works. Look." He took a folded pamphlet from the inner pocket of his jacket. "This is Number 33 of *Sotsial-Demokrat*. It's a manifesto. It says we must turn this Kaiser's war into a civil war in Russia; into a war against the Tsar! This manifesto is being translated into French and English and German, and will be forwarded to many newspapers. Can you imagine this? The world will become so different if people would rise against their rulers!"

"What do you mean, rise against the rulers?"

"I'm talking about people all over the world rising, not against Germany but against the ruling classes in their countries. That's what Lenin and the Bolsheviks truly want."

"Surely that's not possible! And what will happen to all these people you're rising against?" Rebecca asked. "What will you do to them? Guillotine them? Put them in prisons? Take their homes away?"

"Rebecca, don't you understand the injustice of some people having so much yet so many living in starvation and poverty? The families you go to see—they die from disease and starvation with no hope of improving themselves with education or better work. That's what Lenin is trying to change!"

Rebecca felt her fingers tremble, and she balled them into fists. She was torn between shaking some sense into Mark and asking him if she could curl up on his lap and have him hold her tight.

"You are a talented surgeon, Mark. Your patients need you. Why must you abandon them for this political nonsense?" she finally blurted out.

"It is not nonsense to me or my friends. Or my family and my village back home, Rebecca, where I've seen people die time and time again. And it's not nonsense to the families you work with, whose children die from lack of food. Inessa and I are working on international action, no longer just on Russia. This will happen! The world will be different one day."

"What if you get arrested and imprisoned?"

"There is no danger of it, I assure you. I am not doing anything illegal."

"Why can't you be happy with the life of a surgeon, here with me?" Rebecca demanded in frustration.

"You can't even bring yourself to tell your family about me. You know they'll never accept a poor man as your husband!" His eyes were blazing.

"I'm sorry, you're right. I've been at fault. I'll tell them, right away. Will you stop working for Lenin then?"

He rubbed her back. "And what kind of man would I be to do nothing when the whole world is changing, *liebe*? A ghost of a man, a useless man."

"It seems that nothing I say is helping." She bent her head.

"You must allow me to do my duty, just as I allow you to do yours here, in this clinic," he said, kissing her hand. "Come on, I'll walk you home. The sun is setting. We don't want your parents angry at you for missing supper."

When Rebecca arrived at home, Hannah was in the garden, weeding the tulip flower beds. Rebecca watched her for a while, enjoying the sight of someone doing such a simple, peaceful activity. It felt good to just stand still in nature for a moment. The smell of spring was clearly in the air and the birds were beginning to come back, chirping occasionally in the trees. A robin sang brightly on a branch over the garden, and she smiled, despite all the stresses of the day.

"Oh, I didn't realize you were here." Hannah rose

and shook the dirt off her apron.

"I enjoy watching you tend to the flowers. You have a gift with them."

"Mother taught me well. I like gardening, it's very precise. And look at all the tulips that came up this year!"

"They are beautiful." Rebecca touched the velvety petals of a few flower heads with her fingers. "What's for supper today?"

"Lamb chops and potatoes. And a cake. You may want to dress nicely. We have a guest coming."

"A guest? Not another suitor for me?"

"No—it's someone for me." Hannah looked down, blushing.

"What? When did this happen?"

"Ebner came to see Father this morning and asked if he could marry me. He asked me right after."

"And you agreed, I assume?" Rebecca couldn't believe her ears. Ebner Lehman was a pleasant-enough man, although the most boring person she'd ever met. On the other hand, Hannah would likely be perfectly happy with him.

"I think we'll be happy together." Hannah narrowed her eyes, waiting for an argument from Rebecca.

Rebecca needed an ally more than she needed an enemy. "I think you will be, too. I'm glad you made your choice, dear sister." She hugged Hannah to avoid looking into her eyes.

"You are really happy for me?"

"I really am. Why wouldn't I be?"

"You never agree with my choices."

"Well, this time you finally made the right one. I'll

go wash up and change to look good for your fiancé." Rebecca turned and started away.

"Wait, what about you? Is there anyone you hope will ask you to marry?" Hannah asked.

Rebecca paused, her back still to her sister. "There is someone. I will tell you about him later. Let today be about your happiness."

"I knew it. No, please tell me now!"

"All right." Rebecca returned and sat down on a small rock by Hannah. "His name is Mark, and we went to school together at the university. He is a surgery resident now. I'm in love with him."

"Is he in love with you?"

"He is."

"Oh, that's wonderful! When is he going to ask Father for your hand?"

"Well, that's where the problem is. Father doesn't approve of him. Mark is poor. He is from Ukraine. Father caught us kissing a while ago and prohibited me from seeing him again."

"So what are you going to do?"

"I have to convince Father that Mark is a good man. But I don't know how." Rebecca teared up. "And the truth is—if I don't—I am afraid Mark will get tired of waiting and will go back to Ukraine and leave me."

"Surely not if he loves you? He must wait!"

"I don't think any man wants to marry into a family that doesn't respect him."

"We'll think of something. I'll help you." Hannah hugged her shoulders.

"Thank you." Rebecca hugged her back.

She liked the idea of a kinder Hannah. Maybe Hannah getting married wasn't such a bad idea. Would it distract Mother sufficiently to allow Rebecca to see Mark more often? Would it allow her to plead her case with Father more easily? With one daughter successfully married, maybe one poor match would be acceptable? Maybe if Mark could see some hope in their being together, he would spend less time on all this Revolution nonsense.

Chapter 26

Spiez, August, Wednesday—Present Time

The drive to Spiez took a little over an hour. Giant puffy clouds drifted slowly across the sky in my view from the passenger seat of Emelie's car, which we'd borrowed for the day. I counted the clouds, then the tiny pockets of bright blue sky between them. We forgot to turn on the radio, and my mind relaxed, worries and fears slowly dissolving as the clouds disappeared over the snowcapped mountains. It was quiet in the car, with only the hum of the road noise. After some time, I looked at David. He didn't look back, but his hand found mine and held it for a while.

"Shouldn't be too far now," he said, taking an exit off the main road.

I sat up straighter and opened the window. Lake Thun emerged from the mountains now, changing from emerald to blue, then back to emerald as we turned. Only a few sailboats were out today, tiny in this magnificence of water, cloud-covered sky, and mountains. I took a deep breath of fresh air and heard David doing the same.

"Quite a sight, isn't it?" he asked.

"Breathtaking!" I inhaled again.

The car passed through a series of arches carved into the mountainside, and then we began a winding drive into town through turnabouts and small streets lined with picturesque whitewashed homes with brown-slated roofs. I tried to guess which house we were going to. As Ruth had explained, Rebecca used to stay in Spiez with her family all the time. Then the house became her sister's when Rebecca moved away to New York.

The car finally came to a stop on a gravel driveway in front of a large chalet. The house was carved into the edge of a hill, with large evergreens all around and a lake sparkling behind it. I inhaled the fresh air again and took it all in: the mountains, the trees, the fresh rain scent on the gravel. The first floor was whitewashed, and the windows were framed by green shutters. Decorative woodwork ran along the roof and the small balcony of the third floor.

I heard steps behind me and saw David. He set our backpacks down and came toward me.

"I wish we had more time. I would've loved to show you the sunset. Where you are standing now happens to be just the perfect spot. The sun sets over the lake right there." He pointed. His arm grazed my shoulder, then he hugged me closer, reminding me of how good it had felt in the taxi yesterday.

"Oh," I sighed, snuggling closer into his embrace.

Why did it feel as we'd held each other a thousand times before?

We watched the lake and the boats for a few minutes, enjoying the sunshine. Birds flew around the water in formations, but otherwise, it was very quiet. It occurred to me suddenly that we were here alone, and my skin began to tingle in a pleasant sort of way.

"What?" I asked, missing David's question.

"I asked if you didn't mind takeout for lunch?"

"No, not at all."

"You're shivering. How about we go inside and look for those pictures?"

The house proved to be as charming indoors as it was out. Wooden beams, wool rugs, a large fireplace, and cozy furniture were just the basics of comfort in the house. Fifteen minutes later, the coffeepot was going and food was ordered. I could imagine spending my entire life here. Safe. Comfortable. Loved. I hoped my face wasn't showing the thought. But it likely was, because David looked very pleased with himself as he sat down in a large armchair by the fireplace.

"Come, join me. Relax for a moment. Then we'll have a coffee and will start looking." He patted the seat next to him on the chair.

I was about to accept his offer when the room's appearance began to shift somehow and, suddenly, the furniture was smaller and less plush, and it wasn't David at all sitting in this chair. I didn't know who it was, but it was definitely someone very familiar. The image became less fuzzy, and I saw an older man, with graying hair, smoking a cigar. I smelled the sweet scent, well-known to me. There was another scent in the room now. Roses? I wasn't quite sure. As my heart beat a wild rhythm, the man's face changed back to David's, his mouth saying something I couldn't quite understand.

"What?" I asked in confusion, trying to still both my heart and my mind.

"I said you look like you are in another world again. Is this another one of those times when you're seeing things as her? My great-grandmother?" David half rose, seemingly in an effort to catch me if I fell.

"I am. I was, I mean. I'm all right, you can sit back down. I just…for a second… You were gone."

"I was gone?"

"Yes. There was a man sitting in your chair, instead of you. I've never seen him before."

"Was it my great-grandpa Edward, perhaps?"

"I have no idea. I don't know what he looks like. But this man was older and had gray hair. Maybe it was Rebecca's father. I don't remember what he looked like. I only saw a picture of him once, at the Wildflower."

"All right, let's get the pictures then. Coffee will wait."

We went up the large staircase to a small bedroom at the end of the hallway.

"Emelie said this was a junk room where they stored ancient family belongings."

"No attic here?" I asked.

"Everything would get ruined—too cold and moldy, I think."

We walked into a room full of boxes and old furniture. David waved me over to a large trunk by the window.

"The albums should be here." He opened the lid with effort.

"Whew!" I pinched my nose. "I think there's some mold in this trunk."

"I think there's a dead body in this trunk!" David was gagging.

"Trust me, that's not what a dead body smells like," I said. "Let's air it out a bit outside in the sun before we search."

"Excellent idea."

We carried the trunk to the deck outside. I saw now that there was, indeed, mildew inside the trunk and on the photo albums.

"I really hope none of the pictures are damaged."

"Ruth would be devastated," David said.

"Let's lay these albums out on some towels to dry their covers a bit. Maybe it will help," I said.

"Good idea. I'll go get some. We can look through them as soon as they dry a little."

"Maybe we should give them a few hours. The pages maybe fragile."

"Do you have time for this?"

I looked at my phone. "It's only noon, so we have plenty of time. I don't have to take the train to Paris until tomorrow afternoon, and I'm almost packed, so I can be back late tonight."

"All right. Why don't we go to the beach for a while after we set them out to dry?"

We did a quick job of laying the albums out in the sun and took our sandwiches as a picnic to the lake. Sitting next to David on the towel, warm from the sand, my fingers touching his, looking at the shimmering surface of the water, I wondered if it was possible to make this feeling of peace last an eternity. I lifted my face to the sun and enjoyed the feeling of its warmth gently kissing my face and neck. David pulled me down on the blanket and laid me next to him, with my head on his shoulder.

"You fit just right," he said and stroked my arm.

I snuggled in closer, enjoying the warmth of him. He smelled of sand and sunshine, and trees, and clean cotton. I felt almost dizzy with the desire to be kissed by him. His fingers stroking my arm sent my nerves into an excited frenzy. I focused on watching the clouds gently sailing in the brilliant blue of the summer sky.

I hoped this moment would last forever, but I felt David pull away suddenly.

"Do you hear that? I think someone is calling for help!" he said, shielding his eyes from the sun.

"What? Are you sure?" I stood up, shaking sand off me and squinting to see better.

"Yes! I hear it again! Over there! See? It's like a speck in the lake. There is a person waving!"

"What?" I looked again. "Wait, I think it's a kid!"

I ran to the shore, quickly working on removing my jeans and T-shirt. Several people stood nearby, pointing at the lake. I heard faint cries and saw a small head, not too far from me in the water, bobbing in and out, hands beating at the surface frantically.

I kicked off my shoes and started to run into the lake.

"Shit! It's ice cold!"

"Do you need help?" David was standing behind me, staring at me in my underwear and camisole.

Instead of answering, I jumped into the water and swam, the icy cold gripping my chest tightly, making it painful to breathe. *What if the kid freezes before I get there?* My mind repeated the question over and over. I called out to the child, but heard no answer. The little head was still on the surface as I approached, but then it disappeared under.

Shit! Shit! Shit!

I dove, but struggled to see the body. I searched around with half-frozen fingers and grabbed onto fabric. *Thank God!*

I pulled as hard as I could, and a small and very

cold body appeared at the surface. I turned the child over and saw the blue face of a boy who was no longer breathing. I swam as fast as I could, pulling the lifeless body on top of me, no longer feeling cold. David jumped in to meet me halfway. We reached the shore in what seemed like seconds. I fell on my knees next to the boy and gulped air.

"David, I need to start CPR. Can you get someone to call 911 or whatever number they call for an ambulance here?"

I positioned myself next to his chest. The boy was unresponsive; his lungs clearly full of water. A woman kneeled down and began to rub his feet vigorously. Someone brought a blanket and wrapped it around the boy's legs. I was warming up quickly doing chest compressions.

"1, 2, 3, 4, 5…30." I kept repeating as I worked on the little body tirelessly, giving him breaths in between the compressions.

"An ambulance is on its way." David fell on the sand next to me. "Are you making any progress?"

"I'm doing what I can. Here, do chest compressions like this." I showed him quickly. "Count to thirty as you do them, then stop so I can do mouth-to-mouth. Got it?" I proceeded without waiting for an answer.

David quickly moved to the boy's chest and began compressions. We had attracted quite a crowd at this point. We worked tirelessly, but there was no response from the boy. I knew that we had to continue until the ambulance arrived. But I also knew that if we couldn't get him breathing soon, he was in trouble.

Where was that ambulance?

I heard the siren at the same time David exclaimed, "He's breathing!" My eyes closed for a second, in a silent prayer of thanks. The boy was coughing and shivering violently, water spouting from his mouth. I heard claps and excited cries from the crowd. I turned the boy to his side, while David wrapped him in the blanket and said, "You'll be all right. You are safe, my friend."

"Where the hell are his parents?" I whispered to David.

"Who knows? Kids often swim alone around here. They feel safe."

It was only minutes before the boy was taken away in the ambulance. His parents had finally appeared, distraught and confused. There was no time for explanations, as the ambulance left in a hurry to the hospital. The dramatic scene was suddenly over, as quickly as it had begun.

Chapter 27

Spiez, August, Wednesday—Present Time

As the crowd dissipated and the beach returned to tranquility, I began to shake. I tried to wrap my arms around my wet body, but they shook so hard I nearly bruised myself. My teeth rattled, and I couldn't get any words past my throat, which was shut tight. I saw David coming toward me with a blanket and felt him wrapping it around me, as I stood helpless. He pushed me toward the house, but my feet kept getting tangled. I thought I felt myself carried part of the way, but I wasn't sure if it was only my imagination.

Shock, I thought as I came to on the couch.

"I'll get some towels," David said.

I huddled into a ball on the couch. He sat down next to me, and I felt a towel on my hair, his hands gently drying the dripping strands. He pulled me against his chest after, until the lump in my throat dissolved into hot tears.

"I'm sorry," I whimpered, trying to pull away from him. "I…think…I'm…"

"Shh, I got you."

I cried into his shoulder, while he stroked my hair and planted small kisses on my cheek and forehead. His fingers were ice cold, and I wrapped him in the blanket with me. We held each other, wet and cold but slowly warming up, until I was able to speak again.

"I'm just so glad he is okay. I never wanted to be responsible for someone's life again," I whispered.

He held my face in his now warm hands, his eyes kind. "I figured you'd be used to saving lives."

"It doesn't quite work like that." I pulled away and got up. "I think I need to go get dressed."

"Oh, no, you're not running away from me." David frowned. "You just saved that boy's life. I mean, people thought you were some kind of a superhero out there, yet you are in here sobbing. What's going on?"

"A superhero? I don't remember Spiderman saving people from drowning, in his underwear?"

"You're avoiding my question."

"I am." I felt the lump returning to my throat.

"Listen, I think there's something you need to get off your chest. Feel free to carry your secrets around, but I'm here, and I happen to like you. A lot. I also happen to be a good listener." David took my hand and pulled me back to the couch.

I hesitated a moment, then looked at his face, and something inside me burst. I wanted to tell him everything. I wanted to share all my secrets with him, but I also had an enormous fear that he'd never speak to me again if he knew. I looked in his eyes, aching for my troubles to go away and filled with the sudden desire for him to kiss me and make me forget.

I saw David's face suddenly change, eyes focusing on me with tenderness. I knew he was going to kiss me before I felt his lips on mine. He gently lifted me and placed me on his lap, holding me so close his heartbeat echoed through my body. So I slowly told him about how Ella died because of my mistake. And I told him about Hailey dying. And he listened, stroking my arm gently. I worried he'd push me away, but he didn't. He only hugged me tighter.

"There was nothing you could do about your sister dying. She had a heart condition, and you were only a child. You couldn't save her—no one could."

"I forced her to go on a bike ride in the heat, and that's what caused her heart muscle to overwork."

"If it didn't overwork that day because of the bike ride, it would've overworked another day because she ran around playing. You must know this, as a doctor, deep inside. If her heart was going to quit, it was only a matter of time. Did someone blame you for it? Your family?"

"I've never talked to anyone about this."

"Are you serious?" He ran his hand through his hair. Then he hugged me tighter. "Why didn't you talk to your parents about it?"

"I don't have any parents. My mother died giving birth to us. From eclampsia. My father was an alcoholic and left us then. I grew up with my grandparents. Grandmother, really. My grandfather died as soon as we came to the U.S. as refugees. From a heart attack. Heart trouble runs in my family. It's been just Grandmother and me."

"My father died from a stroke when I was fourteen. I know what it's like to lose a family member. But I also know it doesn't help to blame yourself for it. You have to keep going and live your life. It's not your fault, Maya." He kissed my forehead softly, and I lay against his shoulder, absorbing his strength.

He continued, "And all doctors make mistakes, just like lawyers or people in any profession."

"Doctors' mistakes cause the loss of lives," I pointed out.

"That's because doctors also save lives. It has to even out somehow. Look how you just saved that boy."

"That doesn't happen very often."

"I'm sure you've saved plenty of people. And I'm sure you'll save plenty more. You have a gift—I saw it. You can't give it up just because you didn't do something perfectly with one patient, when you were still learning."

"You're very kind. Or maybe you're just saying this only…"

"Because I want to make out with you? You think I have an ulterior motive for being complimentary?" He laughed so hard I almost fell off his lap.

"But you really do have to be nice to me! Because you like me!"

His face became serious. "I really do like you, Maya. More than you know. I also truly believe that you need to forgive yourself for all these things you're holding against yourself. Look, I've made mistakes in my job and in my life, too. I've learned you can't keep them all with you. Otherwise, they weigh you down and don't let you reach your full potential."

I felt the pain in my heart lessen. I also became aware of the sudden deep warmth emanating from his body. Something between us had definitely changed. He drew me closer, and I let him. He was playful at first, giving me gentle teasing kisses, barely touching my lips. I pressed my body into his, begging for a response. I felt his hands slide underneath my camisole as I closed my eyes instinctively. His kisses became more urgent and then his mouth moved and his tongue circled a very sensitive spot on my neck, making me moan. I wanted him more than I'd ever wanted any other man.

"Wait!" Fear suddenly gripped me, and I sat up straight, pushing him away. "What if, while we are making love, I suddenly start having my visions, and…"

"You'll feel like you're not here with me?" He finished my sentence. He looked deeply into my eyes, his fingers stroking my breast gently. "Trust me, you will not be in a different world when you're with me. I'll keep you here."

He laid me gently on the blanket on the floor, and I was lost, once again, in a different world. But it was my world this time, not Rebecca's. There was no me or him, only intense heartbeats and a feeling of flying and falling. And then—love. I felt it in every cell of my body, stronger than I've ever felt anything before. It made no sense, but my heart was full of profound love and a feeling of safety that I hadn't felt in years.

And he was right. I was with him. *Completely.*

I woke with a jolt, in a dark room. To the noise of raindrops beginning to patter on the roof. I watched the shadows on the ceiling and listened to the wind's howling noises. Somehow we had managed to make it to the bedroom from the floor of the living room. I despised the idea of getting up, away from David's warm body. I refused to think that it also meant we would have to say goodbye to each other.

The photo albums on the deck!

I bolted out of bed. "David! Get up! Hurry! We left the albums on the deck, and it's raining!"

I wrapped the blanket around me and was already

running out, ignoring David's confused, sleepy questions. The rain had only just started, and the trees around the deck offered enough protection to the fragile albums we had carelessly left out. David joined me a few minutes later, and we brought the albums in and laid them out carefully on the floor of the library. I wiped them with kitchen towels.

"I think they're fine. Actually, much better than before. I don't smell any mildew anymore," David said, sniffing. "Let's see if we can open the pages."

"Be gentle."

"I will, don't worry." He began to open one of the albums. The pages yielded, with only some getting slightly stuck at the binding. "Here you go!" He pointed at one page. "Here is my great-grandparents' wedding. We have a similar picture hanging in the library at home. This is Edward Fischer."

The man in the picture didn't look at all like the man I'd seen with Rebecca in my mind. "It's not him, not who I've…"

"Imagined?"

"Seen."

"Are you sure?"

"Very sure. Let's look for some more pictures."

He continued to flip the pages. Album after album. There were dozens of pictures of Rebecca and Edward, Rebecca and Hannah, Rebecca and her parents and grandmother. Rebecca and her friends. Even Rebecca with patients in beds, a stethoscope around her neck.

"Wait! This is what Ruth was talking about." David stopped at one of the pictures. "This is the free clinic for women in Bern."

I looked over his shoulder. It was a picture of

Rebecca and another woman standing underneath a sign with the name of the clinic. "And who is the other woman?"

"No idea. She wasn't in the other pictures. Let's bring any picture we're not sure about back to Ruth and Emelie."

I took the picture and looked at it carefully. Rebecca stood next to a smiling woman who was taller than she and had her hair tied back in a tight chignon. Both women wore doctor's lab coats over their dresses. Even though the picture was a faded black-and-white, I could tell that Rebecca's dress was more expensive, with a lace insert, bows, and many buttons. Her friend's dress was darker in color and had no such embellishments.

I touched the dresses, outlining them with my index finger. *Who are you?* I whispered and heard a laughing voice in my head. *Come on, Lara, we have to go. My mother will be furious if I'm late for supper. Tell Vlad you'll see him later.* I closed my eyes and saw the two women running in the rain from the University of Bern's Anatomy building, laughing and jumping over the puddles.

"Her name was Lara," I said to David.

"How do you know?" he asked, his brows furrowed. "Oh, never mind." He shook his head. "Interesting. My mother's name is Lara. I wonder if she's named after this friend."

The clock chimed, and I jumped up in horror. "What time is it? I completely forgot! We have to get back!"

David looked at his watch. "Seven. Yes, we'd better get going. We have plenty of time to make it back

251

tonight. Don't worry."

I dressed quickly, trying not to think of all the things that had happened and the goodbye that would yet have to happen. We packed up a few pictures to ask Ruth and Emelie about. As I opened the door, the wall of rain hit me, and the wind nearly blew me out of the house and down the driveway.

"David. It's raining very hard!" I yelled out.

"I'm sure it's fine." He walked out, then came back in soaking wet. "It's like a tropical storm out there," he said, brushing the raindrops off his shirt.

"Is it safe to drive?"

"Questionable."

"I need to get back to the city," I pleaded.

"All right. We'll go for it, then. Run for the passenger seat."

We were about a mile down the hill when we realized the road was flooded.

"Damn it! These tiny cars can't get through the high water. Give me an American SUV anytime." David hit the steering wheel in frustration.

"Is there another road out? Think!"

"There is, but I think it might be even worse. Let's try." He turned the car around, skidding a few times.

We were stopped by the police less than a mile later, alerting us that the road was flooded. David turned around and drove back slowly. I pressed my head against the cold window, trying to shut my mind, which was screaming profanities.

"Do you really have to return to Paris tomorrow?" he asked gently.

I was at the end of my rope. "I have a meeting with the dean on Friday in New York. If I'm not there, I'll be thrown out of my residency," I said.

"So you have to catch a plane to New York tomorrow. What time is your meeting?"

"Noon. The flight from Paris leaves at seven tomorrow."

"All right, so you need to leave Bern by eleven to travel to Paris on time. Which means we have to leave here by nine to give you enough of a window to go back to Jacob's and pick up your things. The water should recede enough by the morning. You'll be fine."

"You really think I can still make it?"

"Do you consider yourself a lucky person?"

I laughed and cried at the same time. "No."

"Ouch." He placed a hand on his heart, mocking. "I didn't realize I was that awful a lover."

"I didn't mean you and me. I'd love to spend another night with you. You're just about the only lucky thing that's ever happened to me," I said tearfully. "It's the rest of my life that stinks."

"I knew you didn't mean us."

He parked the car, and we ran back inside the house.

"There should be some spaghetti. Emelie always keeps some for the kids," David called out as he worked to light the fireplace.

I went to the kitchen to look for any pantry foods to cook for dinner. There was indeed some pasta, and it was comforting to cook a simple meal after this crazy complicated day. We ate the spaghetti straight from the large bowl, not bothering with plates.

"So tell me exactly why are you in trouble with your residency?" he asked.

"Because when that girl died, it was written in my

file that I had 'questionable clinical judgment.' I was so upset that I asked for a leave of absence. I was supposed to return a few weeks ago, but I didn't. I took a flight to Edinburgh instead. And then they called me to tell me I was on probation because I wasn't back on time."

"It seems rather drastic to place a resident on probation for lateness. I would think there should've been first a warning that you were exceeding your days."

"Residents are abused all the time. Sounds just about right to me."

"Did you look through your residency contract to make sure they had the right to place you on probation?"

"Now I can tell I'm talking to a lawyer." I laughed and took another mouthful of pasta.

"It's not just a lawyer talking, it's common sense. When you go to your meeting, you need to be prepared and question what legal right they actually have to place you on probation. You may be protected more than you know."

"Okay, fine. I'll check into it. I'm sure I have the contract somewhere."

"My guess is they're trying to cover up for the death of that girl, and they want you gone to prevent any further inquiries."

I thought for a moment. "You really think they'd possibly use me as a scapegoat? That seems awfully low."

He pulled me close and kissed me hard. "Come with me, I can distract you. And maybe then I can convince you to stay longer."

"I can't. I have to go back. I have to stop running away from trouble."

"You can call and reschedule your meeting for Monday, which will give me time to find someone over the weekend to represent you at your meeting. It would definitely help to be there with an attorney. The whole thing could be over in minutes, and you'd be back without anything on your record or any probation."

"I need to handle this myself, David. It's really important that I do. I'll let you know if I need help."

Hours later, I lay awake with David's arm across my stomach. Insomnia and worries about my residency aside, the mere thought of being in Rebecca's old house with David sleeping nearby made my heart race enough to make any relaxation impossible. Another reason I couldn't sleep was that after searching through four more boxes of family photos, we had found none of Rebecca with a young man named Mark. Was I looking for the wrong Rebecca or for the wrong man? Was there ever a Mark? Was I only meant to find David? The moonlight was coming in through the window, illuminating David's face on the pillow next to me. I brushed my fingers through the curly mess of his soft hair.

He opened his eyes, and then his own fingers stretched out and he traced the outline of my body. He leaned over and kissed my neck gently, nuzzling it a little, sending shivers all through me. We'd only made love twice, yet he already knew all my sensitive spots. He pulled himself on top of me, and I stopped thinking about the ring or its memories.

Later, as dawn came, we were still talking. Being with David was like being with someone I'd known my whole life. I told him about my life in Odessa and how my grandparents and I came to live in New York City. I told him about how, as a refugee, you never quite felt like you belonged anywhere. That once you lost your home, you never quite felt like you had another. David told me about losing his father and how his mother never dated or married again, because her heart was forever broken. He told me about his childhood dreams of becoming a veterinarian and then deciding to go to law school instead so he could be near his mother and brother. There was a great deal to talk about, and I was grateful for the storm Fate had sent our way.

Chapter 28

Spiez, July 1915

The drive to Lake Thun took all morning and felt endless. Rebecca attempted to relax by watching the clouds floating slowly across the bright blue sky, but her body kept fidgeting in frustration. The car was now making a slow ascent up the winding road to Spiez. She inhaled the crisp morning air, enjoying its sweet taste. She would enjoy it much more if she weren't being dragged here as a prisoner. She coughed quietly into a handkerchief.

She wasn't ill! She was fairly sure it was only a mild case of a respiratory virus. But after seeing Father's concerned face, Mother had overreacted to her cough and ordered them all to the lake two weeks early.

Mother patted her hand. "We'll be in Spiez soon, and you can start your inhalations and hydrotherapy."

"I don't require any of these therapies! It's just a common respiratory virus. It should resolve on its own."

"None of this would've happened if you and Sarah didn't choose to work with those women from the slums," Mother said, her lips pursed.

"We're doctors, Mother. That's what we do. Someone has to help these women."

"If you die, you can't help them."

257

"I won't die. I'm just a little ill. I've not been exposed to some of these illnesses before. My body will get stronger and I won't get sick again. All physicians go through the same experience." She coughed violently from the effort of talking and watched Mother turn pale.

Grandmother intervened. "My dear, when your husband first began working in the hospital, he was terribly ill all the time. I had to ask him to stay in the hospital rather than come home, for fear he would infect us all. With time, his body accustomed, and he stopped catching diseases. This is the life of a physician. Rebecca must bear it."

"How can she ever become a mother?"

"That is quite an irrelevant question at this point, isn't it?" Grandmother asked.

Hannah interrupted. "Mother, can I please spend some time with the Steins, since Rebecca is ill? I don't want to be sick for my wedding. They invited me to stay as long as I wish."

"Of course, dearest. It would be good for you to get away." Mother bent her head to Hannah, and they whispered about what Hannah needed to pack to stay with the Steins. Thankfully, Hannah's wedding kept her and Mother occupied enough to allow Rebecca to do whatever she wanted.

Until this blasted virus!

When they finally arrived at the chalet, Rebecca had to admit she felt exhausted. She wasn't tasked with opening up and airing out the house, and she was grateful for this small blessing. She sat outside on the deck, watching the birds flying from tree to tree and thinking of Mark. Being away from the clinic didn't worry her; Sarah was there to run it, and Lara would come every evening to make sure it would continue running without Rebecca. But being away from Mark made her feel only half alive. She simply could no longer exist without him. She needed him as much as she needed air to breathe. Why couldn't she just fly to him like one of these birds happily flying back and forth?

She got up off her chair, went down the steps off the deck, and walked to the lake. She knew no one would miss her. The surface of the lake was brilliant emerald and calm, settling her mind somewhat. She walked for a while, wondering how she would survive the next few weeks until she could manage to convince Mother that she was well and needed to return to Bern. Thoughts swirling, she picked up a stone and threw it into the water.

"That's not the proper way to skip stones." A voice she loved so much made her spin around. She picked up her skirt to run to him, but he reached her first, embracing her, holding her head to his chest, and stroking her hair.

"I can't live without you in the city," Mark said, lifting her chin and kissing her.

"I'm so sorry I left. I love you so much. I hate being here," she said, kissing his cheeks.

"Is your health really so poor?" he asked, examining her with concern.

"It's only a minor chest congestion. It's going to resolve soon. I'm certain." She looked around to make sure no one was watching, suddenly aware that they were in public. But there were only a few children playing.

"I wanted to surprise you," Mark said.

"I love surprises. But how did you manage to travel here, and where will you stay?" Rebecca asked, worried.

"I'm here with Vlad—we took the train. We're staying with friends; there are many in Spiez."

"I doubt they come for the hydrotherapy." Rebecca raised her brows.

He laughed. "Don't worry, I won't get in trouble. And at least I have a place to stay until you're ready to return to Bern."

"Is it safe for Vlad to leave Lara alone in the city? What if she gets arrested?"

"She's not the one doing anything illegal. It's him they are really watching. If she only works at the clinic, she is safe."

"And where is Lenin?"

"He and Nadezhda are also in the mountains, in Sorenberg. She's been feeling ill after her mother's death, and they're staying at Hotel Marienthal for the summer until her health is better."

"Is he going to make you travel to Sorenberg to work with him?"

"I'm here only for you, that's it. Until you recover."

"I'm not ill." She waved at him in protest. "What of your work at the hospital?"

"I took a leave for a while. I'm entitled to a leave."

"You are so kind to me."

"Kind? I'm desperately in love with you and will do anything for you. Don't you know that?" He kissed her lips gently.

"Then go now. I have to go back before they miss

me."

"When can I see you again?" He wasn't letting her go.

"The family is going for a boat ride tomorrow after tea. I can say I'm feeling dizzy and wish to lie down instead."

His face fell. "Always hiding. Always a secret. Give me a chance to talk to your family, please?"

"No, not yet. I promise I'm going to talk to Mother. Soon, very soon. I love you, my darling. Come by around four tomorrow. See that house over there with a brown roof? That's ours."

He whistled. "Like a palace."

"It's no such thing." She stood up on her tiptoes and kissed him. "I love you. I'll see you tomorrow."

She ran back to the house, heart heavy. She had to tell her family about Mark. *But how?*

The night was sleepless, with Rebecca staring at her dark window, thinking of ways to explain her feelings toward Mark to her parents. She knew she had to get one of her parents alone, or at least with Grandmother present. Grandmother was on the side of tradition, but also not necessarily against the idea of love.

Rebecca dressed quickly the next morning, hoping to catch Mother before anyone else woke up. She ran downstairs and hid briefly in the stairway until she conquered a fit of coughing. She arrived at the morning parlor, still out of breath, yet with enough of it to discuss what she needed. Her face fell when she saw that Mother was entertaining company.

"Oh, Rebecca, good morning," Mother said. "Fräu Einhorn and Fräu Stein have joined us for breakfast.

Come sit down."

"Good morning, Fräu Einhorn and Fräu Stein," Rebecca said, holding back her tears.

"We were in the middle of discussing charity efforts in the city. The last few years we've been helping the Russian students with coats and hats in the winter, but now they seem to all be leaving. So we need a new proposal."

"Mother, I didn't know that was your charity."

"Well, you never ask what it is that I do in my free time. You think you are the only one who does any important work."

There it was—her opportunity to start a conversation with Mother about Mark!

"I apologize," she said as mildly as possible. "I do believe your work is important. Any work women do to help others is important. I'm so pleased to know you helped those students." She turned to Mother's friends. "You know they arrive here with only one change of clothes and sometimes not even a hat?"

"Of course we know that, dear." Fräu Stein shook her head. "What kind of families would send their children so far away with no money and no belongings?"

Rebecca felt her cheeks flush. "Well, I really don't think these families have much choice. The Tsar doesn't allow Jews to attend the university, and there is violence against the Jews in Russia and Ukraine."

"I've heard from some of the students," Fräu Einhorn chimed in, "that Jews have to apply for special permits to live in the cities. They are restricted to living in the countryside only."

"Yes, that appears to be the story," Mother said.

"They have to live within a restricted area called the Pale of Settlement, and may not move outside of the boundary unless they receive the Tsar's permission."

Fräu Einhorn turned to Rebecca. "Is it true? I heard that all the students live together in Bern in what they call 'a colony,' in tiny rooms with no heat or electrification, and eat nothing but stale bread."

"They do tend to live in cramped quarters, but there is plenty of good food that they cook in the common kitchens, or they buy food in the boardinghouse. They have electricity, and they attend concerts and lectures. Their life is not awful at all, and they're all like a family," Rebecca said emphatically.

The ladies stared at her.

"And how exactly do you come in possession of such knowledge?" Mother asked in an icy voice.

Here it goes... "Mother, there are some Russian students I'm friends with. Close friends."

Mother set her cup of tea down. "How close?"

Fräu Stein cleared her throat and set down her teacup.

Rebecca sat near Mother. "Some closer than others. There's one student. He is a surgeon, not a student anymore. He works at the hospital. His name is Mark Minchin, and he has become very special to me. He's helped *Papi* with some of his patients before." She turned toward Mother's friends. "And one time I was hurt and he helped me get home."

"Well, it was very kind of him. I hope you will have no further accidents and we shall have no further need of his services." Mother's face turned a strange ashy color. "Would you be kind enough to excuse me for a moment?" she asked her friends.

Mother grabbed Rebecca's arm and pulled her outside onto the deck.

"Ouch, you are hurting me. Stop!" Rebecca pleaded.

"This is exactly what I was worried about when you insisted on going to the university." Mother raised her voice.

Rebecca straightened up. "He is not just a poor student! I told you—he is a surgeon. He is a kind man. So what if he is from Ukraine? He has suffered so much to receive his education. And he loves me!"

"It is irrelevant whether he loves you or not. You may not get involved with a foreigner who has no prospects of joining our community!"

"How can you be such a hypocrite? You just said you've been giving charity to these foreigners. And now you say you don't want me to be friends with one?"

"But you are not talking about friendship, are you? You are talking about marriage, and that's out of the question. You'll marry who I and your father choose for you, and that's the end of this conversation. If you haven't noticed, I'm entertaining company." Mother left, slamming the deck door.

Rebecca stormed off the deck and down to the lake, kicking at the grass and dirt, and muttering angry words, tears streaming down her cheeks. She picked up a few rocks and threw them as hard as she could into the water. What was she going to do now? This was all ruined!

"Fräulein Miller, may I be of some assistance?" A hand touched her shoulder gently, making her jump.

She turned around, still furious, and found herself

looking at Edward Fischer, the American she'd met at the ball the winter before last.

"Oh, Mister Fischer. I do apologize for my appearance," Rebecca said, wiping at her tears. "You caught me at a bad moment."

He bowed to her. "Just Edward, please. Is there anything I can do?" he asked, his eyes kind and filled with concern.

"Arrange for a new mother for me?"

He laughed. "I have a sister. I know all about difficult mother and daughter moments. Might I help by inviting your family to dine with us later? My mother heard you were in town and sent me with the invitation. We are renting a home just a few minutes' walk from here."

Rebecca thought for a moment. She was definitely going to be scolded for the rest of the day and possibly for several. A dinner invitation from Edward could rescue her quite nicely.

"Yes, I do believe it might help. Thank you." She smiled at him, feeling better.

They walked back to the house, where Edward issued his invitation, to Mother's complete surprise. Rebecca felt smug as Fräu Einhorn and Fräu Stein blushed at Edward's smiles and flirted with him. He really was a handsome man. Rebecca walked Edward back to the lake, torn between feeling awful about her earlier failure and relieved about being rescued.

"Can I convince you to finish my walk with me?" Edward asked. "This time without tossing rocks, hopefully. Although I do happen to be very good at this activity, if you wish to continue."

She smiled. "Thank you, but I think I'd better head

back. I'm very grateful to you for rescuing me. It's awfully kind of you."

"Not at all kind. Rather selfish, actually. I've been quite bored here in the country; these walks around the lake are very dull."

"They are, but the water can distract you from some troubles as well," Rebecca said.

"I don't have any troubles. I'm lucky." Edward took her hand, kissed it and walked away slowly.

Rebecca watched him and thought of how strange this morning had turned out to be. Then her heart began to hurt. What was she going to tell Mark? And how was she ever going to convince her parents to accept him?

Chapter 29

Spiez, July 1915

They dined with Edward and his family two days later, at the house the Fischers had rented for the summer. Mother was bubbling with happiness at having a new friend in Edward's mother, Adele. Rebecca was thrilled that she'd been left alone since Edward's invitation. She and Mark had been able to meet every time the family left the house for an outing. Things really couldn't have worked out any better.

"I wish I had known earlier that you were still in Switzerland," Rebecca said to Edward, who was seated next to her.

"We were not able to leave. We had passage booked on a liner in May, but they haven't been crossing since what happened to the *Lusitania*."

"Of course. What a horrible thing for Germany to do! I'm so glad you chose to stay."

"I'm afraid it wasn't a choice. I feel we are rather stranded here now."

"Well, it isn't safe to cross. You must stay until this war is finally over. It shouldn't take too long; I hear the fighting is fierce," Rebecca said, taking a forkful of trout.

"The devastation in France has been an absolute tragedy. We've been hearing a great deal of rumors here in the Alps from the families displaced by the war," Mrs. Fischer said.

"I certainly hope our country can maintain its neutrality," Rebecca said, suddenly less hungry.

"It's not possible to completely stay out of the conflict. Even a neutral country must be prepared to fight if invaded by hostile forces." Father had joined the conversation.

"Do you really think Switzerland plans to engage?" Edward asked.

"I'm afraid it's already engaged. Not in a traditional military way yet, but through its diplomatic and charity efforts. Physicians and surgeons have been traveling to the front to assist the medical mission," Father answered.

"You're not thinking of going, are you, Joseph?" Mother asked.

"I was, but I've been asked to stay here and supervise the establishment of a special medical service in Bern for the exclusive purpose of serving war prisoners."

"War prisoners? What do you mean, *Papi*?" Hannah asked.

"Our government, together with the Red Cross, has arranged for a charitable medical service for prisoners of war from all countries. There are already medical institutions in Lucerne and Fribourg. And now we'll have one in Bern," Father explained.

"Will the prisoners be transferred from the front?" Edward asked.

"No, they'll receive acute medical treatment at the front and then transfer here for secondary treatment."

"Will the army soldiers come into Bern, then?"

Edward's sixteen-year-old sister, Eva, asked. "Will it be unsafe?"

"I don't believe so. They'll fall under the jurisdiction of the Swiss medical services and will obey their superiors, but there should be no other army presence."

"How interesting. I'm quite looking forward to working with these soldiers. Can you only imagine the stories they will tell!" Rebecca said.

"Rebecca, I feel faint thinking of you working with the prisoners," Mother said.

"Oh, Mother. If you knew what I've seen and done already as a medical student and a resident!"

"Must you shock me every time you speak?"

Rebecca waved dismissively at her mother and turned back to Edward, whispering, "I wish I'd known you were still here. We could've spent time together sooner."

He looked at her for a long time. "I was under the impression that you didn't wish to ever see me again, when we spoke at the ball. I do apologize, but you said you had no desire to marry."

She thought carefully about her next sentence, trying to control her emotions, thoughts, and words. "You must not misunderstand me. I wasn't stating that I wished to see you in a romantic manner. I only meant that I wished to keep your friendship and be of assistance to your sister. You did say she was ill?"

"Yes, Eva is still struggling with her health. In all honesty, I'm glad we stayed, as she's able to follow a new course of treatment here in the mountains. I think she may be finally achieving some relief."

"What is her condition?"

"She suffered pneumonia five years ago, and her lungs and heart have been very weak ever since. Her doctors in New York suggested that Switzerland's air would be best for her lungs."

"So it is helping?"

"Slightly. I still hear her cough at night, but some herbal preparations she is receiving have been easing her chest pain."

"What about your work? How are you able to do it here?"

"I'm managing. I don't have much of a choice. You see, it was my fault she became ill in the first place."

"How was it your fault?"

"Eva and Mother lived in the country, north of New York City, in a town called Poughkeepsie. That's where I grew up. My father was a doctor there. When my father died, I moved to the city to learn banking. Once I became established, I asked Mother and Eva to come live with me. That's when Eva caught pneumonia, at her school. I was very wrong to bring her into a city infested with immigrants and germs."

Rebecca touched his arm as she watched him furrow his forehead. "I'm sure you meant the best for your family. There was no way for you to know that she would become ill. This could've happened to her in the country, as well. She likely was born with weakened lungs, and that's all pneumonia needs."

He touched her hand back in gratitude. "Either way, I will do anything to get Eva better. She means everything to me. She loves it here, so here we'll stay until she recovers."

"It's very noble of you. Please let me know if there's anything I can do to assist. I am, after all, a women's physician. I have my own clinic in Bern now."

"Thank you for your kindness. I'm sure Eva will be very glad to take you up on your offer. I didn't realize you had your own clinic. I assumed you practiced with Dr. Miller."

"Two of my friends and I opened a women's health clinic. We provide health and legal services to those who can't afford them. Father gave me some money to get it started."

"How industrious of you! And is the clinic successful?"

"Somewhat. We have many patients, but not enough resources to help them. I find that going to the women's homes is helpful, but I watch so many mothers and children suffer. We hope more physicians will join us in our efforts. And we need more medications and supplies." Rebecca sighed.

"Are you in need of money? My mother and I would be happy to contribute. We haven't been able to keep up our charity efforts since being here."

"Would you really? That's awfully kind. I wasn't telling you about the clinic to solicit money." Rebecca was embarrassed now.

"I didn't think you were. But I would be glad of an opportunity to help."

Rebecca couldn't wait to tell Lara and Sarah. Not only was Edward an intelligent and pleasant man, but he was also kind and charitable. Not to mention that this dinner and their conversing ensured that Mother had forgotten all about Mark. Dessert was served, and she ate her raspberry soufflé with pleasure, her spirits quite uplifted.

****

The next day was sweltering, and it seemed as if it took an eternity for everyone to depart for the boat ride and picnic they had planned. At first, Mother refused to leave when Rebecca complained of her head spinning. (The day before, it had been a stomach distress.) But when Rebecca assured her that she'd simply remain in her bed, Mother reluctantly agreed. Father rolled his eyes at the list of Rebecca's symptoms, but she stood firm.

She quickly changed into a pretty summer frock and fixed her hair. The maids were busy cleaning, and the housekeeper had gone to the market, so the home was as empty as she could wish for. Mark has been coming to see her every day, and they had found different ways to avoid the family and staff. It was remarkably easy in Spiez—so much simpler than in Bern.

A quiet knock on the door startled her. He was here! She opened the door and was swept up in his arms, her face covered in kisses.

"How beautiful you are!" he said, still holding her.

She wrapped her arms around his strong neck, not wishing for him to put her down. "I love you."

"How do you feel today?"

"I feel perfectly fine."

He sat her down gently on a sofa, then produced a small bouquet of flowers from inside his jacket. "I know you have flowers everywhere, but I picked them on the mountain this morning."

"Edelweiss!" The flowers smelled divine and so did he, of fresh flowers and grass and mountains.

"How long can I stay before your family returns?" he asked.

She knew how much it hurt him that her parents wouldn't accept him. She pulled him down to sit next to her and took his hands. "We have several hours. We have time enough."

"More than ever. In the city, we always have to rush."

"Yes. More than ever." She hesitated. *Was she really going to do this?* Then she got up and took his hands. "Come with me."

"Where are we going?"

"My room. The maids have cleaned there already, so we won't be disturbed."

"Your room?" Mark raised his brows. "We are alone here, and you invite me to your bedroom?" He stood up, a smile beginning to form on his lips.

Rebecca motioned him to follow her. His face changed, and she was gratified to see the hungry look in his eyes. She led him upstairs, watching out for the maids, but it was quiet now, and they reached her bedroom and sitting room without being noticed.

When she closed the door, he gently put his hands on her waist and turned her around. His eyes were as dark and deep as Lake Thun in the winter. She wanted nothing less than to swim in them and feel lost in his soul. She reached for his lips, but they were already on her neck, and she shook with pleasure. He pulled her dress off her left shoulder, then her right, and kissed her collarbone. She started unbuttoning his shirt, hungry to touch him. Her hands stroked the bare skin under his shirt as his fingers worked on the buttons of her dress. She felt his heart pulsing under her fingers, and her own beat in rhythm. His breath was hot as he whispered in her ear, his hands gently circling her breasts, making it difficult for her to breath.

"Are you sure you want to do this?"

She looked at him, her eyes daring, as her hands searched in his trousers. "Are *you* sure?"

He groaned. "You are driving me crazy. I've been dreaming of making love to you for too long. But I can go on dreaming until you marry me. I'll wait…" He groaned again and pressed her hard against him. "If I have to."

"I can't wait," she said, dropping her dress to her feet.

He looked at her in awe as she laughed and pressed against him, her skin hungry for the feel of his body. He picked her up and carried her to the bed, where she finally was lost in the depth of his love and gave herself away to him, happily.

As the afternoon approached, the merciless clock continued to chime in the next room, and she knew Mark would need to go soon. She held his face in her hands, and he ran his hand up and down her side, making her tingle all over again.

"I have to go, right?" he asked.

"Yes, they'll be back soon."

"Your family will never accept me."

"They will. They need time. I spoke with my mother. She listened, but she wasn't ready."

He leaned on his elbow. "What did she say?"

"She was worried about your political activities. She knows the student colony well. She and her friends do charity there."

"I understand. She wants you to marry someone safe, not a Socialist. Someone who can give you a home and children."

"Yes. But I'll convince her." She kissed him with passion.

"Does she have someone in mind?" he asked.

Rebecca laughed. "Are you jealous?"

"Of course I am. You are mine and only mine." He rolled on top of her and covered her face and body with quick kisses.

"Wait." She pushed him away and sat up. "Do you hear that?"

"Yes!" He jumped off the bed and began to dress in haste.

The sounds outside were unmistakably those of an approaching car.

"They are coming back early. I'm so sorry." She began fixing the bed and getting dressed. "I'll show you a quick way out by the back stairs. You can find a path to the lake there."

"I'll sneak away…like a thief," he said quietly. "I do feel as if I've stolen something. We probably shouldn't have done this."

Rebecca hugged his back, but he wouldn't turn to her. "I loved making love to you. You are everything to me!"

She finished dressing and pulled him along. She heard Mother talking to Hannah in the garden in the front. There was no time to waste. They ran down the back stairs, and she showed him the path the gardener took to the back gate. He pulled her tight against him and kissed her quickly.

"Meet me by the lake tomorrow at noon."

Rebecca closed the door and turned back to run upstairs to her room, hoping to fix her hair before Mother saw her. She nearly fell backwards—on the steps in front of her, arms crossed, stood her grandmother.

"You'd better come into my room before anyone else catches sight of you," Grandmother said and proceeded up with no further words.

Rebecca followed slowly, her heart in her throat. She looked back once, but Mark was gone.

Chapter 30

Spiez, August, Thursday—Present Time

I woke when it was light outside. The rain had stopped, and the house was very quiet except for the sound of birds chirping outside. Only a few hours left with David. He was stretched out next to me, with his left leg on top of the down comforter and his palm underneath his pillow. My heart sank. As much as I tried not to allow myself to get attached to him, I could hardly help it. With a feeling of loss gripping me already, I got dressed and went downstairs to the library, where we had left the pictures. We never did solve the mystery of why there were no pictures of Mark. Maybe it was Edward I was really looking for? If only Rebecca would give me another glimpse into her memories.

I took one of the albums and sat by a small lamp in an armchair, legs folded, ready to look again. A sudden *tap, tap, tap* on the window startled me, and I bolted out of the chair, the album falling off my lap. Fear crawled up my spine. I backed up a few steps, wondering if David could hear me from where I was. I searched around for a weapon, grabbed a heavy metal globe, and approached the window cautiously, hoping my vocal cords would allow a scream loud enough if needed.

I saw a large pine tree beyond the window, needles

waving with the wind, rain water still dripping down. I looked for any large animal or human figure outside, my arm ready to strike anything coming at me through the window. Then I put my arm down. My mind didn't believe what I was looking at, but my body calmed down slowly.

My robin was perched on the branch closest to the window, head cocked, watching me intently. We played the staring game for a while; then it flew to the window and tapped with its beak. I set the globe down on a table. *What the hell?*

I approached the window slowly. The bird didn't fly away, just nodded its head at me. I opened the window a crack, stepped back in invitation, and the robin fluttered in, hovering a moment. I whistled to it, and it sang happily back.

"Well, hello there. We're finally going to make friends, are we?" I said.

The bird flew around the room, then landed on a bookshelf and sang another song.

"I wonder if I should give you a name. You are kind of like my pet, aren't you?" I joked. "What should I call you?"

The bird sang again, not moving from its spot, then rose in flight and settled back down in the same spot.

I stood up. "All right, what are you trying to show me?" I cautiously approached the bookshelf, but the bird didn't move. The bird suddenly turned and pecked at one of the volumes, then chirped.

"Okay, I get it. You want me to look at this book. You might want to move, then."

The bird hopped away, and I reached for the old leather burgundy cover it had pecked at, hoping it hadn't made a hole in it. It took me a moment to distinguish the well-worn letters on the title.

Jane Eyre. My fingers shook violently then. I placed the book on a small table and collapsed in the chair next to it. I closed my eyes and, when I opened them a few minutes later, the robin was sitting on the book, looking at me calmly. Did it look sad, or had I totally lost my mind?

"Ella?" I whispered, my voice trembling.

The robin flew close enough to my face to brush its wings against my cheek lightly before it was gone through the open window.

I ran to the window. "Ella!" I called out to the trees and the lake covered by the fog from the rain and morning dew. But she was gone.

The book was still in my hand. I sat back down and flipped through the yellowed pages, even though my nerves felt shattered. I hadn't touched this book since my sister died. It was her absolute favorite. What was that passage she really loved? Something about...the bird? I was searching intently for the passage when I noticed something inserted between the pages. My fingers gently pulled out a small envelope addressed in flowing handwriting to...

Mark Minchin.

"Oh," I whispered. "Rebecca, you're ready to tell me your secret, aren't you?"

I unfolded the letter, careful not to tear the old paper. The letters were beautifully formed, but some were smudged.

Was she crying?

My Dearest Beloved, Mark,

I only say your name when I pray now. But I see

you in my dreams. I feel your hands touching my face and your lips kissing mine, especially when petals fall on my face in our garden. And when first snowflakes begin to fall.

I only have a few minutes to write this letter, yet my hands shake and my eyes are watery. It's been a long time since you said you would return to me.

I wait every day. Every hour. Every minute.

Sometimes, at the hospital, I hear your footsteps in the hall, and I can hardly do my work. Sometimes, I ask the cook to make extra food for dinner in case you suddenly walk in through the front door.

I know your revolution succeeded and Lenin is in charge of Russia now. I wonder if you've been to see your family or if you are working with the Bolsheviks to create a new country. I wonder if you ever made it to Odessa, where you hoped to live. I wonder whether Lara or Vlad are with you, helping you.

The world is different now because of your revolution, and I like to think that it's different because of you. Workers will soon have an eight-hour working day as you always wanted. Germany and Britain have allowed women the right to vote, and more countries will soon follow.

I hear rumors of a war in your country, and I fear the worst. I see you injured and bleeding with no one to care for you. But then I think it impossible, as you were so dear to Lenin and he wouldn't send you into danger.

I search all the newspapers for your name, and then I pray I will not see it. I pray that you are safe. I pray that you are happy. I pray that there's someone who loves you at home.

Mother has forced me to marry. No. That's not a

fair accusation. I've decided to marry. You see, I can't bear to stay here in Bern. Every place reminds me of you. Of us. I've agreed to marry, so long as I can live far away from here. So I'm traveling to America with my new husband, Edward. He is kind and tall. He promises to allow me to practice medicine if the State of New York will allow it. I think they will. There are a few women physicians in New York now and even a hospital where they can practice. It's called the New York Infirmary for Women and Children. I might be able to get a position there.

I am leaving this letter with Grossmami. I don't believe you'll ever read it. But Sarah says I must never lose hope. She is wrong. It's lost already.

I will love you forever.

Your Rebecca.

"It's not possible," I said.

"Couldn't sleep, huh?" David said behind me.

"You have got to stop popping up on me like that!" I rubbed the goosebumps on my arms. "I'm sorry," I said, slowly calming down. "I'm just not a big fan of people startling me."

"Especially in old houses after a rainy night?" he pointed out.

"Yes, definitely not a fan of that," I said. "It's all those years of working in old hospitals late at night and having to walk to my car or the subway in the dark. I'm easily spooked. I'm sorry I'm roaming through your family's house. I just wanted to look at the pictures again."

"No problem. I only got up because I missed having you near me." He came close, sat next to me, and held me tightly until my body began to melt into his. Again.

"Hey, do you believe that coincidences could have meanings?" I asked.

"Coincidences that have meanings? Let me think. *Bashert*—do you know that word? It's the Yiddish word for destiny. Is that what you mean?"

"I thought it meant soulmate?"

"It means both, really, but I don't believe in either. I believe in making my own choices and that nothing in my life is predetermined."

"So you don't think we were destined to meet? You don't think my finding your great-grandmother's ring was a meaningful coincidence?"

"Look, are you going to tell me the universe planned for my father to die? Or for your sister to die? I think that people who believe in Fate or destiny are people who have been very lucky."

"That's not true at all. I believe in Fate and it's been very unkind to me."

He looked back at me, assessing. "Well, maybe you're looking for answers that aren't there."

"Well, I think I have my answers now. You see this book?" I showed him *Jane Eyre*. "I found it here this morning. It was my sister's favorite book. I haven't touched a copy of it since she died."

"Maya, no one can fix what happened to either of us." He spoke with a tone of irritation in his voice. "And things just happen sometimes. A coincidence is simply a coincidence. You shouldn't look for meanings in these things."

"Well, as I picked up this book, I flipped through the pages and found this letter." I handed him Rebecca's letter.

"Not possible!" he exclaimed a few minutes later.

"You still don't believe in Fate or meaningful coincidences? I find a ring that belongs to your great-grandmother, then I meet you, then I end up in a house that used to belong to your relatives; we come here because photo albums are missing, we can't get out because of the rain, and then I find the book my sister loved when we were eleven and it has exactly what I'm looking for. What is this all about? Ever since I found Rebecca's ring, my life has been nothing but a string of messages from the universe or Fate or whatever!"

He ran a hand through his hair. "I don't know. I don't have the answers to your questions. I just…don't believe in things like that."

"Why am I so drawn to you if it's not Fate or destiny?" I whispered, wrapping my arms around his neck. I gasped from the sensation of his body's warmth, and my whole being pulled toward him, with a desperate need, as if I'd been missing this feeling of being touched by his lips and arms forever. I was spinning with sensations, and I grabbed onto his shoulders, trying to keep myself connected to him.

"I don't know," he said and held onto me firmly, his lips first gentle then more demanding on mine, his body fitting perfectly into mine like a puzzle piece. When he slowly pulled away, his face was flushed. He turned away briefly, and then he looked up at me with a deep knowledge in his eyes.

"Do it again," I said. "I feel like it's all just so perfect." I stroked his chest gently.

"It is. Don't go. Stay for the weekend." He kissed my fingers, briefly stopping at the one that wore the ring, as if he were afraid to touch it.

My phone rang loudly, echoing through the small room.

"Let it go to voicemail," David said, as he nuzzled my neck.

"Okay," I said, reaching over to silence it. Then I saw the caller ID.

"I'm sorry, it's my grandmother. I have to pick it up. She worries about me. Baba, what's the matter?" I asked.

"It's Pavel." I heard my grandmother's neighbor's voice.

"Pavel?" I pulled away from David. "Did she ask you to call me? Is something the matter?"

"*Da, beda*. Trouble. Your Babushka had a stroke and died last night."

"What?" I stood up, almost knocking David over. "What are you saying? What do you mean?" I screamed. I felt David's arms around me, trying to calm me, but I shrugged him off.

"Alina was dropping off some groceries for her yesterday and found her in her bed, very weak. We called for an ambulance. The doctors said she had a mild stroke, so we didn't want to worry you. Then, last night, the doctor called to say she had a problem with her lungs. And then this morning she died. It all happened so quickly, there was no time... My wife and I don't know what you'd like to do. About the funeral, I mean."

"What funeral? What do you mean she died? I spoke with her on Monday. What are you even talking about? David..." I looked helplessly at David. "There is a man on the phone, he is saying my grandmother died this morning, but she wasn't even sick. Can you please talk to him?" I handed him the phone, my hands shaking.

I watched David talk confidently into the phone, my ears buzzing with a strange noise as I paced the room. I felt cold, very cold, and there were spots dancing in front of my eyes.

"I think I need to eat something—my blood sugar must be low," I said quietly as I saw David end the call.

"Or you might be in shock again." David gave my hands a gentle squeeze.

"Why would I be in shock?"

He looked at me with watery eyes, and I remembered, grief striking me and making my insides curl up in pain.

"It's true, sweetheart. Your grandmother has passed away. I'm so, so sorry." He hugged me close.

I cried hard, unable to take a breath between sobs. "It hurts so much, I can't stand it, David," I whispered between the sobs when I was finally able to speak.

He continued to hug me without saying anything, and I cried some more into his shoulder, slowly quieting.

"My last conversation with her wasn't even good. I never got to say goodbye!" I blew my nose into a tissue he handed me. "I haven't seen her in almost a year. I'm the worst human being ever."

"I'm sure she knew you loved her. This guy I spoke to said she never came to after the stroke. You wouldn't have been able to say goodbye."

"What else did he say?"

"She died in her sleep; she didn't suffer. That's what the doctor told him."

A new series of sobs burst from my chest, and he

hugged me again. I waited until the wave of grief calmed, then got up and went upstairs to get my shoes and backpack.

"What are you doing?" He came up behind me, touching my arm.

"I have to go. Don't worry. I'll get an Uber to the train station."

"I'll drive you."

"I don't want you to. I have to go right now, and you have to get dressed and lock up the house. I want to be alone. I just need to leave right now." I tripped on my way out of the bedroom.

"You can't just take off. Think. We can go together. We need some time to talk, to think this through. Just give me a moment to get ready."

"I'm done thinking. This is all my fault, don't you see? I have to go *now*! The least I can do is go back home and give her a funeral and say a thousand times 'I'm sorry' to her dead body."

"Oh, God, Maya. This isn't your fault, and there's nothing you can do to make your grief go away. You can't fix this. You have to let yourself be sad. I know! Let me go with you and comfort you. You can't go through this alone."

"Alone is all I have now." I ran downstairs, and he followed me. "Do you understand? I'm completely alone now!" I checked on the status of my driver, then turned to look at him. "I have no family. Nobody."

I stood outside waiting for my car, grateful for stray raindrops falling on me and cooling me off. David followed a few minutes later, dressed now, but still barefoot.

"Maya, please stop running away. You're not alone.

You have me now. I can help you cope with this. And you have my family."

I walked back to him and kissed him. "I wish I could, David. I really do. But I messed things up so badly in my life. I can't bring you into this. It's simply not fair. I have to go."

He took my face in his hands gently, his eyes pleading. "Stay with me. I love you. Stay and let me love you. Let me help."

"I don't know how." I pulled myself away and walked off to the approaching car. I slammed the car door behind me as I got in, and I didn't look back.

Chapter 31

Bern, October 1915

Rebecca hurried to the hospital, as always. The sun had only just come up, but she had already spent two hours visiting the newly delivered mothers from her clinic. The babies were doing well despite the heat wave. She spent some time showing the mothers how to boil the water for the babies' baths and clean them properly, but other than that, there was little to do. She prayed there wouldn't be another attack of dysentery in the city and that more babies would survive this fall.

Now she was needed at the hospital. The British prisoners of war had arrived yesterday, and Father had been with them all night. Surprisingly, the hospital was quiet and she found *Papi* having tea with Dr. Hermann Matti.

"Rebecca! I'm glad you are here. Join us for some tea before you rush out to all the excitement."

"Do I have time?"

"Of course you do," Father said, pouring her a cup. "Hermann and his surgical staff have it quite under control now."

"How many prisoners of war are here?" Rebecca sat down, taking a cup from him.

"Men, my dear. They are men. In unfortunate circumstances," Dr. Matti corrected her. "There are

288

thirty-two of them. Most are officers. All British."

"Are their injuries severe?"

"Not very. We've had to carry out operations on a few to correct some butchery that was done at the front. There are some with infected wounds, as well, which may need operations fairly soon. Dr. Minchin, who I believe you know well"—Dr. Matti winked—"worked all night with his team to repair whatever was most urgent. Now we can all relax a little."

"If we can concentrate on providing the healing effects of air and oxygen on their wounds, I'm convinced we can achieve fast healing and proceed to convalescence for many of them," Father said.

"But keeping the wounds open would expose them to bacteria, in crowded wards," Rebecca protested.

"Your father is correct. If we could supply adequate drainage to the wounds and a constant supply of oxygen, we would most likely prevent the development of bacteria." Dr. Matti set his teacup down. "Why don't we go visit the recovery ward and see about some drainage tubes? I'm sure our talented Doctor Minchin has already managed to think of those himself."

"Of course." Rebecca couldn't wait to see Mark. And what could be better than having Father's friend sing the praises of her beloved?

Mark wasn't difficult to find. Sweat-covered, with dark circles under his eyes, he was moving from patient to patient in an overcrowded ward. She stood at the entrance a moment, admiring him. How assertive he was, giving orders and requesting instruments! How precise his movements were as a physician, how focused on his work! She wondered if she deserved him. She wasn't sure she ever worked this tirelessly to help her patients. She often resented having no chance to have a proper meal and no rest for her aching feet. He only worked harder and was grateful for the work. When she went home, a housekeeper and her parents took care of her and made her hot food. He ate cold meals, which hardly could be counted as meals at all at times, consisting mainly of potatoes and cabbage. How did he find the strength to be so dedicated to medicine? And politics? *And her?* She nearly ran to him, forgetting that she couldn't acknowledge her feelings in public.

"Rebecca! You're here!" He restrained himself from giving her a kiss, noticing her father not far behind her. He bowed to Father and Dr. Matti. "We're almost finished with the insertion of drainage tubes for the four soldiers who have infected wounds."

"Allow me to examine. I'm most curious about your technique," Father requested.

"Certainly. You see, Dr. Miller, the important aspect of the tubes is that they are made of glass, which has the advantage of not allowing the wound to close prematurely," Mark explained.

"Marvelous." Father examined the patient.

"And the gauze is sterilized in a saline solution before it's applied to the wound, promoting drainage by capillary action."

"Very impressive indeed."

Dr. Matti nodded in approval and turned to Father. "Joseph, have you heard of the oxygen chamber that Steinmann has set up in his hospital to provide air to the wounds and decrease healing time?"

"No, is this an effective technique?"

"Absolutely. And we must talk to the Directors

about it if we're to have innovations at our hospital. Why should Lucerne have all the modern devices? All it requires is an air pump with a vessel and a motor. Air pressure is pumped through small tubes to each hospital bed to provide oxygen to the open wounds. It's been most effective in preventing bacterial infections."

Father sighed. "We must find the right time to speak to the Directors about it. I hope Theodor will join us. The more of us asking for funds, the better."

"Dr. Miller, can you help me prepare more saline gauze, please?" Mark asked suddenly, turning to Rebecca instead of her father.

Father flinched, but Rebecca kept her face still. "Of course, Dr. Minchin. I'll be happy to assist."

Rebecca could've sworn Father kept his eyes on her back the entire time she walked to the supply room. Mark seemed unfazed or maybe just exhausted. The door shut with a loud creak, and she was about to scold him for asking her to be so daring. He came closer, his face changing suddenly, and she felt herself flush. His eyes were full of desire. *He couldn't be serious!*

"I have to get back to work, Mark!"

"It won't take long." His hands were on her hips, stroking, pulling her toward him.

"My father is a few doors down," she whispered and stepped back.

"Hermann is talking to him about me right at this moment, convincing him you couldn't make a better match than me."

He took off his apron and threw it down. He smelled of carbolic, fresh linen, blood…and Mark. *How she loved his smell!* His lips closed on hers, and she drank him in, arms around his neck, lost in the comfort of his body.

She pulled away, a horrifying thought suddenly occurring to her. "Does Matti know you are here with me, doing this?"

Mark walked to the door and locked it, then pushed her against the wall, and she felt his fingers sliding underneath her skirt. "Stop thinking," he whispered in her ear.

Mark's lips moved and then reached a sensitive spot on her neck. Rebecca's skin was hot under his breath, and the heat moved quickly through her body. She tugged on her blouse, impatient for his lips to keep reaching other sensitive places.

"No, let me take it off," he said, pushing her hand away and unbuttoning her blouse.

Rebecca's legs shook as Mark picked her up and set her on the desk. She closed her eyes and gave in to the sensations, her breasts rising in anticipation of his lips coming close. *There.* She heard the sound of objects being thrown off. Her hips moved toward him. Mark was hard, ready, and she grabbed his waist and pulled. As he laid her on the table, she arched her back and bit her lip to prevent herself from yelling out.

He was right, it didn't take long. He shuddered in minutes, and then, suddenly, she was so lost in her own wave of release that she almost didn't hear.

"What did you say?" she whispered, her insides still trembling.

"Marry me, *liebe.*" He pulled away and buttoned his pants.

Rebecca sat up, still half-naked, eyes wide open, watching Mark's whole appearance change suddenly, become softer somehow. Then, to her utmost surprise, he kneeled on one knee and took hold of her right hand. She struggled frantically to adjust her skirts.

"What *are* you doing?" She jumped off the table and tried to pick him up by his shoulders. His body wouldn't move; it was rooted to the spot.

"I am asking you to marry me. Love me forever." He opened his hand and she saw a ring.

"Get up at once. I already love you forever. Where did you get this?" It was a small silver ring with a moonstone in a setting of marcasite.

He got up and paced, his steps echoing in the small room. "What does it matter where I got the ring? Do you wish to marry me or not?"

"Why are you doing it now? We've been together for years!" She buttoned her blouse and straightened her hair.

"I've always wished to ask you to marry me. But now we've been making love, and I think it's right." He hesitated. "Your grandmother gave me the ring, so that I can ask you properly."

"What? Did she force you to marry me?" Her blood began to boil.

"Don't offend me, Rebecca! You know I love you with all of my heart. It was difficult for me to accept this charity. Your grandmother wished to know what my intentions were, and I told her I was planning to ask you. She then gave me the ring, so that we could be properly engaged."

Rebecca hugged him. "I don't mean to insult you. I'm just very surprised. The ring is beautiful. When did you possibly speak to *Grossmami*?"

"She came to see me a few weeks ago. She offered the ring to me as a gift. I told her I'd pay her back, as soon as I could. I had a jeweler write words in it," he said.

"Can I see the inscription?"

He gave her the ring. She read the inscription and felt whatever was left solid of her heart melt into hot tears. "I am yours, you are mine," she whispered. "Just like the poem you wrote in my textbook. It is true—we are bound together."

"It's *bashert*," Mark said. "Does this mean you will think of marrying me?"

"I will marry you. Yes." She lifted her head, rose on her toes, and kissed him.

He picked her up and spun her around the room until she squealed with joy. When her dizziness cleared, she asked for him to put the ring on her finger, and then watched it sparkle in the afternoon sun. How beautiful it was as it spread rainbows all throughout the room, making her think of all the magic in the world.

It was two evenings later that she finally found time to see her grandmother. She paced in the small parlor of the home, touching her ring frequently. She'd had to hide it in her pocket most of the time. She hoped another lecture on shaming the family with sexual relations before marriage wasn't coming. She colored, thinking of the last one, at the lake. The only good news that had come from it was that Grandmother agreed to keep Rebecca's secret from her parents. As long as Mark was never seen again anywhere near the lake house. Of course Rebecca continued to meet with Mark. They just had to meet farther away from the house— several miles away, to be precise, to ensure Grandmother couldn't have walked that far. This didn't make Mark any happier. She was more than pleased to return to the city and be able to see him more often and with less effort.

"Oh, good, you are here." Grandmother came in, more slowly than usual, leaning on her cane.

"*Grossmami*, are you feeling well?" Rebecca helped her to a chair.

"Yes, quite well." Grandmother touched her ring. "I see you have accepted."

"Your plan worked." Rebecca smiled.

Grandmother pursed her lips. "I couldn't allow you to ruin your life. Or his, for that matter. That man loves you dearly. Shall I ring for some tea?"

"No, thank you. I wasn't ruining our lives. It's only that Mother and Father won't accept him. I've tried. Mother refuses to hear, and Father has nearly thrown him out of the house. They work together at the hospital, and Father is starting to admire his work, but still he seems not good enough for them."

"No suitor will ever be good enough. You are a precious jewel to them, you must understand."

"Mark was good enough for you," Rebecca said, touching Grandmother's hand. "Please help me find a way."

"Of course I'll help you. I'm already helping you, you silly child. This has to be done right." Grandmother sighed and leaned back in her chair.

"What are you going to do?"

"I don't know just yet, but I always find a way. I told you, I do believe in love. But not foolish love. Only love that deserves a chance."

"And does our love deserve a chance, then?" Rebecca asked.

"I spent some time with your doctor a few weeks

ago. He is not like us. There is a fire in him I don't understand. He'll never have a quiet, respectable life like your father. You must understand this as well."

"I know. I fear it sometimes. But I love him desperately."

"And he does love you. I believe he deserves you and you deserve him. But life with him will not be easy." Grandmother stretched out her arms, and Rebecca accepted the hug gladly.

"I've loved him for too long; there's no going back. It's already been difficult. But I can't live without him. He owns my soul," Rebecca whispered.

"And you clearly own his. This is why I gave him the ring. He can't possibly afford one himself. He'll pay me back by protecting you from harm."

"Thank you, dear *Grossmami*." Rebecca wiped tears from her cheeks. "I don't know if I can ever fully express my gratitude to you. Your blessing means so much to me."

"Pfft," Grandmother said. "Save your gratitude for when you can marry him in front of your whole family, with my son's full blessing. It will not be an easy task to change Joseph's mind."

"Am I forgiven, then? For what happened in Spiez?" Rebecca asked.

"You're always forgiven." Grandmother kissed her. "Now run along. This conversation has exhausted me. I'll have some tea and think of a way to talk to Joseph."

Rebecca nearly ran home, her soul singing and her heart lighter. It was all going to be settled. She and Mark would finally be together. It would take some time, but she could wait a while longer. She had waited forever already. And there had been no further talk from

Mark about Lenin and the revolution. Mark seemed so focused on his surgical work lately. He wouldn't have proposed if he wasn't planning to give up his activities on behalf of the revolution. He would never put her in danger. Maybe all the political work had been forgotten, and Mark would finally settle on being here in Bern, with her. *Yes, that was it!*

Chapter 32

New York, August, Thursday/Friday—Present Time

I called Pauline from the train. This was no longer an exciting ride through the Alps but a nail-biting tedious journey on two trains: the first from Lake Thun to Bern, and the next from Bern to Paris. I was exhausted, yet I couldn't sleep. I called Pavel, then the hospital. I received the phone numbers for the funeral home, but every time I turned on my phone to dial one of the numbers, something inside me cracked.

Texts from David flashed across the screen, but I deleted them without looking. He had somehow managed to get hold of my phone and add all his contact information. I thought I should probably delete his number, but couldn't bring myself to do it. The memory of his body pressed against mine, his arms holding me last night as I lay on his chest, was too strong. His words, "It's not your fault" when I told him about Ella's death, and the way he stroked me when I cried on his shoulder… I wiped the tears and stared at the mountains, willing them to give me their silent, stoic strength.

I was going through the security checkpoint at Charles de Gaulle Airport when I saw Pauline waving at me, a plane ticket in her hand, from the other side of the security scanner.

"What are you doing here, you crazy woman?" I cried out and rushed through the scanner, barely avoiding a body search.

She held me tight. "I had nothing else to do this weekend. Nicolas is in South Africa, scouting locations. I was alone. And so were you."

"But you can't just run out to New York! Can you?"

"Of course I can." She shrugged her shoulders. "I am the queen of my own business. Also, I need to buy more photos for my gallery. I was planning to go in September, but now will work too. Let's go, or we miss our flight."

During the long flight, she listened to all of my stories about Bern and Spiez and David, then put on her sleep mask and slept peacefully. I took off the darn ring and tucked it away on the bottom of my backpack. Living someone else's life hadn't been helpful for me at all. I prayed. Prayed that a mistake had been made and my grandmother was still alive. After all, I had yet to see her body. I counted the minutes until landing.

"You look like shit," Pauline remarked when we landed in New York ten hours later.

"I love you so much," I said, dragging her through Customs.

"I love you too, stupid."

It was after midnight when we arrived at Pauline's hotel, where I finally collapsed from jet lag and exhaustion. The next morning, Pauline held me while I learned the details of my grandmother's passing at the hospital. She did die peacefully in her sleep. She arrived in the ambulance with Alina, her neighbor. My phone number wasn't given as a contact, only the neighbor's, so the hospital never knew to get in touch with me. She never fully regained consciousness after the stroke and never suffered. She was too old to live any longer, with her advanced heart disease and kidney failure. I should be glad she went peacefully, the doctor explained.

Pauline forced me to eat some food before meeting with the Dean about my residency. She wanted to come with me, but I told her to meet me afterward. This was something I had to face on my own. All terrible things happen in threes, Baba always said, so I might as well get this all over with in one day and start a new life next week. I took a long walk to help gather my thoughts and calm my nerves. Three cups of street coffee later, I was able to approach the tall gray hospital building looming sinisterly over me.

The revolving door, so familiar for many years, felt heavy and squeaked loudly in my ears as I pushed it. The sounds of the first-floor emergency room grated on my raw nerves.

I can do this. I know what to say.

I walked to the security desk to check in. I no longer had my resident ID badge. I was no longer welcome here.

"I need a visitor's ID," I said to the security officer. "I have a meeting with Dr. Haber. In the administrative suite."

"Name and ID."

A loud voice sounded behind me. "Maya? Dr. Radelis? Look at you! You look so good!"

I turned around, a smile forming on my face despite my nervous state. I would know that voice anywhere. Gayla Cole was a pulmonary nurse and one of the last nurses I had worked with, a kind, generous person who was motherly to every sick child and universally loved by all doctors and residents. I stretched out my arms and was rewarded with a warm hug.

"I wondered what happened to you! I haven't seen you in ages! I thought maybe you changed your mind about Pulmonary after what happened with Hailey. It was such a shame with that poor girl—I just can't stop thinking about her. That asshole, Dr. Asher, I just can't believe he drove her to take her own life. She was such a darling girl." She shook her head.

"Thank you," I said to the security guard, taking my Visitor sticker.

Then I shuddered as the full force of Gayla's rambling words hit my consciousness. I swung around.

"*What* did you say?"

"About what, dear?" She was rummaging in her purse for something.

I wanted to shake her. "About Dr. Asher? And Hailey?"

"Oh, that? The day she hanged herself? I went to give her the lab slip and prescriptions you ordered, and she was sobbing, heartbroken. I asked her what was the matter, and she said Dr. Asher told her she was going to die in less than a year. He saw her right after you did. He had to sign off on your charting."

My knees threatened to buckle under me. "But I thought he wasn't there that morning…"

"Oh, he was! But he was busy having breakfast with the donors. You know how it is—everyone always wants to give him money. He's such a big star and all. Then he showed up as you left for your hospital rounds, just to take credit for seeing her."

I grabbed her by the shoulders. "Gayla, do you understand that this is really important?" I couldn't find the words. "Didn't anyone ask you about this before? About Hailey?"

"No, why would they? No one at this hospital cares what the nurses have to say. Nurses and residents are invisible."

My vision was going in and out. Little spots danced in front of my eyes.

"You're turning white, Dr. Radelis. Should you sit down? Are you ill?"

"I'm actually fine... I just never knew it was Asher..." Strangled words came out of my throat.

"You got blamed for this, didn't you? Is that why you've been gone?" She pointed at my Visitor sticker. "They asked you to take a leave? The girls and I knew it!" She tossed her head back, eyes blazing with fury. "Those bastards. I just knew they would find a resident to blame. That's how it always is. Nurses or residents!"

"I did get blamed for this. But now that you've told me about Asher and I know it wasn't my fault, I think it will all be better," I said. My vision had recovered and I straightened up, energy surging through me suddenly. I felt all my guilt and all my fear vanish forever.

"You thought it was *your* fault? Oh, but of course you did... You thought you were the last person who spoke with her. Oh, dear." She grabbed me in another hug and patted my back gently.

"I'll be all right now. Thank you." I smiled at her. I was certain, absolutely certain I would be fine now.

"Why are you here today? Are you starting back up?"

"No, they're holding a meeting to place me on probation. But they won't be able to do that anymore, because I'm going to fight."

"Don't let those administrative suits and asshole doctors make you think you're not a good doctor. Your patients loved you. You are a great doctor. You go get them! And then come see the rest of the girls."

"I will. I promise. I'm back now. For good."

"Oh, and as you're meeting with them up in administration? You may want to mention that the nurses know how to file an ethics complaint against Asher. And we have several in mind. This isn't the first time he's driven a patient to do something desperate and blamed it on a resident."

My jaw dropped, but she was already walking away. I laughed to myself and marched to the administration department. I had nothing to fear now.

I walked confidently past the reception desk and straight into Haber's office. Madeleine ran after me, protesting, but I ignored her. I had the upper hand. The residency director stood up, face reddening, then waved dismissively to his assistant.

"Great to see you, Dr. Haber. Madeleine…" I turned and gave her a fake smile. "Can I have a coffee, please? Cream, two sugars?" I threw my bag on one armchair and sat in the other, legs crossed, arms stretching.

"Dr. Radelis," Haber began.

I stopped him with a wave of my hand. "I know, I know. I've violated policy. Whatever. You want me on probation. I see the thick packet of papers you have sitting there." I nodded toward it. "But let me tell you what I also know. I had exemplary evaluations until I got to Pulmonology. I was headed for the Chief Resident position. I'm a great doctor. I left and didn't want to return because you and Dr. Asher wrote in my file that I made a mistake and caused a patient to kill herself. But I know now that it was actually Dr. Asher who caused Hailey's suicide."

He narrowed his eyes. "That is a highly inappropriate accusation, and it is not helping your case in any way."

"I have several witnesses, Dr. Haber, who will be happy to report to the Ethics Committee today. They'll also write to the Medical Executive Committee and to the American Council of Graduate Medical Education. I can also draft a nice long statement about resident abuse at this hospital."

"Are you threatening me? Do you realize that, as a resident, you still have three years to spend at this hospital?"

"I do. Very much so. I'd like to get on with it. So please call down to Security so I can get my badge back and we can forget the whole thing ever happened."

Madeleine walked in, carrying my Styrofoam cup of coffee.

"Thanks." I took a sip. "It's perfect. I think Dr. Haber needs you to toss something in the confidential shredder?"

I gave him a challenging look. The air in the room hung heavy. Then I smelled my victory.

"Yes, Madeline. Please shred this," he said through his teeth. He handed her the ominous stack of white papers with my name on them.

I stood up, adrenaline still pumping through me, and started to leave with my head held high.

Then I turned, remembering. "Oh, and Dean Haber, I'd have a talk with Dr. Asher, if I were you. I'm going to be here for another three years, so I'll be paying attention to patient stories now about his interactions with them, and I happen to have a strong interest in Pulmonology."

I walked out, ignoring the murderous look on his face. I left the administrative suite, ran to the bathroom, and leaned over a sink, breathing heavily.

Did I just stand up to Dean Haber? Did I threaten him? Did it *actually* work?

I opened the tap and splashed cold water on my now burning cheeks. The face in the mirror looked defiant, angry, with eyes blazing. Why wasn't I scared? I began to laugh, first little giggles, then bursting into full, loud laughter. His face when I threatened him! I think he was frightened. Why was I ever scared of him before? I took a deep breath to settle down.

I was back!

I couldn't wait to tell Pauline. I couldn't wait to tell… *Oh…David!* I would fix it with David next. Right after I'd buried my grandmother and dealt with my grief over losing my only family member. But one thing was certain—I would never allow anyone to ever take Medicine away from me again.

Chapter 33

Bern, May 1916

Wisteria bloomed wildly at the Botanical Garden, and Rebecca inhaled the sweet scent briefly, but it gave her little joy this morning. Her knees kept shaking, the bicycle rattled as a result, and she nearly fell off. Where was Mark? Every second without him was wasted!

She had sent a note to Mark's boardinghouse an hour ago and then rode her bicycle to wait for him. He'd forbidden her to come to the student colony for fear she'd be followed and would be in danger because of her association with revolutionaries. She heard the creaking of the black iron gate at the garden's entrance and then the crunch of the gravel path under his feet. She slowly lifted her head, worried, terribly afraid it wasn't him walking quickly next to his bicycle. But it was!

"I was hoping you would come!" She almost sang with happiness, stretching her hand to him, her heart full of love. And terrible worry. Kids played around them, but she hardly noticed.

Mark was here! Father would be saved now!

She started pedaling, beckoning him to follow. There was no time to stand around.

"Your note?" he asked, pedaling behind her. "How long has your father been ill?"

She took a moment to catch her breath. "He started having pains last night. He went to bed saying he suffered from indigestion. Then, this morning, he began to moan and scream from sudden attacks. Nothing gives him comfort. We've tried tonics, heat, and enema."

"Is it possibly appendicitis?"

"He says it's gallbladder disease. I agree. He has all the symptoms of it. He asked me to send for you."

They reached the house in minutes. Mark rushed into Father's bedroom, past her crying mother. Father was moaning loudly and holding his right side. The housekeeper stood helpless at the bedside, holding a hot water bottle.

"Can everyone please leave and allow me to examine Dr. Miller? Rebecca, where can I wash my hands?" Mark asked.

"I remember you," Father said weakly, as Mark gently palpated his abdomen a few minutes later.

"Do you?" Mark's eyes were closed. He was intent on his examination.

"I remember I saw you kissing my daughter. Without my permission."

"Father! Never mind this now. Concentrate on feeling better. Mark is a great surgeon. You need his help."

Father waved her away. "I didn't ask for a woman's opinion. We are having a conversation like men. I know who he is. I asked for him, remember? Leave us!"

Rebecca looked at Mark, and he nodded his head. She found Mother in her parlor, Grandmother next to her, teacups in front of them, untouched.

"What did Mark say?" Grandmother asked.

"You know him, Fräu Miller?" Mother asked.

"That's a tale for a later time. So what is it, my dear?" she asked Rebecca.

"I don't know yet, *Grossmami*. Mark is examining him. But Father is in a delirium; he is confused about the year."

Mother burst out crying again.

"*Mami*, it's only a simple case of gallstones. He will not die from this if Mark removes the gallbladder." Rebecca paced in agitation.

"What do you mean 'removes'? Does Joseph require an operation?"

"Most likely. Unless it's something else." Rebecca regretted saying this as soon as the words left her mouth. Mother turned paler than fresh snow.

"Shush, Rebecca. It will not be anything else, Helene. Joseph will have the operation and live a long happy life yet," Grandmother said in a firm tone.

"He will. I promise, *Mami*." Rebecca poured herself some tea, but her hands shook so hard she had to set the cup down.

Mark came down the stairs minutes later and went directly to her mother. "Fräu Miller, I'm afraid your husband was right. It is indeed an attack of gallstones. He requires an operation. I am going to phone the hospital and have him transported there."

"Will he…die?" Mother grabbed onto Mark's hands.

"God willing, he will live a long life still, Fräu Miller." Mark gave her hands a firm squeeze and went to the phone to make arrangements.

Hours later, Rebecca sat by her father's bedside and held his hand. Grandmother had gone home, reassured that he was out of danger. Mother was asleep in a small chair nearby. Rebecca felt a squeeze on her fingers.

"He's done well, your young surgeon," Father said, voice cracking and weak.

"*Papi,* try not to talk too much. You must rest."

"On the contrary, Dr. Miller must cough to clear his lungs of ether. It will prevent mucus from becoming stale in his lungs," Mark said, coming near her, fingers lightly brushing her arm.

Father's eyes focused on the two of them, narrowing, but he kept his observations to himself.

"And how is your pain now?" Mark asked, listening to Father's lungs.

Father coughed, then answered, "I'm much improved, thanks to you, it seems. You have good surgical skills. Very impressive."

"Thank you. This means so much to me." Mark examined the dressing.

"And yes, you may be allowed to spend time with my daughter," Father said.

"What?" Rebecca stood up.

"I may be ill, but I'm not without my mind, Rebecca. I'll speak to your mother about this when she wakes up. Now, both of you, go. I must sleep." He turned his head to the side and closed his eyes.

Mark took Rebecca's hand and kissed it. "It's done now. We'll be able to marry."

"Yes," she said. "I'll have you forever." She took his hand and pulled him outside the room where she could kiss him happily. There was no need to shock her parents.

****

A few days later, Mother decided to move Father to

the lake house from the hospital, to recuperate. He insisted he would have done just fine resting up in his study, reading, but she packed up the house and had everyone traveling almost before they realized what was happening. Rebecca could also have remained in the city, but she needed a break from the hospital routine and her clinic and thought a week's rest would not harm her patients. She also thought this would be an excellent opportunity to discuss her engagement to Mark with her parents. Father hadn't spoken to Mother yet, due to his illness, but nothing would prevent them all from talking about it now. Hannah was married, and it was Rebecca's turn.

She was settling Father into his bed and airing out his room for him when she heard Edward's voice downstairs.

"You may go." Father leaned back on his pillows. "I'd rather like a nap. The journey exhausted me."

"Edward can wait, of course. I need to give you your medicine."

"Nonsense. Go greet your guest. I'm capable of taking my own medicine."

"Well, if you're sure."

She slowly backed out of his room and ran downstairs. Edward and his sister were seated in the parlor, talking to Mother.

Eva jumped up at seeing Rebecca. "I'm so happy to see you here, so early in the summer. I hardly ever see you in the city anymore, now that you've cured me."

"I do apologize for not visiting more often."

"Oh, not at all. I know how busy you are as a doctor." Eva hugged her.

"And we will forever be grateful to you for Eva's restored health, of course," Edward added.

Rebecca turned to him. "Thank you for coming to visit."

"We're very glad your family is here to keep us all company. And your skills will be quite useful over the summer if you stay."

"Oh, yes, you probably haven't heard," Eva said, her eyes wide.

"Haven't heard what?" Rebecca asked.

"We have hundreds of prisoners of war here for convalescence. They're living in hotels and pensions and even in family houses," Eva explained.

"I thought this was only happening in the cities. How are they receiving medical care?" Rebecca asked.

"These soldiers are the ones who don't need medical care, just fresh air and exercise, mainly. Anything better than what they received in German prison camps," Edward explained. "My sister and Mother are working with the Red Cross to arrange visits for them with their families."

"That's wonderful!" Mother exclaimed, walking in with a tea tray.

Eva blushed, not accustomed to receiving praise.

Rebecca examined her flushed face, concerned. "How is your health, Eva?"

"Perfectly fine. I just wish we could finally go home."

"We'll go home soon enough, dearest. The war is nearly over," Edward said, touching her hand gently.

"It must be nearly over, if the Germans are allowing so many soldiers to rest in the Alps," Mother remarked.

"I guess I could stay here for a while," Rebecca said. "I suppose the Red Cross would appreciate my efforts here as much as in Bern."

"I prefer for her to be near me and Joseph and not in the city alone. And if she has your company, so be it," Mother said.

"Colonel Hauser heads the internment program. I'll introduce you to him, Rebecca. He'll be pleased to have another physician around. The spas and sanatoria have many physicians, but not enough to care for the thousands arriving every day," Edward said.

"Yes, would you believe it? We had twenty-seven English officers and four hundred-eighty-eight English soldiers arrive yesterday. Last week, it was two hundred French and American ones," Eva added.

"Are they only coming to Spiez?" Mother asked.

"They are coming to all the villages and towns in the Alps. Any place that can provide accommodations and is easily accessible by rail, for transport," Edward explained.

"How remarkable," Rebecca said. "I definitely wish to be involved in this. Thank you for telling me. I suppose Lara can manage the clinic without me for a little while."

After tea, Eva stayed to talk with Mother about the efforts underway to arrange the wives' visits for the soldiers, while Rebecca and Edward took a walk to the lake. The air was still rather chilly by the lakeside, but the promise of spring was definitely near. The grass and leaves were brilliantly green, and the scent of spring flowers permeated the air. There was mist hanging around the mountains, but the lake was emerald clear, as always.

"I'm sorry your father's been ill," Edward said.

"I do believe he's on the mend now."

"And how have you been since I saw you last?"

"Very well. More than well."

He turned to her. "Your clinic is still successful, then?"

"Very successful, thanks to your support. We had enough medicine last winter to take care of hundreds of families. You helped save many lives."

"Surely it wasn't just the medicine. Eva told me you have a gift for healing. She said it seemed magical, the way you eased her breathing."

Rebecca laughed. "Some of what I do may seem magical, but most is pure medical science. I'm proud of my work. I think Lara and I have accomplished a great deal with the poor families in the city. And the hospital has seen hundreds of prisoners of war, as well, so I feel I've contributed to helping in this horrid war somehow."

They walked in silence for a while, watching the birds fly from tree to tree, building nests. Rebecca hesitated, then asked, "You've been caring for your family for a long time, but you haven't thought of starting your own yet?"

He laughed. "I have indeed thought of it. But I haven't found anyone worthy of the honor of becoming my wife."

"Maybe when you return to New York."

"Maybe," he said, turning his head and examining her. "And when will you make the leap into marriage, dear friend?"

"Not any time soon, I'm afraid," she said. "I do love someone, and I've agreed to marry him." She looked carefully at Edward, wondering how he would take the news.

"Well, I hope he deserves you," Edward said firmly, turning toward her. "You're a unique woman and should only have the best man to share your life."

"He does deserve me, and I hope I deserve him. I have some concern that he may love his work more than he loves me. And then there's a matter of my mother approving of him."

"Your mother will come to see reason, if he is a worthy man. You must forgive his devotion to his work. It's important for a man to be proud of his work. Family life alone is not enough for a man's happiness."

"I'm afraid marriage is rather complicated for a woman. It's much easier to avoid it. I might just do that. I do have my own means of earning an income." She wasn't sure why she was telling Edward all this, except that it seemed they'd been friends for a long time and she knew he was someone who never passed judgment.

"Nonsense. You are someone who should be loved and married."

She laughed. "Sometimes I feel as if you are my brother."

His face scrunched up. "I hate when beautiful women only see me as brother potential. But, in your case, I'll accept it."

"We should probably walk back. I must check on *Papi.* He was feeling ill from the travel."

They walked back to the house on the worn path still muddy from the spring rains. Rebecca thought of how kind Edward was to step into the role of a brother for her. She missed Karl still, and likely always would. She wasn't sure she and Hannah could ever be fully kind to each other. But she could accept a stranger's kindness if freely given.

Chapter 34

New York, August, Friday—Present Time

We took a long subway train ride to Brooklyn to take care of funeral arrangements after my meeting with the Dean. I had just enough time to fill in Pauline on what happened at Haber's office. I didn't feel like celebrating. I just wanted my life to get back to normal. Of course, it didn't feel like it ever would. I checked my phone, but there were no more texts from David. I desperately wanted him to know how I managed to get my residency position back, that I had finally stood up for myself. And that he was right that it wasn't my fault that Hailey died.

Baba Zoya had chosen her funeral home. She also had a plot, next to my grandfather, at the Jewish cemetery. They would take care of all the arrangements. When we entered Baba's apartment to pick out a burial outfit, it still smelled like her. I automatically peeked in the kitchen to look for the fresh tea and cookies she always had ready for me. Her glasses were on the table by her reading chair, next to an open book. Her plants were still alive. She had a gift for growing indoor plants, and they covered her living room floor, making it look like a tropical greenhouse. I touched the leaves of the plants and then the wool blanket she kept on the reading chair because she got cold often. I imagined her sitting there comfortably, with her book and a cup of tea, waiting for me to return. *Except that I never did.*

"She has many pictures of you. I love these," Pauline said, picking up one of the hundreds of photographs standing or hanging on every surface of the room.

"She does." I wiped my eyes. "She did."

"And what are all these paintings?" She pointed at the artwork hanging on the walls. "Was she an artist? These are really good."

"No, she was an English professor. But she started to paint when my grandfather died. She painted all the time. I think it helped her with her grief."

"How touching. I can see your grandmother in all her things here, she has so many special little objects. It must be hard for you to see it." Pauline came close and gave me a hug.

I cried quietly into her shoulder, and she held me closer.

"We should probably hurry for today and just pick out her clothes. This is too much heartbreak for one day, right? Where is her bedroom?" Pauline gently pushed me out of the living room.

"There are even more things in the bedroom." I took a deep breath.

"Oh, look at this," Pauline called out from the bedroom. "This is such a beautiful box. Is it Ukrainian?"

"What box?" I walked in behind her. "I don't remember this." I examined a large hand-carved wooden box standing on top of her dresser. "It must be new."

"It's beautiful. See what's inside."

"I feel like I'm prying. She never liked for me to look through her things without permission."

I stood paralyzed in front of the box, then took a deep breath and opened the lid slowly. It was filled almost to the top. An envelope with my name on it was taped to the inside of the lid. I gently peeled the tape off and opened the envelope. There was a note, written in Babushka's calligraphic Russian.

My dear daughter,

You know you were always like a daughter to me. I fear my memory is not as good as it used to be. It's been too long since we saw each other, and I don't know when you will return to see me again. I thought of this when we spoke last. I want you to remember where you come from, and I know we haven't talked enough about it. I collected a few items in this box for you to remind you of your childhood, of the life you have likely forgotten.

You said you wanted to know about my father. He was a great man. I've missed him ever since he passed away. I was only a young girl when he died. As he lay dying, he asked me to bring him his journal and a pen. He wrote something in it, right before he took his last breath. I've never wished to look at this journal, as the memory of that day has always brought me to tears. But you asked if he has ever been to Bern, and I thought I would give you his journal to help answer your question.

I found many pictures of you and Ella. You said you lost the one you kept with you. Don't ever forget your sister. She should always be a part of you. I know you blame yourself for her death. But it was never your fault, dear girl. Your sister was born ill, and every day

*she was alive was a gift to us all. We didn't wish to
protect her; we wanted her to live the full and happy
life of a child. The doctors told us she wouldn't live
long. Be assured, every day Ella was happy, every day,
and no one has ever blamed you for her death. You were
a gift to me and your grandfather. You still are.*

Your Baba Zoya.

I clutched the letter in my hands. Then, sniffling
and crying, I looked inside the box for more. There
were pictures, lots of pictures, on top of other items.

"It's a memory box she put together for me,
Pauline," I finally managed to say in a strangled voice.
"It's like she knew she was going to die."

Pauline sat down next to me as I stared in disbelief
at a picture of myself, age five, wearing a white plaid
dress, red sandals, and a red bow. My hair was pulled
back to hold the bow, but curls were bursting out on all
sides. I was smiling widely at whoever was taking the
photograph.

I looked closely at the picture. It was taken
somewhere outdoors. I stood near a picnic table
covered in vinyl; a plastic yellow bucket was on its side
nearby. Over my head, grapevines hung low. Next to
me stood a girl, about my size, in a white dress with ivy
leaves on it, her face strikingly similar to mine, her hair
wearing the same red bow, her feet in the same red
sandals. Behind the table, the shape of a woman in a
housedress was visible, her back turned to whoever was
taking the picture.

Suddenly, a spasm of grief shook me as a memory
flashed in my mind of the day Ella and I got new
dresses for our birthday party. I closed my eyes and felt
Baba's hands in my hair, pulling and tugging to put the

red bow in. I smelled the leather of my new red shoes. Grief came in waves, and soon I was drowning in it. Pauline held me until the sobs stopped wracking my body.

"I think you need tea," Pauline whispered when I was calm.

"Thank you."

"And I think you must stop looking in that box for today."

"Let's just have some tea."

We drank tea, away from the box. There were still my grandmother's favorite "Maria" cookies in the pantry and a jar of raspberry jam in the refrigerator. It wasn't difficult to tell Pauline about Ella, but it was heartbreaking to realize that I would never drink tea with my Babushka again.

I pulled myself together after our tea and chose Baba's favorite outfit. I found her cameo earrings she always wore out to dinner. As we were leaving, I also grabbed the wooden box. In case of a sleepless night.

"Are you sure it is a good idea? How about we come back tomorrow?" Pauline asked, her hands ready to take it back to the apartment.

"No, I need it," I said firmly.

I could have gone back to the apartment I shared with two other residents and still paid for, but Pauline convinced me to stay another night at her hotel. The funeral was not until Sunday, and she was planning to stay in town that long. I was grateful for her company. I would start my new, different, lonely life on Monday.

Chapter 35

Bern, September, 1916

Rebecca wiped the sweat off her forehead and stood up straighter. Her back ached from the strain of bending over so many patients in one day. It had been an exhausting summer in Spiez, working with the Red Cross mission. More than two thousand soldiers had arrived in the last three months and needed the help of the locals for meals, clothes, and exercises. She, Mark, and other physicians from nearby towns had worked tirelessly to assess the soldiers for medical needs. Then, as the soldiers' families arrived, there were days and nights spent with women in labor, infants needing care, and children needing to be vaccinated. She had only been able to check on her patients in Bern once, and all hopes of a summer rest had long been forgotten.

At least there was little time left to worry about what Mark was doing. She saw him often enough, and he was entirely too exhausted to do any work for the revolution. He was dedicated to medicine these days, and there was tremendous need for his skills. She knew she had the gift to heal bumps, bruises, and minor illnesses, but he could mend bones better than any surgeon in Switzerland and take out a tumor with no risk of infection.

The best news had been that she had finally

convinced Mother to accept Mark as her future son-in-law. Of course, Grandmother and Father helped her with this impossible task as well. Either way, Mark was now welcomed in their home occasionally for dinner. She could see that he was slowly winning Mother's opinion, and even Hannah and Ebner were pleasant to him at times.

"*Liebe*, do you have a moment?" Mark's head popped through the door behind her.

"Of course, darling. What is it?"

He led her to a chair and gave her a kiss before sitting down next to her. "I'm afraid I have some rather sad news for you."

"What is it?"

"I just received word from Vlad. He is leaving Bern to travel back to Russia. And he is taking Lara with him, of course."

"But why? What's happening that they have to leave so suddenly? She hasn't said anything to me!" Rebecca was sure this was a mistake.

"He's made the poor decision to join the Menshevik Party in Russia. They believe they're ready to start the revolution now."

"So Vlad and Lara are going to be part of the revolution? Are they in terrible danger? Will they be imprisoned?" Rebecca gripped Mark's hands, hoping this wasn't true.

"They will be captured and sent to Siberia if they fail. I don't know what will happen."

"Who are these Men-she-viks?"

"They disagree with Lenin and the Bolsheviks who want to organize the working class. They think the revolution should be done by the educated class, by the middle class. They are frightened of the power of the working class. They have officially split from the Bolshevik Party now and are planning to take down the Tsar any minute." Mark's eyes were dark and sad.

Rebecca was at a loss for words, her heart beating painfully with fear for her friend. Mark kissed her hand, and she leaned against his shoulder, the two of them sharing their sadness.

"Wait," she said. "You are not going anywhere, right? You are not any part of this plan, right?"

"No, *liebe*, I'm not. I have to wait for my orders from Lenin. The Bolsheviks will need to see what happens with this Menshevik Revolution before making their attempt. We want a proletariat revolution. We don't believe the educated elites would ever work to accomplish the democratic goals of the revolution."

"But you can't ignore the wisdom of the educated people. You must have everyone working together: the educated and the working class."

"Lenin says the Menshevik Revolution would result in the dictatorship of the bourgeoisie and not the true power of the people."

"But the educated class are you and me. My father. Lara. Vlad. Sarah. How can a new world be built without people like us? What do *you* think? Don't answer as Lenin, but tell me what's in your mind."

"I don't know enough to answer. I just want to do the best for my family, and I know that the Tsar is not the best. If the Tsar is gone, I'll be able to keep my family safe, maybe even bring them to live in Odessa, in some luxury. And maybe you and I can even live there."

"I don't know if I can abandon all my work here.

My patients need me."

"There are many more families needing your help in Ukraine. You don't know what it's like there. There's terrible poverty and famine in most villages. There is so much need for physicians. We can live in the large city of Odessa and prosper, but give free services to the poor in the villages."

"I'm worried about how unstable things will be politically for a while in your country if you do have the revolution."

"There is a war going on all around us in Europe right now." He laughed. "I am afraid the entire world is unstable. The Bolsheviks are just hoping all this chaos will result in better lives for the people who are suffering the most."

Rebecca sighed. "I don't know. Maybe you are right."

He kissed her and got up. "I'll try to catch a train to see if I can say goodbye to Vlad and Lara. They've been my best friends for years. They've been my family."

"I have to go with you. I can't imagine not saying goodbye to Lara. I'll never forgive myself. I just have to ask my parents for permission. Come pick me up at the house in two hours."

****

Two weeks after Lara and Vlad left, Rebecca returned to the city. There were just as many soldiers to treat at the hospital, and she was the only doctor left at her women's clinic now. She couldn't neglect her patients forever. Losing her friend was difficult to bear, and she needed to spend time with Sarah. Although Edward's sister proved to be a lovely companion in

Spiez, she was somewhat too young and frivolous at times.

"We ought to consider hurrying up with Rebecca's wedding, my dear," Father said at dinner one night.

"It's not something we can simply hurry up, Joseph." Mother stopped her fork in midair. "The preparations required are extensive. She'll have a winter wedding, as planned."

"I hear the Russian students are leaving the community urgently."

"*Papi*, that's not true," Rebecca said. "Only a few have left. They think they are ready to overturn the Tsar."

"Well, in a few days almost all will leave, if they haven't started leaving today."

"Oh, what a relief," Mother said. "They've been a major disturbance here for years. They should never have been allowed to stay."

"How could you say this, Mother? You know I'm marrying one of them!"

"Well, your fiancé is an exceptional man. But most of them have been mainly a nuisance to the city. Now there will finally be more opportunity for the Bernese to attend the university."

Rebecca ignored her, turning to her father. "How do you know they're leaving?"

"Rabbi Hirsch was told that all the revolutionaries have been ordered to leave by their various political parties. The revolution they are planning is very near. Whoever hasn't left will likely be asked to leave by the Swiss authorities. Their temporary visas are expiring and will not be renewed."

"Do you think they'll really rise against the Tsar

and his family, Joseph?"

"They appear to be quite organized, my dear. I don't know if they have the numbers or a strong enough leader. Who knows? I just think we should make an effort to keep Rebecca's surgeon here with us, so that he doesn't get swept up by the romantic notions of the uprising."

"I'm glad they are leaving. Between the threat of war, the prisoners arriving here every day, and the constant disturbance of these revolutionaries, we've had little peace in Switzerland," Mother said.

"There is something else you must know, Rebecca," Father said, setting his fork down and sighing. "Rabbi Hirsh told me there have been some rather tragic stories from the Jewish villages in Ukraine and Poland, in the Pale of Settlement."

"What has he heard?"

Father took her by the arm. "Come to my office for a moment. It's best your mother doesn't hear such stories."

He closed the door behind him quietly, as she sat in a chair, trembling with worry.

"It seems as if hardly any Jews are going to be able to survive this awful wartime in the Pale. The Rabbi has received many letters and has heard stories from the soldiers about entire towns being burned to the ground. There's cholera raging in many of the villages, and no medicine or help has been provided. The Germans burn any village where cholera is suspected, and so do the Russians. The Cossacks pillage the homes, hang the adults, and spear the children on their swords. It's not clear which army is the worst, as all seem to hate the Jews equally. Whoever survives the pogroms and the murders is likely to die of starvation or cholera."

"These must be rumors! Surely soldiers are not capable of such horrors." Rebecca pressed her palm against her mouth, refusing to believe.

"Unfortunately, this appears to be true. You'd be surprised what angry men are capable of during war." He kissed her head. "And Jews are always targets. Especially in wartime. The reason I'm telling you is because you must tell Mark. His family might have perished already. If not, maybe there's something he can do to save them still."

"I'll go see him right away, *Papi*."

Rebecca grabbed her hat and ran out the door, forgetting to ask Mother's permission. The rain beat sharply on her face, but she hardly noticed as she raced through the dark wet streets, worry filling her mind and giving her legs strength.

She reached the door of Mark's boarding house, bending over and gasping for breath. She listened for the usual sounds of the house, in vain. No one was playing piano today, there was no laughter coming down the stairs, and no Yiddish prayers. Father was right—students had been leaving!

Her breath came back, and she yelled "Mark!", suddenly terribly afraid that he was gone as well. Her legs shook, refusing to carry her upstairs to find him gone.

God, please let him be there, don't let him leave!

"Mark!" No answer.

She collapsed at the bottom of the stairs, her skirt in a wet puddle, shivering from the cold and sadness, too much in shock to cry. How could he abandon her? How could he abandon their love?

She didn't hear him come out, but she felt the warmth of him.

"You are here," he said, sitting down next to her, gathering her in his arms.

"Father said that all your friends were…leaving or…being sent home." She choked on the words as she spoke.

"He is right. The war is almost over, and the Tsar will fall any minute. Everyone's preparing. People want to be home with their families, to participate in what's to come, in whatever way they can."

"You are not leaving! Please tell me you're not!"

He looked away, then turned back, took her hands, and kissed them. "My love, I need to go on a short trip home to deliver a manuscript for Lenin and see my family. I'll be back in a month, long before our wedding."

She pulled her hands away in agitation and jumped up, the rain beating hard on her face again. "So you *are* leaving! How does a surgeon become involved in such a task? Why can't this man deliver his own manuscript?"

"He would be arrested or likely killed. You know that. But I'm…a nobody. This manuscript has to get to Russia to get published, so that people hear the truth."

"You are not a nobody!" She hugged him and held him. If only she could stop him. "But the war is going on. It's too dangerous for you to travel—you'll be killed on the way."

"It's not dangerous anymore. There're safe routes now. The trains are running, and people travel all the time. And I won't be alone. I'll travel to Zurich first to pick up the manuscript, and two other people will join me."

"I don't understand. I'm trying very hard, I really am. You have everything here. You have worked so hard. You have the admiration of all your colleagues. You have my love." She struggled to put words together, they swirled in her mind at a dizzying speed.

She had to convince him. She had to make him stay.

She pulled back and watched Mark's face for any sign that he understood and agreed with what she was saying.

He held her face in his hands. "My love, my darling, I do have everything here. I have you. I have the respect of your family now. And I love medicine. I don't know how to explain, but can you try to understand? I'm not a whole man if I don't help with what's happening in my country."

He got up and paced, oblivious to the rain soaking his hair and glasses. Rebecca felt her blood was draining from her body. She knew she was losing him.

Please, God, she prayed silently, *don't let him go! Oh, please, God, don't take him away from me.*

Then she remembered. "Mark! Rabbi Hirsh said there was great danger in the Pale of Settlement. The German and Russian armies have been killing the Jews at will, burning and pillaging and starving people. There's also cholera. I was coming here tonight to tell you about that and to ask you to get your family somewhere safer. Maybe here. Instead you are going there!"

"I know, *liebe*. My mother has written to me. They are worried for their lives every day. I have to bring them to Odessa, to safety. It's one of the reasons I'm

329

going now. I'm glad you understand."

"Isn't there anything you can do to help that won't take you away from me?" she cried.

"I could maybe say 'no' to Lenin. But dearest, I haven't seen my family in years, and now they can be killed or die of cholera any day. My father is ill. How can I live here every day in my success and prosperity if Father lies on his deathbed grieving over my cold heart while my mother and sisters are starving?" Mark was crying into his hands now, sitting next to her.

Rebecca kneeled down by him and held his head in her hands, kissing his salty tears, feeling his pain, and knowing she had no choice. "What am I going to do? How will I live without you, my heart?" She heard herself sob.

She must let him go. She must bear it. She had no choice.

Mark picked her up and set her on his lap. He stroked her back lightly. "I will only be gone for a month. This is how long I can be gone without jeopardizing my medical practice, yet still make an impact for the revolution and see my family. You'll not even notice me gone."

"I won't be able to breathe without you. But if this were happening to my family, I would go, too, or live with the guilt forever," she whispered.

He kissed her tears. "Thank you. I knew you'd forgive me for leaving you."

"There's nothing to forgive. You must go. It's your duty. They've done so much for you. I understand what it's like when your family needs you or your community. I haven't stopped caring for my father or the people of this city for more than a day. I wouldn't stop if you asked me."

"I love you for understanding." Mark looked at her, eyes smiling now.

Grief gripped her chest tightly. What if she were making a mistake? Yet, what else could be the right choice?

"Hold me," she whispered and cried some more into his chest.

She *was* making a mistake. She was sure of it.

He won't be back, her mind whispered as her heart shattered.

Chapter 36

New York, August, Saturday—Present Time

I woke up early, feeling strangely rested, in a plush hotel bed with crisp white sheets and a soft feather duvet. I rolled around restlessly, then remembered the memory box. Pauline was still in a deep sleep. I dressed in the hotel robe, grabbed the box, and locked myself in the giant bathroom. Coffee could wait.

I positioned myself on the bathroom rug and took the items out gently, holding some to my face, and looking carefully at others. They smelled like Baba; they smelled like my childhood; they smelled like home. There were small handkerchiefs I remembered using as a child, my stuffed animal from when I was in elementary school, a wedding picture of my parents, my silver baby spoon, and my baby earrings.

I read Baba's letter again, every word precious to me. When did she write this? It must have been right after we spoke Monday. How long did it take her to put this box together for me? Did she have time to put all the items in it before she… I wiped the tears and searched for my great-grandfather's journal.

The journal was in a simple brown cardboard-covered spiral notebook, somehow well preserved. *So Baba brought it all the way from Ukraine, even though she says she'd never read it? Interesting how we manage to keep our most painful memories with us.* I re-positioned myself more comfortably on the rug and flipped through the pages. A great deal was filled out, in tiny letters, in Russian. I scanned through it, finding some entries on World War II, marriage, my grandmother and her sister being born. So did he write a memoir of sorts? I flipped to the first page to check if he started with his childhood, and dropped the journal.

Not possible…

The first page did have a title.

My Life by Mark Minchin.

Mark Minchin was one of the names on the list of students I still had from the University of Bern Archives. And it was the name on the letter I'd found in *Jane Eyre.*

I somehow never knew that my great-grandfather's name was Mark. How did I not know? What was wrong with me? Did I know his wife's name? I quickly looked through the journal. It was Anna.

All right, calm down. This doesn't mean anything.

I flipped through the early pages of the journal. Stories of childhood in the village of Lepetikha. He was one of thirteen siblings. The village was in the Pale of Settlement, where the Jews were restricted to live by the Tsar. I flipped further. He was sent by his family to study medicine at the University of Bern, because the Tsar only allowed a small number of Jews to attend the universities in Ukraine. I flipped frantically through the pages, nearly ripping them, but there was no mention of Rebecca. He wrote that he had returned from Bern and worked with Lenin and the Bolsheviks in Leningrad for some time after the revolution. He eventually returned home and moved his family to Odessa and established a medical practice. He said something about him being in hiding during Stalin's time because he feared being arrested as a Jewish physician.

Nothing about Rebecca. Must be the wrong Mark. Another dead end.

Then I remembered and slowly turned the journal pages to the last entry, where Baba said he wrote on the day of his death. And there it was, in barely legible writing, written with the shaking hand of a dying man:

Dear Zoya, this is for your eyes only. You were always my best helper.

When I was a young man, I attended the University of Bern in Switzerland and then practiced surgery in Bern. I was engaged to marry a Swiss physician. Her name was Rebecca Miller. I went home to check on my family's safety during the Great War and to perform an errand for Lenin and was unable to ever return to her. I tried. Many times. But there was a great deal of fighting and trains weren't able to go through. And then, when the Revolution took place, the Red Army wouldn't allow me to leave. I was recruited as a surgeon and told I would be killed as a deserter if I left. I regret every day of my life that I didn't try. She must think I abandoned her.

If you ever get a chance to find her, please tell her I loved her until the last breath I took. Just as I love you and your sister.

I closed the journal and held it to my heart. "I found her for you, Mark, but too late." So that's what happened. That's why Mark never came back. Rebecca never found out. I wondered if Rebecca ever found happiness in her life with Edward. I wished I could ask David or his mother. I wished I could ask my grandmother if her parents were ever happy. I set the journal gently back in the box. I knew it all, now: the love, the separation, and the heartbreak.

I had to tell David. But how could I call him after the way I'd treated him? I washed my face and decided to think about it later.

I touched my sister's photograph before closing the lid on the box, and I thought of the robin. "Is this what you wanted me to find out, Ella? Is this why you led me to the store to buy the ring and follow you to Bern? You wanted me to know our great-grandfather's story? Thank you."

Pauline knocked on the bathroom door, and I heard her tired voice: "I'm awake now. You don't have to hide. I called for breakfast."

I waited until she had coffee to tell her about my great-grandfather's journal.

"Well, this all make sense now," she said, spreading jelly on her toast.

"How exactly does this all make sense to you?"

"Mark and Rebecca couldn't be together and have their love. So Rebecca put her love in the ring—for her descendants to have. You were meant to find it and then meet David. Don't you see?"

"How could something so abstract as love be preserved in a piece of jewelry? And I'm not Rebecca's descendant. I'm Mark's." I shook my head.

"Well, somehow Fate led you to find this ring and then find David. Look." She showed me her phone. "Nicolas messaged me from Johannesburg this morning. I asked him what he thought about all this. He says he hopes we believe him now about the meaning of coincidences."

"Well, yes, I do believe him now. You can tell him that," I agreed. "But the whole trapped-love-in-a-ring thing eludes me."

"Be patient. There is more. He says that quantum physics—I have no idea what that is—has a theory that souls are made of negative potential energy electrons that have a memory. Do you understand any of this? He said you would."

"I had to study quantum physics in premed. I don't remember any discussions about the energy of souls, though."

"Here, read it yourself. I don't understand physics." She handed me the phone.

I read the rest of the text.

So if a soul is made of energy, it could stay somewhere in the universe. And maybe this energy could be then transferred into an object or a person? And a certain, somehow sensitive, person could be able to perceive this energy.

"Wait," I said. "I think I understand. He's saying that some of Rebecca's energy was transferred to the ring, and then, since I was related to the man she loved, I was able to perceive some of this energy!"

"I guess?" Pauline shrugged her shoulders and poured another cup of coffee.

"All right. And what if great love had strong energy associated with it, as well? And the energy of it could also stay in the universe until it found the right people who could sort of absorb it?"

"You mean that you and David absorbed the love Rebecca and Mark had? From the ring?" Pauline asked.

"Right!"

"That's exactly what I said before! But without

needing quantum physics. I think it's very romantic."

"The only problem is that this somehow feels very predestined to me. As if I had no control over who I fell in love with," I said.

"Did you feel you had control?"

"Yes and no. I did try to resist the feeling. I think I did. And I did run away from him. But I also felt absolutely incredible when I was with him." Memories of David holding me in his arms suddenly flooded my mind. "To be honest, I can't imagine living the rest of my life without him," I admitted to Pauline, as well as to myself.

"If you feel so strong, what does it matter if it was choice or not? Fate is not such a bad thing. Many people dream about it."

"You're right. I'm being stupid. Now I just need courage to go find him again and apologize."

"You'll find courage. I know you will. Until then, I am here with you." Pauline hugged me.

"Thank you." I hugged her back.

It was after I got dressed for the day that I realized that what Nicolas said could explain the bird that accompanied me in Europe. Maybe the energy of my sister's soul transferred to the robin, because she loved those birds. I hoped I would see it again. The truth was I didn't mind that I'd been sensitive to Rebecca's and Ella's energies. I'd enjoyed my adventures and feelings I'd experienced. I was grateful for the strength Rebecca's ring had given me when I stood up to Haber.

I touched my finger out of habit and realized the ring wasn't on it. After a brief moment of panic, I remembered that I had taken it off on the airplane. I'd faced Dean Haber all on my own, without the ring.

Well, what do you know... I dug in my backpack for Rebecca's ring and put it back on. I liked being on my own, but I missed her company.

Chapter 37

Bern, April 1918

The last of the snow had melted away, but the trees still stood with their black branches naked. The city was left with the ghost of winter lingering among its orange roofs. The promise of spring was in the air now, and Rebecca smelled it as she came to the front door of her home. She was in a hurry, as always, but she noticed the bird. It sat on a small patch of wet grass by the front door with its orange chest puffed up, likely trying to keep warm. *A robin. Mark's favorite bird. He said it meant new beginnings*, she remembered.

Grief came swiftly, throwing heavy waves at her chest and making it hard to breathe. Suddenly, she could feel it soaking into every cell of her body, and she felt unable to withstand its force. Her legs shook, her stomach felt a punch, and she held her throbbing head with both hands. She gasped for breath, then sat down on the steps. She'd become used to these attacks since Mark had disappeared. So many things reminded her of him. She lost control of her senses frequently these days. There seemed to be no way to stop the pain. She almost welcomed it now. Craved it. That's how she knew she was still alive and could go on doing her work.

"Oh, Rebecca, not again!" Sarah's hands were

holding her, trying to stop the shaking.

"I saw a robin," she cried.

"There's always something to see." Sarah lifted her from the steps and knocked.

The housekeeper opened the door, and Sarah took Rebecca to the living room. The house was quiet. Her parents were out visiting tonight, but Rebecca had insisted she needed some time to catch up on correspondence.

"We're going to need some tea," Sarah said to the concerned housekeeper, who was removing Rebecca's coat.

Rebecca lay unseeing on the lounge chair, holding the ring Mark had given her.

"We'll have some tea, and you'll feel better." Sarah rubbed her feet.

"He is never coming back," Rebecca whispered.

She saw tears in Sarah's eyes and knew the truth. She was right. He was never coming back. He was dead. *Or worse—he'd stopped loving her.*

"He loves you. It's not possible for him to forget you," Sarah said.

"It's been eighteen months since he left. Anything is possible."

"He's probably fighting with the Red Army and can't write. You know what we read about what's happening there."

"If what we read is true, he's been in grave danger and is likely dead," Rebecca replied.

"I won't believe that."

"I'd rather believe this than the alternative."

"He would never stop loving you. Just look at your ring," Sarah said gently.

Sarah was right—tea did make things better. Tea with Sarah always made things clearer.

"I don't think I can keep on living like this," Rebecca said, then got up and paced, turning the ring on her finger.

"You certainly can't. You must stop grieving him. Then you can find someone else to love," Sarah agreed.

"I mean that I can't keep on living here. In Bern. Where everything reminds me of him. Everywhere I go. Everything I look at. Everyone we knew. I won't ever recover from my grief."

"What are you saying?"

"I have to leave Bern. I have to leave Switzerland, maybe."

Sarah walked up to her and grabbed her shoulders. "Rebecca, there's a war going on. You can't go anywhere."

"I know. But it will be over soon. Germany is losing, and Father says it's only a matter of months now. I can leave as soon as it's over."

"My God, Rebecca, you can't just leave your home!"

"It's not my home anymore. It's just a place where my broken heart aches every minute of every day." She looked at her friend, pleading with her to understand.

"No one knows more than me about broken hearts, remember. But the heart will heal, if you allow it." Sarah hugged her and held her head, stroking it. "It will get better, I promise. Don't despair. And don't run away. I have to go now, but I'll phone you later to check on you."

Rebecca closed her eyes and relaxed in the lounge chair as Sarah left, but she was interrupted by the housekeeper after what felt like just a few minutes.

"What is it now? I need some peace, Magda."

"Pardon, Dr. Miller, but there's an Edward Fischer requesting to see you."

Rebecca jumped up in surprise. Edward? What was he doing here? She did enjoy his company, yet she was so tired and so desperate for some rest…

She sighed. "All right, I'll see him," she said. She straightened up her hair. Why was she doing this, exactly?

"I was beginning to worry you'd send me away. The rain has just started again." Edward walked into the room, smiling.

"I apologize I kept you waiting. It's been a bit of a difficult day," she admitted.

"Won't you tell me about it?" He kissed her hand and sat down.

"I don't wish to bother you with my medical stories."

"Well, what are friends for?" He smiled again.

She did enjoy his company very much. "Let's forget about my troubles. How's your effort on behalf of the American soldiers?"

"I'm working with the ambassador, Mister Stovall, on an appeal to Switzerland to establish a unit here to treat all those who are severely wounded and can't be transported home. We're proposing to send a few American physicians to Switzerland to work with the Swiss Red Cross to help treat them."

"That would be very much appreciated. We're badly in need of additional help at the hospital. All the physicians have been working day and night with no time off lately. The strain is showing." Rebecca was thrilled to hear the news.

"What I'm really hoping is that we can negotiate for the release of many of the prisoners of war. The war is coming to an end. Mr. Stovall is arranging for a conference, here in Bern, in September, to discuss with the German government the soldiers' repatriation and internment, if the war is not over before then."

"And how is Eva?"

"Desperate to return home. Both she and Mother are quite homesick and keeping me busy looking for a passage home."

"But it can't possibly be safe yet?"

"Any moment now, I hear. The difficulty seems to be a lack of available ships. All of them have been in use in the war and are no longer equipped for transatlantic passenger travel."

"How long will you have to wait?" Rebecca asked. She needed to know. She must leave herself.

"I hear that it's barely a few months. We hope to leave this summer, maybe after another stay in the mountains."

"It's probably for the best that you must wait. Influenza has been raging in America, but it's beginning to slow down. It's dangerous for Eva's lungs to be exposed to it. One more stay in the Alps would do her good."

"Yes, I've heard about the influenza. We do wish to prevent exposing her to any new illness."

"I shall miss you," she said, smiling. She would be able to leave Switzerland after the summer then too. This was good news indeed. Should she tell him of her plans?

Edward blushed, then turned away. What was the

matter with him?

"Shall I call for some refreshments?" she asked, concerned.

He stopped her with his hand. "Dear Rebecca. What if you didn't have to miss me?"

"What do you mean? You're thinking of staying here, while your family returns home?"

"No, that's not what I'm thinking." His eyes were watery, and he suddenly got up and kneeled in front of her.

"What are you doing?" But she knew.

He took her hand. It felt like lead. Still, she couldn't stop him.

"You may have noticed that we've become close friends in the last few years. It may be the case that this was just a friendship for you. But I'm finding that, for some time, I haven't been able to think of you as a friend," he began.

She shook her head and opened her mouth, but words wouldn't come out.

"Don't say anything yet. Please," he pleaded. "I know that you don't share my feelings because you still love Mark. I don't mean to be cruel, but it doesn't seem as if he is coming back. I thought, rather selfishly maybe, that I might have a chance. You know I'm a good man. I can provide for you, even though you don't need it. I'm kind and gentle and will always treat you with respect. The truth is—I love you. I have loved you for probably longer than I realized. I can't imagine leaving Switzerland without you. Please consider my proposal."

What to say? Her broken heart lay in pieces in her chest. "Dear Edward, I care so much for you, and I'm so honored by your love. But…I think my heart may always belong to another. I don't think it's fair for me to marry you. I care too much about you to hurt you."

She felt the tears coming and then felt him kiss them.

"Marry me, and I will love you and care for you and help soothe your grief."

"But you will know that I don't love you!"

"I accept that. I know you care for me. We're good friends, and that's a great start for any marriage."

Thoughts raced through her head. Was this the answer? She could leave with Edward and his family, go to America, and never have to see Bern again. And never have to think about Mark again. She gave Edward a shy smile.

"You will marry me then?" Edward's face was happy and hopeful.

"Will I be able to practice medicine in New York?"

"Of course you will. I'll never stand in your way."

He took her face and kissed her cheeks gently. Then he took a small box out of his pocket and opened it. A diamond-and-ruby ring on a blue velvet pillow lay inside. She shuddered. Another engagement ring.

"Can I put it on you?" he asked.

She gave him her left hand. Her right hand would always wear Mark's ring, until the day she died. Edward's ring shone, and she couldn't help but open her eyes in surprise at the beauty of it.

"Do you like it?"

"I do. It's beautiful."

"So? Is this a yes?"

Her broken heart beat wildly, protesting, as she whispered, "Yes."

He kissed her hand. "It's all settled, then. I can't wait to tell Mother and Eva. Will you and your family please dine with us tomorrow? To celebrate?"

"Of course," she said. "Oh, but my parents…"

"I've already asked their permission. This morning."

"That's why they told me they would be gone for the afternoon," she said, realizing her family had plotted against her.

She watched him leave later with joy in his step. He blew her a kiss from the door. She smiled. It was good to see him happy. And she now had a chance to forget too. Edward was a kind, good man. She believed he loved her. He'd take care of her broken heart. She knew it would never heal, but she also knew she'd be better if she left for America.

Chapter 38

New York, Tuesday, August—Present Time

Grandmother's funeral took place on Sunday, a quiet sunny day. There were only a few of her friends present besides me, since most of my family was already dead. An empty hole had been dug next to my grandfather's grave, and I stared at it, feeling just as empty. I put a rock on their joint memorial stone, and Pauline and I walked away—she to the taxi to the airport and I to the hospital.

Two days later, I tossed and turned on the mattress in the resident on-call room, unfortunately falling over and over into the hole in the middle. I'd been on call for twelve hours, with multiple admissions for late summer enterovirus, and thought I'd have no trouble sleeping, but my thoughts swirled around in my head at a dizzying speed. I still hadn't come up with a plan on how to apologize to David.

I also couldn't stop thinking of the little girl brought in by her family in the middle of my shift yesterday. I had just poured my third cup of coffee and was trying to get the instant creamer to dissolve, when my pager went off and I was forced to rush to the children's unit. It was housed in a smaller but newer building of the hospital complex, painted in bright yellow shades. There were no patients hospitalized there, usually. Most families sought emergency treatment only and then took their children home, fearful of spending too much money in the city. So the unit remained empty, untouched, and eerily quiet.

As I approached, I heard a child screaming over and over. It sounded very much like a tantrum and not like pain, so I slowed down, my earlier headache letting itself be known. A group of doctors and nurses stood in the hallway, looking helpless. Strong wails were coming through one of the doorways.

"What's the story?" I inquired, gulping down the coffee.

"Five-year-old girl, just admitted with grandparents and a brother," one of the nurses explained hurriedly. "She got sick ten days ago, was throwing up for a day, and has refused to eat or drink since then."

"So, dehydration?"

"Yes, she's here for IV fluids and also so we can figure out why she's not eating or drinking. GI's been paged."

"Oh, good, you're here, Dr. Radelis. Let's examine her," Dr. Williams, my new Attending, said.

After a thorough exam and a confusing story from the family, we gathered that Katelyn had been briefly ill with a stomach flu ten days before and was taken to the local ER. Since then, she had refused to eat or drink or allow anyone in the family to do either. Her twelve-year-old brother kept trying to explain something to me about the time she had stopped eating, but the little girl began to scream and thrash on the bed again.

I left the room wondering if there was something I could do to help Katelyn start eating. Dr. Williams had spoken to the rest of the medical team and then placed orders for a series of tests. I looked around the nurses' station and found a banana muffin. The girl's eyes had opened wide when I presented her with the muffin, and then she threw it at the wall, crying, "You're going to die, you're going to die!"

The grandparents and her brother looked at me scornfully, while I tried to explain that I was trying to tempt the child with different kinds of food, but they wouldn't hear me, as they focused on soothing the distressed child. I ended up backing out of the room slowly.

"What do you think is wrong with her?" I asked one of the nurses.

"I don't know, but let's try Jell-O. All kids will eat it," said Ally, the most experienced pediatric nurse.

"How about if we play feeding dolls? Maybe she'd respond to that?" I suggested.

Ally brought me an old doll from the playroom. I also grabbed a stuffed teddy bear and a matching game and tried to return to the room.

No luck. Katelyn hid behind the bed at the sight of me, screaming, "Bad doctor, leave now!"

I shook my head and walked out, feeling so much like a failure. Her grandmother walked out with me and finally explained that, three months ago, Katelyn, her twin sister Amy, her brother Jack, and their parents were in a car accident. Katelyn's parents and twin sister died, while Katelyn and her brother had survived with only a few scratches. Katelyn seemed just fine for a while; playful, happy, watching TV as she used to, until she had suddenly stopped eating and drinking.

Grief. I knew it well.

Now, hours later, as I lay in the dark of the on-call

room, I felt the little girl's pain, paralyzed by being unable to help her. I thought of David and wondered if he still felt love toward me. My heart ached for him. Every cell of my body ached for him. I looked at my phone. No more texts. I typed a text to him, then erased it.

Don't be a coward, Maya. I touched my ring. *Rebecca, I need more courage.*

I got up and went to peek in on Katelyn. Her grandmother was asleep in a sleeper chair, but Katelyn was up, playing with the doll I had brought her earlier. I took off my lab coat, grabbed another doll and a set of play food from the playroom, and put a juice box in my pocket. I cracked Katelyn's door open and put the doll through, pretend-waving her hand.

"Hi, I can't sleep. Can I play with you?" I asked in a little girl's voice.

"Okay."

I heard the little girl's laughter, slowly entered the room, and sat on the floor, spreading out the items I'd brought. Katelyn sat next to me with her doll. She named it Katelyn. She named my doll Amy, after her sister. The dolls played school, dance, and then they had a picnic. And Katelyn fed them juice from the straw, then sipped some herself.

"You know," I said, "we have a lot in common, you and I."

"Like sisters?" she asked.

"Like friends," I answered.

"So we can be friends?"

"Yes, we can. Because, you know, when I was little, my sister died too. And I was sad for a very long time, just like you."

"What was your sister's name?" Katelyn's eyes were large and filled with tears, as she set her juice box down.

"Ella. I've always missed her, and I'll always love her. She will always be my sister, even though she died."

"Can Amy always be my sister?"

"Of course. You don't have to stop eating and die to be close to her. You can always love her. And you can always talk to her in your mind or even draw pictures for her if you want."

"I can?"

"Yes. She'll always love you and hear you."

"Do you still have muffins? I'm hungry."

"I do. Would you like to come with me to a special snack room? We'll see what we can find. You can have any snack there you want."

Katelyn placed her hand in mine, and we walked to the nurses' station. Her hand felt warm and solid in mine. I knew she'd be fine. And I knew I'd be fine.

I left the hospital several hours later, exhausted. Yet I couldn't stop thinking about David.

I felt him in my mind. I felt his arms around me. I felt him in my heart, stronger than ever.

"Taxi," I yelled.

Chapter 39

Bern, May 1919

It was raining. Rebecca opened the window and inhaled as the fresh smell of wet leaves, flowers, and grass filled the room. She needed to remember what the rainy morning smelled like in her home. She needed to remember every last moment in her home. Nothing would ever be the same again.

The robin was there, perched on the tall branch of the linden tree. It had been there, every morning, for weeks. She smiled and waved it in.

"Come in, then. You know the way."

The bird flew in, making circles around the chair where her wedding dress was carefully laid out. It landed on her writing desk, where paper and pen lay at the ready. It turned its head and looked at her, questioning.

"Yes, my friend. Today is the day."

The robin hopped closer. She stretched her hand out, the way she had seen Mark do it, and the bird hopped into it, its feet tickling her palm. She gently brought the palm closer to her face. The little bird held on and showed no fear, chirping happily and puffing up a bit.

"I have to leave my home today and live with my new husband. In a few months, I'll leave Switzerland forever. Edward says birds like you look different in America, so I'll miss you, my little friend. I'll miss everything about my home."

She wiped at the stream of tears coming down her cheeks. "One day, though, I will die. When that day comes, I want my soul to fly back here and become a bird just like you. Then I can soar free and go wherever I'd like and not feel the pain of a broken heart. Because it's too much to bear sometimes, little friend."

Rebecca set the bird down on the desk. "We have to write a letter to Mark now. Be quiet, no chirping! We don't want anyone to come in yet and catch us doing this. This has to be our secret, all right?"

The robin hopped to the corner of the desk, standing still as if understanding.

"Where do I start?" Rebecca looked down, tears falling on the paper in front of her. She wiped them. It wouldn't do to mark the paper, the letters would come out all smudged.

My Dearest Beloved, she wrote. And then the rest came easily. She needed him to know. She couldn't marry Edward without Mark knowing. She didn't want him to think she had abandoned him. It's just that she wasn't strong enough to live with a broken heart, without him, here in Switzerland.

"Well, that's done now, birdie. You'd better go," she told the robin. "I don't want anyone to shoo you away. Good-bye now. If you get a chance to fly to Ukraine, maybe you can find Mark for me and tell him about my leaving."

The bird heard her and flew out. Rebecca closed the windows. The rain had stopped now. It was time to announce her being awake to the rest of the house. The awful process of preparations for her wedding was about to begin.

Hours later, she stood examining her reflection in the mirror. She didn't look anything like herself. The dress had been purchased by Mother and Grandmother, without her consent. Well, they did ask her to participate in the selection, but she was busy at the clinic that day. And on every other day that they wished for her to shop for the wedding dress. So the end result was this hideous white frock that made her look like a pile of snow. The layers of satin, silk, and lace got all puffed up and tangled when she moved. She would've preferred to get married in a simple suit as many women did these days, but Mother wouldn't hear of it.

"You look beautiful," Sarah said, coming up behind her.

"No, I absolutely don't. This dress is hideous."

"I think you look rather nice in white. Where is the veil?"

"Grandmother is bringing it in a few minutes. She wanted to put it on."

"Maybe, if it were a bit longer, it wouldn't look so odd," Sarah said.

"Maybe if I were a truly happy bride, it wouldn't look so odd."

"You're not the first woman to marry without love. It may come later." Sarah hugged her.

"It never came for you."

"I married a monster. You're marrying a kind man who loves you."

"You're right. I'm being ungrateful."

"I understand. I know you still think of Mark. It will be easier, perhaps, when you start your new life in

America. Oh, I will miss you terribly! I don't know how I'll live without you." Sarah squeezed her hands tightly.

"What if you come with me? We can do the same work there as we did here. New York is badly in need of physicians, I hear. You could use a fresh start, as well. Oh, please think about it."

"I don't need to think about it. I can answer now. I can't go with you," Sarah said, letting go of Rebecca's hands.

"But why not? What could possibly keep you here?"

"I've met someone. Someone who loves me. He is very kind to me, and I think I might be very happy with him." Sarah's eyes were full of love.

"What? You've said nothing about this. When did this happen?"

"About two months ago. I didn't want to speak of it until I was certain of his feelings toward me. And mine toward him." Sarah sat down on Rebecca's bed.

Rebecca sat next to her and held her close. "Where did you meet him? And what's his name?"

"He was one of the officers here for convalescence. I helped the Red Cross to arrange a visit for his mother and sister. His name is Hugh Fergusson; he is from Edinburgh. His family owns antique shops there. He wants to marry me and bring me back to Scotland with him. I could have a law practice there, I think."

"So I will go to America, and you will go to Scotland. Both of us leaving Switzerland to go far away."

"When will you go? Has Edward secured a safe passage?" Sarah asked.

"He has booked us a passage on the *Mauritania* when it starts crossing with passengers again in September. When will you go?"

"Hugh was waiting for me to tell him when I was ready. I think I might tell him I'm ready to be engaged now and marry in the fall. I wasn't sure how to tell my parents."

"With ships going transatlantic all the time soon, maybe we could see each other every once in a while."

"Of course we will. I'll never be too busy to visit my friend in America. And how exciting will that be!" Sarah smiled.

"Come now, we'll not have tears on this wedding day," Grandmother announced, walking into the room with her face hidden behind the yards of tulle veil in her hands.

"Happy tears, Fräu Miller, not sad," Sarah said, winking at Rebecca.

"This mountain of veil, I hate it," Rebecca said.

"Now, no granddaughter of mine will marry without a veil. You will like it once I arrange it on your head." Grandmother began the process, pulling and tugging on Rebecca's hair.

"Hurry up! It's almost time to leave for the ceremony," Mother called from downstairs.

Rebecca paled. This was it; the time to lose her heart forever was coming. She was to become Edward's wife and not be Mark's beloved any longer. She'd never be the same person again; it was simply not possible. She would be someone living a lie, every minute of every day. Yet she couldn't imagine not going through with it. She swayed.

"Are you feeling faint, my dear?" Grandmother

steadied her.

"I'm well. Just a bit tired from all the preparations. I think the veil looks good. Thank you." The lies began already. The veil was hideous; it matched the ghastly dress very nicely. Now she fully looked like a snowy mountain. And the veil itched her hair terribly.

Suddenly she remembered. "Oh, *Grossmami*, I have to give you something. Before I leave tonight and forget." Rebecca ran to her jacket and pulled out a letter. "Here, please take it for safekeeping. It can't stay here."

"And who is this for?" Grandmother checked the name on the envelope and pursed her lips. "Why do I need this?"

"In case he returns." Rebecca swayed again and held onto the back of the chair.

Grandmother grabbed her arm and brought her face close, looking intensely at her. "Rebecca, you must remember—he's never coming back. Today, of all days, you must repeat this to yourself. It won't do you any good to still pine for him. It'll ruin any chance you have with your new husband."

Rebecca pulled away from Grandmother's hold. "Don't you think I know this? I just want him to have a note from me, just in case. Because soon I'll leave here forever. Please, won't you keep it for me? It makes me feel happy to know I left it. I can't leave here without that. If you want me to be happy in my new marriage, please keep this letter for me!"

Grandmother sighed and tucked the note into the pocket of her jacket. "All right, I'll do what you wish. I've always spoiled you. But you must forget him."

"Time to go now," Father said from the door, then

gasped when he saw Rebecca. "How beautiful you are! I never thought I'd see such a sight!" He offered her his elbow.

There it was, time to say goodbye to her old life and start her new one. She looked at her room quickly and said goodbye to her things: her furniture, her walls, her window, her rugs. She would never come back here the same person again. She would be Rebecca Fischer in a few hours and never Rebecca Miller again. She fixed her veil and walked to the car, not looking back. It was time to marry Edward and move on.

Chapter 40

New York, August, Tuesday—Present Time

I knew exactly where to find David: East 26th and Park. The house was clear in my mind, I didn't need to look for the address, which I was sure he had added to my contacts. It was a four-story narrow brownstone that Rebecca had loved, and a small set of steps with black wrought-iron railings led to the first floor. Ten steps after you opened the little gate, up to a set of double doors made of maplewood. No decorations on the facade. Rebecca had wanted it rather plain, to remind her of the house in Bern. Large windows looking out at the tall, sweet-smelling linden tree in the front.

The cab flew through the city, stopping only at lights and at a few spots of congestion. He lived so close to the hospital, I hardly had time to think about what I would do if it was too early and he was still asleep, or if he had already gone to work. I wasn't worried about what I'd say to him. If he opened the door, I knew the words would come to me. I just needed to see him. I needed to have a chance to apologize for running out.

There it was. 26th Street. "Right here is good," I yelled out to the driver.

The cab came to a quick stop. I paid and jumped out, looking for the house. There it was, standing with its windows brightly lit, between a large apartment building and a smaller building with a bakery. Birds jumped happily on the branches of the linden tree. I inhaled the sweet smell. How had I never noticed these trees before? The house was small, but I knew Rebecca loved it. And so did David.

Oh, David. How could I have been so stupid?

It was always him. I should've known.

I ran up the steps and slowed down only for a second before raising my arm toward the brass knocker. I nearly fell forward as the door was opened by a handsome man who looked shockingly like David. He waited patiently as I struggled to find the words to explain what I was doing there. I finally gathered my thoughts and was about to introduce myself, as he stretched his hand out and said, "You're looking for my brother, aren't you?"

"Oh, you are Nate," I managed to say.

"I see you're well familiar with our family. Should I know your name?" He smiled.

"Maya," I replied. "And no, your brother wouldn't have mentioned me. At all," I added, looking away.

"Well, come in." He pointed inside.

"No, it's fine. I really was just looking for David. We met in Europe, but he doesn't know I'm here. He wasn't expecting me. Is he around?"

"Ha, you're planning to surprise him." He rubbed his hands together and laughed. "I can't wait to watch this."

"He's not great with surprises. Not his thing, right?"

"I see you *have* met him." He laughed again. "Can I offer you some coffee?"

"Sure." I couldn't stop fidgeting.

"You do know David doesn't live here?" Nate asked, while pouring the coffee a few minutes later.

"What?" I sat down on the kitchen stool, my legs unsteady now.

"Sweetheart, who is it?" A woman's voice called out from upstairs.

"It's a friend of David's, looking for him," he yelled back to her. "This is our mother's house. We are meeting her for breakfast here this morning. David is getting some things from the bakery next door. How did you know to find him here?" He handed me the coffee and pushed over the milk and sugar.

I bought myself some time mixing my coffee. How could I possibly explain this to a stranger? "He gave me all his contact information. I just wasn't sure which one was his address. I figured I'd try him here. I work nearby."

"We grew up here, and we visit Mom all the time. She gets lonely." He smiled. "Mom, come down here. Meet David's friend."

I got up off my chair. "You know, I think I'd better go. Thanks for the coffee, but I really don't want to intrude on your family breakfast. Can you just let David know I'd like to speak to him?" I headed toward the door.

"Please don't run away!" David's mother, a beautiful woman with a kind smile, wearing a sunflower print dress, came downstairs and approached me with her arms open. "We don't meet David's friends very often. I'm very tempted to trap you here. I'm Lara Fischer, David's mother. You see, all he ever does is work, work, work. I'm very happy to learn he has a bit of a social life."

Lara Fischer pushed me back to the kitchen, her arm around my shoulders. "You're wearing scrubs. Are you a doctor?"

"I'm a resident. Mrs. Fischer, I apologize for showing up uninvited. I just…" How could I possibly explain?

"Had to see him, didn't you?" Mrs. Fischer smiled in understanding. "It's all right, dear. And call me Lara, please." She looked at me thoroughly. "You look familiar. Has David introduced you to me before and I've forgotten?"

"No, we really have just met," I said.

"Well, I can't wait to hear all about it," she said, sending a mischievous smile to Nate.

I sank back into the chair, noticing Nate responding to her with a smirk. This was a mistake; I was sure of it now. But a minute later, the front door opened, then slammed closed, and I stared at David, paralyzed by both excitement and worry. As he saw me and his eyes lit up, my worry disappeared and my heart filled with deep love.

I ran to him, words struggling to come out, trying to explain. Nevertheless, happiness filled my entire being. He set his groceries down, took my face in his hands gently, and kissed me softly, whispering something I couldn't hear. Here, even in front of his family, I felt as if I was in paradise alone with him.

"I knew you'd find me when you were ready," he said.

"David," I finally managed to say. "I have so much to tell you."

"I can't wait to hear this," Nate said behind me.

"I see you've met Maya." David blushed and nodded to Nate and his mother.

"You have some explaining to do, looks like," Lara said, giving him a quick hug.

"I know. Hold on." David took my hand and pulled me along to the dining room. "I have to show you something." He took a photo album off a shelf and pulled out a picture. A picture of Rebecca and a man who bore a striking resemblance to my grandmother.

"This is Mark. It says it on the back. I found it in one of Rebecca's books."

"I have something to tell you, also," I began. "My grandmother left me her father's diary. His name was Mark Minchin. He studied medicine at the University of Bern when he was a young man. One of the entries was about his regret that he left behind a woman he loved—Rebecca Miller. He couldn't return to her because he was forced to fight with the Red Army."

David whistled.

"You both have a story to tell, I guess." David's mother stood next to me.

"Let's go eat some breakfast, and we can explain everything. It will take a while," David said, giving me another kiss. "I'm not even sure where to begin…"

"I know exactly where to begin," I said. "With the bird I saw in Edinburgh."

Then my mouth dropped open, and I nearly tripped over a chair in my path. "The painting," I gasped, grabbing my throat.

"Oh, this? Of course you'd notice, if you are interested in my grandmother. She loved robins. They reminded her of Bern, she always said. She collected any paintings of them she could find. We have them everywhere. I rather like them," Lara said and proceeded to the kitchen.

I looked around, holding onto David for strength. Small and large paintings of robins hung on the walls of the dining room, living room, and the small library off to the side. The same robin I had seen so many times during my week in Europe, guiding me, helping me find my way, and giving me clues.

The robin I had thought was Ella's spirit…was really Rebecca's, all this time.

Rebecca was the one who found me and led me to David.

She wanted to make sure her love for Mark never died.

Chapter 41

RMS Mauritania, *October 1919*

The wind was merciless on the open deck, whipping her shoulders, bare arms, and neck with icy sharpness. But being in the open air and seeing nothing but darkness all around her was what she needed at the moment.

Have I made the right choice?

She felt a warm jacket being placed around her shoulders and turned. Edward. Always so thoughtful and kind to her.

"My darling, I've been looking for you everywhere. Dinner is about to be announced."

"I just needed some air. I'll be down in a moment."

"Can I join you? Do you mind my company?" he asked, his eyes worried.

She hesitated. It was wrong to keep hurting his feelings. "Of course you can join me. It's ghastly out here with the cold wind, but also, somehow, so beautiful."

"I know what you mean. The ocean is very ominous in the night." He wrapped his arms around her. "I think you'll be pleased with a surprise I've planned for you at dinner."

"More surprises? You've been so generous already!"

"Nothing makes me happier than seeing you smile. You should be learning this by now." He kissed her neck gently.

The warmth of his kiss on her cold neck made her shudder in his arms, and she felt his arms tighten around her. To her enormous surprise, she had discovered that she could respond to her new husband's touches and didn't mind them as much as she had expected.

Edward whispered in her ear, "Darling, I know you love another. But I'm very happy that you respond to my affections." He turned her around and kissed her mouth, first gently, then more demanding. "I love making love to you."

She felt herself blushing, and her body shook, her mind torn between remembering the enjoyment of lying with him last night and remembering all the times she had made love with Mark. Edward was a gentle, careful, and thoughtful lover. Mark was passionate; always surprising, always demanding, and always in a hurry. She never felt like she had lost her soul to Edward when the lovemaking was over.

"So what is the surprise you have planned? Can I have a clue?" She switched the topic, pulling away from her husband and her memories.

"Oh, I might as well tell you. I've arranged for us to sit next to another female physician at dinner. And not only is she a physician; she is one of the doctors at the New York Infirmary for Women and Children, and she teaches at the Women's Medical College. Don't you think she'd make a lovely dinner companion for you?"

"Edward!" Rebecca hugged him. "I can't thank you enough. You are ever so kind to me. Let's hurry to dinner."

Later that night, Edward stood by her vanity table, watching her getting ready for bed. His smile signaled he was not at all planning to go to sleep. She didn't mind. He was charming at dinner and afterward, impressing her new friend, Dr. Elizabeth Stokes. Elizabeth had been married, but her husband has passed away and she had decided not to remarry, finding marriage an impediment to being a physician in New York. Rebecca hoped that would not be the case in her marriage. She rather liked Edward.

She was rubbing in hand lotion when she noticed it.

Mark's ring was gone!

She screamed and crouched on the floor, searching, thinking she must have allowed it to fall on the floor with slippery fingers.

"What's the matter, darling?" Edward's hands were on her back.

"My ring! It's missing!"

"Don't exert yourself. Call for the maid."

"No, I must find it now." She panted, fingers searching, nails clawing at the floor and furniture desperately.

It wasn't there!

She ran to the bed, dropped on the floor, searched under it, then riffled through the bedding.

"You must calm down, darling. You will work yourself up to a fit." Edward's arms were around her.

"I'm not prone to fits, Edward!"

"When was the last time you saw it?" Edward asked.

She sat down, holding her chest, trying to gather

her thoughts. "I don't remember…" In truth she didn't. How she had betrayed Mark! Wrapped up in Edward's affections, she had forgotten to stroke Mark's ring and talk to him, as she had done for the past two years. How could she have done this?

Oh, now she remembered! "I think I haven't seen it since France," she whispered, horrified.

"Check your jewelry box," Edward suggested.

She was already running to it, tripping on the rugs. She dumped the contents on the marble counter. *Not there.* She collapsed on the chair in tears. She remembered now. She had taken it off one night in France when she wished to be just with Edward. She had felt she owed it to him. She had placed the ring in her jewelry box and closed the lid. *Stay safe, Mark, I love you,* she had whispered her daily prayer and gone to bed with her husband.

"It was that French maid! She hated me. I couldn't understand a word she said. She stole it, I'm sure."

"Cecile Thomas? I'm so sorry for her, again. She was terribly rude."

"I know it wasn't your fault. I don't blame you at all. But the fact is she despised me and would steal something from me out of spite!"

"I'll buy you many new rings when we come to New York, darling. I love giving you gifts." Edward kissed her fingers.

"Thank you, but this ring can't be replaced." She pulled her fingers away, shaking in anger and grief.

He lifted her chin rather roughly. "Was it given by him?"

She couldn't lie. "It was."

"Then I will consider it an intervention by Fate.

You have a new husband now and no need for an old lover's ring."

"Oh, please don't be angry with me, dear Edward. I'm already so much in pain."

"I'm not angry. I'm hurt, Rebecca. Hurt that you'd still cry so hard about this man who abandoned you."

"Not this man, but something that reminded me about my old life in Switzerland. I might never see home again." Fresh tears appeared.

He held her then. "You're right. I'm being unkind. But I thought you wished to leave Switzerland. You begged to leave as soon as possible. I don't understand this sudden nostalgia."

"I didn't know I'd feel so much pain. I'll be quite all right soon. I just need a little time. You can return to bed. I'll be right there. You're correct—I need to let it go."

She could tell he was pleased, very pleased. He kissed her as gently as during their tender moments. "I'll let you calm yourself, then. Have some rest and join me when ready."

"I should be better shortly."

She was grateful when he left and she could compose herself. Her broken heart couldn't handle any more guilt or explanations to him. It wasn't fair to him. He was right; it was likely Fate that she lost the ring. It was time for her to let go. Of course she knew her heart would never let go.

She heard his gentle breathing as he fell asleep. She took out her smaller suitcase, opened a book inside, and found the pictures she kept secret. There was Mark, sitting next to her, hugging her. *How happy we were together.* How careless with their time, never thinking that it would end one day.

"Stay safe, Mark. I love you. Fate tells me I have to let you go. But you'll be locked in my heart forever. I'm yours, you're mine, remember?"

She placed the photographs gently back into the book and went to join her new husband. And her new life.

Epilogue

New York—Present Time

It was one of those perfect New York autumn days when I enjoyed walking around the city in my precious spare time. The sun persistently snuck in between the buildings, trying to warm up the streets. Here and there a rare yellow leaf could be spotted on the street, blown from one of the tiny hidden parks, and the smell of the city changed from dust and garbage and sweat to river and coffee and fresh pretzels baked on every corner. The river still welcomed sailboats and rowers in large numbers, but the city's pace was becoming slower and more relaxed.

I walked to my favorite cafe on Stone Street and sat down, waiting. David announced himself with a kiss on my lips a few minutes later.

"You coming over tonight?"

I laughed. "I just left your apartment this morning!"

"I want you there all day and all night."

"You'll get sick of me."

"Never." He handed me a small envelope.

"What is it? A jury summons?"

"A bill. For my coffee services."

"Fine, I'll open it." I ripped the envelope open and a small shiny key attached to a key ring featuring a robin fell out with a clang onto the table.

My heart pounded. "What is it a key to?"

"Our apartment. Enough of this staying over. I want you to move in."

"Bossy! What if I want you to move in?"

"You have two roommates!"

"Fine," I said. "I'll abandon the TV-bingeing twins for you."

He leaned over and kissed me. "Thank God. I didn't know what I would do if you refused."

"I have a present for you too." I handed him a thick, large envelope.

"Papers, you are giving papers to an attorney?" He read the address on the envelope and raised his brows. "What?"

"Yes. It's an application to Cornell."

"It's for the College of Veterinary Medicine," he said slowly.

"I know. I requested it for you. Your mother has already sent them your transcripts. You just have to provide them with a letter of recommendation and they're ready to accept you for next year. You have all the prerequisites completed."

"Where did you get this insane idea that I want to abandon my career?"

"Your family in Bern told me, and then your mother and Nate told me. Your mother gave me your old application and the acceptance letter she saved. But it's your choice, of course."

David rubbed his forehead. "It's like you all plotted against me. I've worked hard to become successful at what I do. I'm well respected in law. I'm known internationally."

I took his hand. "You don't have to do this. No one is forcing you. But there are two of us now, and your brother is well taken care off. You can finally think about yourself. I wanted you to have this option. But only if this is what you wish for."

"I need to sit on this a while."

"Absolutely." I put the key in my pocket. "But I'm coming over tonight, and I will expect dinner and a few empty hangers. And a drawer in the bathroom."

He groaned. "I'd heard that I'd lose my bathroom space, but closet space as well…"

I kissed his nose. "I love you. Have to get back to bloody noses and broken bones. I love schnitzel, if you happen to have any for dinner."

I walked back the long way to the hospital, enjoying the fall air and the feeling of lightness in my heart. I touched Rebecca's ring on my finger. It had been a long time since I'd had any dreams about her and Mark. I guess she figured it was time for me to build my own life. With David.

A word about the author...

Elena Mikalsen grew up in Ukraine but came to New York City as a refugee with her family at age 17. She knew her husband was her soulmate when their eyes locked in an elevator at the Lenox Hill Hospital in 1996.

She is somewhat obsessive about travel, but when at home in San Antonio, she can be found browsing through bookstores or antique shops with her husband and two children. When not writing stories, she is a Pediatric Psychologist helping children with chronic medical illness.

This is her first work of fiction. Visit her at: www.elenamikalsen.com

Thank you for purchasing
this publication of The Wild Rose Press, Inc.

If you enjoyed the story, we would appreciate your
letting others know by leaving a review.

For other wonderful stories,
please visit our on-line bookstore at
www.thewildrosepress.com.

For questions or more information
contact us at
info@thewildrosepress.com.

The Wild Rose Press, Inc.
www.thewildrosepress.com

Stay current with The Wild Rose Press, Inc.

Like us on Facebook

https://www.facebook.com/TheWildRosePress

And Follow us on Twitter
https://twitter.com/WildRosePress

www.ingramcontent.com/pod-product-compliance
Lightning Source LLC
Chambersburg PA
CBHW050027030726
47506CB00001B/150